Mint Condition

A Classic Car Romance, Book 1

By

KAT DRENNAN

KP PUBLICATIONS, OJAI, CALIFORNIA

MINT CONDITION

ISBN 978-0-9996714-2-9 Trade Paperback

ISBN 978-0-9996714-3-6 ePub

KC Publications
Ojai, California

More Books by Kat Drennan

The Love on the Faultline Romantic Mystery series
Borrego Moon

Love on the Faultline Historical Novella
Lies In White Satin

Love on the Faultline Standalone Romance
High Tide

Serpent's Coil Historical Time-Travel
The Cloisonné Brooch
Lesidi's Coin
The Serpent's Coil

A Classic Car Romance - Romantic Suspense
Book One - Mint Condition
Book Two - One of a Kind
Book Three – Hotrod Lincoln
Book Four – Five Window Pickup Coming Soon

Award-Winning Women's Fiction
The Goddess of Undo

Acknowledgements

A book idea can come in a flash of inspiration; after that it takes hundreds of hours to recreate that flash in words and images in someone else's mind. It doesn't happen overnight or in a vacuum. I owe thanks to many who helped along the way:

To my crit group homies, The Blockheads, who only flinched a little when I said my next project was a romance; to the wise and wonderful freelance editor, Lynnette Labelle for helping me submit the best manuscript I could; to crit partner/authors Kate Collier and Kimberly Keyes, for their invaluable feedback and support; to beta readers Heather Faulkingham, Meredith Jaeger Githens, Connie Goldsmith, Jan Lloyd, and Chris Wade—your responses were golden; to my sweet and talented editor at Escargot Books and Music, Mayo Morley for opening the door; and finally, to my own private hunky boy husband, Fred Drennan, who fostered my love of classic cars and who allowed my wild and crazy affair with Nick Berlin.

To my sweet Miss Connie.

I miss you every day.

Chapter 1

A black car entered the cemetery parking lot and stopped. Maddie's heart stopped with it. A limousine. Not even the dead rode in limos in this town. Tinted windows hid the face of the person in the rear seat, but it had to be him. The coward. Sneaking a peek without having to make an appearance.

"Ashes to ashes," the pastor droned, as emotions banged around in her heart like trapped ghosts. Anger. Grief. Dread. Twenty years since her father had dumped her on Grandpa's Kentucky farm. She hadn't seen him since. Did she want to? Hell no.

What could he have to say to her after all this time? Sorry? Forgive me?

She dragged her gaze from the coffin back to the limousine just as a black-tinted window slid down, revealing a young, strikingly handsome face. One she didn't recognize.

He was pure California. Had that deep tan, sandy-haired, not-quite-shaven look.

He opened the door and unfolded his tall frame from the back seat of the limousine. She caught her breath. *He's coming over here?*

"Maddie." Flo nudged her back to the moment. Walt and Flo, a few neighbors, shop owners, and people from the church fidgeted or simply stared into the gaping hole. The ones who *had* been there for her. The ones who counted. The ones she would protect now.

Maddie forced white-knuckled fingers to open. The compacted lump of dirt fell with a thud on the plain, wooden coffin Grandpa had specified.

The mechanism squeaked under the strain as the attendants cranked it down into the earth. Maddie blinked back stinging tears as reality sunk in.

"Follow the goddess, Grandpa." Her throat closed on what would have been *goodbye*.

She stepped away from the hole, her long sigh producing a wisp of frosty cloud, as she joined the other mourners making their way to the parking lot. She wiped the dirt off her hands down the sides of her little black dress, leaving a smudge where dirt mingled with the fine mist on the fabric. Didn't matter. She would never wear the dress again.

"He was a good friend," one of her neighbors said as he fell into slow step beside her. "Best I ever had."

Maddie trudged along, her eyes on her muddy rubber boots, her only concession to the freezing wet of an early Kentucky sleet. She circled the old man's shoulders and gave him a squeeze. "You're coming back to the house now, right? Flo's got a big spread waiting."

They stopped at the edge of the gravel lot and she let her arm drop away from his shoulders and glanced up to give him a warm smile.

"Wouldn't miss it," he said.

She stood a moment longer as lingering mourners offered condolences and headed for mud-spattered cars. Her chest hollowed out. The burial, the food, and then, she would have to figure out how to live without her grandpa in her life.

She saw him standing next to the limo, his back to her, rubbing his hands together against the cold. Whoever it was had a lot of nerve, showing up at her grandfather's burial without so much as a phone call of warning. The hollow feeling vanished, replaced by the heat of old resentment.

She stalked across the pitted gravel lot and stopped a few feet away, remembering the shattering moment their eyes had met across the graveyard.

Maddie squared her shoulders. She didn't care how good looking he was, she would set this guy straight right now and send him on his way.

"So what is he? A coward? Or just too important to bother?"

He whirled at the sound of her voice.

"Excuse me?" A matched set of startled blue-green eyes locked onto hers. Dreamy, seductive eyes. The kind a wise woman avoided.

"No excuse." She stepped closer. "A *man* shows up to his father's funeral. Regardless." Heat bloomed at her chest and neck. His quick glance down said he hadn't missed it.

He took a gentlemanly step away, shoving his hands in his pockets. "That lets me off the hook. My old man's alive and kickin'." He fished his cell phone out of his jacket to show her. "Just blocked a call from His Highness a minute ago."

She angled away, some of the heat melting away. "My father didn't send you?"

"Not unless we're related." That smile again, warmer, wider.

She cocked her head. Tears she'd held at bay all morning stung the corners of her eyes. She raised the back of her hand to her cheek, tightening the dress over her breast.

His gaze went there, the reflex of a man interested in more than a funeral.

She dipped her head, folded her arms, and to her own surprise, emitted a low chuckle. "I sure hope we're not."

His smile faltered. "Not what?" he asked dryly.

"Related." Warmth blossomed on her cheeks, and she had to look away. It had been far too long since she'd let a man's stray look get a rise out of her. Her mind might be on a funeral, but her body had a mind of its own.

"And you don't know my grandfather?" she asked, willing the blush away.

He shook his head.

"When I saw the limo, I thought…" She cast her gaze around the now empty parking lot, then off into the distant cold. "If my father didn't send you, and you don't know Grandpa--"

She massaged her forehead with shaky fingertips, suddenly sorry she hadn't at least grabbed a piece of toast before she left the house. *Too late to be sorry.* Her knees went liquid.

He stepped in, caught her by the elbow. A long, lean thigh pressed against hers, and a whiff of sandalwood and citrus filled her senses. *Cartier?* Her vision narrowed to the size of a fist. All she saw was the intensity of those sea-green eyes. The anger that flared when the limo first appeared smoldered and went out.

"Steady," he said, supporting her elbow, his breath warm against her ear.

"Thank you. I'm all right. It's just that…I should've eaten."

"It's cold out here." He reached for the limo door. His hand slid from her elbow to the small of her back. "Let's talk inside."

His fingers were cold, but heat radiated from the pressure points at her back just the same. She stared at him a moment. He was smooth, charming, and the kind of handsome that revved a girl's engine and sent her thoughts down the wrong road.

She stiffened and turned away from his touch. "Talk?"

He hunched his shoulders and shoved his hands back into his pockets.

She crossed her arms over her chest and took a step toward her Toyota pickup, irritated by her physical response. "If you're a bill collector, you'll need to get in line, and today is not the day for it," she said, emphatically.

His eyes darkened as he closed the distance between them once again. "Wait. You put an ad on eBay? A Cadillac?"

All right. Now he had her attention. Besides, bill collectors didn't show up in limousines. Or wear Cartier cologne. "With blind contact information," she said. *Explain that.*

"The obit—".

"There's been no obit." She fisted her hands against her hips.

"I came all the way from California."

"In a limo? Must've cost a fortune." Her fingertips had lost their feeling, her stomach was doing flip-flops, and any moment, her teeth would be chattering. Handsome or not, it was too cold and she was too weary to play games. "What *is it* you want?"

He fixed those eyes on hers. She sensed a battle going on behind them. "My father, *the king of self-important fools,* is interested in your car. He wants me to…photograph it."

Maddie cricked her mouth to one side and studied him once more. She couldn't help admiring the cut of his shirt and the perfect knot of his very expensive tie. She might live on a farm in Kentucky, but she knew quality when she saw it. She'd made a business of knowing.

Don't be too hasty, Grandpa would say. And he would be right, as always.

She took a deep breath and relaxed her shoulders. He seemed harmless, after all.

"Didn't mean to be rude. I don't know how you found me, but I do have a car for sale. Maybe."

He exhaled and his eyes brightened.

"There's a memorial reception back at the house. There'll be food and we can take a look at the car." And there would be plenty of people around in case she had misjudged his character.

She climbed into her pickup, rolled the window down and handed him her business card. "Here's the address. The road back to Lexington will be messy later. You should book a room in Georgetown."

❧

Maddie glanced in the rearview mirror as she pulled away. She couldn't suppress a grin. She'd been numb to almost every sensation for days. Now, the corners of her mouth twitched with amusement. A tiny seed of warmth took hold in her heart. Not full blown, but there. A little promise that she might one day breathe all the way to the top of her lungs again. Might live through this. It was absurd that on the saddest day of her life, up walks an inconveniently handsome stranger, squeezing a smile through frozen lips. A stranger who might have the wherewithal to buy the Cadillac. The thought hit her hard, again. Something she'd have to get used to. The eventual sale of the Flying Goddess, though necessary, was too sad to think about. Especially today.

She down-shifted, and turned on the highway toward home. A jangly refrain bubbled out of her cell phone. She grabbed it off her dash before the call went to voicemail.

"Mad Monkey, how can I help you?" Her teeth chattered around the words. She cranked up the window and flipped the truck's heater dial to full.

"It's me. Clay. Those parts showed up. I'm out of town next week, but we could start on the '55 as soon as—"

"I'm kind of busy right now." Maddie tried to find some enthusiasm but it just wasn't there. Maybe it never would be again. Clay was a good friend who had helped her grandfather and her restore dozens classics, but she didn't have the patience for him right now.

"Do you *ever* listen to your messages?" she asked.

"I saw the box on the doorstep and punched your number. You don't sound so good."

She couldn't bring herself to say the words out loud again, not so soon after putting her grandfather in the ground. "Go in and listen to your messages. Come by after."

She clicked the phone off and threw it on the dash before he could question her further. Stale air belched out of the heater vent, warming her feet. Still, she couldn't stop shivering. By the time she reached the farm's turnout, several cars already lined the long driveway. Flo, her housekeeper and one-time nanny, greeted people at the front door, collecting covered dishes.

Maddie surveyed the arrivals as she pulled into the garage. She recognized most of the cars, had worked on them at one time or another as favors for mowing or putting up tobacco in the barn. She glanced out to the highway a moment before heading for the back of the house.

A blast of warm air met Maddie at the kitchen door, but no amount of heat, not even a few moments respite talking to a handsome man, could touch the cold stone anchored in her heart. Opening the door to the kitchen left her bare and vulnerable to memories of her grandfather's love. It would take a while to get used to this house without him in it.

Flo pulled her inside with an arm around her waist as Bébé, Maddie's yellow Labrador, shot past them toward the dining room. "Child, you're shivering like a wet kitten. Get on upstairs and into a hot shower."

Maddie eyed the people milling near the dining table. Flo pushed her toward the stairs. "Never mind, I'll take care of them."

Relieved, Maddie dropped her bag in the foyer. Flo was every bit a member of the family as she was. She had to be hurting too, but true to form, she had everything under control. Despite the sadness of the day, Flo's salt and pepper hair was scooped up into a French knot, her white work shoes were polished, and the pearl studs her husband, Walter, had given her on their wedding day glowed on her earlobes. The two of them had helped her immeasurably since her grandfather's illness. Just like they had every day for the past twenty years. If the sky fell, Flo would be there to hold it up until Walt built a support under it.

"Thanks, Flo." There weren't enough words for the gratitude Maddie owed the couple.

"You take your time, girl. No one's goin' to leave as long as there's ham on the table."

Maddie trudged up the stairs, the weight of the day bearing down on her. In the shower, hot water battered the top of her head and streamed down over her face and shoulders, taking with it some of the chill. She clenched her eyes shut against the aching memory of the casket lowering into the ground.

Don't wallow. Grandpa's voice played in her head. He was right, again. He'd died an old man, had a good, full life. He would want her to get back to hers.

She turned and let the water sluice down her back. As the steam poured over the top of the shower door, another image filled her mind. A stranger in a black limousine. Sandy, well cut hair, the deep tan of a person with big wads of money and the time to spend it, and crisp lines down the front of his trousers.

Not from around here.

Someone, if she was any judge, who may actually have enough money to buy the Cadillac. *And, don't deny it, that sinewy thigh felt good against yours.*

She shook her head, cranked the faucets off, and stepped out of the shower, flipping a towel over her wet hair, pleased with herself. For the first time in days, months maybe, she had actually thought beyond her grandfather's imminent death and the mountain of responsibility that came with his estate. Something—a slice of life and light in Limo Man's sea-green eyes—made her think forward not back. Something sincere and inviting, the first sign of color in a world that had lately faded to gray, made her think about her future. She hadn't so much as gone for coffee with a man since Grandpa got sick two years ago. He'd have been the first to remind her of that.

Slipping into her terrycloth bathrobe, she peeked out the back window and surveyed the property. Rain had turned to swirling snow that settled on tractor seats and bird feeders hanging in bare limbs of the backyard trees, and caught in ruts on the gravel driveway in front of the main garage. Bébé was outside, bounding across the backyard, nipping at snowflakes and skidding her nose along the ground.

Maddie pulled the towel off her head, ruffled her hair, and peered out the dormer window to the front of the house. There was the limousine, parked right up front, quickly collecting snow on the windshield. Maddie's heart kicked like a new born filly, a little wobbly but definitely on her feet. She needed a little kick right now. A kick out of the wallow. Grandpa would've wanted that. He'd been after her for closing herself off after the breakup of her college affair. *Wouldn't hurt to make friendly.* He wouldn't have wanted solemn, he would've wanted a party, complete with Kentucky Bourbon punch. And he'd have wanted her to move on.

She owed him a good send off. She hung her black dress in the closet, and pulled a fuchsia cashmere tunic over a pair of skinny jeans, then took her fancy turquoise cowgirl boots out of their box. Grandpa had bought them for her birthday, three years ago when he still had his wits about him. Seemed fitting to wear them to his going away party. Feeling good about her decision, she pulled on a pair of warm socks, then pushed her feet into the boots and went downstairs.

She spotted him right away. He gazed across the property through the telescope at the parlor window. He looked up suddenly, as if he could feel her eyes on him. Flo turned a gaggle of kids away from the parlor and back to the food, where the driver was already pushing something around his plate with a block of cornbread.

Limo Man turned to face her as she stepped to the window.

"Madonna. You look…*warmer*," he said. His eyes took a slow walk over her cashmere curves and sexy boots without apology.

"Considerably so." She appreciated the double entendre. "Please call me Maddie. I never much appreciated being named after a rock star."

"Like a virgin," he said with a grin. He fumbled his wallet from inside his jacket and drew out a card. His eyes lifted to hers. Sea green shot with gold around the pupil. She could be peering into a tropical lagoon. Her face heated, caught in the fantasy. And for a brief droplet of time in a tide of grief, it felt good to be her.

She glanced down at the card.

Nicholas Berlin, Jr., President and CFO
Central Coast Real Estate Investment Trust, Inc.
Montecito, California.
www.ccreit.com

Real Estate. That explained the expensive clothes and charismatic smile. It took a conscious effort to keep her hand steady. "You *are* a long way from home, Nicholas Berlin."

"Believe me, I know." He studied his flimsy shoes which were clearly soaked. "And please. I'm Nick. My father is Nicholas." He said the words as if they left a bad taste in his mouth.

"Nick, not Junior," she observed.

"Thanks."

Maddie stepped closer to the window.

"I don't hear Kentucky in your voice," he said.

"My family's from California, too. My parents, that is. Grandpa's been here since the thirties. This land, some tobacco, and a few cattle are all he has…*had*…to show for it." How long before she could speak without her throat closing?

"Nobody has fences around here. How far does the property go?" He turned to gaze back out the window, politely changing the subject.

"That line of trees goes along the river." Maddie moved closer still, brushing shoulders with him as she spoke. She trailed her hand in a wide arc. "Across there to the top of the ridge. That's pasture for the cattle, and there is a fence, it's just down in the hollow. Out there and around to the back are paddocks we rent long term to folks coming in to Lexington for events."

"Horsey people."

"Um hum. Grandpa used to grow tobacco out there, but there's not much money in that these days, other than just keeping up the tradition. My garage is right there behind the house, and—"

Flo peeked into the parlor.

"You two planning a trip down to the *holler* or are ya going to eat?" She dried her hands on her apron.

"It smells better than anything since I got off the plane," Nick said, giving her a broad smile.

Flo gave him the once over, eyebrow up, then turned and hurried back to the kitchen.

Maddie grinned, nodded her head toward the dining room. "She's right. I'm starving."

His warm smile as he motioned her to lead the way did as much good for her spirits as the hot shower. In the dining room, neighbors and her customers sampled various dishes and forked up slices of ham.

"Our condolences, Mad," a neighbor told her, his mouth already full of food. "Heard he was sitting behind the wheel of that old car when he crossed over. Must be some relief, though, after all."

Reality rushed in again. For a moment, in the parlor, under the gaze of an interesting gentleman, Maddie had kept it at a safe distance.

"Thank you, Adam, it is, but…" turning to Nick she said, "Grandpa had a heart attack, but he'd been suffering from Alzheimer's for quite some time. I promised I'd never put him in a home. Turned out to be a tough promise to keep."

"But you're glad it's over," Nick said quietly, lifting his eyes to hers.

She studied them as she considered his words. Sometimes it took a stranger to point out the obvious. "Yes. I'm glad. But there's a big empty space where he used to be. It's going to take more than a table full of food to fill that up."

He surveyed the table a moment. She got the sense he was looking for the right words. "Maybe start with a few bites," he said at last.

Here was a man who'd lost someone dear. That seed of warmth expanded a little. She offered him a plate and took one herself, picking out a few morsels as he loaded his full.

"I expect things will get back to normal someday," she said. A flurry of activity at the front door signaled the arrival of another group of guests with a passel of kids in tow. Distant neighbors she hardly knew. The dignified memorial was over and the feed was on. No one, not even the gas station attendant down on the highway would be turned away. Maddie smiled. Grandpa would have wanted it that way, but she was tired of the crowd, the condolences, the obligatory intrusion into her usually private life. She touched Nick's arm. "Let's go to the kitchen."

Nick scooped up another spoonful of butter beans and a chunk of cornbread as Maddie pulled him away. "What are these? I've never seen lima beans this big before," he asked.

Maddie allowed herself a little laugh. "You really aren't from around here."

The kitchen door swung closed on the voices in the rest of the house. Tucked into the small dining nook, Maddie felt insulated from the world. She forced herself to finish the morsels she had selected from the table as Nick cleaned his plate. Watching him brought back her appetite.

She was eyeing the rest of Nick's cornbread when Flo slipped through the swinging door and slid a platter loaded with a selection of dishes in front of them. "You read my mind."

"Thought I'd better save you some. Food's almost gone. Makes me wonder if these people eat between funerals."

Nick lowered his head, a grin teasing his lips.

"I'll come out and help you in a minute, I promise." Maddie covered Flo's hand with hers. "Thank you for this. For everything."

Flo rolled her eyes to the ceiling as if that would keep tears from falling down her cheeks. "Don't get me started now."

She gave Maddie's shoulders a hug.

"Doin' it for him as well as you." She propped her hands on her hips. "You going to introduce Mister Fancy Shoes?"

Maddie's cheeks warmed. "Sorry. Flo, this is Nicholas—*Nick*—Berlin. He's here about the car."

Flo mouthed a silent "*Oh*", wiped her hands on her apron and then shook his, an uncharacteristic smile on her lips. "They don't make 'em like her around here anymore."

Nick smiled at Flo and then back at Maddie. "No, I'm sure they don't."

Flo raised that discerning eyebrow of hers, and with a quick nod, she turned and headed for the door. "I'll have everybody out of here by three o'clock. Don't you worry yourself."

Flo had known Nick less than thirty seconds and it seemed they'd already shared a private moment. She quickly slipped out of sight before Maddie could protest.

"She likes you," she told him, pointing at the swinging door with her spoon full of scalloped potatoes.

"Mister Fancy Shoes?"

"If she didn't like you, you'd have never made it to the kitchen."

Nick scooped some banana pudding onto his plate and looked up at her with a boyish grin. "My mom used to make this stuff."

He devoured the pudding.

She wiped her mouth and dropped her napkin on the table with a big sigh.

Why was it that this stranger from all the way across the country, wearing the wrong shoes, felt so right sitting in her kitchen nook? She had known him for what? An hour? It defied reason, but his presence had somehow managed to break through the cold that had seized her heart when she first arrived home.

The snow thickened outside, erasing ruts in the driveway as cars drove away, pushing down on the barns like lids closing softly on hat boxes. Before long, it would be dark. Not a good time to be out on the roads. "We'd better get you out to see the car before I have to shovel us a path to the garage."

Nick looked up as if noticing the changing scenery outside for the first time. He shook his head. "I guess we should have done that first."

"No worries. You finish up." Maddie got up from the table, scooted in her chair. "We've got extra outdoor clothes. Something there'll fit you, including some rubber boots."

Maddie headed for the mud room, feeling better than she had in months. Grandpa was gone and that hurt, but she wouldn't spend the next hour like she had every day for the last two years trying to convince him that his wife, long dead, wasn't waiting for him out in the barn. A little bit of weight lifted from her shoulders.

On an impulse, she slipped a bottle of red wine into a canvas bag on her way through the kitchen, along with an opener and two plastic cups from the counter. Her healthy grandpa, the one she grew up with, would've suggested the bourbon.

Riffling through the various coats—Grandpa's, hers, Flo's—she was pulling an old camouflage Gore-Tex off the hook when something out the back window caught her eye. A figure, near her garage. Wasn't it? Must have been Bébé, still chasing snowflakes. Yes. That's what it was.

She pulled a pair of boots from under the bench as Nick joined her in the mud room, a finger pointed out the window. "Did you see—"

"—Something out there?" She glanced over her shoulder at the glass storm door. "Yeah. I think it was my dog."

"Hmmm." Nick shifted a doubtful gaze back to the window. "Looked like a guy to me."

Maddie shrugged it off. No guest of this house would wander around outside with Flo's food on the table. If she balked at every bird or critter that traipsed across their land, she'd never get anything done.

"C'mon, get your shoes off. I think these'll fit." She drew his attention back to her with a tug to his sleeve. "And try this coat."

Her smile grew as he swapped Brooks Brothers for camouflage drab. It was impossible to take her eyes of his flat, muscular stomach where his shirt tucked below his belt. Just the kind of distraction she needed today.

"And this…" She pulled her grandfather's knitted cap down over his ears to complete the picture and turned him to face the mirror above the row of coat hooks. His laugh was low and satisfying.

No sooner had she put her hand on the back doorknob than Bébé came trotting in from the dining room. She pushed her wet nose into Nick's hand, then sat, her tongue lolling out the side of her mouth.

They looked at the dog, looked outside, and back at each other.

Chapter 2

Nick was in over his head. He'd thought Kentucky was all horse racing and fancy hats. He'd been wrong.

From the moment he realized the address his father had given him was a cemetery, to the freezing cold, to the shattering look the woman had given him when their eyes first met, Nick had the sense that nothing was as it seemed. He'd run his thumb over the raised letters on her card as his driver navigated the slick back roads to her property. Kerrigan. The name had a familiar ring to it he couldn't quite place. The image of those taut points popping up under the soft fabric of her clingy dress sent a scintillating charge below his belt that lingered as he'd waited for her arrival in the sitting room of a surprisingly well-kept farmhouse. Her appearance had not disappointed. It had taken every ounce of his business skill to keep from swooping in on that long column of neck for a taste of more than lima beans and corn bread.

When Maddie buzzed open the door to what had appeared from the outside like an ordinary country barn, his expectations were once again shattered. He expected a bare bulb swinging on a wire, and the smell of dirty oil sinking into splintered planks and pitted, uneven cement. Instead, they stepped into a climate-controlled fantasy garage large enough to work on three cars at once.

They shook snowflakes off their coats and hung them by the door. Maddie flicked on a row of light switches illuminating Epoxy coated floors, glossy white walls banked in immaculately clean work benches, and a hydraulic lift recessed into the floor in the last bay. It was state-of-the-art, all the way. Shiny red tool boxes as big as deep freezes sat at the ready, the kind of setup Nick had seen in homes of his wealthiest clients. He was pleasantly surprised. Henry Ford would have been working the screws loose under the lid of his casket. A neon sign flashed on and off above the roll-up doors at the far end of the space. It would have been at home on a wall in any classy venue in Vegas.

Nick's gaze slid from the sign back to Maddie.

"Mad Monkey?"

Maddie shrugged. "Grandpa sent me to college to study business and I came home and started Mad Monkey Motorcars." Pride shown in her eyes as she swept the shop with her gaze. "Not what he had in mind, I expect, but I love the work."

Smack in the middle of the space, gleaming like a scene from a fifties movie premiere, was the Cadillac. With her spreading chrome grin and classy continental kit, she dominated the scene like an automotive version of Marilyn Monroe. Nick feathered his fingers along the voluptuous curves of her pale yellow sides as he slow-walked the length of her. "My new Beemer would beat her in performance, but it's hard to beat the look."

Maddie opened the wine, filled two cups and handed him one.

"Depends on what you mean by performance." She slid in behind the wheel and switched on the accessory power. The black top lifted with a confident *pumph*, folded, and settled into the boot behind the backseat, revealing pale ivory leather upholstery edged in deep red piping, and a dashboard right out of a drive-in dream.

Nick completed his circle and stood at the front of the car admiring the generous bumper. "Nice tits."

Maddie's easy laugh drew his gaze to her face.

"Those would be Dagmar bumpers." She draped her arm across the back of the seat, inviting him to sit behind the wheel. "Named after artillery shells, not a woman's anatomy."

"Coulda fooled me." *Missed that on my web research.* He came around to the driver's door.

"Common mistake." Maddie glanced away, pressed her lips together a moment. It was refreshing to talk to someone outside the car restoration business for a change. "Feels good to laugh a little. I hope you don't think it's crass, right after a funeral."

Nick slid into the driver's seat. He palmed the hard plastic knob on the big steering wheel, like a door handle into the past. His senses filled with the smell of leather upholstery, the gleam of chrome, and the warm scent of the woman sitting next to him.

Her eyes went darker blue when they turned serious. Dark eyes, short dark hair, creamy, white skin. His taste in women had always run in the opposite direction—blonde, busty, belligerent. Easy to let go of. But something about this girl piqued his interest. She was tall, graceful in an angular sort of way. Her syncopated walk spoke of confidence few women he'd known could pull off in real life. She wouldn't take shit from anyone, least of all, a man. She made her living in a man's world, that was for sure. Still, there remained something vulnerable about her. The tug below his belt grew more insistent.

"Grief brings odd things to you," he said, adjusting his posture. "A dose of guilt—mood swings." *Flashbacks. Anger. Regrets.* "Comes with the territory for awhile."

He pulled the heavy door closed and propped his elbow on it.

Her expression changed as she gazed through the windshield. Silence stretched comfortably between them, marked by the faint ticking of the analog clock in the dashboard. At last, she turned her gaze back to him.

"I am glad, really. Relieved." She swirled the wine in her cup. "I took care of him full time for the last two years. Diapers, feeding—not the kind of thing you want to see in a man who took care of you all your life—but owed. Definitely owed."

She dipped her head and swallowed hard. He could almost see a wave of emotion as it swept over her.

"If you don't mind my saying," he said, changing the subject back to safer territory. "Seems more likely you'd find an old Ford F150 truck out here on a farm. This car's not your average country ride." He sensed her looking at him closely.

"It's family baggage. You don't want to hear it."

His interest was piqued, but it was obvious by the tone of her voice she didn't want to talk about it. He'd try a different tack.

"Two hundred and ten horse power, Hydra-Matic, right?" He ran his hands over the top of the wheel. "Worth at least, what? Fifty thousand?"

He cocked his head, checking her reaction.

Maddie slid across the bench seat to the passenger side, her mouth tilted in a half smile. "For a minute there I thought you'd done your homework."

She stretched out her long legs, crossing them up on the dashboard.

For a minute, so had he. "Seriously," he said, recovering as best he could. "She's beautiful. And a classic, that's a given. But what's so special about this car?" *So special his father would lie to him to get it.*

Maddie leaned on the armrest, staring at the row of toolboxes. She could almost see Grandpa standing in the garage long before its modern renovation, coaching her as she set the points and timing, a socket wrench in his hand, a red rag half stuffed in the pocket of his overalls. How many hours of her life had she put into this car before she was even ten years old? Nothing had made her happier than scooting around the garage on his creeper, polishing hubcaps, and climbing up on a metal stool to hang his tools in their proper places on the pegboard.

She sighed as the image came up, lifted her spirit, and let her down again softly.

The car was a member of her family, her only connection to her parents. Whatever their weaknesses, they were after all, her parents. The ache of longing for those lost to her was perhaps undeserved, but not something she could easily control. The car was different. A hunk of steel couldn't desert you or break your heart. And it only rusted if you neglected it. It had been the solid object in her life when everyone else had abandoned her.

What was so special? How could she explain to a stranger?

She turned back, forcing a smile.

"Around here, everybody works at the Toyota plant. I mean *everybody*. They finish five thousand cars a day out at Georgetown. Five *thousand*."

Her eyes stung and she forced back the tears. She was determined not to break down every other minute, even if it was the day for it. She scooted back to the center of the seat, poked at the Bakelite keys of the radio tuner, producing satisfying *ca-chunks*.

"This car…" she realized she was delivering her grandfather's speech. "This is a '53 Cadillac Eldorado Special Edition. They only made five hundred and thirty-two of them."

Maddie straightened and wiped her eyes clear.

"No one knows how many are left. This one's never been publicly listed." Her throat closed again. She tried to breathe out of it, but it was no use. All the emotion of the day bore down on her and she was helpless to stop it.

"I'm sorry." When his arm slipped around her and pulled her close, she let it happen. Never mind that he was a stranger. He was there.

"It's me who should apologize." His hand lingered on the back of her neck. "I showed up here with my own agenda, never thinking about your circumstance. I should have known better."

The small kindness pierced what she'd hoped until this moment was an impenetrable veneer of composure. Any pretense of holding up well dissolved under waves of grief as though every hurt she had ever suffered had come back to pummel her. All the while he pressed her head against his chest, letting her ride it out with the patience of a close family friend.

Her first sense of ease returning was the sound of his beating heart, and the awareness of his cheek resting against her forehead. His heat, the pressure of his hand on her neck, and a faint remnant of Cartier blended together in a heady, sensual combination inviting her to linger. She pulled away just far enough to look into his eyes. They *could* be old friends. The second stretched until the truth welled up in her eyes. "I'm not sure I'm ready to let her go."

He ran a finger across her cheek, drawing away some of the moisture that lingered there. "I wouldn't blame you."

The quick intimacy set her senses on alert. It would be easy to forget she had only met him this morning and let things progress farther than they should. She angled away a bit, just to be sure she could. "What about your father?"

Nick cocked his head to one side, apparently considering his options. His eyes darkened around their centers. "You said there were five hundred and some of them. Let him find another one."

"Just like that? You'd give it up?"

"I'm not the one crazy for the car." The look in his eyes said he was more interested in her.

"Fifty emails in my inbox can't be wrong. The market's hot for her." She wagged her finger at him playfully, pushing past another wave of grief. "A rabid collector wouldn't be amused at losing the chance at the Flying Goddess."

Nick shrugged. "Not my job to amuse my father anymore," he said. He leaned in to almost touch her forehead with his, so close, she could feel the warmth of his breath on her lips. Excitement sizzled in places she'd ignored for a long time. She'd felt it at the cemetery. She felt it now. "It's a shame though. I was hoping to get to know you better over the deal."

"Seems like you're skipping the deal part and going straight for the get-to-know-you part." She pushed back a little, losing herself in those startling eyes again.

"It's not every day a man gets to make out with a gorgeous brunette in the front seat of a Cadillac."

Maddie knew she could push him away. His touch was light, not demanding. Instead, she let herself enjoy the lightness of the moment. After a day full of sadness, a playful conversation was welcome relief. "Make out? Is that where this is headed?"

"If you want."

She leaned her head back against the seat and closed her eyes. "My grandfather died in this car you know. Right there where you're sitting."

Nick straightened in the seat. "Geez. I'm…sorry. I—"

Maddie waved her hand dismissively. "No worries. I didn't think I'd ever be able to sit in here again." She opened her eyes and rolled her head to look at him. "It helped, your being here."

Nick's smile broadened as he relaxed a little in the seat. "That's good, because I sent my driver on his way."

She sat up with a snap. "You let him go? That was a little presumptuous, don't you think?"

"Not on purpose. His meter was running, and he was worried about getting a hotel, so..." He sat up straighter. "I'll call a taxi when I'm ready to go. No problem."

"Yes, problem. The only taxi around here is the flatbed trailer the Barnes boys use to haul their family car to the Walmart."

"You're joking, right?"

"No, I'm not. Every Saturday they all pile into this old Dodge van that quit running years ago, and he hauls it on the flatbed down to the store so they can go shopping."

Nick shook his head, his eyes alight with pleasure. "Looks like I'm sort of stuck then."

A giggle worked its way up her throat. Grandpa would love this predicament. She could almost see him grinning at her from the front of the car. Nick reminded her of Grandpa in a quirky, go-with-the-flow sort of way. He made her laugh. Something she hadn't done in a long time.

She put her hand against his chest. "Then you have time for a little more wine."

His grin broadened. "Absolutely."

He grabbed the door handle to let himself out and it immediately fell off in his hand. He stared at it like it might bite him. "Sorry. I seemed to have broken it."

Maddie let go a full-blown laugh. "I've got a new part being made for that. Hold on." She leaned over his lap, jiggled the handle back on until it engaged, then popped the door open. In less than thirty seconds she retrieved the bottle from the office and slipped back across his lap to where she started.

"Try that in your Beemer." She refilled the cups. His laugh rolled out warm and wonderful, and hearing it released some tension from the day.

Nick turned the bottle in his hands and read the label. "Paso Robles?"

"Best bourbon in the country's right here in Kentucky. Wine? Not so much. You can't ship it into Kentucky from another state. I order it online and have it shipped to a friend of mine in Cincinnati."

"California wine is worth it, I suppose. I'm spoiled, having local vineyards practically in my back yard. But it seems like a lot of trouble."

Maddie shook her head. "We do have some vineyards starting up, but they'll never take over the bourbon, at least not in my lifetime."

He filled the cups, handed her one. "To the Internet and good friends then."

Maddie tipped her cup to his. "To the Internet, and early snow."

The Zinfandel slipped down her throat like California sunshine, taking the edge off the cold and the day's events. She deserved a break and good company. She knew Flo would manage things in the house, seeing the guests out. Maddie had no more heart for condolences. Whatever Nick's intentions were for coming, she was glad he was here. Something in his eyes set her to thinking about warm and wonderful.

"Does the radio work?" He reached across to the fancy knob and gave it a twist. The power antenna rose just outside the wraparound windshield. "Mmmmmm."

A Kenny Chesney song whined out of the dash speaker. They both went for the knob, their hands brushed, sparking a static snap.

"Ouch!" Maddie jumped back, shaking her hand. "Clayton must've been in here last. He loves his country music." She punched the clunky buttons until something a little softer played through.

"Clayton?" Nick sat back at a polite distance. The look in his eyes teased.

"Old school buddy. Great body man."

Nick tipped his glass, lifted an eyebrow. "My kind of guy."

Maddie enjoyed the tease, light and breezy after a long dry spell. "*Car* bodies."

"Bet this baby purred when she was new."

He settled back in the seat, slipped his arm around her shoulders. He was smooth, all right. Practiced at the art of charming. A delicious chill shot up the back of her neck. She liked his style.

"Purrs now." She turned the key in the ignition. The engine jumped to life.

Nick closed his eyes, and stretched his legs out under the Caddie's ample dash.

She scooted closer, pressed the gas pedal with her toe, the motor raced. "She's a collector's dream."

Leaning forward to turn off the key, Nick finished with his hand on the small of her back, his forehead once again nearly touching hers. "Unexpected."

He brushed a light kiss over her lips, drew in a shallow breath, and waited, his hand eased up her side, just short of brushing against her breast. Maddie felt alive and sexy, like the girl in the Vargas Pin Up poster on the garage wall. For a moment, she let herself indulge the fantasy: She'd unbutton his shirt and throw off her sweater…

"Feels like high school," he said, his lips moving to her earlobe. Heat spread up her shoulders and flushed her cheeks.

She bit her bottom lip, slipped a hand against his chest and pressed him away firmly, and let go a low laugh. "We're not in high school and this feels like trouble," she said, reluctantly. She straightened her tunic, willing her heartbeat to settle.

"You'd better shoot those photos before we do something we'll both regret."

She leaned across his lap again to work her magic on the broken door handle just as Nick straightened in the seat. His arousal was obvious. "I can't imagine how I'd have any regrets."

Maddie swallowed hard, grabbed the door handle and prayed it would work. Just then, a *crash bang* came from outside. The next instant, Nick's expression was lit up in a flash, frozen somewhere between ecstasy and shock.

Maddie yelped and sat up just as another flash lit the shop.

"Holy shit!" Nick pushed the door open and clamored out of the car.

Maddie got to her knees in the front seat, heart pounding. She looked out over the hood of the car to the front window of the shop as Nick sprinted for the door.

Maddie ran after him, grabbing Grandpa's Louisville Slugger from behind the door.

She was standing at the ready, her pulse banging in her ears, the baseball bat poised to waylay any intruder when Nick came back, huffing and chuffing.

"Wait!" His arm shot out to block a potential blow.

Maddie lowered the bat, her pulse racing in her ears. "I take it that wasn't my dog."

"Not unless she's six feet tall, obese, and runs on two legs." Nick pulled a camera out from under the borrowed coat. "I scared him off. He dropped this."

Maddie turned it over in her hands, a standard pocket model, simple enough to operate. She switched it on, punched the memory key, bringing up the last few shots. Daylight close-ups of the outside of the garage, several of Maddie in her truck leaving home for the burial, and finally, Nick's face caught in surprise along with Maddie's as she rose from his lap. Her stomach took a dive for the floor. The photo was misleading, to say the least.

"Did you get a look at him?" she asked.

Nick leaned against the office desk, shaking snowflakes out of the neck of the jacket. "He wore one of those stupid hats. You know, with the floppy things?" He flapped his hands next to his ears.

"A Yukon," she said, breaking the tension with a laugh. "Damn Peeping Tom." She cycled through the shots again. "We had one around here a while back. Walt fired off the shotgun and I thought we'd seen the last of him."

"What about your buddy, what was his name, Clayton?"

"Clay? He's got his own key to the garage. Why would he prowl around? Besides, he's shorter than I am."

Nick looked uncomfortable. He glanced around the shop like a fish out of water. "We should call the police."

Maddie sniffed. "Cops may roll out on Peeping Toms in Montecito, but…"

"Did you see anyone?"

"All I saw was you, and a big bright flash." She smiled at him, then went thoughtful. It was the truth. She had let things get out of hand.

Nick ran his hand through his hair; the stray shock of sandy blond fell right back on his forehead. "He wanted pictures of the car. What about the locals?"

"Locals? Geez, everybody around here knows about the Flying Goddess."

Nick frowned and looked out the office window into the shop.

"What are you thinking?" Maddie asked.

"I'm thinking that if my father can get your address, so can anyone else who really wants this car."

He lifted the camera out of her hands, flipped through the photos again.

"This guy's casing—the house, the garage, your car—" He held the camera up so she could see the screen. "See that? A great shot of your video cam above the door, and the lock type. We see this in the real estate business all the time. Someone puts their property on the market, right away, they get robbed."

"Well, they can't get in here. Nobody can." *Really? And what about the man standing next to you?* She had been too trusting, too drawn in by his pleasing looks, easy manner, and—remembering the warmth of his hand on her side—all that.

"I'm just saying, maybe my father's not the only one obsessed with the car."

Maddie's hands went suddenly cold. She was young, but she'd been in the classic car business long enough to know that guys got *wonky* over a car if they wanted it badly enough. The insanity usually amounted to paying thousands more than a car was worth because it was just like the one they'd had in high school. But this guy, whoever he was, had obviously been following her all day. She'd been so wrapped up in the funeral and Nick, she hadn't noticed anything else. The thought of it sent a jolt of cold through to her bones.

"I'm sure it's much simpler than that," she said, pushing the fear away. She flipped the intercom unit to the house. "Flo. Is Walt in there with you?"

"No. He rode into town with that limo driver. Took him into his brother's and he decided to stay because of the storm."

"Okay." Maddie interrupted what she knew could draw out into a long story. "I'll be out here a few more minutes," she said, her eyes intent on Nick's. "Lock up tight. I've got my keys."

"Uh huh," Flo crooned. "You be careful now."

Maddie let go a little laugh. "Go to bed."

The simple explanations were running out. She'd promised Nick a look and some pictures. At least he'd had the guts to ask instead of prowling around on his own. And she liked him. Yes, she did. People have met under weirder circumstances. But the incident had set her off. Grandpa would have told her to take stock, weigh her options. And he would have been right. Something was going on and it had nothing to do with *kissy kissy* and chills up the nape of her neck. She needed to step back and take control of the situation. Now. Before things went any further.

She pressed his cup into his hand, tipped hers in a quick toast, and drained it.

"Take your pictures," she said, tossing the empty cup in the trashcan by the office door. "There's a bed and bath in the back of the shop. And a space heater. You'll be comfortable."

Nick stepped back as she swept by. "Fair enough," he said. Maddie heard the disappointment in his tone. She was sorry about that, but she was thinking with her brain now, not with her panties. He would get over it. And she would too. She stepped out into the snow. If there was any trace of the intruder, it had already been erased by a fresh layer of white.

The house was dark except for the light above the stove. Maddie considered pouring herself another glass of wine and taking it up to her room but thought better of it. Her mind was already a blur of conflicting emotions. Chalk it up to the grief roller coaster. She regretted now that she had let her levelheaded nature destroy the few moments of pleasure she'd had in a very long time. But the regret was immediately replaced by doubt. It was bad enough that Nick had tracked her down, but someone else had done the same and taken pictures of her house and the car on the sly. Who's to say Nick wasn't just cleverer? Found an easier way in? Her gut told her that wasn't the case, but she wasn't sure she could trust her gut right now.

She flicked off the light and climbed the stairs to her room. It had been fun to invite him home, enjoy a glass of wine and a little company, and watch his interest pique. He had been a gentleman. But who had played whom? This wasn't the old college days when getting laid was as much a part of her agenda as getting her degree. This was real life and Grandpa wasn't here anymore to make sense of it for her. Not now. Not ever again. Her heart ached at the thought.

There was something about the man out in the barn that she liked or she wouldn't have invited him home. And he had passed Bébé and Flo's inspection too. But who was to say he hadn't charmed her to get to the car?

She stole through her darkened room to look out the window. The moon hung half mast, lighting the snow-covered landscape is an eerie glow. Clouds shifted overhead, but there was no movement on the ground. Even the cows were smart enough to huddle together out of the wind. Her thoughts went back to the silent barn and to the man she had left alone there so abruptly—the image of his face close to hers, those sea green eyes, the way the cleft above his lip repeated in his chin, the way he tasted in that one, brief whisper of a kiss—all of it combined to send heat to her cheeks.

Stop thinking about it. She turned away from the window. He was an intruder, after all. She'd let down her guard. Days before the funeral, he'd checked the car out on the internet, gotten her address, and showed up unannounced. He knew a lot more about her than she did about him.

She moved her grandfather's strong box from the bed where she'd been going through the contents that morning. Deeds to the property, birth and death certificates, trust documents, and her grandparents' stack of love letters tied with a yellow ribbon. The pink slip to the Cadillac was folded inside a creased photo of her mother. Maddie slowly sat and studied the image. She'd be about Maddie's age in the picture. Twenty-five, give or take. Without her mother's wild, darker version of Farrah Fawcett's hair, it might have been Maddie standing there in a mini skirt. Long legs, tall boots, peasant blouse open one button too far. The body language said she must have had the hots for whoever took the picture. Maddie brushed across the face with her thumb. She had a feeling her mother had always had the hots for somebody, a weakness that eventually got her killed.

She set the photo and the pink slip on the pedestal table near the bed and stacked the rest of the contents on top of the box. She was beyond thinking about all that had to be done. Physically and emotionally drained, and desperately in need of sleep, she climbed between the sheets.

Morning brought the sun through her windows too early. Dark clouds that had hunkered over the funeral had been chased off by a brisk, overnight wind. Her sleep was fitful, filled with dreams of frustration and fear. She'd been advised by the county social worker to expect sleep trouble. It was part of the grieving process. Well, it could just go. She had too much to do to spend her time worrying about sleep.

Item one on her agenda was to check out Nick's story. A quick internet search on her laptop had popped the Central Coast Real Estate Investments Trust to the top of the Google list. By the look of the prospectus, Nick Berlin was the head of a very successful investment group. With the salary he likely pulled down, he could outbid anyone in the car market if he wanted to. So why had he come all this way when he could have contacted her through the listing? He had a confident manner, a bold approach. He was used to getting his way. Maybe he just wanted to hedge his bets, get a jump on everyone else.

Her shoulders slumped. She huffed out an exasperated sigh. She was making excuses for someone she didn't even know.

A light tap sounded on her bedroom door and when Maddie answered, Flo shouldered in with a mug of coffee. "Must be important, you clacking away up here on your computer before getting your coffee."

"You have radar ears." She accepted the coffee from her in one hand and scrolled down the computer screen with the other.

"You're welcome." Flo caught her hands on her hips and peeked around the bedroom door to the bathroom. "So, where's Mister Fancy Shoes?"

Maddie smiled at the woman who'd managed their house since her grandmother passed away. "You never miss a thing, do you?"

Flo shrugged. "Hard to miss a handsome guy shows up in a limo in the middle of a snowstorm."

"He slept in the garage."

Flo scrunched up her nose and pushed her hands in her apron pockets.

Maddie had to laugh. "Sorry to disappoint you." She sipped the hot brew. "I saw that you had a little thing for him."

"Me?" Flo clucked her tongue.

Maddie put the mug down. "Give Clay a call for me. See if you can bribe him with some of your biscuits and bacon gravy to drive Mr. Berlin to the airport."

Flo slipped back out the door muttering something about *kids* and *failing to understand.* Maddie turned her attention back to the computer. Her inbox was clogged with mail. With the exception of a few more expressions of regrets and condolences, the rest had been forwarded from website inquiries about the Cadillac.

Maddie cruised through several messages, her eyes getting bigger with each one.

"No need to be hasty," she told herself. The level of interest in the car and the sheer dollar value of the suggested offers told her she should hold off on a private sale and list the Goddess at one of the upcoming high stakes auctions. Bad news for Nick and his father. But that was the breaks. She needed a big infusion of cash if she were going to keep the farm, and her business, going. Handsome wasn't worth much where classic cars were concerned. Nick and his father would just have to get in line with everyone else.

"Rise and shine, Mr. Berlin."

Nick bolted upright in a dark room. One minute he had his hands on the most beautiful brunette he had ever seen, the next he thought he was back on tour with the surf team.

He rolled his gaze over to a row of red tool chests on wheels. *Oh. Yes. Maddie's garage. Nice.*

"Breakfast in fifteen minutes and it gets cold quick around here," a woman's voice said. Flo's not Maddie's. He dropped his head back on the pillow.

Just then his phone chimed out *Viva Las Vegas.*

Louise.

What is it with the women this morning? He'd slept on his arm and it had gone numb on him and didn't respond quick enough to pick up the call. He was still wiggling his fingers to bring them back to life when he heard the voicemail tone. Pulling the quilt around his shoulders, he crossed the small sleeping area and stumbled to the bathroom.

Could have been worse.

Could have been down his regular five thousand at the Bellagio's VIP Salon.

Overall, finding the car, getting the girl—well, almost getting the girl—and surprisingly, after watching back-to-back car auctions on the garage flat screen TV, getting a good night's sleep—he was ahead of the game.

He didn't have to listen to the message. He knew what his croupier friend Louise would say. "Where the hell were you last night?" Read: "Where's the five thousand you usually dump on my table?"

Safely in my pocket, thank you. He'd give his friend a call later. Right now, he had more pressing things to think about.

Last night he'd grabbed a few shots of the dashboard and cockpit of the Caddie with his cell phone and sent them off to his father, but the images that stuck in his mind had nothing to do with the car.

He ignored several texted responses from Nicholas Sr. and let the night wind of the passing storm lull him to sleep, even though his feet stuck out over the end of the small twin bed. The prospect of sharing breakfast with Maddie had him dressing hastily, ignoring the wrinkles in his pants. After her abrupt dismissal last night, he'd half expected to be hauled out of bed by Walt and sent packing.

Sun sparkling on the night's snowfall was cruelly deceptive. It was cold as hell outside. Nick zipped the borrowed coat all the way up to his nose and sprinted for the house.

Flo met him at the back door "My, we're energetic this morning."

She pulled the coat off his shoulders and hung it in the mudroom.

"There's coffee in there." She pointed him to the kitchen. "Maddie will be down in a minute."

Hearing their voices downstairs, Maddie shut down her laptop and shifted it to the nightstand, enjoying an undeniable frizz of excitement at the back of her neck. Despite the mystery surrounding his arrival, she couldn't deny her interest in Nick Berlin and the quirky notion that Grandpa had sent him for her personal pleasure. She scooped her grandfather's papers into the strongbox with the intent of putting it on her closet shelf for a while longer.

But as she closed the lid, she noticed a letter on top of the stack had different handwriting than the rest. The envelope was smaller and more creased, as though it had been flattened in someone's wallet for a long time. But it was the return address that stopped her pulse: R. Kerrigan, Lompoc, California.

Her father? The postmark was two years old. Resentment shot through her. Had her grandfather hidden a letter to her from her father for two years? No. That wasn't fair. Grandpa had been mentally out of it for at least that long. Maybe longer. She slipped the envelope out of the stack and sat on the bed. Her fingers trembled as she ran them under the open flap.

Two years ago, Maddie was still commuting back and forth from Lexington to school. Grandpa could easily have misplaced the letter and forgotten to tell her about it. But if that were the case, how did it end up in the strongbox? Had he stored up enough anger against his son to stick it away without telling her? Funny how Alzheimer's sufferers couldn't remember what happened yesterday, but they could hold on to twenty-year-old drama.

Maddie remembered. She was only five but she remembered. She and her father were running away. Days riding across the country in the big Cadillac, red rocks and deserts, rugged mountains and greasy-spoon diners, nights laying quiet in the big back seat while the engine thrummed her to sleep. Waking in a different hotel room each morning. Away from the ocean. Away from California. Away from something her father couldn't explain. Or wouldn't.

She saw snow for the first time on the country roads that would define her new life and in the ruts on the gravel driveway that led to her new home. The memory she had of her father was him waving goodbye in front of the Lexington Greyhound station where Grandpa had dropped him off.

He'd called on her sixth birthday and after that, nothing.

Until now.

Maddie unfolded the yellowed paper.

Dad,
The money's gone, no more comin'. Sorry.
Can't help it. I need the car to settle accounts,
or I'm gone too.
Ross

Her stomach did a flip-flop. Money? From her father? Her grandparents lived well, but they weren't anywhere near wealthy. Yet modeling school, the best tutors, and tuition at the University of Kentucky had somehow been within their reach. And then there was Mad Monkey…the seed money, the state-of-the-art garage…

How could she have been so dumb? Of course, they couldn't afford it. The money had come from *him*. All the old feelings of anger and abandonment welled up inside her chest. She would have rather had him in her life. Why couldn't he see that? The probable answer deflated her spirit like a flat tire on Sunday morning. He didn't care about her at all. All he wanted was the car. Just like everyone else.

"Sonofabitch." Maddie scooped the letter off the floor and threw it in the box. The car was all she had now too and she wasn't about to give it up to someone who hadn't the decency to even show up at his father's funeral.

She stared at the return address on the envelope as if she could transport herself there by the force of her will. Lompoc, California. It wasn't that far from Ventura, where she was born. She had an address for where he was. Or had been two years ago. It was a place to start.

Still, she found it hard to believe Grandpa would hide the knowledge from her without good reason. The only answer had to be that someone, probably her father, had manipulated him, coerced him, or held something over him. Something about the car. Something that her grandfather would hide from her.

But he hadn't hid it from her. He'd told her to look in the strongbox. He knew she'd find the letter one day. After he was gone. The finality of his loss descended on her like a mantle, heavy and thick and cold. If she ever had a child, she swore, she'd fight Heaven and Earth to make sure it knew it was loved.

She dragged her duffle bag from the closet and yanked clothes out of her drawers. Her ideas were scattered, half baked, but pulling together in a raggedy plan. For better or worse, her father was the only kin she had left. He may not want her, but she wanted the truth, and now she knew where to get it.

Thoughts circled round in her head like crows squawking for attention. She turned the laptop back on and drummed her nails on the keyboard while she waited for it to boot up. *There's seven hundred in petty cash. Tell Flo you're going to Louisville to pick up a bumper. You're Mad Monkey, after all. She'll believe that.*

The laptop chimed on. Maddie opened a map program and entered the address, making a mental image of the purple line leading across the map from Kentucky to California. It was only four inches long, give or take. She could be there in a couple of days. Grandpa would advise against taking off impulsively. He would have good reasons. Practical ones. But he was gone.

It was time she made the important decisions on her own.

She closed the computer and shoved it in the duffle. As soon as Clay left with Nick, she would put her plan into action. With cash and a sleeping bag, she could be halfway across the country in the old Caddie before anyone could talk her out of it.

Chapter 3

Clay jabbered to Nick about his "history" with Maddie all the way to the airport.

"Hey, you got off lucky, man. She's trounced a few hearts, including mine," he'd confided around a mouth full of country biscuit. "Learnt my lesson back in the fifth grade. When that woman says no, she means *no.* I got the gold tooth to prove it."

He pointed out the hunk of gold in the front of his smile with his tongue, as if Nick could miss it.

It was hard to imagine Maddie's friend in the fifth grade. His oversized gut barely cleared the steering wheel of his old pickup. Nick could see Maddie popping him one. He'd have laughed out loud at the thought if he hadn't been holding his breath. *Surely you shouldn't drive so fast in the snow?* But Maddie's childhood sweetheart managed to control the skids, running his mouth the whole time, unfazed.

"She's a great mechanic though. Makes those old cars sing."

Nick took a death grip on the door handle, tried to focus on his business. "What's a car like that worth? In your opinion."

"IMO?" Clay's eyes lit up, eager to offer it. He might be wearing greasy overalls, but he was obviously no stranger to the truncated text talk in automotive chat rooms.

"Like that un?" Clay shrugged a shoulder. "Couple hundred thou. Maybe more."

Clay rummaged his left hand through a nest of coffee-stained papers stuffed in his door pocket, sending the car into a temporary skid. Nick slammed his foot on an imaginary brake pedal. Once they'd recovered, Clay came up with a photo and passed it to Nick.

"I redone all the chrome on that Chevy, inside and out. Maddie restored the engine and tranni. Ran like a brick shithouse."

Nick tried to imagine what that would sound like, but another sliding maneuver brought his attention back to the road. He held his breath as Clay used cockeyed momentum to exit the freeway.

"Owner got eighty-five thousand for it at auction," Clay said without missing a beat. "Heard it got stolen not long after."

He pulled under the airport departures shelter and stopped. "Shame."

Nick exhaled. He pulled a hundred-dollar bill out of his wallet and tossed it on the console, hands trembling from more than the cold.

"Thanks for the ride," he said, relieved to be out of the truck.

Clay leaned across his cluttered console, snapped up the bill, and tossed it back.

"Way too much, man. I get good mileage in this thing." He slapped the dashboard.

Nick silenced his jangling cell phone for the third time and looked around, marveling that the old pickup was the only vehicle at the curb. He pulled his carry-on bag out of the truck bed and came back to the passenger door.

"If I were driving, we'd have finished that last slide in the ditch." He leaned in and made direct eye contact with Clay. "Oh, and tell Maddie thanks for the sleepover."

He relished the other man's expression as he shut the door and headed for the terminal.

Nick rolled his carry on through the revolving doors into the warm terminal, renewing his belief that snow should stay up in the mountains where it belonged, not on the interstate.

He wasn't exactly sure what had gone down at the farm house. Maddie was a no show. One minute he was eating a twenty-five-hundred calorie breakfast, and the next he was whooshed away in a trashed pickup by a fat man in greasy overalls.

He told himself he'd dodged a bullet. The last thing he needed in his life right now was a long-distance girlfriend. Until he was sure Central Coast was safe from his father's meddling—and his reputation—he needed to keep things neat and tidy. Still the scent of her lingered in his mind as he ordered a syrupy coffee. *Forget it, Berlin.* If he'd learned any lesson watching his father's decline, it was that beautiful women could be the downfall of a wealthy man if he wasn't careful. With new determination, he sipped his coffee and studied the departure boards. He could get out by noon if he was lucky, seven in the morning if he wasn't.

There was only one worker behind the ticket counter and she was checking in a family of four. Nick couldn't decide if the emptiness of the ticketing area was the prelude to a terrorist attack, or an airport wet dream. Before he could make up his mind, his phone jangled an electronic version of Cold Hearted Snake. *Christ.*

"What's up, Dad?" He tried to keep the impatience out of his voice. His father was mostly retired, but that never stopped him from trying to run Nick's life as if he were the President and CEO and Nick was the mailroom boy. Between Nick Senior, his frozen feet, and his wild skid down the freeway, Nick was ready to abort the entire mission and head back to Vegas.

"*Whaddya* mean, what's up? You got the car?"

"Not exactly." No. That wasn't what the old man wanted to hear. "Yes. I mean, I found the owner."

"You've seen it?"

"Yes. And now I'll probably miss my flight back to LAX. Did you look at the documents I left you?" He was anxious to sever the business relationship with his father and Berlin & Berlin Associates once and for all. If his father thought this goose chase was going to distract him from his goal, he was mistaken.

"I don't give a shit about your real estate investments," his father said, following up with a coughing spell. "Don't let that car out of your sight." His father's face would be red on the other end of the phone.

"We're too late, Dad. She's decided not to sell, besides—" Nick shouldered his phone and pulled out his driver's license.

"What do you mean, she decided not to sell. That's *the car.*"

"There's more than five hundred of them out there." Nick yelled into the phone over the blaring airport security recording. "What's stopping you from picking another one?"

The empty hall became suddenly silent again, leaving his question hanging out loud like a curse in a church pew.

"None of your goddamn business is what's stopping me."

"None of my business?" Nick lowered his voice, switched to the other ear and fished his now invalid e-ticket out of his back pocket. "*I'm* the one standing here in a business suit and tie in the middle of horsey country. It's *frickin* twenty degrees outside. *Twenty.* It sure as hell is my business. Pick another one for *chrissake.*"

Nick heard his father flick his lighter and pull a drag on what he knew was an expensive, illegal, and forbidden-by-his-doctor cigar. Nicholas Berlin Sr. coughed and sputtered. Nick coughed back at him.

"That's none of your business either."

The family ahead of him trudged away toward security with their carry-ons, ignoring the youngest who dragged along ten feet behind, thumb in his mouth.

Nick's chest tightened a little as he caught himself staring.

"Fine."

He stepped up to the counter. "I'm *outtalk* here."

His father was still growling and coughing when Nick laid the phone down. He slapped his ID and e-ticket a little harder on the counter than he meant to and the ticketing attendant flinched. “Sorry.”

Dutifully, she scanned the ticket and gave him a sympathetic smile. She pushed the ticket back to him. “You’ve missed your flight, Mr. Berlin.”

He sent her an exaggerated grin and shifted his eyes to the phone and back to hers, then spoke much louder than necessary.

“Can you get me a ticket to Vegas instead? Direct?”

She pressed her fingers against a smile as she heard his father carrying on over the phone.

She grinned back, obviously up for the game. A maelstrom of frantic keyboard clicking ensued.

“Sure. I’ve got a direct flight. It’s in first class.”

“Perfect,” Nick said. She was a quick learner.

A fresh round of expletives burst from the phone. The young woman covered her giggle. A lady with purple hair stepped up to the queue line, a pet carrier stacked on top of her air conditioner-sized bag. Nick waved her forward, slid his paperwork across to a closed ticket window, and knocked his cell phone hard on the counter.

“What was that Dad? I didn’t hear you.”

“Initials,” his father shouted and went into another coughing convulsion. “On the steering knob.”

Nick shouldered the phone again, shoved his ticket and ID into his inside coat pocket, trying to picture the knob. He’d had his hand on it as he sat behind the wheel, but he didn’t remember any…wait. There was something.

“A red swirly pattern?”

“Yeah. Her initials, you know, if she’d married me, they would have been—”

“Wait.” Nick’s stomach knotted. He was just beginning to enjoy life without that old familiar nausea and now, at just the thought of the woman who had marked his life with misery, it was back. After all this time, and a shit load of consequences his father had dumped on his family, he had sent Nick across the country in the earliest, heaviest snow storm in recent history because this car had once belonged to *Corrine Webb*? Nick couldn't believe what he heard. He often held back his feelings to preserve the tenuous relationship with his father, but he couldn't hold back any longer and he didn't care if the whole damn airport heard it.

"You ruined your first marriage, drove another good woman crazy with your belittling abuse, alienated one son and have damned near lost the other one over a woman who's been dead for twenty years—" The ticketing agent and the purple haired woman stopped their transaction and stared at him with their mouths open. His ears burned and he turned away.

"Just tell the girl you won't take no for an answer, make her an offer she can't refuse—no holds barred—" Clichés kept coming as if his father hadn't heard a word.

Nick swallowed bitter anger. Madonna Kerrigan had every right to her privacy and her dignity. He wasn't going to impose his father's mania on anyone else. He moved himself back into the ticket line, renewing his vow to keep Miss Kerrigan—and any other woman who came his way—at arm's length. He would never let a woman poison his life the way his father had allowed Corinne Webb to poisoned theirs. "*You* make her an offer. I'm done with it."

"You sniveling little bastard. You think you can crap out on me? You'll find the locks on my doors changed by the time you get back."

The bilious burn crept up again. It was an empty threat, but the thought that his father continued to try to manipulate him stopped him in his tracks.

"What, cat got your tongue?" Nick heard the lighter flick again, heard the drag. "Everyone has their price, son. Even you."

Nick pulled the phone away from his ear when the coughing erupted. Next his dad would go into his *you're-no better-than-I-am* speech, followed by his usual dig that Nick's fiancée had dumped *him* because he was a spineless mama's boy.

Purple hair cooed into the pet carrier and moved away. The woman at the ticket counter motioned him forward. Nick stared at her as his thoughts tumbled into place. The knot in his stomach relaxed even before he said the words.

"I am better than you, Dad. That's what goads you," he said into the phone without emotion. "I'm better than you because I know when to call off my bets and walk away."

ɞ

"Why, Nick. I didn't expect to see you back so soon. Maddie's…not here."

Flo stepped back from the doorway, inviting him in.

"I'm sorry to hear that. I was hoping to catch her. I didn't get a chance to say goodbye." He tilted his head to see into the foyer, half expecting the dog to come trotting down the hall. "How long since she left?"

The smile that greeted him slipped off her face, replaced with a look of thoughtful concern. "It's an hour or so into Louisville, hour or so business, then lunch. If I know Maddie, she'll hit her favorite mall…I'd say she left pretty early to get all that in…"

"So, you don't really know?"

For the second time today, Nick's stomach knotted up. Despite his vow to get back to Vegas, he'd found himself standing in the rental car line instead of the ticket line shortly after he'd broken the connection with his father.

"Soon as the road cleared, I went for supplies. She was gone when I got back. Left me a note." Flo poured herself a cup of coffee and plopped into a kitchen chair.

Nick declined coffee and paced the kitchen. He was more confused by his own behavior than Maddie's at this point. He'd been in the airport, a boarding pass away from getting back to reality and, the next thing he knew, he was driving back down the interstate in a red mustang with Kentucky plates.

Flo sipped her coffee, following him with her gaze.

"It was kind of strange, now that I think about it. Maddie taking the Goddess out to get bumpers. That's Clay's job."

Nick stopped in front of the window where he'd first seen the garage. The roll up door was open, revealing the empty bay.

"You like her, don't you?" Flo stirred more sugar into her thick diner mug.

Nick turned.

"No. I mean, yes. I—" He waved his hand vaguely at the garage. "We should close that door."

"Maddie hasn't brought anyone home since high school, gives all her attention to those cars. It's time somebody paid attention to her." Her gaze flicked back up to Nick's. "I saw the way you looked at each other over dinner."

Therein lies the problem. His gut told him to forget the girl, but his mind wouldn't let go of those long legs stretched up on the dashboard of the Cadillac, those cobalt eyes, or the fragrance of her heated skin. Nick drew in a slow breath. *Crap.* "Yeah. Well. Sure. She's…" *Fascinating.* There. He admitted it. Fascinating and unforgettable. Regardless of what his intellect told him to do, Maddie Kerrigan stimulated his desire, hit him on an emotional level that triggered his curiosity. There was something about her he'd missed, something that compelled him to see her again. Regardless of the alarm bells going off in his head, he wanted to see her one more time, if for no other reason than to convince himself he'd be better off staying away.

"…She really knows her cars," he said, feebly. Flo raised a knowing brow at him.

Flo was on his side, he might as well take advantage of it. He was no longer interested in what his father wanted. He was interested in Maddie. The fact that she wasn't there, that he couldn't see her right now, made it that much more compelling to find her. *Dammit.*

She seemed like the kind of person who could go off on a whim. She had almost gone over the edge right along with him last night in the front seat of her car. But she didn't seem like the kind of person who would put that car in jeopardy. It meant too much to her.

"Does it seem off to you?" he asked, following a spindly, twisty thread in his brain. "Taking the car out in bad weather on an errand her employee would usually do?"

Flo looked worried now. "Seems off she would take Bébé. She takes her everywhere she can, but she wouldn't take her on business when she'd have to leave her in the car."

She got up and poured more coffee into her cup. "Sure you don't want some?"

His pulse was already racing with caffeine, or maybe the thought of seeing Maddie again, but if having a cup of coffee kept Flo talking, what the hell. Maybe if he hung around long enough, Maddie would show up. He pulled a thick, diner cup from a hook under the cupboard and held it out. "Black."

Flo smiled, her face creased with years of caring for others, and filled his cup.

"You do that with an experienced hand. I bet you were once a classy waitress at some fancy restaurant." He lifted a brow, sipped from his mug. "Good coffee too," he added, eyeing her response to the compliment.

Flo adjusted the collar on her blouse, straightened in her chair. "Well, I wouldn't have called it fancy, but that's where I met Maddie's grandpa. Walt and I came here from Florida when Maddie was seven. Been here ever since, taking care of the house and the property. Mr. Kerrigan mostly worked on his cars."

"So, this is your only home?"

"Yes. I guess you could say that." Flo looked off into the backyard through the kitchen window. "I suppose, now that old Jake is gone…" She closed her eyes and pressed her lips together.

Nick put down his cup. *Raw hearts in this house.*

"I'm sorry. I should go."

Flo pulled a corner of her apron up and touched it to each eye. He started to get up but she held up her hand. "No, no. It's okay. I just…It would be nice if you stayed a little longer. I'm sure Maddie will turn up."

Go easy. You've got her in your pocket if you go easy. "Lost my mom last year. Cancer. But I really think it was stress, you know?"

Flo looked up. "Oh, I'm awful sorry. That had to be hard for you."

She reached over and patted his hand.

"She was my stepmom really, but yes. It was hard. She's the one who raised me, mostly." Nick always felt his father pushed her over the brink. Pushed her hard to measure up to some ideal he had of the perfect woman, based on that Corrine, of course. Nick held his coffee in both hands, letting the wave of loneliness pass through. Someday, he'd get over it. He hoped.

Now they both watched out the kitchen window as Walt pulled up in a small tractor, scooped away the tracks of the Cadillac leading out of the garage. He shut down the motor and scuffed into the garage bay. A moment later, the rollup door lowered.

Nick cleared a lump out of his throat. This was no time to mush around. Flo obviously didn't know what Maddie was up to, but Nick was worried. Who was that prowler last night? What if he was still up to no good? Maybe Maddie had left something in her room. Something to help him gauge his next move. Even if that was to turn back around and get on a plane. But he had to get up there without alarming Flo about the prowler. He could see she didn't need any more worries right now.

He drank the rest of his coffee and put his cup down. "You know, Maddie said she had some papers for me. About the car?"

"I don't know anything about the cars. If Maddie had anything, it would be out in the office, or upstairs."

"You wouldn't mind, would you, if we maybe looked? They weren't in her office last night." He stepped to the window, deliberately pulling back. It was one of his specialties. He waved his words away in the air. "You know, I'm sorry. Forgive me. I'll call her when I get back to Montecito. I was just hoping I could look at them on the plane."

Flo pressed her lips together, covered them with her free hand for a moment, and then blew out a big sigh. "I don't see as it would hurt. Let's go up."

Nick hesitated in the doorway to Maddie's room, and couldn't help but breathe deeply. The air was filled with her scent. He pressed his lips together hard.

Flo bustled past him into the room.

"She was going through her grandfather's things." She opened the closet. Her eyes went to a strongbox. "I see she's put them away."

Nick stepped into the room, overwhelmed by the artful layering of color and texture. Maddie was a garage monkey with a sense of style. A pair of terrariums flanked the window seat, preserving a bit of green in the otherwise white landscape beyond. In the corner, a pedestal table held an antique mercury glass lamp. The wooden sleigh bed would have cost a pretty penny. The bed had been made, the clothes in the closet hung neatly by color and length, shoes lined up in pairs on a shelf beneath a row of shirts and jackets. Everything was tidy and in its place as if the occupant had simply gone shopping on the first sunny day after a snowstorm.

Nick caught himself missing her. What the hell was he thinking? One passionate moment with a woman and he was a goner? At thirty years old, he was no stranger to one-night stands, but when they were over, they were over, he seldom gave them another thought.

He stepped to the bedside, looked out on the garage, and swallowed hard against the memory of Maddie only a breath away. *Give it up, Nicky boy.*

Flo gasped.

He turned around sharply to see that the color had drained from her face. She stepped back, one hand over her mouth, the other holding an envelope.

She turned it over and back again, shaking her head.

"What?" Nick started to reach for it but checked himself when Flo slapped it to her chest.

"Oh my god, she *knows*." She shook her head, looked up to Nick.

"Knows…" Nick prompted.

"I think she's gone to see her father."

She backed to the bed and let herself plop down to sit on the edge as if her legs could no longer hold her up.

Her father. Nick remembered now how Maddie had attacked him the moment she saw him at the memorial. She thought he was her father at first, or someone her father sent. He couldn't tell if she was angry or disappointed, but she was definitely agitated. Her father had hurt her deeply. He had recognized it in her eyes.

Flo shook the empty envelope. "There must be a letter here somewhere."

She put the envelope on the table and glanced around the floor, then lifted the bed skirt. "I'm not one to snoop into someone else's business, but…"

Nick cast his gaze around the room to the dresser, the nightstand, the pedestal table. Then he saw it, propped against the lamp. The photo. The face of the young woman in the picture stopped him cold, shocking his senses like an unexpected needle stick. He steadied himself with his hand against the window frame.

"What is it?" Flo slipped the photo from his trembling fingers.

"Oh." Her voice carried a note of relief. "That's Maddie's mother. Corrine."

She handed the picture back to Nick.

"She died a long time ago, poor thing."

Maddie's mom, Corinne. Poor thing. She said the words so matter-of-factly. *Paper or plastic? Have a nice day. How about those Giants?*

Never mind that the same picture had sat in a frame on his father's bookshelf for as long as Nick could remember. Corinne. The woman who had destroyed his father's marriage, stole his car, and run off with his business partner. The woman his father had obsessed over for more than twenty years. *Poor thing.*

Gold diggers. Whores. His father had hated women ever since. But more than the words and the face nearly identical to Maddie's, it was the background that sent Nick's stomach through the floor. The woman in the picture leaned provocatively against a classic yellow Cadillac. This was no wild goose chase. His father had known exactly what he was after since the moment he saw it on the Internet.

Nick dropped the photo back on the table, fighting old images he didn't want in his head.

"Nick?" Flo asked, bringing his thought back to reality. She gazed at him expectantly.

"Well," he said, still stunned by the shock of the discovery. He picked up the envelope and he read the address, then tapped it on his palm.

"Lompoc. Huh."

She pulled a tissue from the sleeve of her sweater and cut her gaze away. Nick took the opportunity to slip the envelope into his pocket.

Flo frowned at the floor. If guilt had a face, she was wearing it. He left his business card on the table. "Thank you, Flo. I want to know if you don't hear from her soon."

He hesitated at the door. She didn't look up. Instead, she pressed the tissue to her eyes.

"I'll let myself out," he said softly.

Nick slipped the envelope and a road map under the sun visor and got out of the car. He'd topped off the gas and cleared the windshield, undecided about which way to go. A smart person would take a southern route to get out of the severe weather. But maybe that wasn't right. Nick straightened and scanned the highway running out of town, not much of anything but white covered hills and a few black barns in either direction. A person who thought they might be followed might do the opposite. Take the tougher route. Or, he could jam across country the central route and wait for her to show up at the address on the envelope. But that wouldn't get him what he wanted. He wanted an explanation. He wanted an end to the Corinne curse.

He wanted to show his father who was really in control.

One thing he did not want was to be led around by his dick.

"You goin' to pay for that gas buddy or just stand there till the squeegee freezes to the windshield?"

Nick blinked at the attendant who seemed to have materialized out of nowhere. And then it hit him. It was a small town. If Maddie filled up here, and chances were she did since it was the only station he could see in either direction, the attendant would surely remember the car, if not the woman.

"Yeah, she filled up here around eight thirty this morning. Had Bébé with her." He looked Nick up and down. "You're the guy in the limo. Saw you at the burial."

Nick nodded. He dug a fifty out of his wallet and handed it over. "She left some documents with me, trust deeds and like that." The words tumbled out of his real estate repertoire. "I thought I could catch her, but…" He stuffed his wallet back into his jacket pocket.

"I can mail them to her…" he said, trusting the man would accept he had some business to conduct as reason enough to ask.

"Too bad about her granddad. Nice people, the Kerrigan's." The attendant stared at the bill before he folded it into his shirt pocket. "She's a sweet girl. Asked about my brother-in-law up in Cheyenne, how he's doing, if the weather up there's okay for his cattle these days, about his kids. She restored a forty Ford for him last year. Present for his wife. Ha."

Sweet girl. Right. The kind that sucks the life out of you and then runs off with your business partner.

But Nick had a clue on the come line and he played it. Better than flipping a coin. "How *is* the weather up there right now?"

"Well, like I told her, this was a freak storm, early for this part of the country. It was light up that way. Not much happening over there yet, but soon."

Nick slipped into the car. "Thanks man. I'm happy to be heading back to Cali, as they say here in the east. See you next time through."

☙

Georgie banged the steering wheel of the coughing heap. "I told you to watch her till I got out of the john." The car belched black smoke then kicked back into a reasonable rhythm. "We'll be lucky if we can catch up with her in this dog."

Leon crammed the remaining half of a stale bacon biscuit into his mouth and licked a glob of melted cheese off his fingers. "How would I know she'd take off so fast? My blood sugar was getting low, George. You know what happens when my blood sugar gets low."

Georgie looked over at him like he was dog shit on a plate. He was still mad about losing the camera. It wasn't Leon's fault the bucket collapsed under him when he took that last shot. Had to be rusted out or something. He already had what he needed, but damn, he could have sold that picture. His hands had been so numb he could barely squeeze the button, never mind keep a hold of it in a full-on sprint in the snow. Once the guy picked up the camera there was no goin' back.

He washed the chewed mass down with a slug of Mountain Dew. "Just think good thoughts, Georgie. Like, you know, the Stay Puft Marshmallow Man in Ghostbusters."

"How 'bout I think about you left out on the roadside. It'd lighten my load by about three hundred pounds."

Leon straightened his shoulders. "I don't weigh no three hundred pounds."

Georgie snorted and rolled his eyes. "Right. You just keep your eyes open. She's heading for the Interstate, we'll catch up soon enough."

Chapter 4

Nick's hunch paid off.

He'd driven straight through heading north, breaking speed limits in four states. The night was clear and cold, a quarter moon hung low over the Mississippi river. It would have been an eight-hour drive for the old Cadillac, adding a couple pee stops for the dog and fast food for Maddie. He'd followed the MapQuest route as bright city lights gave way to private horse farms and eventually to frozen golf courses where he'd expected to link up with Interstate 80 for the long haul. There, he checked hotel parking lots.

He was on the phone with Louise when he saw it. Tucked into the far corner of the lot behind the Hampton Inn, the signature taillights of the classic, yellow Caddie stuck out behind a hedge of twiggy branches. Nick's senses went on alert.

"Holy Christ, I just got lucky."

He tapped the brake and slowed to a stop about fifty yards away.

"Not luck, Nicky boy. Fate."

He'd been apologizing to Louise for not returning her call and trying to explain what he was doing in a rented car in Davenport, Iowa at ten p.m. on a Monday night when she'd interrupted him with her usual insight.

"What do you mean, fate?" He knew exactly what she meant, but he wasn't going to let her go there. "When the car goes up for auction, I'll bid against my father." *We'll see who locks the doors on whom.*

"Don't change the subject. She's got a hold on you." He could hear the smile in her voice. "You and I both know the only thing that could keep you from my Friday night crap table would be the girl of your dreams."

Louise purred, letting him know that she knew she was right.

Maddie, the girl of his dreams? Not likely. His fingertips tingled when he thought of the silky softness of the skin on her neck. But the image of her eyes darkening to cobalt stopped him cold. "Nightmare's more like it."

"Oh, you *are* in trouble."

Nick redirected his approach. "It's the car, Louise. That classic Caddie I told you about?"

"Um hum."

She wasn't buying it. He pictured Louise luxuriating like a fat cat on a windowsill, slow-blinking at the truth. But this time, she was wrong. Maddie Kerrigan would never have a hold on him. Now that he was on to her, knew where she came from and what she was capable of, she was one Mad Monkey he could resist.

Mad Monkey. She had him going there in the front seat of her fancy car, her long legs stretched out on that buttery leather seat… Nick groaned inwardly, and dragged his mind away from the image.

"No way. I'll take care of business and—" He had just checked the rearview mirror and backed up, when another car pulled into the lot and cruised behind him.

"Nicky boy. You can't fool old Louise—"

"Later Lou. I have to go." He clicked the phone off before his friend could protest.

❧

Between the dog's furry coat and her faux down sleeping bag, Maddie was plenty warm in the backseat of the Cadillac. She stretched her back and readjusted to accommodate Bébé's sprawl.

Try that in your Beemer, Mr. Fancy Shoes.

She couldn't help thinking about Nick as she settled in. She had been so occupied taking care of her grandfather, she scarcely had time for Mad Monkey Motors, let alone her sex life. But in only a few hours, Nick had awakened her sex kitten. Here in the backseat, with only Bébé to keep her warm, it purred loud and clear. Hungry, for the first time in months, all right, years.

Good vibes, bad timing. Nick would likely be home in LA by now, his sensual presence relegated to dream material.

She rolled to her back and bent her knees up. Lights from occupied hotel rooms glowed invitingly through the Caddie's foggy windows. Forget it. Her travel cash didn't allow for fancy hotels and she didn't want to use her credit card unless it was absolutely necessary. The parking lot would have to do. Think about something besides smooth white sheets, a pillow topped mattress, and Nick Berlin. How about a mental list of men whose company she'd enjoyed in the last year? A worthy distraction, like counting sheep. Maddie squeezed her eyes shut as if the simple action might conjure a lineup, but it only made her laugh, realizing it had been a very long dry spell.

Her sex kitten would have to wait until this business with her father and the car was over. Once the money was in the bank, a little R & R wouldn't hurt. She forced a purging sigh and cocooned deeper into her sleeping bag.

A moment later, Bébé's bark brought her straight up in the seat.

"Shhhh." Maddie hooked her arm around the dog's neck and listened to a car cruise by, slowing as it passed behind hers. She rubbed the side window to clear a small hole in the moisture collected there and peered out just as the car disappeared behind the building.

Bébé woofed under her breath.

"It's okay, girl." Maddie rubbed Bébé's ears as much to calm her own nerves as the dog's. "It's just someone looking for a parking place."

She pulled the sleeping bag over her head and willed her heart rate to slow down.

Bébé jumped into the front seat and continued grumbling, nosing her own peephole clear.

"Bébé. Lay down."

The dog continued to pace back and forth, restraining a nervous whine.

Maddie sat back up. If the dog was going to alert at every car that drove by, she'd never get to sleep.

"Get back here." She snapped her fingers and jabbed the seat. Bébé reluctantly obeyed. But before they could get situated again, a car pulled in next to the Caddie. Bébé went nuts, jumping at the window and barking like a maniac. Bébé's eyes widened and followed the sound of footsteps coming around the back of the car, her bark quieting to a low growl.

Maybe sleeping in the car wasn't such a great idea after all. Maddie stroked the dog's neck as hairs lifted on the back of her own.

There was a knock on the window. Bébé leapt to the front seat.

"Bébé?"

A man's voice. A man who knew her dog?

Maddie threw the sleeping bag off and climbed over the seat, heart racing. Bébé's crazy bark filled the car with chaos, her tail banged frantically against the steering wheel as she lunged at the window.

The knock came again, harder this time. "Maddie. It's me."

A pair of blue-green eyes appeared at the cleared spot in the window and shifted back and forth.

Maddie pushed the wiggling mass of fur out of the way, rubbed the spot bigger and peered out.

"What on Earth? Nick?"

She looked him up and down, her mind still not grasping the whole picture. He wore the same shirt and jacket he'd been wearing the day before, and a serious five o'clock shadow that made him look like he should be advertising a pair of low slung designer jeans.

She rolled the window down a few inches. "What are you doing here?"

"Me?" He hunched his shoulders against the cold, a plume of vapor streamed out of his mouth. "What are *you* doing out here like a homeless person?"

The dog whined and nosed to the window. Maddie pushed her back. "You can't have the car so you're stalking me?"

Nick straightened and threw his hands up in the air. "No, I'm not stalking you." He pulled his jacket closed around him. "I just want to…"

He ran his fingers through his hair and swept the parking lot with a hurried look. Then he hunched close to the window. "Can we talk inside? It's twenty-frigging-*two* out here."

Maddie glared at him. Had she conjured him out of thin air? One minute she was thinking about how wonderful it might be to have his hands on her hips and the next, here he was pounding on her window in the middle of the parking lot.

Her pulse settled from *scared-shitless* to *what-the-hell?* She wasn't about to go into the hotel with him. But it was stupid to make him holler at her from out in the cold.

"Tch." She huffed out a breath, unlocked the car door, and scooted over.

The moment he slid behind the wheel, Bébé attacked, her pink and black tongue scouring the side of his face. Nick pulled the car door closed with one hand and fended the dog off with the other. Maddie ordered Bébé into the back, then leaned breathlessly against the passenger door.

Nick's gaze swept over her, feasting for one long, transparent moment on the curves beneath her thin T-shirt before returning his eyes to her face. "You're freezing."

Maddie folded her arms across her chest, hiding nipples which had pulled achingly tight. "Not until *you* got here."

Nick scanned her makeshift bed in the backseat. When his gaze came back to hers, his eyes narrowed, then one maddening eyebrow lifted. "This was your plan? Drive across country, sleep in the car?"

It wasn't a question, but an accusation. Maddie's back stiffened. She'd never done ridicule well. Especially when it came from a man who didn't know *diddly* about her. And even more maddening was the fact that his tone and the expression on his face made her question herself. She let some of the air out of her puffed up resistance.

"It's none of your business." She got to her knees and reached over the backseat to snag a sweatshirt she'd been using as a pillow. "I screwed up, putting the car on eBay. All kinds of weirdoes crawled out of their closet, yourself included, apparently."

"So, you took off across country driving a Number One car all by yourself?"

His critical tone set her off again. "What do *you* know about Number One cars?" She pulled the sweatshirt over her head and yanked it down. "You only offered me a measly fifty thousand for it yesterday."

Nick rubbed his palms on his pant legs, avoiding her eyes.

"All I know is that I wasn't the one sneaking around your place with a camera." Then he turned back. "At least I was honest."

"Honest? Or just clever enough to get a front row seat?" What was it with the men in her life? Her father dumps her, her grandfather up and dies on her, and now this perfect stranger thinks he can come out of nowhere and tell her what to do? *Wait, did I just refer to him as perfect and in my life?* She had known him less than forty-eight hours.

Nick straightened in the seat and checked the rearview mirror like he was expecting someone. "I went back to your house to apologize. I'm sorry. I barged in on a very personal moment because of my father's—"

He interrupted himself as though the mere thought of his father set him off track. Muscles bunched in his jaw. "When I got back to your place, you were gone."

His tone changed from apologetic to something else entirely. Maddie curled her legs up under her, settled further into the seat, and shivered.

She had forgotten about the guy with the camera. All she remembered about last night was Nick undressing her with his eyes, the heat of his fingers teasing her earlobe. The sound of his breath catching when she pressed her hand against his chest, and yes. Those eyes, damn him. They were the kind of eyes you could pour your soul into. The kind you could learn to trust and then realize too late they had led you to trouble. She had come so close to taking the moment to the next level. Her ears burned at the memory. "So? I have a business. A life." She waved her hand at the dashboard as justification.

"I'm just saying, a woman alone. That guy could have followed you."

The suggestion stung, then startled her as a memory of a couple of sleazebags back at the Quick Stop played through her mind. She chewed her bottom lip. *Don't be paranoid.* They were just poor town boys getting off on seeing a pretty girl alone.

"That's ridiculous. How could anyone have followed me?"

Nick raised his eyebrows and rolled his eyes at the headliner.

He was right, damn him. She slumped down in the seat. If he'd followed her, anyone could have. She had been completely impulsive. Gone off without thinking it all the way through. She ran over the plans in her mind. There had to be something redeemable. Some defense. "I only had seven hundred cash, I won't use my credit card unless it's an emergency and…I have Bébé."

Bébé was busy licking Nick's ear. "Some deterrent."

Once again, he nudged the dog away, and focused his attention out into the parking lot. After a moment, he flexed his shoulders back and cracked his neck, let out his breath, and turned back to her. Maddie saw something in his expression she hadn't seen before. He'd closed off, pulled back a notch, shut down.

He fingered the steering wheel knob a moment, spinning it slowly. “If you want to get this car to California—”

Maddie gasped. “How do you know that’s where I’m going?”

Nick rubbed his fingers over his mouth. “Maddie. I’m sorry. I know I’m going at this all wrong. Flo—”

She put a hand up. “Oh. Now I get it.”

She remembered her conversation with Flo. They must have conspired. She couldn’t help but smile a little. Flo had been taken with him as much as she had.

Nick glanced into the mirror again before he focused his attention back on the big steering wheel. “I’ll rent a car hauler in the morning. A closed one, and trade the Mustang in on something that’ll tow it, but only—”

“Wait a minute. You may be some fancy schmancy CEO, but that doesn’t mean you can just show up here and take over.”

That seemed to stop him a moment. He leaned his neck over slowly until it cracked, then refocused on her. “But only,” he went on, his voice lowered, “if you sleep *inside* the hotel.”

He held up his finger at her expected reaction. “Your own room—tonight and every night—until we get there.”

Maddie understood the *how* of everything. How he had found the car, how he had tracked her down. He was relentless, used to getting his way, even if he had to pay for it. What she didn’t understand yet was the *why*. But the scent of him filled her senses. His masculine presence drew her like gravity and the space between them shimmered with the possibilities. She could almost taste it.

“I can’t afford that kind of expense.” She knew it was a feeble excuse even before she said the words.

“You can pay me back out of the proceeds when you sell the car.”

Maddie drew her finger through the condensation on the passenger window. The offer had merit. And, assuming the information on his web page was credible, he was no criminal, and, damn. She could gaze into those gorgeous eyes all day long. She was out of excuses.

❧

Maddie filled her coffee cup from the hotel buffet for the second time. She'd already eaten a chocolate croissant and a bowl of fruit, let Bébé out for a short run and fed her some kibble, and so far, Nick was a no-show. She'd been awake since five-thirty, waiting for the buffet to open. She had to admit, the hot bath and smooth sheets had been everything she'd dreamed of. Well, not *everything.* And with Bébé assigned to the car, she'd had the entire king bed to herself. She would pay him back, of course. As soon as the car was sold. She'd assured Nick, it would *not* be sold—to anyone—until she'd confronted her father. And, she'd told him at the door to her room, it would be to the highest bidder, not in some sweetheart deal made in a moment of passion. She actually thought she was being cute, flirty. She couldn't help herself. Back at the farmhouse, they'd been close. Soooo close, just thinking about it made her shiver.

But Nick didn't seem to hear her declaration, flirty or otherwise. The moment he'd hauled her bags up to her room, and waited through her pronouncement, he'd left her standing in the doorway with a curt good night.

So. A moody guy. She'd seen it in the car. She'd keep it business. If the *why* was simply for the car, and it seemed that is was, that could work in her favor. If there was anything she knew, anything she was really good at, it was driving bidders wild at an auction.

She was about to make another run at the buffet when he slipped into the booth facing her. "We're all set."

He carried himself like a man who'd just made the deal of a lifetime.

"We are?" Maddie had to stop herself from laughing. His five-o'clock shadow was gone, his sandy hair still wet from a shower, his athlete's physique pushing the limits of a white T-shirt. The words "Hog Stampede" were emblazoned across the chest of an upright, snarling hog in running shoes. She giggled.

"What?"

Maddie pointed at his shirt.

Nick shrugged. "I didn't plan on staying more than one day, okay."

He went to the buffet, filled a large Styrofoam cup with coffee, and came back.

"A gentleman was selling them, over there." He tipped his head in the direction of the lobby. "There's girl sizes if you--"

"No thanks. I planned this trip, so I have a spare." She fixed her eyes on her coffee, repressing a grin. "That'll look nice under your suit jacket."

Nick stiffened a moment before he let go a laugh. Their eyes caught and held. Maddie broke the connection, dipped her head down and stirred her coffee. "What's all set?"

Nick scooted into the booth opposite her. Her laughter caught him off guard. It felt good to laugh. Hell, if he had a tail it would have been wagging out of control. Something about her short-cropped hair above the collar of her Mad Monkey sweat shirt, the clear blue of her eyes without the interference of makeup, and the way they crinkled at the corners when she looked away, took him to a free and easy place inside. A place that was foreign to him.

He cleared his throat. *Stay focused on business. Strictly business.* It was his new mantra. Help the girl get the damned car to auction and be done with his father's crap—past and present—once and for all.

Everything had been fine until he slid into the front seat of the Cadillac where they'd had their last…*conversation.* It had taken every ounce of his will to walk away from her hotel room door last night. And now, here she was, lighthearted and free, making him laugh.

Reeling him in.

He wasn't going to let that happen.

He straightened his shoulders and cracked his neck.

Maddie's head popped up. "You do that a lot."

"What?"

"Cracking your neck like that."

Nick shrugged a shoulder. "Make's it feel better."

"Could be what's making it hurt in the first place," she said, then pursed her lips.

He cracked it the other direction.

Maddie held up her hands. "Okay. None of my business."

She sipped her coffee. "So, again, what's all set?"

Nick's brows drew together as if he'd forgotten the original question.

"Come on. If I were alone, I'd have been on the road for two hours already." She pointed to the Hog Stampede T-shirt. "You've made your fashion statement for the day, so, what else?"

He started to crack his neck and straightened instead. "We pick up the car hauler and swap the Mustang for a Silverado in…" He stopped to check his watch, "…twenty minutes."

"Chuh! Good thing I brushed my teeth."

"If we leave by ten, and drive straight through, we can be in Cheyenne before midnight." Nick nodded, satisfied with his plan. *One less tempting hotel room.*

Maddie wrinkled her nose. "Straight through? That's twelve hours."

Nick popped the lid on his coffee and stood, the snarling hog flexed across his chest. "It's a guy thing."

Chapter 5

Maddie awoke to the brawny purr of a V8 engine pushing them along the highway. A colorless landscape rolled flat under a drab gray sky. Patches of snow left over from last week's early blizzard clung to clumps of gray grasses on the soft shoulder. Her lower extremities felt like folded cardboard and she had to pee. She unfolded her legs slowly and propped her feet on the dashboard.

Nick's head bobbed in a deep, private groove, iPhone buds firmly implanted in his ears. He'd eased his tall frame back in the driver's seat, one arm stretched across the seat back, the other draped over the steering wheel at the wrist. Being on the road suited him. Sinewy muscles played in his forearms as he tapped his fingers on the wheel. She pressed her lips together, savoring the rush of pure heat brewing at her center, a sensuous promise. What was it about this stranger that pushed all the right buttons? He was moody and preoccupied. Not her favorite combination. A sudden image of her father hunched over a cup of coffee at the breakfast bar jolted her a step back. That similarity in itself should have sent her running for cover.

But there was something else. Something that went beyond appearances and mood and a little girl's first hint at love. Nick had a tender spot under that edgy exterior. She'd seen it, been wrapped in its warmth. Where had that gone?

She pulled her legs down from the dashboard and pushed herself up in the soft leather seat. They could have rented any truck on the lot with a tow package. But no. Nick had to have the swankiest one. She'd protested as they scoured the lot. She was the one who would ultimately pay.

Maddie smiled, remembering. When Nick had stepped up to the counter, the stampeding hog snarling out from under his Armani jacket, then rented the most expensive tow package on the lot, the agent's jaw dropped.

"You ever towed a heavy payload down the highway, *Miss* Maddie?" Nick had lifted his chin a notch as if he'd been towing cars across country all his life.

She doubted it. *Truck drivers don't arrive in limos.*

"As a matter of fact, I have. It's my business, and I don't need captain's chairs and surround sound to do it."

"Well, I do," he said, and leveled a self-assured glance at her. But there was something else in that look, something veiled, vulnerable. Embarrassment? Guilt? Their eyes held a mutual challenge several heartbeats, until he dragged his focus back to the road.

Maddie tilted her head, studied his profile. "Some people simply enjoy the aesthetic of a classic car, the ambience, the romance—Like Prince Rainier and Princess Grace winding down the coastline, hair blowing in the wind."

"I didn't say they aren't romantic." Nick relaxed in the seat a bit. "The trouble with old cars in my opinion is that they're not practical. There's no spare parts if you need them and no service center to install them."

"This Cadillac's original sticker price was under eight thousand dollars. Now she's worth…a small fortune." She wasn't about to name her price. Not yet. "Will you get more than you paid for it when you turn your Beemer in?"

Muscles tightened in Nick's jaw.

Time to bite her tongue. She didn't want to argue with him. This truck was indeed more comfortable than her old Toyota, and a lot less vulnerable than the Goddess would be on a long trip. The road had drastically changed since they'd passed through Omaha where Nick suggested she "hold it" until they got through the city. It wasn't snowing, but it was still winter bleak and unfriendly to automobiles.

And much as she'd tried to ignore them, a couple of jerks at the last stop she'd made before getting off the interstate had paid way too much attention to her and her car. Knowing the Goddess was safely out of sight in an enclosed car hauler eased the tension in her stomach.

Maddie propped bootless feet in the corner of the dash and stretched to pull the visor down. She licked her finger and rubbed a black smudge out from under her eye. She might feel like a stiff piece of cardboard, but she didn't have to look like one. Anyway, it was a distraction from an unrelenting fantasy—climbing over the console and into Nick's strong arms.

"Don't worry, your precious car is still back there."

Maddie jumped, flipped the mirror visor up.

"I see that," she said, her ears heating up. "And I still have to pee."

A pile of fur erupted from the backseat and seconded the motion, licking the back of Nick's ear. He tipped his head away, pulled the ear buds out, and straightened in the seat, both hands on the wheel. "Can you make her stop that?"

"You must taste pretty good." Maddie drew in a breath through slightly parted lips, remembering the scent of him just before he tested a kiss back in her garage. Maddie caught a brief flash of amusement on his features before his hands tensed on the wheel. He readjusted in his seat.

She snapped her fingers, pointed, and Bébé's rear end plopped down obediently. Maddie'd seen the play of emotion across Nick's brow through miles of silence. The playful Nick who'd relished their encounter in the front seat of the Cadillac had been replaced by someone else. A distant, closed off someone else. If they were going to spend several days on the road together, Maddie wanted Playful Nick back. Handsome Stranger Nick. The one who made her pulse rush. The one who made her forget her circumstance, at least for a few precious moments at a time.

He checked the passenger mirror and flicked the right blinker on. "Diesel at the next exit," he said without looking at her. "We should have plenty of room to park there."

"I'll park it, if you're worried," she told him, half playful, half serious. That was her car back in the trailer, after all. She wasn't about to let his demons or his ego damage the Flying Goddess.

They pulled through to the diesel fuel pumping shelter and stopped. She led Bébé on a quick stroll and watched from a distance as Nick filled the tank, cleaned the windows, and headed for the convenience store pay counter. An invisible force seemed to ride his shoulders, weigh him down.

What did you expect, Maddie? You let him into your life on short notice. And the moment you did, he shifted gears.

Whatever it was, it was his problem, not hers. She had problems enough of her own without having to tiptoe around somebody else's. But she missed Playful Nick. Hoped he'd return.

Bébé headed for the barrier around a dilapidated phone booth. Maddie urged her on, her own need to pee trying her patience.

That's when she saw them. She recognized the heavy set one right away. He'd watched her from the entrance of the Quick Stop when she'd pulled off the Interstate in Des Moines. Seen them in her rearview mirror as she pulled away, getting into a battered coupe. Now they were parked behind the building, between her and the restroom she desperately needed.

Damn.

Maddie quick stepped behind the booth and peeked around. Surely it was just a coincidence. Anybody traveling the Interstate would stop off at the same gas stations and markets along the way. But a zip of chills prickling the back of her neck told her otherwise. It was the car all right—primer paint, bald tires, bailing wire coiled recklessly where a hood latch ought to be. The heavy-set man on the passenger side hunched his shoulders and leaned away from the older gray-haired driver who gesticulated wildly. Maddie knelt and ruffled Bébé's neck. "Hold on, girl."

Finally, the two of them got out of the wreck and sauntered around to the convenience store entrance. Maddie glanced back at the gas pumps. Nick was nowhere to be seen. She'd have to move fast.

She pulled Bébé's leash and sprinted to the trash heap car. Bébé squirmed, excited, in on the game, whatever it was. Working the bailing wire, Maddie freed the hood and lifted. The odor of burnt, dirty oil attacked the back of her throat. She leaned in, quickly found the distributor coil wire, and yanked it off.

Bébé growled and got to her feet. Maddie pointed at her. "Shhhhh."

The dog had alerted on a noise at the side of the building. Maddie let the hood down quietly, then sprinted back to the phone booth. Holding her breath, she watched a woman shuffle around the building with a restroom key dangling from a dirty length of wood. Maddie exhaled and closed the distance between them in a few long-legged strides.

"I'll take that, thanks," she said, grabbing the key out of the woman's hands before she could object.

The way was clear when she came out of the ladies' room. Dropping the key outside, she sprinted across the lot, hurried Bébé through the rented truck's passenger door and tucked the coil wire under the front seat. She had the side doors open, pouring kibble in Bébé's dish when Nick returned, a paper sack in one hand, his cell phone in a white-knuckle grip in the other.

He clicked the phone off as if it had bitten him and handed her the sack.

"Hope you like mustard on your hot dog," he said. "It's all they had."

Maddie leaned against the passenger door, arms folded and legs crossed.

The Double J Truck Stop offered the Who's Who of fast food's finest. Across the street a bedraggled sign advertised the Platte River Archway Monument somewhere in their vast, gray future. The only other structure, as far as she could see, was a bit of broken fence where someone had miscalculated a right hand turn out of the driveway.

Her stomach grumbled. She climbed into the passenger seat and pulled the heavy door closed. "Mustard's fine." She squeezed a packet of mustard on a dry dog, licked her fingers and held it out to him. "Next meal's on me. My choice."

Nick grinned, but the full-blown smile she was going for was once again a no show. His cell phone broke into another round of urgent. He ignored it, both hands busy as he maneuvered the truck toward the driveway, checking his mirrors.

He saw the car in his driver's mirror. The hair stood up on the back of his neck. It was the one he'd seen at the hotel.

"Hold on," he said, his tone a warning. He jammed his foot on the gas. Maddie braced herself with one hand, the other shot up, wiener flying out of the bun. Bébé lunged from the backseat and snapped it out the air as they squealed out of the driveway dangerously close to an oncoming semi.

"Come on, damn it." Nick gritted his teeth, his foot to the floorboard. The semi driver laid on his air horn as the back end of the trailer cleared his lane.

Nick finally exhaled and shook his head. "Crazy sonofabitch."

He settled into the seat.

"Really? You swerve into oncoming traffic with a five-thousand-pound car in tow and call *them* crazy?"

Nick cracked his neck. Sure it had been close, but they'd made it. He held his hand out for the hot dog.

She slapped a fist full of crushed bun and mustard into his waiting palm.

"What?"

"You've *never* pulled a trailer before, have you?"

Nick scowled at the mess in his hand. "I could use a napkin."

"I could use an answer." She shifted her weight, stuffed a napkin in the driver's cup holder on the console. "I don't care much about this rented beast, but that's my Number One car back there."

He could feel her glaring at him as he scooped the remains of the bun into his mouth. "We're okay." He licked mustard off the corners of his lips. *What was the big deal?*

"No. We're not okay. Whatever's eating you, you need to get over it, or let me drive."

Nick straightened in the seat. "You see that car back there at the gas pump?" He cocked his head toward the rear. "Gray junker?"

Her face broke into a self-satisfied smile. "I wouldn't worry about them."

"Wouldn't worry? They've been following you since the cemetery."

Her wide-eyed expression told him she hadn't noticed.

She pulled a thick, kinked wire from under the seat and waved it at him. "Anyway, they're history."

Nick glanced at the wire then back to the road. "What's that?"

"You're kidding."

Nick shrugged. "Told you I don't know old cars."

"Trust me. Those guys are stuck. Besides, they don't know it's us in this rig." She tossed the wire to the floor. "Question is, *why* are they following us?"

"It's your car. You tell me."

"Your father maybe?"

Nick stared down the road, his shoulders hunched. A new irritation clouded his mind and clamped his jaws shut. Anger at his father, but also at himself.

"My father doesn't need low lifers to get what he wants, he's got me."

"Maybe he doesn't trust you."

Nick snorted. She hit close to home there. Nicholas Senior believed he had him by the balls, and for the last few years that had been true. But not anymore.

"You're refusing his calls. Why?"

Nick eased into a comfortable speed and set the cruise control. "What makes you say that?"

"Just a hunch."

She relaxed against the seat again, propped her foot up on the dash.

The curve of her thigh pulled a lever in his gut every time he checked the passenger side mirror. Nick had to look away.

The sight of the old junker *had* caught him off guard. He'd overreacted and put them at risk. But Maddie was right. The conversation with his father at the airport had been on his mind and each new ring meant another threat on his voicemail:

"I'll crater the business."

"Expose your bad habits."

"You're just like your mother…"

He released a slow breath, reminding himself that his mother was not to blame for his father's misery.

Nick was plenty capable of supporting himself without help from his father. He had more than quadrupled his assets since he went solo with the real estate investment trust. He'd moved the corporation to high-end commercial investments in time to miss the real estate crash and parley the pot into dream territory. His father had fought him at every turn and he knew this very well. Nick got his *I-told-you-so* moment when he'd still had cash to buy investment property at bargain prices, his rental properties were full of families who'd chosen to wait until the market cooled to buy.

Bad habits? He'd known people who spent thousands a night on cocaine. He'd never touched the stuff. He was a social gambler, good at playing the odds-on craps and seldom lost his initial stake. And the women? Vegas girls were realistic about their love life, happy to spend an evening with a gentleman of means, and cheaper in the long run than the gold digging daughters of the rich and famous. His father had no room to talk. Since Nick left the family business, it hadn't grown at all. The threats were nothing but a new tack on the old warfare between them.

That was a bad habit he would no longer entertain. The war was over except for dividing the spoils. He'd draw up the papers severing himself from any remaining assets between them when he got back to California. Nicholas senior would soon find out what his own bad habits had bought him.

"Hel-*lo.*" Maddie's voice penetrated his thoughts.

Nick blinked away the nagging dialog. "I'm sorry. What did you say?"

"I said, your shoulders get all *hunchy* when you talk about him."

Nick tried to relax his shoulders.

"What happened between you?"

"It's old crap." Personal crap. He shrugged and slipped her a quick glance. Both of her feet were up on the dashboard now, her tight jeans emphasizing the curve of her thigh. Did she have to sit like that?

"You know how it is with fathers."

"No. I don't know how it is," she said softly. They rolled on several minutes before she lowered her legs and turned toward him in the seat. "I haven't seen or heard from my father since I was five years old."

Nick flinched inside, unsure he wanted to hear this right now. But Maddie went on the way people do on a long stretch of road. He kept his eyes straight ahead and let her talk.

"We probably drove out here from California on this very road. We were living in some rented rooms at the beach in Ventura before that. I guess raising a daughter on his own was too much for him."

"I could see how that could be…restrictive," he said, glancing at her a moment.

"Oh, he dated plenty of women, if that's what you mean. He was a good-looking man. One of his girlfriends said he reminded her of a young Sinatra, especially at the wheel of my mother's car. Didn't know anything about that then, though now, I see the resemblance. But, you're right. None of them ever stuck around for long. A kid already in the picture, no one to take her away on weekends. And, he was moody, irritable. Chain smoked hunched at the bar in the kitchen most mornings till late. Then he'd leave me with the landlady."

She stared out the windshield. Her shoulders relaxed a little, and that foot went up on the dash.

"I guess he went to a job of some sort. I don't know. All I remember is lying in bed with the sound of the Pacific Coast waves pounding outside my bedroom window until I fell asleep at night. Then he'd be there, next morning."

She fell silent. Nick shifted in the seat. His mind reeled with questions. What about her mother? How did she fit in to the story? Maddie fisted her hand over her mouth and faced the passenger window. When he realized he was studying the white skin under wisps of dark hair at the nape of her neck instead of the road, he reset his shoulders and concentrated on his driving.

"I thought we were just going to shop or out to eat." Her voice came from someplace far away and fragile. "Didn't realize the car was packed for travel until it got dark. We drove and drove…and drove."

"I'd fall asleep to the drone of the motor and changing music on the radio, then wake up in a tiny motel room to tractor trailers rolling out on early starts. Once we passed the Rockies, the land got flatter and greener until we finally turned up at my grandparents' driveway. I didn't even know I had grandparents. Next day, we all went to the train station and left him there."

Maddie turned to Nick.

"I never saw or heard from him again…" She picked at a loose string on the edge of her jeans. He heard a bit of himself in her voice. The child that longed for the love of a father. "...until I found the letter in my grandfather's strongbox."

Nick felt himself cave a little, responding to an ache in his own heart. He squeezed the steering wheel. *Stay focused.* She could be playing him even now. She was, after all, her mother's daughter.

"What about your mother?" He had to ask. There was no point in any of this if he didn't.

Maddie sighed and curled her legs back under her in the seat.

"I don't remember her at all, really. Only what my father and my grandparents told me. As a kid, I bought their stories. Now I can read between the lines enough to understand that she was her own worst enemy."

Nick pressed harder. He needed to know about the woman who destroyed his family and what was so goddamned important about the Cadillac. "And the car?"

"They showed it a lot. Arizona. Pebble Beach. The Goddess was popular, a showpiece since she rolled off the showroom floor. I don't remember any of that, of course. I was too young. Grandpa told me stories. How she was the Glamour Girl of Vegas. How the casinos used her in marketing ploys to get people using the slots."

"And your mother. What happened to her?"

She retreated into her thoughts, worried the red piping in the leather upholstered seat.

"Short version? She OD'd."

A little shockwave snapped in his ears. His father had always talked of the woman in the past tense, but he'd left out *that* little detail. He blinked at Maddie, then fixed his eyes back on the road.

"And the long version?"

Maddie shut her mouth and resettled in her seat, facing ahead, then huffed out a sigh. "I don't know why I'm telling you all this." She glanced at him a moment. "Or why you care."

Nick tapped his thumbs on the steering wheel. "It's a long drive."

He could feel her eyes on him. "Make's the time pass, you know," he said, lifting a shoulder. He needed to keep her talking.

After an uncomfortable silence, she turned and gazed ahead as if she drew the memories from the stark landscape--dry grass, and hard, cold rocks.

"There's not a lot I know, really," she said. "Her parents were grifters. Got jailed in some scheme. Child Protective Services picked her up. She lived with fosters till she was eighteen. By then, she was no different than hundreds of other girls in the eighties. Buzzed on pop-club glitz and cocaine. A material girl. Who else would name her newborn daughter Madonna?"

Maddie let go a mirthless laugh. She had shredded a napkin, a twisted pile of mustard-stained paper littered the leather seat beside her. "She was pretty. Nice body."

Like Maddie's. Except for the short-cropped hair, he could be looking at Maddie's mother right now.

"First guy she meets," Maddie went on, "…promises her the moon. Takes her to Vegas, buys her nice clothes, fancy meals...puts her up in an apartment…. Girl like her? She thought he loved her. Wanted her. Couldn't see he just wanted a secret place and a girl to cheat on his wife with."

Maddie sighed, ran her fingers along the dashboard. "Gave her the Caddie. Guess he registered it in her name so his wife wouldn't find out."

She snorted. "At least she got something out of the deal."

Nick clutched the wheel. The words cut him deep. His mother had cried when his father sold her station wagon. *Money's tight*, his father had said. *We can't afford two cars.* They'd eaten macaroni and cheese out of boxes for days while his father was away on what he'd called *sales trips to get more business.*

Maddie stopped picking at the upholstery as if she'd just realized she was doing it. "She'd have died before I was conceived if my father hadn't found her running the car in the closed-up apartment garage. I think they were business partners, the guy and my father. That's how he met her. Anyway, my father actually married her."

Nick's hands went cold and the back of his throat thickened. Maddie's story brought it all into focus. The anger, the hurt, the betrayal, the loss. And something he didn't know: Both women had attempted suicide because of his father; only his mother had been successful. Nick swallowed a hard lump of crow. There were two sides to every story. He'd never considered the other woman's dilemma.

A sheen of perspiration broke out on his face. He rolled down the window, leaned toward the flow of cool air.

"The partnership went south, the money stream ended, of course," Maddie said. "But they had me, and once that was done, she went back to the clubs. When I was two, she left with a guy she met at a disco who said he'd make her a pop star." Maddie cleared her throat. "When she…died…Daddy put the car in my name."

Nick's ears were ringing and his head suddenly ached. If they weren't driving down the road at seventy-five miles an hour, he would have taken off running. Instead, he did what he had to do. He checked his mirrors, exited the highway, and slowed to a stop at a strip mall anchored by a Cracker Barrel restaurant.

"Something wrong?" There was a tone of true concern in her voice.

Nick swallowed again. "Your turn to drive."

Leon was headed into the convenience store when a skidding screech and a truck's air horn shattered the relative silence of the lonely gas stop. He hopped-skipped back to the car and shouted at Leon. "Wow! Did you see that? They almost crashed!"

They watched the fancy truck and trailer fishtail and recover then barrel down the road, kicking up gravel from the shoulder.

Georgie turned the key in the ignition. The starter groaned, but nothing happened. "Get in."

"But I didn't pay yet."

Georgie twisted the key again. Nothing.

Leon scratched the roots of his thready goatee. "Told you we should've give those ladies back at the Quick Stop a hand with their flat tire. Paid it forward."

Georgie banged the steering wheel with his fist. "Shut the fuck up with your voo-doo-karma-bleeding-heart bullshit."

He slammed out of the car and threw up the hood. "Go pay."

Leon slump-shouldered away. "I don't know why you're in such a damned hurry. We ain't seen that Caddie since last night. They ditched us good."

A quick scan of the engine had Georgie scratching his head. He'd just filled the tank and they'd charged the battery up before they left. He'd poured in a quart of oil not more than a month ago, if he had it right, and beyond that, what he knew about cars was as useless as wheels on a sled.

Something tickled the top of his head. He straightened to see the bailing wire swing free of the hood latch and drop to the ground. That was weird. Usually, it was a pain in the ass to fumble the thing off. He'd yanked the hood up without realizing it was undone until it hit him in the head. Now it hit him like a sledge hammer.

"Fucking A."

He turned back to the highway and shaded his eyes to look after the truck and trailer. They were nothing more than tiny dots in the distance.

"Drop kick me Jesus," he said, growling.

He leaned back on the car and spat in the dirt. Sighting the phone booth, he hollered at Leon as he sauntered out of sight, "Get me some fuckin' quarters."

Chapter 6

Nick hadn't touched his burger plate or said a word since they'd ordered. Maddie had devoured half a mountain of Cobb salad. What was he thinking about that so occupied his mind? She'd bared her soul to him in the car, hoping to draw him out, but he'd clammed up tight. She might as well be traveling solo. At least she could have belted out her favorite Christina Aguilera songs as she drove.

She stabbed the last pieces of lettuce off her plate and held the fork aloft. Who was she kidding? It was comforting to have him along for the ride, sulking or not. She'd wanted to crawl into his lap since the moment they'd climbed into the truck together.

The moon rode low on the horizon, a bright halo all around in contrast to the mocking grin on its face. Nick stared out the restaurant window.

"Rain's coming," Maddie said, hoping to draw his thoughts back to the table. Nothing. Not even a blink. She'd have to do better than talk about the weather. A little chill snuck up the back of her neck. That familiar chill she got when she was about to succumb to her impulses. She wiped a drop of salad dressing off the table with her thumb, rubbed it on her napkin and cleared her throat.

"I liked you better with your hands in my panties."

She added a scraping of bacon and blue cheese onto her fork, slipped the bite into her mouth, and waited, resisting the urge to squirm in her seat.

Nick flinched, as if waking from a dream.

Bingo.

He shifted his gaze to her eyes. "I'm sorry. What did you say?"

Her ears warmed. She gave him a sincere smile. "You looked miles away just now. What were you thinking?"

He pulled in his breath and grinned back at her.

"I distinctly heard the word 'panties'."

"Wow. Really? Is that what you heard?" Maddie's eyebrows arched as she sluiced a tomato wedge through a pool of salad dressing and captured it in her mouth, slowly licking the remains of dressing from her lips. Her face felt flushed. It had to be as red as the tomato. She'd never deliberately played the tease, and she had never been a good liar. But she couldn't help relishing the way Nick's eyes locked on to her mouth. His reaction heated her straight to her core.

She ceremoniously blotted her lips with a napkin and took time smoothing it back onto the table as she composed her next line. "What I *said* was, 'I think I'll stop by in Cheyenne and visit my auntie.'"

Nick leaned back in the seat and folded his arms. His face broke into half a smile. "The color of your eyes changes to cobalt when you lie, did you know that?"

"I never lie." The tips of her ears flamed with heat. She laced shaking fingers together and clamped her hands between her legs.

He reached across the table, lifted her chin gently with his fingers, his thumb resting near the corner of her mouth. "Tell me another one."

Her heart rate jumped to the red zone, the heat of his fingers touching her skin registered deep inside. The panty comment was no lie. She *did* like him better with his hands on her. Just the memory of him poised above her in the front seat of the Cadillac had her crossing her legs and adjusting her hips on the banquette cushion. She looked over her shoulder. It was late. Way past the dinner hour. The waitress was taking an order from a couple at the far end of the dining room, otherwise their side of the restaurant was quiet.

She exhaled slowly. It took every ounce of her willpower to maintain composure as she worked out the next line in her head. When she was ready, she drew a finger across the plate and sucked salad dressing off it, then grazed his thumb with her tongue. "My auntie in Cheyenne lives in a shanty." She gave him a wide grin.

"Deep, dark cobalt." Nick shook his head slowly. "You're running out of rhymes."

"*Okaaaaay.*" It was fun, but she'd grown tired of the game. Her pulse sent blood racing through her veins, shooting endorphins to her brain. She would tell the truth.

"When you got out of the limo, at the cemetery…"

"Um hum."

"Before I knew who you were…"

His eyes narrowed, blue-green irises closed around pinpoints of black.

Maddie released her hands and rubbed her palms slowly on the tops of her thighs.

"I felt you."

❧

Nick pulled away with a start. He was used to suggestive banter. It was an entertaining way to pass time with a sexy woman. The girls at the Beaver Ranch were experts—professional women who skillfully created a safe place to have a little fun, no strings, no problems—and they were paid well for their efforts.

Maddie was clever. She had lulled him into his comfort zone and then zinged him below the belt. Laid open the emotional no man's land he'd avoided for nearly eight years.

He'd felt her too. Felt her grief, her anger, her passion. She had shattered his defenses with one look. He wished to God he could roll everything back to the moment before he knew what the car meant to his father.

Before he knew who she was.

But life just didn't work that way. It was like a judge asking a jury to disregard what they'd heard. It couldn't be done. The amusing, innocent, fascinating, and utterly captivating Maddie was fun to be with, could make a road trip worth the time. But the serious Maddie. The one with the cobalt eyes that drew him in. She was the dangerous one. The one who scared him.

This was no time to stumble or let her get to him.

He needed to keep things in focus. Maddie, daughter of Corinne, was someone he could deal with. A person to which he could attach no strings. Keep it light, impersonal, playful. Two could play her game. He shifted in his seat, put on his gambler's grin.

"You should feel me now."

Her eyes flashed fire. She threw down her napkin and scooted out of the booth.

"Maddie, wait—" He slid to the edge of his seat and swung his legs out.

She whirled back on him. "No, *you* wait."

She leaned so close he could feel the heat radiating from her face. "*I* was serious."

Nick swallowed, his eyes intent on hers. "So was I."

She stood staring at him for a heartbeat, then turned and headed for the restrooms. He watched her ass as it shifted up and down under that maddening, runway gait. When she disappeared down the corridor, Nick suddenly felt abandoned. *Man, you are so dead meat.*

"Looks like you got your hands full." The waitress stood at his shoulder with a steaming pot of decaf and a *seen-it-all* smile. He knew her. She worked in every restaurant in Vegas. Ambitions derailed or past their prime, she lived vicariously, aching to connect.

Nick smiled at her and slipped back into the booth. "We have some things to work out."

"Can I get you anything?"

Nick scrubbed a cold French fry through a pool of catsup. "A piece of humble pie, maybe?"

"Good choice."

Nick stood when Maddie came back to the table. She slipped in quietly, eyes averted. Her lips gleamed with a fresh application of lip gloss.

The waitress slid a plate of strawberry shortcake between them along with two spoons and silently removed their dinner plates. Maddie folded her hands in her lap, shoulders hunched.

Nick cleared his throat. "Can we start over?"

She lifted a shoulder, pressed her lips together.

"You wanted to know what I was thinking."

She looked at him. "I wanted…"

Her eyes were astonishingly beautiful without any make up at all. His heart tightened a little, knowing he'd been the cause of some of the pain he saw there.

She dragged her eyes away. "I want to know more about you," she said.

Nick shuddered. She was serious. And she had been painfully forthcoming with him. Now it was his turn. Revealing his soul had never been his forte.

He unfolded the paper napkin, slipped his hand under and smoothed it over his fist, then took a slow, deep breath.

"When I was ten, I hated math. I knew my multiplication tables cold. But those long division problems? They were stacked up all wrong. At least to my ten-year-old brain."

Maddie's aloof expression dissolved to curious.

"My stepmom helped me." Nick pulled one corner of the napkin up through his fingers, forming a paper ear. "Moral support, mostly. At the kitchen table. Over glasses of chocolate milk."

He pulled another corner through his fingers. Now he had two ears and a nose of a paper rabbit covering his fist. Maddie gave him a half smile.

He slipped out from behind his side of the table and slid in next to her until their shoulders touched.

"My stepbrother, Luke, is a couple years younger. He always blew right through his math, but not me. This one night, I don't know. I was having a really tough time. Luke's mom and I had our heads together, working it out. Dad storms into the kitchen and kicks her chair. 'You're wasting your time,' he yells, and 'He's an idiot, just like his mother and you're an idiot for trying.'"

Nick opened his fingers and let the crumpled napkin float to the table. When he lifted his gaze briefly to Maddie, their eyes connected. He wet his lips and continued.

"He pounds his fist between us and swipes the glasses of chocolate milk off the table and they shatter all over the marble floor." Nick shot his hand at imaginary glasses of milk.

"Where was your brother?"

"Dunno. Watching some cop show on TV."

"So, what'd you do?"

"I ran to my room, did the rest of the problems under the covers by the light of a Batman flashlight and sound of his voice bellowing downstairs."

"You had marble floors in the kitchen?" Her words pulled him out of the drama, settled him back to an adult perspective.

"Yeah. It was part of his control. An 'I give you marble, you have to take my crap' kind of thing."

He handed Maddie a spoon. "Anyway, I aced math from then on, right through business school at Pepperdine. Dean's list."

Maddie scooped a pile of whipped cream off the top of the shortcake and lifted it to his lips. Nick allowed her to feed it to him.

"What about your brother?"

Nick shrugged. "He left home right after high school. Couldn't stand to watch his mom grovel to live in a mansion. Being a little older I saw it differently. She did what she did to protect us."

"Where is he now? Your brother."

"I don't see him much. He was a cop. But finished law school, now he's a prosecutor. Wants to be a DA someday. No surprise."

Nick scooped a mouthful of strawberries and cream into his mouth.

"Some fathers," he said around the mouthful of sweetness. "They deserve all the love and respect due them for years of devotion."

He scooped another spoonful into his mouth and looked out the window as he chewed. "My father? I don't owe him a thing."

Maddie loaded her spoon and held it to her own mouth as she nudged him playfully with her shoulder. "Sure we're not related?"

Oh, now that was interesting. He quickly did the math. No. Their fathers had both been bastards, his for being there and hers for not, but thankfully, there was no chance they'd had the same mother. And he was warming to the idea that his father had been wrong about Maddie's.

❧

Maddie white-knuckled the steering wheel through blinding rain all the way to Cheyenne while Nick slept in the passenger seat not moving a muscle. She could just make out the freeway sign through the hellacious downpour. Only five miles to go.

She glanced over at Nick, the deep cleft that rode between his brows for most of the trip had relaxed, returning his face to that easygoing Nick she had first seen back in Kentucky. The scene in the restaurant played over and over in her head. Right or wrong, she felt a little easier herself. *Sometimes you just have to get things off your chest*, Grandpa used to say.

Another mile, another scene that'd been haunting her. She was five years old and back in the garage with Grandpa, hands splayed out against the Cadillac's yellow hood. Blue eyes reflected at her in the shiny chrome hood ornament. Innocent eyes, willing to forgive anything.

"Why does the car have a goddess on the front?"

"So you'll never lose your way."

It had been twenty years and she could still hear his voice, warm, solid, and true as American steel.

Now, Maddie hoped he was right.

She breathed a sigh of relief as she pulled through the heavy liquid veil into the Holiday Inn check-in parkway.

Nick yawned. "Well, that went quick."

The sight of his bed hair, his eyes half-mast, and the rumpled hog T-shirt might have made her laugh if her nerves weren't so jangled. "For you, maybe."

"Oookay." He combed his fingers through his hair. "I'll get the rooms."

Bébé was eager to run and wasted no time finding a spot. Maddie fed her and bedded her down in the backseat of the truck.

Road noise and too much coffee fueled a *churring* buzz inside her head. She was dog tired but nowhere near ready for sleep. When she finally dragged her overnight bag into the lobby, Nick stood waiting with a key card.

"Room 303."

She took the packet and headed for the elevator. She lifted her finger to punch the Up arrow and then stopped. "Room? As in one?"

She turned, and Nick was gone.

The room was cozy enough with a king-sized bed banked by nightstands bolted to a plank headboard and a pastel reproduction screwed into the wall above. An aqua glow radiated from the pool area and a cluster of bright lights in the distance defined Cheyenne's downtown business district. It was as far west as she'd been in twenty years.

She felt suddenly hollow, alone. What the hell was she thinking leaving just when Flo and Walt needed her most? She'd thrown her stuff in the car and taken off because of a letter that was two years old. For all she knew, her father wasn't in Lompoc anymore. Could be anywhere. Nick had been right about him. She didn't owe her father a thing. But Grandpa had left the letter in the strongbox, told her to go to it, open it. He wanted her to know.

Maddie shivered. She had been thoughtless in more ways than one and now other people, good people, Walt and Flo, were left in a lurch and it was her fault.

She pulled the drapes and turned away from the window. She should call Flo. See if everything's okay. But it was late. Too late. *Better wait till morning.*

Three short knocks pulled her out of her thoughts. Nick was at the door with two beers in a bucket of ice, his eyes alight.

"Corona," she said, stepping aside to let him in.

"Mexican champagne."

"You're making an assumption."

His smile widened. "Only that you'll need a little something to dull the road noise."

Maddie leaned against the door until it closed. He put the ice bucket on the table next to the bed.

How long had it been since she'd shared a beer, or anything for that matter, in a hotel room with a man? Maddie didn't want to think about it. She rubbed her arm against a fresh set of chills. "Thanks. I'm glad to be off the road. Glad for the beer. And glad for the company."

"You're cold," Nick said. He stepped to the window and punched buttons on the heater unit below it.

She pushed away from the door. She had the chills but it wasn't because of the cold. It was a full load of road nerves and the thought of what she might do if he put his hands on her.

Another impulsive move she'd regret later?

Maybe. But it was Playful Nick. The one who had put his arm around her in the restaurant, the Nick she'd met back home on the day of her grandfather's memorial. The one she missed. She felt empty and alone and he was just what she needed. To hell with it. He was right. She didn't owe anybody anything. And she owed herself a break.

❧

Nick popped the tops off the bottles and handed her one. She stepped closer and clinked her long-neck bottle to his. "To road warriors."

"To road warriors," he said, echoing her toast and they drank together.

She gave the bed a testing bounce, put her beer on the nightstand and sat Indian style, then pulled off her sweatshirt, letting go a long sigh. "This is a lot better than the back of the Caddie."

Nick sat in the club chair next to the nightstand. He smiled at the memory of finding her in her car, freezing in the little T-shirt like the one she wore now. He had wanted her then and he wanted her now. No doubt about that. Wanted to bury himself inside her and never come up for air. He swigged the rest of his beer and put it down.

Maddie caught his eye, as if she could read his mind, and pulled off a boot. "Have I thanked you yet?"

"Almost." He could think of a thousand ways, but he was afraid to say the wrong thing and find himself outside the room. He'd watched her pull off a boot before, something he'd grown to enjoy in the car.

"It's been my pleasure. Can't let anything happen to that number one car. Or her owner."

She was looking at him with those deep blue eyes. They were warm, inviting, without a hint of hesitancy in them.

"Need help with the other one?" he asked.

Maddie drank long from her beer and put it down. "Absolutely."

Moving to the bed, he sat beside her and lifted her leg over his lap. He held her boot heel in one hand and slid it off her foot, massaging her calf with the other.

She stretched into the massage as the boot came off. He moved slowly, watching her expression. They had been cheated of this moment the first day they met. He wasn't going to let that happen again. He pulled her into his lap, savoring the warmth of her against him.

He exhaled as she circled her arms around his shoulders and settled closer.

Nick savored the tension in her thighs as she reacted to the hardness between them and then he pulled back just far enough to see into the eyes that had shattered his senses the moment he first saw her. It had been only two days, but it seemed as though he had known those eyes forever. Eyes that really saw him, saw into his soul. Not her mother's eyes, but her own.

"Maddie." He whispered her name, husky, without demand. More than he simply wanted this, he wanted this to be right. He dropped his forehead to hers. "Are you sure? I can get my own room."

"Not on your life, Nick Berlin." She turned her face up to his, nipped his bottom lip, then watched his eyes as she kissed him again. "Not this time."

Maddie deepened the kiss, relishing the taste of him, the texture of his shoulders under her hands and the muscles flexing under his skin, then waited breathlessly for his answer. One, two, three heartbeats in, the answer came in a rush. His mouth caught hers, tasted, then devoured, leaving her breathless. She moved her hands over shoulders, down his flexing lats to the place where his T-shirt dipped into the back of his pants. She slipped her hands under it, pulling it off as she slid her fingers up his sides. He captured her lips again, took possession of them as she shrugged out of her own T-shirt.

Nick pushed gently away, just far enough to look at her. Maddie relived the moment in the front seat of the Cadillac—the scintillating, searing moment she had dreamed about ever since. Only this time it was real. This time no one could take it away from them. She rocked against him, inviting him back until his hands moved up her sides and captured her breasts.

Thumbs moving over dark nipples under a lace bra…

Hips moving in unison, slow, rhythmic, building…

Mouths tasting, demanding, gasping for breath…

Clothes frantically pulled away…

Maddie felt him moan deep in his throat when she released his zipper and reached for him.

"Please, I want you inside me," she said. She let go of him reluctantly so he could slip out of his pants, barely breathing as she waited. And then he was back. The hotel room, the road, all reason and sanity dissolved in the magic of slick bodies coming together, seeking, finding, exploding in passion.

Nicholas Alexander Berlin slipped behind the hospital room curtain and stared at the silent form in the bed, his thumb running nervously over the keys of his cell phone. The man Nicholas had once envied was reduced to little more than a pile of sharp angles beneath a drab cotton blanket, his face turned to the wall.

A hot stone of bitterness burned in the middle of Nicholas's chest, tinged with a pinch of fear. "Looks like I'll outlive you after all."

If the man heard him, he made no response.

A wave of satisfaction rose to replace the bitterness. Why shouldn't he gloat? He was the last man standing. One by one, the fools had met their ruin, and now, he would collect his rightful reward.

Just the thought of having the Cadillac back in his garage sent a sizzle through his gut, fueling the images that had kept him awake at night for more than twenty years. The Flying Goddess, Corinne in hot pants. An attractive diversion for the perfect heist.

Nicholas moved silently around the end of the bed. His old colleague's gnarled profile pressed deep in the folds of a dingy pillow.

Better you than me, Kerrigan. The words were tough, but tinged with a stab of fear. He had to face down a wave of anxiety most mornings lately. Seeing Kerrigan in this state gave it a whole new perspective.

Ross had been good looking back in the nineties. Robust, charismatic—could've given Tom Cruise a run for his money.

Women fell quickly under his spell, even when it was against their own best interest.

He was brilliant too. His classic car show idea had worked faultlessly. Corinne on the revolving platform, long legs disappearing into tight-assed Daisy Dukes and the quintessential classic car—the '53 Cadillac Eldorado—drew gamblers' eyes away from their dice, dealers' hands away from their cards, and pit bosses' focus away from their posts.

In a matter of moments, JR and Nicholas had palmed thousands in chips, while Ross, working his job at the hotel front desk in an impeccable Brooks Brothers suit, made the switch, transferred neatly wrapped packs of hotel guests' cash into his own, blind-registered safe deposit box. Who could blame the men upstairs for missing the hand off with Corinne's firm, ripe ass filling their monitors? They were salivating, wishing it were their hands on her ass. Their chance to get inside those hot pants.

Nicholas's lips stretched into a thin smile. His own deception had been the best of all.

It was his job to drive the Cadillac off the lobby floor, past the sliding glass walls to the valet parking area and out into the night. No one on his team suspected a thing when they opened the velvet jewelry box and found the centerpiece missing. As far as anyone knew, the fifty-carat teardrop of yellow diamond was never in the box with the matched set of earrings, bracelet, and necklace. Who would, in all honesty, leave an item like that in the hands of a hotel desk clerk?

Nicholas had feigned disappointment, but it was Ross himself who cooled any suspicion.

"Makes sense," he'd said. "I wouldn't travel all the way from Belgium like our little thief, evading authorities and risking my life, only to leave a piece like that in a hotel safe. That woman's got it on her. Hidden someplace nice and warm."

Nicholas remembered his sizzling satisfaction when Ross unwittingly created an alibi for him. As it was, the box contained more than a hundred thousand in sellable diamonds, stolen goods to begin with that could never be reported. The guest cash had been an opportunistic plus. Casino cash would have been traceable.

"We'll all do just fine out of this," Ross had assured them, splitting the cash into equal piles of fifty thousand. "Bide our time. No fancy stuff. Keep our heads."

Nicholas had never been good at biding his time. He waited only a couple of months to stake a down payment on his first real estate investment. An insatiable passion for roulette left JR happy with his pile of chips. Ross slipped his fifty thousand inside his jacket like he did it every day. A characteristic gleam in his eye told Nicholas he'd had a girl waiting back in his room.

Rage leapt up again, this time burning the back of Nicholas's throat. It *had* been a perfect plan. Spend the cash, hold the diamond, sell it on the black market just in time for his retirement. The only flaw in the plan had been trusting Ross.

A ripple of fear swept up his spine as Nicholas took in the gravity of his old partner's condition—the fragile form under the sheets, the stack of diapers in the cubby hole beneath the nightstand, the pale skin stretched over gaunt cheekbones. Twenty years disappeared in a flash and now it seemed only a year or so ago that they had been friends. He worried the bulging veins on the tops of his own hands. He had been the strong one. Ross had been the handsome one. "Not so handsome anymore, eh Ross?"

The man stirred, his jaws clamped once, then relaxed. Nicholas caught his own breath and held it until, barely perceptible under the sheets, the other man's breathing started again.

The cell phone vibrated in Nicholas's hand. He drew the speaker close to his lips and turned to the window before he answered. "This better be good."

The man on the other end of the connection breathed hard, coughed.

"We lost her."

Nicholas deflated. "Lost her? How do you lose a woman in a huge yellow—"

"She got the Caddie into a toy hauler somewhere out of Omaha. Didn't catch on till halfway to nowhere, then the Valiant broke down, and—"

The hot stone returned to Nicholas's chest. "She's a Kentucky holler hick, for chrissakes. How hard can it be?"

"She's picked up some guy and some major horsepower. They're long gone. Even if we got another car, they'd have five hundred miles on us."

Nicholas backed up to the visitor's chair and plopped down, pulled a small tube from his jacket pocket, and squirted a tiny blast under his tongue. A vague suspicion prompted him to ask, "What'd he look like?"

"How the hell should I know? I didn't see 'em."

Nicholas leaned his head back on the chair, waiting for the brain freeze to pass. It eased the hot stone in his chest but didn't improve his mood.

"You want to get paid, you better start makin' sense." He heard another Kentucky drawl in the background.

"A blond guy, Leon thinks. Tall, fancy coat. Bought some hot dogs inside the Quick Stop when we were there, and—If you want, we can—"

Nick Jr. Sonofabitch.

"No. You guys lay off. I'll handle it from here."

"Yeah, sure. But how're we gonna get—"

Nicholas clicked off the phone and his gut heaved up a tarry belch. His head hurt. His body shuddered. He was tired. Tired of chasing the Cadillac and tired of thinking about it. In fact, right now, he was just plain tired of thinking at all. He relaxed into the chair; the sounds of the hospital faded a moment before the squeak of rubber-soled shoes on the tile floor along with a metallic clatter announced the imminent arrival of a dinner cart.

Light from the hallway stabbed into the room as a nurse's aide backed through the door pulling a cart.

"Afternoon."

She turned with a start. "Oh. It's you, Mr. Berlin. I didn't see you come in."

"Just checking up on our boy, here. Not too talkative today."

He stuffed his medication back in his pocket, eased himself up from the chair and edged toward the door.

She slipped a covered dish on the bedside table. "Not that I'll get anything down him. I'm afraid he's slipping away on us. You've been a good friend, stopping by and all."

"Least I could do."

"We could feed him with a tube if I could locate family. The social workers haven't had any luck."

"Pity."

Chapter 7

The pillow next to hers was empty, except for a note neatly printed on hotel stationary that read "Gone for clothes."

Clothes?

Maddie propped herself up on an elbow. Red numbers on the bedside clock clicked to ten thirty. The last time she'd slept in until ten thirty was the morning after her college graduation.

So much for getting an early start.

Again.

Bébé lifted her head from the mangle of covers at the end of the bed.

"Looks like you got lucky too." Maddie leaned up to rub the dog's ears. Nick must have snuck her into the room before he left.

The thought of the kind of clothing "Mr. Fancy Shoes" would find in Cheyenne, Wyoming gave her a smile. Hard to beat Hog Stampede.

She stretched deeply into the blissful memories of a woman who'd been up most of the night making love. Nick had been everything she'd imagined, and more. If there was an afterlife, Grandpa was out there somewhere congratulating himself on sending her a "Doozy". She shook her head at the thought, and padded barefoot to the bathroom.

A leather bag open on the vanity erupted with shaving gear, power cords, and the heady scent of fresh-washed man, dispelling any lingering funk about waking up alone.

Maddie floated into the shower. Wouldn't hurt to freshen up before they went for round three. Or would it be four? She'd been laid up one side and down the other and everywhere in between. Just thinking about it gave her goose bumps.

Hot water stung her skin and sluiced down her back. "Yes-s-s-s-s-s."

It was good to feel like a woman again.

But when she emerged from the bathroom in nothing but a towel and found herself still alone, some of the glow dimmed. Fighting a frown, she tousled her hair dry in front of the mirror. Sex in a hotel with a handsome almost stranger satisfied some delicious, erotic desire within her, but morning had a way of bringing things back to reality. She could fit what she knew about Nick on the business end of a spark plug. There was more to Nick than a delicious smile and blue-green eyes. Something cruised under the surface, not menacing by any stretch, but there, like a pothole in the road, ready to knock you sideways when you least expected it.

Maddie crawled over the bed with the towel slung low around her breasts and pulled her computer into her lap. What was the name of his real estate office? Central Coast something…Montecito? She tapped her fingers over the keys and watched the names scroll across the computer screen.

Central Coast Real Estate Investment Trust's website had just topped her search list when Bébé's ears perked up and alerted Maddie to footsteps outside the door.

"Damn." She snapped the laptop closed.

No sense running for cover. Nick had already seen every blessed inch of her the night before. Despite her doubts, the thought sent a scintillating shiver through her.

Bébé woofed and leapt off the bed.

The dog's rear end plopped down just as Nick bungled in, hip first, wrangling a fist full of bags in one hand and a cardboard tray of fu-fu coffees in the other.

Damned if it wasn't Cowboy Nick, complete with a black Stetson hat cocked low on his forehead, shiny black shirt studded with white pearl buttons, and a pair of pointy-toe boots.

"What? No fringe?" Maddie adjusted the towel a little tighter around her.

Nick's brow furrowed a moment before he let the bags slide to the floor. "Hope you like mocha."

She sampled one of the coffees and relished the heady hit of strong caffeine and chocolate. "You are absolutely forgiven."

"Forgiven?"

"I don't like waking up alone after a night like…"

Nick stroked her body with his gaze, sweeping from her eyes to her mouth to the top of the towel where she'd tucked it in and down to where it grazed the top of her thighs. Her body heated under the intensity of his inspection as the moment stretched between them. She pulled the towel down a bit further and tucked her legs under her.

Nick cleared his throat and turned his attention back to the bags. "To answer your question, *podnuh*, I recon I got some free-*inge* in here somewhere."

"*Podnuh*?" Maddie laughed softly. In all her years in Kentucky, she'd never picked up an accent, but somehow, in two days, Nick had affected a Texas drawl that belonged somewhere south of the Pecos.

Nick dumped the contents of one of the bags on the bed. Maddie couldn't resist pawing through the packages—a pair of five-pocket jeans, a pack of white T-shirts, some socks, and a long-sleeved plaid shirt.

"You did all this in an hour?"

"I told the sales clerk I had a hot woman waiting back at the hotel." A pair of black, boot-cut pants and a package of underwear joined the pile from another bag.

Maddie snatched the underwear. "Silk? Oooooh."

"Hands off." He slipped them out of her hands and emptied the other bag. "Ah. Here's the fringe."

With a lopsided grin, he unfolded a black suede jacket and held it up to her body. Maddie caught her breath. Leather strips dangled over the sculpted bodice, across the yoke in the back, and all around the bottom.

He let his eyes wander again. "Looks like that would just about cover it."

He tossed his hat on the bed and moved in closer as Maddie rolled the luscious suede between her fingers. It probably cost a fortune.

"Oh, no," she said, wagging her finger at him. "This is definitely out of my—"

"A gift, Maddie. For last night."

Hand to the top of her towel, she moved away from him. He felt the need to pay for her attention? That wasn't going to happen. Not now, not ever.

"Don't get all flustered—"

"Flustered—"

"Just…try it on." He held the jacket up enticingly.

If his grin hadn't grown to a genuine smile at just that moment, she might have ruined the whole morning on a lecture about how she couldn't be bought. Instead, she savored the twinge at the memory of his fingers touching, dipping, and exploring where his eyes were focused at that moment.

Not a good time for a woman coming out of a dry spell to pick a fight.

She slowly stood up, slipped her arms into the sleeves of the jacket and let the towel slide away to the floor.

Nick was right.

It was just long enough. The fringe at the bottom grazed the tops of her thighs.

The cool satin lining sliding against her bare skin sent ripples of pleasure straight to her center. She caught her image in the full-length mirror on the bathroom door, turned to look over her shoulder at the back, then cinched the soft tie belt and flipped the collar up. Maddie had always wanted a soft leather jacket but never let herself spend money on frivolous things. The last personal purchase she'd made was a pair of red Jimmy Choo stilettos, and she only wore them when one of her cars went up on the auction block. She hunched a shoulder up and felt the soft leather against her chin.

"That guy must have been a really good salesman to get you to throw this in with your jeans and underwear."

He crossed the room and pressed close behind her, smiling at her reflection in the mirror. The blue in his eyes overtook the green.

"Girl."

He pulled her back against his chest. "She said this jacket was guaranteed to get me more of whatever had put the grin on my face."

&

Nick slipped his hands under the leather, slid them over the silky skin of Maddie's bare hips and up to fill them with her breasts. Firm nubs rose against his palms sending a shot of heat through his bloodstream. She leaned her head back against his shoulder and let out a soft sigh.

He wanted her again, felt the need rising. The intoxicating warmth of her body and the freshly showered fragrance of her skin drove every other possibility from his mind. Since the moment he'd awakened beside her, he could think of nothing but the taste of her, the way her hands moved over his back, and the way she'd opened to him. It had taken every ounce of his will to let her sleep in without him.

Her neck's silken whiteness tugged at an ache he had suppressed for way too long. He closed his eyes and skimmed his fingertips along the contours of her throat. Her vulnerability touched him somewhere he wasn't sure he could go.

She was trouble and he knew it. He could just as easily have hired a freight service to deliver the car and flown them to California. Or bailed on the whole thing. What did he care about the Flying Goddess? His father had a garage full of old cars. What good was adding one more to the neglected lineup? Why should he let himself be governed by an old man who had managed to destroy the women in his own life? Who was of late showing signs of bad judgment?

Nick had settled into a life rhythm that worked for him. Everything in its place. Neat and tidy. Montecito for business, Vegas for pleasure. Women were never an issue for him. So, what the hell was he doing in a hotel room in Cheyenne, sporting a righteous woody and a pair of cowboy boots?

"Hello?" Her voice startled him. He opened his eyes to meet her intense gaze in the mirror. Those slate-dark, soul-shattering eyes.

God help me.

He dipped his head, nuzzled into the softness of her neck, and kissed her there, just below her ear.

"Maddie…" He exhaled on her name, giving in to the moment and every male impulse in his body. He loosened the tie belt from around her waist, let the jacket fall open, the taught skin of her nipples impossibly pink against her white, white skin. She let the jacket slip off one shoulder without taking her eyes from his in the mirror. His mouth went dry, desire strained at the button-fly jeans. If there was any doubt as to where he should be right now it was lost in his longing to meld her body to his.

He traced his fingers across her chest from the shallow dip where her collar bones came together, to the curving muscles in her shoulder, watching her eyes darken. He slid his fingers down the white skin over her ribcage, her hips and into the soft curling hair hidden under the fringe of the jacket. As she pressed against him, her soft cry segued to sigh.

"We really should be on the road…" Her lazy, breathless tone told him she didn't mean it.

"Really?" He dipped his fingers into her warmth, toyed with the quickening bud nestled in the folds. "I was thinking somewhere a little more comfortable, like on that bed over there."

"Here," she gasped. She shrugged the coat off, letting it fall slowly from her fingertips to the floor, then slid her hands over his. "Right here."

His eyes met hers again in the mirror, then his gaze shifted to admire the way her tall, slender body complemented his taller, harder frame. He circled an arm across her chest, rested his hand on her shoulder, and smoothed his other down over her hip.

A low moan built from deep inside him as his hand floated back up to her neck, lifted her chin and tilted her face to his. Those slate blue eyes captured his in a scintillating gaze and he caught his breath. Louise and Luke had been right. Something had changed inside him, and it had nothing to do with a car and everything to do with a woman. This one.

"Maddie," he said, half whispered.

Then, just like he imagined when he turned his credit card over to the sales clerk at the Boot Barn—mixed with the memory of the frenetic first to the last, mind-numbing thrust of the night before—he let himself tumble, free-fall into her, losing himself in the intensity of her response.

He worked his fingertips in slow circles until she rocked against him, her breath warm and impossibly close to his ear. He added his thumb to the mix, massaging until she moaned and arched her back. He went down on a knee, his hands gripping her sides as he brushed his tongue along her belly to join the play. It circled and dipped and tasted, taking turns with his fingers as they moved, parting her folds one moment, thrusting inside the next, in a syncopated rhythm that had her pumping against him on tiptoe. She whimpered and he held back, taking her higher until she nearly lost her balance.

"I can't…I have to…" she gasped, gesturing toward the bed.

Nick scooped her up. Bébé jumped out of the way and scurried to the corner as they fell together over the bed. Maddie rolled up and straddled him, pulling impatiently at the snap-front shirt as he worked to open his fly.

His pulse thundered in his head. "Hold on."

He rolled her off, stood, and kicked off his jeans remembering another purchase he'd made. At least he was trying to keep the big head in control. He hopped to the pile of bags and pawed through, coming up with a box of condoms.

"Hurry," she said on a throaty sigh. She pulled him on top of her as he spilled the tiny packages all over the bed.

"Let me do that." She grabbed for a packet, shifting them both off balance. They rolled, laughing, onto the floor. She split the package open.

"Here, here," he said, snatching the lubricated latex away from her as he rolled back on top.

"No. I've got it." Winning the battle, she slicked it over him, then pulled him toward her with an intensity that didn't come with a price tag.

"No. Wait," he said. He breathed deeply, fighting for control. "This one has to last, all the way to Wendover."

He hesitated to take one more long look at her and then poised himself just to touch her warmth. He covered her mouth, seeking her tongue with his.

She circled her arms around his neck and arched her hips to receive him. As he slid into her, she bit his lips gently and opened herself to him. She was wet and delicious, moving under him like a rogue wave, building, cresting and carrying her to a shuddering break.

When at last he let himself go, it was as though he'd diffused into her, leaving himself and joining with something he hadn't believed possible. It scared the living daylights out of him.

Maddie lay, spent, her tummy slick with the sheen of their passion. Nick's cell phone jangled like an alarm clock shattering a dream. It played a tune she hadn't heard before.

He propped himself on one elbow, slipped from playful to serious, and reached for his phone.

"Sorry Maddie. I have to take this one." The set of his shoulders and the tone of his voice told her it wasn't his father on the line.

She untangled her legs from his, retreated to the headboard, and settled into the sheets.

Crossing the room, Nick stood at the window, his attention focused in the distance, the muscles along his backside tensed as he listened. She had to drag her eyes away.

"...I'm not worried about that…" His voice lowered. "That's to be expected. Lodgings would be the last to recover..."

He glanced over at Maddie. His eyes narrowed, then he turned his back again. "The retail numbers should reassure the Board …"

Trying to ignore his conversation, she pulled her computer onto her lap and opened the lid. The Central Coast Real Estate Trust webpage refreshed on her screen. Her breathing went shallow as she scanned the images and charts. Nick Berlin, Jr., CEO of the Central Coast REIT, wasn't selling mid-town bungalows in Ventura like she'd imagined. A set of chills turned the skin on the back of her neck and arms to gooseflesh.

"Of course I'll be back in time. My father has never had a vote…That's what he thinks…" His tone changed again, impatient, annoyed.

Maddie pressed her lips together and closed her laptop with a quiet snick.

"…Thanks, Alice. I appreciate the heads up…"

He clicked the cell phone shut and looked at Maddie. The furrow between his brows deepened as he regarded her, pushing fingers through his tousled hair.

"Business," he said, as if she couldn't tell.

Maddie crossed her legs Indian style under the comforter. "A hot listing?"

She knew damn well it was nothing of the kind, but she didn't want him to think she'd been eavesdropping. The color came up in his cheeks and he glanced away as he tossed the cell phone on the nightstand. "Something like that."

The truth about his business hunched like an elephant in the room. If he wasn't willing to tell her, she was certainly not going to ask. Maddie caught his eyes for a moment before he broke their gaze. He fished his Levi's off the floor, wadded them in front of him and slipped into the bathroom.

Maddie exhaled when the door snicked closed. She wished she hadn't seen the website. It was hard to ignore financial numbers that started with B's. When a man's title included letters like CEO and CFO, his life was subject to business in the middle of pleasure. She understood why he kept women at an emotional distance. He was the kind of guy women stalked, hoping for a big diamond ring, or if they got lucky, a positive pee test.

She saw now that he wasn't kidding about the coat. A little fling, a little gift, and *hasta la vista,* baby.

Well, maybe that was just fine with her.

She had things to put in order too.

And Mad Monkey to revive.

He'd been nice enough to offer his help, but once this trip was over and the car auctioned, they would go their separate ways. And it sounded to her that for Nick, the sooner the better.

The sex was good. No, the sex was incredible. But it was just that. A lusty re-acquaintance with her libido that was long overdue. No harm, no foul. The last thing she wanted was to be that cloying female he wished he'd never met.

She exhaled again, purging some of the hurt she denied. If she needed a lie to get through this, then so be it.

When he came back into the room, he searched her eyes as if trying to read her mind and then, apparently coming up empty, he scratched the back of his neck. "Sorry, Maddie—"

"It's okay," she said, trying to sound like it was. And, as much as she'd enjoyed their closeness, she'd make sure it didn't happen again. "Like I said, we'd better get on the road."

Lifting her chin, she retrieved her towel from the floor and sprinted for the bathroom. To hell with that little sting forming in her throat. She closed the door behind her without looking back.

Maddie's cell was tinkling when she got out of the shower. She peeked out the bathroom door thankful to find the room once again empty.

The caller ID said it was her body man back home. "Hey, Clay. How's the new build going?"

"Where are you?" Clay was a practical man, not given to drama. The tone of his voice put her on full alert.

"I'm in Cheyenne." Clay would figure she was visiting her friends. "Why? What's happened? Are Walt and Flo all right?"

"Nothing. I mean, Walt and Flo are fine. It's just…"

Maddie swooped around the room, hooking her clothes off the floor, phone shouldered to her ear. "Spit it out, Clay. You're making me nervous."

Holding her Mad Monkey sweatshirt over her chest, she pushed the vertical blinds aside and peeked out the window. Nick had already pulled the truck around to the loading area. He looked up from the back of the car hauler as if he felt her eyes on him and gave her a little wave.

"They broke into the shop."

She let the blinds fall back into place. Her fingers suddenly went cold. "The shop. My shop?"

"I didn't want to scare Walt, so I called you. Nothin's missin' that I can tell, just messed up, you know…like makin' a show of it?"

She ran shaky fingers through her hair. "What would someone want in the shop? The car's gone, once they saw that—"

"I don't know, Mad. They dumped over toolboxes, smashed up the sign."

"My sign?" Her Mad Monkey neon sign? It was like a stab to her heart. That made it personal. Why was someone trying to hurt her? What had Mad Monkey done to cause such rage?

"Want me to call the Sheriff?"

"Yes, I…I mean…" She peeked out the window again. Bébé sat in the driver's seat of the truck, her tongue lolling out the side of her mouth. Nick wasn't there, likely on his way back to the room. The tight knot of fear in her stomach expanded to anger and disbelief. "...No…not yet."

If Nick was involved, she was in a better position to learn the truth than the Sheriff back home. And if he wasn't… "Do you have your camera with you?"

"Just my cell."

"Good enough. Get some pictures, then clean up." She hopped into her Levis. "I don't want Walt and Flo involved. Do you understand? I don't want anyone to know about this, not yet."

"Yeah, sure. But…"

Footsteps stopped at the door. "I have to go."

She threw the door open just as Nick reached it.

❧

The look on her face—drained of color, eyes wide with fury—stopped him cold.

She threw her bag up on the bed, stuffed the sweatshirt in, and pulled out a fluffy sweater. The pink one she'd worn on the night of the memorial. She shot her arms through the sleeves and yanked it down.

"What?" He shook his head, trying to figure what had set her off this time.

"You're the only one who knows I have the car, yet people followed us. I threw them off the track, and now my shop gets tossed."

"Tossed?" He reached the bed in two steps and grabbed her wrist. "Maddie, what's going on?"

"Let go of me." She wrenched away, her eyes blazing. "You want the car, *mister* CEO? You can have it. A million bucks, and she's all yours. But leave Mad Monkey out of it."

She zipped up her suitcase in three sharp strokes, mumbling to herself.

Nick stood next to the bed, watching the flurry of activity without a clue as to how he figured into it. When she straightened to look at him, those slate blue eyes, as dark as he'd ever seen them, brimmed with tears.

"What? You thought you could buy me with a fancy coat? I'd be all sweet and sexy until you were done with me?"

She scooped his cell phone off the night stand and slapped it into his hand on her way to the door.

"Call off your goons. Anything happens to Flo and Walt, and I will hold you personally responsible." She yanked the door open and turned back. "Don't forget your wardrobe, cowboy. I wouldn't want you out in public without your silk underwear."

Nick stared at the closed door, the loud bang still ringing in his ears. "Goons?"

It wasn't the first time a woman had left him standing on the wrong side of a slammed door. Usually, it was a relief—the moment when a nice little piece of ass realized that's all she would ever be to him. A smoldering night of sex…a no strings exit. A distraction. Okay, a deviation from plan, but he was on vacation, right? A man could take a few days off for a lark once in a while?

So why did he feel like half of him just stormed out the door? He banged his hand against the wall, paced back to the window, and looked out in time to see Maddie throw the latch on the car hauler and drag open the heavy doors.

"Crap."

He scooped up his shaving kit, crammed his half open carry-on under his arm and charged out into the hallway. A frail woman leaned on a walker in front of the elevator doors herding a gaggle of odd sized bags and boxes. She gave him a hopeful look.

He opted for the stairs, skidding through the lobby and out into the parking lot. A pair of socks bounced out of his bag onto the ground. Bébé barked wildly in the truck's front seat.

It took a moment for his eyes to adjust to the dim light inside the trailer.

"Maddie?"

He could see her silhouette in the driver's seat of the Cadillac.

He dropped his bag to the pavement, sidled in alongside the car, and knocked on the window. She stared straight ahead, fingers white-knuckled on the steering wheel. Tears collected along the sharp edge of her jaw, leaving shiny tracks over her flaming cheeks.

"You want to tell me what the hell just happened?"

She shook her head violently.

Nick paced back a few steps, threw up his arms, and turned around. "I can't help you if I don't know what happened."

"I don't need your kind of help."

He lowered himself next to the window to get to her eye level. "You were wrong about me once. Maybe you're wrong again."

She rolled her eyes to his, the fury gone out of them. Instead, their light had dimmed, lost focus. "They wrecked my shop. Mad Monkey. Why, Nick?"

He tried the door handle. "Just let me in. I can explain. I think."

"You think?"

"If I had a clue what you're talking about…"

Maddie stared at him for several heartbeats. At last, she closed her eyes, lifted the door lock and slid over to the passenger side of the seat.

"What do you want from me, Nick? Sex? Because, I'm a big girl. I can do that." She turned to him. "I *like* to do that."

She shifted in the seat and straightened. The hint of defiance in her chin was dampened by the hurt in her eyes. "But this bit with the car? I don't get it."

"We had a deal. I'm still good for it." Nicked softened his voice and searched her eyes. Once again, he'd set her off and he wasn't sure why.

"What do you gain by trashing my business?" She curled her legs up under her and hunched toward the door.

"I'd gain nothing." He fought to hold his tone even, reassuring, but pressure built in his chest. The crazy thing about letting a woman inside was that you started to see what made her tick. Her patterns. Her moods.

Strings.

Like the ones that pulled at his gut when boyhood memories crept in. The look in her eye told him the anguish he saw there went beyond someone breaking into her shop.

"Tell me what really happened."

An ache ran up her insides and stung her throat. She suddenly felt childish, defensive. But he was absolutely right. It was shocking to hear that her shop had been violated. She had struck out at the nearest person and he'd seen that. But that's not what had really set her off and he'd seen that too.

"You *lied* to me."

"About what?"

"You said you were a real estate agent, not some big shot CEO with a trust company worth billions."

"I never said I was a real estate agent." His eyes narrowed and the sharp angles of his brows softened. Was it compassion she saw, or pity?

"I'm not one of your hoity-toity girlfriends, living off my granddaddy's estate. I have to work for a living." She lifted her chin.

"Maddie—"

She sniffed, turned away, and tried to get herself together. They were back in the car where they started, but they would never be the same again. She had never been good at lying to herself. She had actually entertained the thought that maybe—maybe they had something worth holding on to. Something special. But she had been wrong.

"We live in different worlds, Nick. Yours pays fortunes—what amounts to a lifetime's earnings for people like Walt and Flo—for art, for classic cars. Mine builds them. CEOs from Montecito don't bring grease monkeys to their fundraiser-ball-of-the-month club."

Nick looked at his hands, drew in a long breath, then blew it out. "Maddie. We need to clear up a couple of things."

"No, no. I get it. You're out of my league." She waved off his attempt to touch her arm.

Nick straightened in the seat, taking it in. For a moment she thought he would deny it, but he didn't. His jaw worked in that maddening way she'd seen back on the road.

"We had an agreement. I'm willing to stick to it. I don't know anything about any goons."

He twisted the steering wheel knob between his thumb and forefinger, traced his fingers over the swirling pattern.

"But you can be damned sure when I find out who trashed your shop, they will pay."

"I've got insurance. That's not the point." Her next thought stung the back of her throat, tortured her words. "They invaded my home. It's no Montecito estate but it's mine now, damn it. And it's all I've got."

Nick huffed out a breath.

"I was hoping to get to Wendover before midnight," he said finally, opening the driver's door.

Maddie arched her back and glared at him. "I don't take orders from—"

"Fine. Ride back here." He swung his long legs out of the car and stood. The angles of his face turned hard. "I'm locking that door in two minutes. And FYI, despite what you may have inferred on our website, I gave up *hoity toity* a long time ago."

Chapter 8

"Well, there's a voice I haven't heard in a while." His half-brother answered his call on the first ring.

"How's it goin' man?" Nick lowered his voice, not wanting the occupants of nearby booths to hear his conversation. No sense trying to keep the tension out of his tone. Luke could always read him like a stop sign. A Miranda Lambert song drifted over the patrons, masking the slot-machine din out in the casino, but not enough to keep Nick's fingers from itching. He fisted his hand and flexed it.

"Same ol' gang-stabbings and bum fights," Luke said.

"I thought moving up to Santa Barbara would have changed all that." Nick hadn't talked to his stepbrother since he'd left the city of Oxnard and taken the job as detective in the Santa Barbara DA's office.

"Only difference is tourists and cruise ships added to the human salsa. You?"

"I'm in the black and holding."

"That's a plus in your business right now."

"Cash talks." In more ways than one.

"Glad to hear it. Been meaning to come see you in Vegas. What's a good hooker at the local bump and run cost you these days? A thousand?"

"In your dreams. And don't call 'em hookers if you want to get laid."

"Professional sex technicians?" A high-pressure cappuccino machine discharged in Luke's background.

Nick rolled out a satisfying laugh. "Sounds like you're on duty at that fancy coffee house on State Street."

"Who, me?"

"Hold on." Nick shifted his cell phone to his other ear, scanning the darkened restaurant. "I need your professional services."

"I don't give head."

"Funny."

"I thought so."

"Seriously." Nick could almost feel Luke's arm around his neck, wrestling him to the floor in a sweaty, make-believe head lock. The two of them had stuck together when life at home got scary. But they'd both made it through.

Another slurp. "Okay. Shoot. I have three minutes left on my break."

"What do you know about Dad's partnership? Way back. Before he married your mother?"

"Dude, I was an egg in my mother's ovary back then."

Nick craned his neck to see Maddie at the casino bar. She'd sulked the entire run from Cheyenne, barely saying a word. Then two guys showed up in the hotel lobby and, all of a sudden, it's old home week. She and her friends had apparently ordered another round and were heading his way. Nick settled back in the booth.

"Running out of time here," Nick said.

"Go."

"That picture on Dad's bookshelf? A classic car and a girl?"

"Long legs, dark hair, big tits."

"Forget the tits. Dad's story is she ran off with this guy, an old partner. I need to know everything you can tell me about him."

"He's still on about that slut?" Luke let go a little laugh. "I thought she was dead."

"As a doornail, but his obsession is alive and well."

"Crazy son of a bitch. Still yanking your chain?"

"He's up to something and it's starting to stink."

"It's not like there's a case, Nick. I can't go poking around for no reason." Nick heard voices prodding his brother to leave. Luke held them off, and then came back to Nick. "So…"

"So, get me what you can, okay? I got a lot riding on it."

"Yeah? Well I hope she's worth it."

The question hit him hard. Louise had nailed him with the same MO.

"I gotta go."

Maddie crossed the dining room. Heads turned, male and female, to follow her progress. Nick didn't blame them. She looked good enough to eat. Her laugh, music he hadn't heard since leaving Cheyenne, triggered a leap in his heart rate. The tousled hair, fresh Mad Monkey tank top, stretch jeans, and those fancy turquoise cowboy boots added to the heat. He couldn't stop his gaze going to the sweet spot where her zipper ended as she closed the distance between them.

"You changed." He stood.

She lifted her eyebrow at him as she slid into the booth and kept going all around the horseshoe shape to the other side. The big guy she'd introduced as Robert slid in after her, three schooners of beer wedged between his fat, scarred fingers. The third guy, Robert called him Ray, carried a coffee cup. Nick motioned him in and sat opposite Maddie.

"So we were here in September for the World of Speed?" Robert slid a beer across the table toward Nick, continuing a conversation that must have started at the bar.

"We heard about this Hunters' Widows' Weekend thing and decided to come back." He pressed his shoulder into Maddie's, eliciting a half smile. "Like golf widows, you know? Bored, neglected. Looking for a little excitement."

His grin framed a mouthful of perfectly straight teeth.

Maddie sipped her beer. "What's a classic car guy like you doing at Speed Week?"

Her tone was chatty, light, the opposite of the last six hours she and Nick had spent together on the road, but a glimmer behind those dark eyes told Nick her mind stewed on something else.

"Speed Week is for qualifiers." Robert drank half his schooner in three gulps and plunked it down hard on the table. "World of Speed is for the big boys. Crazy fast."

He turned his gaze to Nick. "Maddie said you're in real estate. Tough times. It's the same with classics right now. No money in it."

Robert picked up his beer and sipped, his gaze slipping to his friend. "Right Ray?"

The skinny man lifted a shoulder. He'd passed on the beers and sat stoic, wary. "Depends."

He shot a glance at Nick, then settled on an indifferent stare over mirthless, thin lips.

Nick cracked his neck.

Robert gulped more beer. "Anyway, I'm just layin' low, waiting for things to turn."

The guy was no backwoods holler boy. Fresh cut, dark hair, logo golf shirt from some private club Nick didn't recognize. An expensive watch and a conservatively impressive diamond ring on his right pinky proved that. No Kentucky in his speech. Nick envisioned Robert and Maddie meeting at auctions, trading stories and car parts. He didn't see them trading anything more intimate. Just the thought of it shot a bad taste in Nick's mouth. *Asshole.*

Something about Ray set Nick's teeth on edge. He looked uncomfortable in his boxy, silk shirt, like he'd just pulled it off a hangar in the gift shop and walked out. A little withered around the edges, this guy didn't seem the type to be with Robert on a chick hunt. In fact, he didn't put him with Robert at all.

Nick sipped his beer, pasted a smile on his face, and switched his gaze back to Robert. "So, how long have you all known each other?"

Robert pushed his shoulder into Maddie's again. "Maddie and I met at her first auction."

She looked down into her beer as if there was an escape hole in there somewhere.

"What was that, Maddie? Three, four years ago?" Another nudge.

She shrugged a shoulder and kept her eyes down.

Robert turned his attention back to Nick. "She had a smokin' hot '48 Merc. Big V8, all copper-orange and chrome and hunkered down. Copper Jamm."

He signaled the bar waitress to bring another round. "But Maddie stole the show. Man, you should have seen her."

Nick put on his game face, but his stomach tightened into fight mode.

"She drives it herself, up on the block, bright lights gleaming on the paint. Lots of ooohs and ahhhs." He stretched his hand out over the table, laying out the scene for his listeners. "She gets out of the car in a jumpsuit, you know, a grease monkey suit? Starched collar all turned up and spotless white, Fuck Me red heels and a red scarf around her neck…"

Nick's thought flipped momentarily to the first time he'd seen her, in mourning black, snow boots, and that silky red scarf. Under the table he drummed his fingers on his thigh.

"And that ponytail… The guys go ape shit. Bidding like fools." He slipped his arm from the back of the booth to Maddie's shoulders and pulled her hard to his side.

"I paid about five thousand dollars more for that car than I should have, but it was worth it. Right Maddie?" He winked at Nick.

She pulled away slightly, the color coming up in her cheeks. "And you sold it the next year for twice what you paid."

"That's the way the game is played, my love." He finished off the rest of his beer. "Buy low, sell high. Like that Caddie of yours out there. The market's not that hot right now."

Maddie lifted her head. "I'll decide when to sell it," she said. "And to whom."

Nick recognized a familiar flash of fire behind her guarded eyes.

"*Whom* now is it?" Robert pressed a finger under her chin and lifted. "You know, I think I still have a picture of you in my wallet."

Maddie pushed back as he rolled up a haunch and pulled out a polished leather billfold. She glanced briefly at Nick, offering a reluctant smile as Robert riffled through a stack of cards and tossed a photo out on the table. "Quite the pair, huh?"

In the fraction of a second before Maddie slapped her hand on the photo and dragged it to her lap, Nick saw Robert's arm possessively around her waist, a red bandeau top under the open jumpsuit, and an enticing display of cleavage. There was no doubt as to which pair Robert had been referring. Nick felt his jaw working and fought to mask it.

"Nick isn't interested in our history, Rob." Maddie scooted out of his embrace. Her eyes went dark and she glanced at Nick as the waitress brought the tray of beers to the table.

Robert smiled good-naturedly and held up his hands in surrender. "No, I don't suppose he is."

"And neither am I," Maddie said.

"So, nothing's changed, I see. Except that hair. Whew." Robert gave Maddie's short, tousled do a disapproving look.

The waitress cocked her hip and lifted her order pad. "Anything else? Dinner?"

Maddie relaxed a little and took a deep breath. "Let's order something. I haven't eaten all day."

"Aw, baby, that's why you're so cranky." His hand went below the table. "Nick here hasn't been feeding you."

She jerked further away from Robert.

Nick flexed his jaw, fished a hundred-dollar bill out of his wallet and threw it on the table. You all go ahead." To the waitress he said, "Get me a shot of Patrón…to go."

The Utah side of the sprawling building was dominated by a bountiful buffet. The Nevada side was dimly lit chaos. It took Maddie's eyes a moment to adjust. Against a dark backdrop, slot machines flashed colored lights and spun bright images of cherries, lemons, bells, and jackpot signs in front of the players who fed them. Deeper into the dark, workers in white shirts and black satin bow ties presided over a few green felted tables. Most of the players hunched over mixed drinks and piles of chips. One woman, overweight and proud of it, did a happy-dance as a dealer dealt her a winning blackjack card. Only a few tables were active, the rest hunkered under translucent plastic, awaiting better times.

Bells and buzzers and country music added to the assault on the back of her head, which had started to throb the moment she turned in response to a pat on the butt and found Robert Hogue leering at her breasts.

Robert was harmless, but she'd never intended to spend more than a few minutes with him, let alone dinner, a quick look at the Flying Goddess, and a beer-fueled detour down memory lane. A detour she had to remind him several times would lead to the same place it had four years ago.

A dead end.

His creepy friend stuck to them like dog poop on a boot. She was surprised and a little annoyed when he followed them to the parking lot. He made no excuses for checking out the Caddie over their shoulders. Maddie had to glare him out of the way so she could get the trailer doors closed and locked.

She spotted Nick at one of the two open craps tables, and headed toward him, relieved. Robert followed her, his hand at her side. He gave her a possessive squeeze just as Nick looked up.

The croupier tapped his stick on the green felt table to draw Nick's attention back to the game. "Still with us, sir?"

Nick's gaze lingered on Maddie's a moment, unreadable, before he turned and dropped a stack of chips on the Pass line. He leaned down to rest his elbows on the padded railing.

Maddie imitated him, moving close to his side, suddenly regretting the time she'd wasted ignoring him in the car. In the space of the hour or so she'd spent away from him, she'd sensed something missing. Something annoyingly necessary, it seemed, for her peace of mind.

The stick tapped twice on the table in front of her.

Nick's eyes lifted only as far as her lips. "Croup wants to know if you're in."

The croupier waited, castles of brightly colored chips stacked in front of him. A short man, he appeared to be standing on a box, but he was every bit in charge of the table in his white shirt, black satin tie, and somber expression.

"I've never played," Maddie said. But she would. She wasn't about to leave another opening for Robert, who never could take no for an answer.

"Gambling's for suckers." Robert's brash announcement drew annoyed looks from the other players at the table. "You'll get luckier back in my room," he said in a stage whisper close to Maddie's ear.

Nick stared at the chips in front of him, his hands clasped together, knuckles whitening.

Maddie picked up the cue, turned on Robert, her hands fisted at her hips. "Don't you have an appointment with a neglected widow or something?"

Chuckles from around the table.

Another rap of the stick just in front of Robert had him snapping his head up.

"If you're not playing sir, move away from the railing."

Robert's neck reddened. He shoved his hands in his pockets and stepped back. "If you need anything, Maddie, I'll be in the coffee shop."

Robert had always suffered what Maddie called the center-of-the-universe syndrome. She guessed he was here on a tighter shoestring than hers. He talked big, but she knew better. If he had any cash, he'd be at the auctions now, when the prices were low. She glanced at Nick as she turned to the table. Was that a glimmer of amusement in those hooded blue-green eyes?

Nick slid a short stack of hundred-dollar chips in front of her. Her eyes widened.

"Oh no. I'll play with my own."

"Give the man your money then. People are waiting on you."

Maddie pulled five twenties out of her pocket, her stomach doing flip flops. The last thing she'd expected to spend her cash on was the craps table. But there was no way she'd rack up a gambling debt to Nick along with everything else. She could see Robert out of the corner of her eye, arms folded across his chest, just waiting for his chance to glom onto her. It was worth the hundred bucks to stick by Nick's side instead.

The croupier snagged her money and pushed it through a slot in the table in front of him with a nod to a woman standing in the center of the ring of tables, a gold brocade vest added to her staff uniform. The croupier slid Maddie one chip.

"One chip?"

Nick leaned in to her. "Just put it on the Pass line."

He nodded toward a little sign bolted to the inside of the table: Minimum bet $100.

The croupier gave her a stern look. Her headache helmet tightened.

"And don't let your hands go below the table, or this guy…" he inclined his head toward the croupier, "…will hit you with his little stick."

Maddie blew out a breath and slid her only chip into position. The three other players at the table had been watching the exchange, apparently mesmerized. The croupier broke the spell.

"Players, place your bets," he said, gazing over their heads.

Nick slipped a five-hundred-dollar stack of chips alongside Maddie's bet.

"You win, I win," he said into her ear. "Just like Jack and Rose."

"Jack and Rose?" She could smell the alcohol on him, along with the heady scent of his skin. She'd never seen him quite so loose.

"On the *Titanic.*"

Maddie gripped the railing, shaking her head.

The croupier selected a fresh set of dice from his stack, placed them precisely on the table in front of him and pushed them to Maddie with the hook end of the stick.

"New roller," he called out, practiced and sing-songy.

Nick's eyes sparked with excitement like someone had lit a firecracker behind them. "Okay. This is it. Bounce 'em off the rail down there, Maddie."

The other players pushed their chips into position, all eyes on her. Maddie felt a sensation like a train leaving the station. *Or, the Titanic…*

Nick nudged her arm.

"Okay, okay." She rubbed her hands together, scooped up the dice and tossed them hard. They bounced down the green table, caromed off the foam-padded railing at the opposite end, and rolled back, one dice settled on a five, the other a two.

"Seven." The other players whooped and hollered. The croupier scooped up the dice and, working his way around the table, paid them off. Maddie was surprised that he left a hundred-dollar chip next to her original bet, but when he moved on to match Nick's stack of five hundred with another just like it, she realized her jaw was hanging open.

"I thought seven was a loser."

"Not when you're coming out." Nick smiled genuinely for the first time this evening and stacked his chips in one pile. He placed her first hundred-dollar chip in the groove on the rail in front of her. "You're on their money now, Mad Monkey."

The croupier sent the dice back to her. "Coming out!"

Nick leaned in, smiled into her eyes. "Put your bet out there, girl."

She slid her chip back on the Pass line and rolled again, putting nines in play. She continued to roll with Nick coaching, each time matching her hundred-dollar bets with a stack of his own, until his stacks multiplied by tens. Her chips were all over the table, at his instruction, wining on practically every throw. She had rolled more than twenty passes without crapping out, her original hundred dollars stacked safe in the railing. She jiggled the dice in her hands and jiggled again.

"Roll Mad Monkey." A man across the table slid a stack of chips into the Field. "Nine, baby, nine."

Maddie was confused a moment until she remembered she wore one of her shop tank tops, a replica of her neon Mad Monkey sign brightly printed across the chest.

She jiggled the dice some more. "Come on, Maddie. One more throw."

Excited, Nick slipped a stack of chips on the Horn in the center of the table.

"Thousand-dollar *yoh*," the croupier called out over his shoulder.

"Roll an eleven, Maddie."

She looked at Nick, breathing hard. "But you just put…"

She leaned into him, familiar, like breathing, his warmth radiating through her whole body.

"Just roll for chrissakes. Everybody's waiting." His head tilted into hers, his wrist resting casually over the railing.

Maddie huffed in a couple of deep breaths and fingered the chips safely in her tray. Nick was right. What did she have to lose? She picked up the dice, rubbed them together in her hands and let them go.

"E-*yoh*-leven," the croupier called.

Shouts around the table. The woman in the gold brocade vest stalked from the center of the cluster of tables and nodded at Nick as the croupier measured out three stacks of five chips with his thumb.

Maddie leaned into Nick. "Who's that woman?"

"The pit boss. You've made thirty-three passes since you rolled that seven. Everybody's raking in chips. She's going to—"

How did Nick know exactly how many passes she'd thrown? The woman picked up the dice and looked them over.

Maddie's stomach churned like it did when the bidding stalled out on one of her cars right at her break-even point. It was a surge of energy she hadn't felt in more than two years.

A casino waitress delivered two shots of tequila on a silver tray. Nick laughed, his eyes bright. "All told around this table, you probably cost the casino about fifty thousand so far. It's her job to make sure you aren't cheating."

"But how would I—"

The woman put the dice down in front of the croupier, shot Maddie a thin smile and said, "Good luck."

Nick handed her one of the shot glasses and downed his. She followed his example, heart banging against her ribs. All eyes were on her. The sounds of the casino—the *clickity* whir of the roulette wheels, bells gonging relentlessly from slot machines, and the heat of the tequila—all added to a deafening buzz inside her head. What on earth was she doing? It was fun. It was exciting. And it made her a little woozy.

Walt and Flo were on the verge of being kicked out of their home. Her shop had been broken into. For the first time in her adult life she actually had some choices to make completely on her own. She couldn't afford to take chances. Not now. Much as she hated to admit, Robert reminded her that the car auction business could be fickle as hell. She could score big, but it was a gamble, just like this. A big one.

The croupier slid the dice back to Maddie. She stared at the oversized, red cubes, the dots blending together, losing their patterns. Her throat stung.

"Nick…" She lowered her voice so only he could hear. "I'm going to throw a seven. I just know it."

Nick fixed his gaze on hers, connecting on a string of fire for one heart throb, two. At last he stood, got the croupier's attention, and cut his hand across his neck.

"All bets off, hers and mine."

Mumbles went around the table as the croupier made eye contact with her to confirm. A few others pulled their bets as well.

The buzzing stopped as if someone had turned off an engine somewhere deep in the bowels of the casino. In the silence, Maddie straightened, squared her shoulders, and then rolled the dice.

"Seee-ven out," the croupier called.

Sound rushed back to Maddie's ears. Those who had left their bets on the table watched the croupier scoop them away.

"Good call, Mad." Nick restacked his chips. "Time to let someone else roll."

Her hands shook as she piled her winnings into a plastic cup, light headed. She had turned her hundred dollars into nearly two thousand and her nerves into shattered glass. She was excited to have won the money, but she was acutely aware that she could just as easily have lost. Suddenly, she questioned every decision she'd made since she first laid eyes on Nick Berlin.

Apparently, the casino server was under a standing order to bring him shots of tequila. He had just downed another as she turned to leave. "Where you goin', Mad Monkey?"

"Back to the room. I've had enough crap for one night."

"Craps."

"That too."

"Aw, come on, Maddie. Have little fun."

His words slurred, his eyes lacked focus. She wasn't doing much better. She put a hand on his shoulder for support. "Sure Nick. We can have a lot of fun. But for how long? How long 'til it comes back and bites us in the butt?"

Maddie slipped into the room, let herself fall back against the door as it closed, and exhaled tension out of her neck. The room was dark except for a neon pink glow cast by the casino sign outside the window. Nick had reserved separate rooms when they arrived. She didn't blame him, the way she had treated him in the car. Now, she wished he hadn't. The warmth in his smile and the glint in his eye in the casino had her libido tapping her on the shoulder with an impish grin of her own.

Why did life have to be so complicated? Couldn't a girl just get laid and go on about her business like a guy? Let the orgasmic waves pass through without leaving an imprint?

Noooo.

For a woman it had to mean something, go somewhere. Count.

She pushed away from the door, crossed the carpet, and scanned the parking lot a moment before pulling the curtains closed. She hoped Robert hadn't seen her leave the casino and followed her from outside where she'd walked, fed and bedded Bébé down. It would be like him to assume she'd want his attention. Talk about things coming back to bite you.

She and Robert's short-lived romance had been fueled by a shared passion for old cars and too much Jack Daniel's. For an entire weekend car show and auction, Robert stuck to Maddie like dog fur on the back of her pants. No matter how she tried to scrape him off, there he was, hovering, hand at her back, her self-appointed personal escort. If there had been anyone interesting to meet, they would have been instantly put off by Robert's possessive presence. She'd cancelled her contract in what had promised to be a lucrative auction in Des Moines when she saw his name among the registered bidders.

It was obvious by his reaction to the photo of Robert and her that Nick hadn't caught the pained expression on her face along with the generous flash of cleavage.

Sure, she'd had a moment of wild temptation in the backseat of that Mercury. But who keeps a photo of a girl who pushes the hotel room door closed in their face at the moment of truth?

Didn't Nick see that Robert was harmlessly self-absorbed and completely clueless?

Did she care?

She let go a deep sigh. The rivalry between the two men had been exhausting. All she wanted was a hot shower and clean sheets.

She twisted the switch on the bedside lamp, spilling soft light over the corner of the room, a baggage stand, a small desk, and a boot shuck. Using the shuck, she removed the boots her grandfather had predicted would bring her luck in the love department. Well, they'd brought her luck all right. A couple thousand dollars' worth of it. But love? Love was another matter entirely.

She sat on the edge of the bed, shrugged off the tank top, and squirmed out of her jeans. The room shifted again as if a tide rose under her. She leaned back against the headboard, reliving the warmth of Nick's hand on her hip, wanting to feel it again. She closed her eyes, but the face she saw on the inside of her eyelids was Robert's.

"No." She shook the image away. Not Robert. Her *liquored-up* brain was playing tricks. Or was it? What was so different about Nick? Hadn't they played out the exact scenario? Love scene in the car? A weekend fling?

Robert had taken advantage of her weakened condition, her elation at selling the Mercury. Nick charged her up. Each time they had come together, she'd wanted more.

Robert was forgettable. Nick was…dangerous. Dangerous to her future, her plans, her responsibilities. He could buy her a thousand times over, and would, if she gave him the chance.

He had helped her. She would pay him back. But she couldn't afford to be pulled off track. Not now. Not with her future—and Walt and Flo's—in the balance. She had already taken a detour because of the letter. A necessary distraction. The thought of seeing her father after all this time sent a jolt to her stomach.

It would probably have been smarter simply to write back. *Smarter and weaker.* There was already one coward in the family. Maddie reset her shoulders. She would not be following in his footsteps.

In the shower, she was grateful for the handrail, a lawsuit-saving device against the careless falls of wobbly old people and too much tequila.

Hot water steamed through layers of alcohol and doubt. She had made some progress, after all. She would still have to sell the Cadillac to move forward, which had always been the plan. But she was two thousand dollars richer than she had been in the morning. She could make it the rest of the way without Nick. Trouble was, she wasn't sure if that was what she wanted.

She tipped her face to the water and let it wash the confusion away. She'd get out her map and—"

A hard bump at her door made her jump nearly out of her naked skin. She pulled back the shower curtain. She'd left the bathroom door open. Her pulse revved up a notch and throbbed at her throat.

Was that the room door closing? Shoes hitting the floor?

She flipped the water faucet off. Steam settled around her and droplets of water fell from her hair.

The footsteps came nearer, uneven, slow. A hand gripped the door jam. Maddie caught her breath. Tanned, slender fingers, manicured nails.

"Dammit, Nick. You scared the crap out of me."

Nick appeared, unsteady, pushing the door all the way open, that half-assed grin at the corner of his mouth.

His gaze traveled over her wet body, lingering on her breasts before he continued his blatant appraisal, settling in the nest of curls between her thighs. "Thought that's what you wanted."

"What, to be scared?"

"To cut the crap."

He had indeed removed his shoes. And his shirt and pants. He took an uneven step toward her. Feeling a pulse of heat between her legs, Maddie swiped the shower curtain around her.

"Nick, I'm tired now. Okay? I just want—"

"I see. The old flame shows up and it's bye-bye Nickie."

"Nickie?" Maddie narrowed her eyes. It never hurts to see a man high on tequila to check out the worst-case scenario. She lifted her chin, then gripped the shower curtain. "I'm sorry. Has there been some kind of contract or claim I'm unaware of?"

&

Nick took a step, shot his hand into the shower and flipped the water back on. "I seem to remember this one."

In one quick move he was in the shower, his mouth on hers, demanding, surging, taking her breath, her mind, her soul. They swayed together, off balance as he ran his hands down her back. She grabbed the handrail, standing firm as his fingers sought their mark, the trembling flesh between her legs. She pulled her mouth away, catching her breath. "Nick. No. I don't—"

He covered her mouth again, carelessly, rough. She turned away. But there was no going back. He captured her jaw in his hand and twisted her into the kiss. The water pelted his back adding to the heat building inside him as he pushed her into the wall. When he pulled away, his eyes focused on hers. "Oh yes you *do,* Maddie."

He rolled his shorts down and pulled them off.

His mouth covered hers again, demanding, then slipped down to her neck, to her breast, taking it in, teasing the hardening nubbin with his tongue. He pulled her to him and lifted her up, one hand on her ass and the other braced on the handrail, his gaze burning into hers. His need for her had even surprised himself. But when his hand touched the inside of her thigh, instead of resistance, her gaze turned brilliant, cobalt blue. She lifted, parted, and melted into him.

Steam fueled his passion as he pushed deep inside her. She moaned and rolled her head back. Her breasts begged to be tasted and he closed his mouth over one and then the other. Her body responded with a scintillating grip as he rocked against her, harder, faster, losing control until her arm slammed back against the shower wall and went limp.

"Nick, I can't—"

"Good idea."

He lifted her off her feet, stepped out of the shower and had her across the room and on the bed without losing their connection. He buried his head in the curve of her neck, inhaling the fragrance of her skin in deep, desperate draughts. Her legs wrapped around his middle and her arms pulled him down. Not the moves of a woman who'd just been with another man. His head spun on a single mission: get as deeply inside Maddie as he possibly could. Deep enough to mark her, claim her, keep her for his own.

The distinct, feral scent of Maddie aroused him and took him higher, faster, until there was nowhere to go but into the pulsing, weightless center of himself and then into her—deeply, maddeningly, undeniably—into her.

They lay together. Bodies spooned long and heated on wet sheets. Spent. Heart rates slowing. He was heading for trouble.

Deep trouble.

And he was helpless to stop himself. How that squared with the image of her mother in a photo, he hadn't a clue. All he knew was from the moment that jerk-off Robert had appeared, his mind twisted up and the tequila finished the job. The thought of Maddie under Robert's hands, under anyone's hands, took his brain in a direction he didn't want to go. He was jealous, *dammit.* And not of any woman. He was jealous over *Her* daughter. *Not good. Not good at all.*

Nick's attention dissolved into a tequila haze, loosening his brain, his lips. "I can see why he did it, though."

Maddie propped up on one elbow, rolled him on his back, her blue eyes deepening to slate. "He?"

Nick's eyes rolled under closed lids. He could swear the room spun continuously to the right. He slipped a leg down off the side of the bed, touched the floor with his toe, and continued. "She knew the power she had over him."

Now Maddie sat all the way up, ran her fingers through her hair. "She *who?*"

He opened an eye, touched her ear, and stroked the side of her cheek. "You look just like her, you know. I saw the picture in your room."

"What on earth are you talking about?" If he'd been the least bit sober, her expression would have brought him fully around.

Instead, he closed his eyes, sealing himself in a safe, reddish glow.

"Just…like…Corinne."

☙

"Corinne?" Maddie rolled off the bed and stood, hands fisted at her waist.

"In the picture. Eyes, hair…" Through eyes open a slit, his gaze immediately shifted to her bare breasts. "…tits."

Maddie covered herself. "What picture?"

"My dad took that photo. The day he bought the Caddie for her."

Maddie stalked across the floor. The only place he could have seen that picture was in her bedroom. When had he been in her room?

Nick rolled onto his back, eyes closed, arms gesturing as if he were talking to someone on the ceiling. "He was a jerk. A real asshole. I see that now...not your fault…"

His words deteriorated to a mumble as his arms dropped limp to the bed covers.

Maddie stared out the window as pieces of the story flew around in her head and settled in a tight, hot knot in her stomach. Nick's father was the married man who bought the Cadillac for her mother?

She crossed to the bathroom in three fierce steps. Suddenly, it all made sense. Her instincts had warned her the moment she'd seen that limo at Grandpa's funeral. She'd been fooled by a handsome face. Another of Grandpa's favorite sayings rang in her ears: *Fool me once, shame on you. Fool me twice…*

A moment ago, the swollen warmth of recent sex had her head floating on clouds. Now, it was a stark reminder that they'd skipped the protection phase and gone straight to insanity. She grabbed a towel off the floor and stomped back to the bed.

"This?" She wiped frantically at her legs as if she could take it all back. "And all this," she moaned, waving her arms around the room. "…was about my mother and the car?"

A deep snore ripped through the room like a giant zipper.

Chapter 9

Bébé had spent the last hour alternately sulking in the passenger seat or whining, eyes and nose fixed out the back window of the car. Maddie didn't blame her. She felt like bawling too, which made her angry. She had promised herself to keep her distance from Nick Berlin and had failed miserably. She had let him in and enjoyed every second of it, even the tequila-fed sex fest that ended with his admission of guilt. He and his father had conspired to get the Cadillac back in their family.

Maddie spun the steering wheel knob with her thumb, refusing to feel like a victim.

Men.

Men like her father who lived on the edge and ran from responsibility. Men like Robert, pathetic, clueless, and in your face long after you made it clear you wanted them gone. Good men like her grandfather, who had the gall to up and die on you. Good looking, well-heeled men used to getting their way. Men who endeared themselves to your dog then broke her canine heart.

Bébé was in the middle of another low, dog sob when Maddie's cell phone jangled.

"What in the world is wrong with your dog?"

Maddie recognized the tone in Flo's voice, motherly concern that both annoyed and endeared.

"She has to pee," Maddie lied. "And so do I, but I'm not stopping until dawn."

"So you're alone."

"I've got Bébé."

But Flo had her pegged. Maddie felt more alone than ever. She had covered the distance between Wendover, Utah, and Ely, Nevada under a full moon and a dark cloud of righteous anger, at Nick and the whole damn masculine gender. But most of all, she was mad at herself.

"Girl, a dog is hardly—"

"I'm fine," Maddie interrupted. "Sorry I didn't call last night. Things got a little dicey and—"

"—you and Mr. Fancy shoes parted ways," Flo said.

Maddie sighed into the phone. There was no point in denying they had been together. "Nick has his agenda, I have mine."

"That's what I wanted to talk to you about."

"What?"

"Your agenda."

"I'm sorry. I took off in a hurry and I haven't been keeping in touch, but I know what I'm doing."

Right. She was out in the middle of nowhere, heading to a place she'd never been to meet a father she likely wouldn't recognize for a reason that wasn't exactly clear. She wouldn't call it an agenda. She wouldn't even call it a plan.

It was more like a rash. Ready to flare into a raw, consuming ache no matter how hard she tried to calm it. An ache she had kept to herself, not wanting to discount all the love and devotion she'd received from those who'd stuck by her, but there anyway, just under the surface, ready to put a sting in her throat when she least expected it. The years hadn't dulled the pain of the image in her mind. Her father—handsome, intelligent, strong—the first man ever to hold her hand, stroke her hair, plant the love of the ocean in her heart, then spirit her away to a distant, flat place.

She needed an explanation, an apology, something…

"I just don't want to see you hurt. You're vulnerable right now and…"

Bébé launched into an all-out howl that ended with an impatient yip. She leapt into the front seat, cocked her head at Maddie, and pawed her leg.

Maddie tossed the phone into the seat, letting Flo ramble on. She would run out of platitudes soon and feel that she'd done her duty. Nothing she could say would change Maddie's mind. She had already spent too much time following someone else's agenda instead of her own.

Right now, there was a wide spot in the road up ahead that looked like as good a place as any to hang her fanny out on the highway. She needed both hands and her brain to slow down and angle safely onto the shoulder.

At least with Flo on the phone, if a bear came out of the woods while Maddie squatted by the highway, someone would know what happened to her. She shut down the engine, opened the door and stepped out.

Bébé circled, her nose fully occupied with what must be a thousand new and interesting smells, until at last she returned, squatted next to Maddie, and peed luxuriously.

Maddie ruffled her ears. "We girls stick together, right?"

Bébé wagged her tail in agreement, nosing Maddie's pocket where she knew there were treats.

"Back in the car."

"People just aren't always what you think..." The sound of Flo's voice filled the air.

Maddie picked up the conversation as if she had never left. "What people? Is something wrong? Where's Clay? I thought he was—"

"Clay's fine. He's been working in the shop. Says clients are looking for you. It's not that…"

Again, Flo's words faded away. Maddie leaned against the curving hip of the Cadillac, let her head tip back against the top, and exhaled, really exhaled, for the first time since she'd backed the Flying Goddess out of the trailer. The image of the parking lot at Wendover filled her thoughts. She should have at least taken a minute or two to slide the ramps in and close the trailer gate. True to form, she'd gone off half-cocked. The thought triggered a familiar pang of guilt.

Crap.

Off in the distance, she saw what must be headlights wending their way toward her from Ely. She realized for the first time since she got out of the car that it was quite cold. *Time to go.* She shivered and slipped back into the driver's seat.

"You know, your grandpa always took care of things, and…"

"I'm a big girl, Flo. I'm going to take care of things, so don't you worry." She pulled the door closed. "I…just need some…time. I'll be on the road 'till about five this evening. I'll call when I get to Lompoc, okay?"

"You see, now that's just the thing—"

In the rearview mirror, the headlights came closer. Maddie did not want to be sitting here like a lost soul when whoever it was drove by.

"Flo? I've got to get going. I'll talk to you later." Maddie clicked the phone off before Flo could argue further. Bless her heart.

Walt sipped his coffee and watched Flo's shoulders slump as she slid the phone back into its cradle on the kitchen wall. She rinsed her china coffee cup out in the sink and inverted it on the drain board.

He'd been highlighting ads in the classifieds. "You didn't tell her."

He knew she wouldn't.

His wife of thirty years spun around and sent him her injured look. "Dammit, Walt. She wouldn't let me get a word in edgewise."

"Oh, I heard a *lot* of talk."

"And you would have had an easier time tellin' that child you kept a secret from her all these years?"

Touché. Flo had always been good at the touché. Most of the time she was spot on. Walt rolled his gaze to the window, his only defense. A light snow had added a clean layer over the muddy driveway. It'd still be warm in Key West right now. Or Sarasota, where his brother lived. He let go a deep sigh.

"No. Don't suppose I would."

He pushed his highlighter pen away and dabbed at his nose with a plaid handkerchief. "Child will learn the truth soon anyway, so I guess warning her won't make no never mind."

"I should have told her the day her grandpa died. Or at the memorial, at least."

Walt drained his cup, the last of it a slow-moving slug of sugar. "It was her grandfather's choice not to tell her about Ross, Flo. Not yours."

He paused to smack his lips. "You shouldn't take it on yourself."

"Liam wasn't in his right mind and you know it. She wouldn't be off on this…this…" She waved her hand in the air between them.

"Adventure?"

Flo leaned back against the sink and wiped her hands on her apron. "Only a man would see leaving home with nothing but a dog and two pair of jeans an adventure."

Walt rustled the newspaper in front of him, flattened it out again, and retrieved the highlighter. "Here's one. Two bedroom, two bath, only five years old. My railroad pension would cover the mortgage."

Walt glanced up. Flo had turned to gaze out the window over her sink, her back straight as her ironing board.

It took Nick a moment to make sense of what he was seeing. He pinched the bridge of his nose, squinted, and looked out the window again. Sure enough, the truck and trailer were there, but something wasn't quite right.

He had awakened to find himself alone in Maddie's room, double sledge hammers pounding inside his skull, a horny-toad tongue dry and spiky in his mouth. Lurching out of bed hadn't helped any.

Maddie must have felt better than he did, already up walking Bébé.

He pressed the side of his face to the glass. It felt cool against his skin and gave him a better view into the parking lot. Either someone had dropped lumber against the back end of the trailer, or…

"Holy shit."

He scrambled around the room, snagging his clothes and then realized Maddie's overnight bag was gone. The morning's reality hit him in the chest like an unexpected rock thrown up from the road.

He hauled on his pants and shirt, stumble-clumped down the stairs, and sprinted across the parking lot. The doors to the trailer were folded back against its sides, the wheel ramps extended to the ground. The only thing inside was a pair of scuffed yellow chocks.

Nick climbed up one of the ramps and gazed out from the back of the empty trailer bed. He should have known better. Like mother, like daughter.

Beautiful, sensual, ruthless.

He'd been right about her, hadn't he? Should have taken that plane back to Vegas and dropped five thousand on craps instead of wasting his time on her.

But what was he out? Really? The cost of the rental was nothing. And the hotel bill? Well. They'd had fun. He was used to paying for that. But down inside, where he added up the plusses and minuses, he knew. Knew it was more than fun. And that hurt more than he was willing to admit.

He fisted a hand at his hip and ran shaky fingers through his tangle of hair. "Drop kick me, Jesus."

The hammers pounded harder. He sat on the edge of the trailer bed, head in hand. It hurt like hell.

"You're going to have to move those ramps."

Nick's head snapped up at the sound of the voice. The concierge humped across the lot toward him, waving his arms.

Nick blinked at the man. "You see her leave?"

"Who?"

Nick squatted down, focused on the concierge's name tag. "The woman, Ron. In the yellow convertible."

Was the man an idiot? Couldn't he see what happened here?

Ron shook his head.

"No, sir." He pointed at the ramps.

"Trailer's been just like this since I come on at eight. You're going to have to—"

Nick stomped around to the truck cab. The keys had been left on the seat. "Why in hell didn't you come and get me?"

The man shrugged. "Tried."

Nick shot him a raised brow.

"Your room was empty, sir."

Nick understood the hotel's *don't ask, don't tell* etiquette. Patrons were allowed a certain amount of privacy where room sharing was concerned.

Images of last night ran hot and cold in his head. Maddie wet, in the shower, water dripping from taught nipples down over her flat stomach... Resistant, then warming, pliable, then full throttle Maddie in play. He swallowed hard. The concierge gave him a knowing smile and headed back to the reception area.

Nick stared at the trailer's flat, wooden bed as if the Flying Goddess would materialize from the effort. His eyeballs felt dry in their sockets. He slid the ramps up into truck bed runners, one by one, the force of anger assisting his strength.

They were heavy. Too heavy for Maddie to do on her own?

Maybe.

Maybe not.

If there was one thing he knew for sure about Maddie Kerrigan, it was that she was tougher than she looked. She had probably had done it alone plenty of times. He shook off irrational suspicion. Robert was still here, after all, wasn't he? With that other creep?

He checked the parking lot, realizing when nothing jumped out at him he had no idea what Maddie's irritating old friend had been driving. He stepped to the street, looked off to the west and scratched his head, sucker punched.

Nick pulled into the first station he saw and filled up the gas tanks. The double dose of Excedrin had dulled the pounding in his head but done nothing for his mood. To hell with her. To hell with his father too. The last thing he needed was to be pulled off track by a redneck female garage mechanic and a greedy, self-absorbed old man.

He was done with the whole deal. A quick stop over in Vegas to recharge, then back to Santa Barbara for the stockholders' meeting. He'd shoot down to Montecito after the meeting and put the old man in his place once and for all. His Vegas condo lacked the soul of the Montecito estate, but at least it was a refuge from the ghosts that haunted their coastal property. There was no need to go there every other week. He could hire someone to check up on the grounds, or maybe Luke would give in and help him out. He lived in Santa Barbara after all.

Nick checked the truck's GPS. A straight shot down US 93 would have him rolling the dice or visiting the Beaver Ranch in under six hours. A purging sigh and a crack of the neck had him seconding the motion.

He adjusted the seatbelt, the mirrors, and the radio. Maybe he'd just buy this truck. It was a good fit. Great power. A different image than the Prius he kept in Vegas and the Jaguar he kept at The Compound, but hey. It felt good to get out of a suit and tie and let his hair down a little. If the truck could tow that heavy old Cadillac, it could tow just about anything. A boat, maybe, or a Wave Runner. That thought took him back to Montecito and the knot that wouldn't let go of his stomach.

He pulled out onto the highway, the load noticeably lighter with the Cadillac gone. It rendered Maddie's absence all the more real. He rolled his shoulders against the nagging feeling that none of the things he dredged up from the pages of Playboy or GQ would fill the ragged hole in his heart. He could push the blame off on her all he wanted but he knew deep inside he'd been the one to screw up. He should have told her about his father's connection to her mother on the day they'd met. But he hadn't known. Not then. Now, it was too late.

He cranked the radio up loud to block out the circle of thought that kept bringing him back to Maddie. The speedometer was well into the seventies, an Eagles' song playing over the road noise, when his cell phone vibrated under his left haunch.

He lifted his hip and slipped the phone out of his back pocket.

The caller ID said it was Luke.

Damn. Nick had forgotten all about Luke. "Hey, buddy. Sorry. I should have—"

"Where the hell have you been? I've been calling you all night." Nick heard muted voices in Luke's background, then a loud engine roaring to life. He propped the phone on the console and squeezed the wheel in a frustrated grip.

"Took myself off line. What are you driving?"

"Moving van."

"You and Gina finally split?"

"Woman doesn't appreciate a detective's schedule. Thinks I can just up and marry her at a moment's notice."

Nick sipped terrible coffee from a plastic foam cup, which only reminded him Maddie wasn't around to steer him to something better. "In whose world does three years qualify as a moment?"

It was easier to talk about Luke's on again off again romance with his girlfriend than think about his own misadventure.

"Mine. A man's got to be sure about these things."

Echoes from their shared past. A bitter taste settled at the back of Nick's throat. Their father had turned both his sons off commitment. "What is it about us Berlins women don't get?"

"That would be the self-centered, egotistical, thoughtless part."

"There must be an acronym for that. I've been hearing it a lot lately."

"Yeah. J-E-R-K. I thought you swore off free-range pussy."

Nick recoiled at the term which seemed somehow crude connected to Maddie, a feeling he wasn't sure he wanted to own. Better to switch the focus back on Luke.

Maybe Luke's newly homeless situation could work in his favor. He cleared his throat. "There *is* the guest house at The Compound."

"In your dreams, pal. I said I'd never go back home and I meant it."

"*Mi casa, su casa.* Besides, I could use some help with the old man."

"*No comprende, hermano.*"

"*No comprende*, my ass. We'll talk about it later, little brother. Which reminds me, forget about that background check on Dad's old partner. I decided I'm better off without—"

"Oh, no. It's too late for that, brother." Luke's voice went serious, his detective persona kicking in.

A semi passed Nick on the left. The air horn blast drowned out all but Luke's last word, "…*Lompoc.*"

"What?" Nick stepped on the gas.

"I said, the guy's in Lompoc."

"*I* told *you* that."

"No man. I mean, he's like *in* Lompoc. You know. Club Fed?"

The fist that had hold of this stomach all morning tightened its grip. Nick jammed his foot on the brake and squealed to a stop on the side of the highway, nearly jackknifing the truck and trailer. The dust cloud caught up with him and billowed through the open cab window. He grabbed his phone off the console and slapped it to his ear.

"We're talking Ross Kerrigan, right? The partner."

"*Ex*-partner. Record shows a conviction on embezzlement, big bucks, from the real estate company they put together."

"Shit."

"Story goes they had a falling out over some chick. She splits with the partner and a Cadillac Dad claimed he paid for."

The picture of Maddie's mother leaning seductively against the door of the Cadillac flashed through Nick's mind and his stomach pitched.

"They end up in a lawsuit over the business," Luke went on. "Then evidence surfaces that Kerrigan had his hands in the till, big time."

Deep-rooted anger rolled in Nick's gut as the magnitude of their father's hate took shape in his mind. "The old man can't make a stink over losing the car and the woman because he's a respectable, married man, so he takes revenge on the partner."

"You think he framed Kerrigan?" Luke asked.

"He's capable of more than you know." A remnant of childhood guilt stung Nick's throat. "I wouldn't put it past him."

He heard Luke's turn signal tick and an engine surge. A car's horn blared in the background. What outrage did Luke know about their father that he'd never told?

"Asshole," Luke muttered under his breath, obviously meant for some driver that got in his way. "Anyway…the jury didn't think so. Kerrigan got twenty years."

"And Nicholas Alexander Berlin Sr. gets away with murder," Nick said under his breath.

"What?"

"Nothing. I'm just…thinking out loud." Nick wasn't ready to face the truth himself, let alone tell someone else, especially Luke.

"Look, if you want my help, you need to let me in on this thing."

Another semi passed him on the left, blaring its horn. Nick could hardly breathe. He sucked air hard in through his nostrils and a hardened frown. A haunting image swam up from the cold cellar where he stored the memories of his sixth birthday. He froze, just as he had back then.

The memory of *that* night was forever seared into his heart. He and his mother had celebrated alone in the kitchen, his father late coming home. He was high on gin and delusions of grandeur at having outwitted his partner on some business deal or other. From Nick's adult perspective, he saw it as another in a series of manic episodes. But the boy in him still raged under the covers, small and helpless.

Within minutes of his father's arrival, his mother, sensing trouble, had sent him to his room with a piece of birthday cake on a paper plate.

She seldom argued with his father, knowing it could lead to a scene. But that night, she fought back and accused him bitterly. Nick buried his face in his pillow, praying to a god he didn't believe in to stop the screaming. But it went on and on.

"You crossed the line, Nicholas Berlin, and I won't let you get away with it."

"So I missed his birthday. So what? He'll get over it."

"That's not what I'm talking about and you know it."

"You want the good life, you make the sacrifice."

"We make the sacrifice. Nickie and I. Not you. Nothing's good enough for Nicholas Berlin. Even if it means destroying the family of an innocent man."

"Family. What would you know about family?"

"Enough to stay here and raise your son while you're out sleeping with other women."

Nick Jr. had clamped a pillow over his head, but he couldn't block the sounds of his father's strident voice as he followed his mother upstairs.

"That man stole everything I held dear," his father ranted.

"That woman and that precious car were dearer to you than your own blood?"

"That idiot kid's no blood of mine."

"How dare you accuse me," his mother cried out. Something crashed. Glass shattered. His father bellowed something unintelligible.

"Let go of me," she yelled. Nick heard them struggle back to the stairway next to his bedroom door.

He should go out there. Do something. Help her. But he was riveted to the bed, his fingers clenching down on the pillow as hard as he could.

The next thing he heard was her scream and the sickening sound of something heavy, tumbling, hitting the walls, the stairs, and then quiet.

Horrifying, paralyzing quiet.

Nick gasped for air, reliving the memory for the thousandth time, as the anxiety built in his chest, driven by the indelible image.

An accident, his father had told the police that night. A fall that left his mother at the bottom of the stairs, eyes open, her head bent at an impossible angle. A fall that happened while Nick hid like a coward under the covers and wet his bed.

Imbecile. Worthless. Not my blood. His father's words pounded ruthlessly in his mind. *Not my blood.*

Nick wished it were true. Too many times he'd lashed out in anger and recoiled at the reminder that he was his father's son. He was a murderer every bit as much as his father. His mother needed him and he'd done nothing but hide under covers. And never told a soul.

And now, because of him, this was all coming down on Maddie's head. His father had used her mother, lied to her, and robbed Maddie of her future. He had been the one to send her father to jail. To separate her from the ones she loved.

Nick had to stop her before she stumbled blindly into a world of hurt. He had to explain.

Ha. That was a laugh. What was there to explain? The fact that he hadn't known in the beginning didn't change a thing. He couldn't turn back time and rewrite history. He was a coward then and a coward now. Running away. Hiding from the truth. Maddie had awakened a part of him he'd given up on. The part that had a right to love. He couldn't bear the thought of never seeing her again or touching her or holding her close.

Yet here he was, running back to Vegas where he could buy love whenever he wanted without any of the baggage that came with it or soothe his loneliness with a date at the craps table. Where he could fool himself into believing he was innocent.

The truth crushed in on him. The only person who had ever made him feel innocent had been Maddie Kerrigan. She made him feel like someone with a future and a heart and a soul.

He stared at the empty passenger seat. Anguish twisted his gut until it burned. Maddie, so giving, so fragile, so alive, was heading for a train wreck. And all the wealth and prestige Nick had come to take for granted were useless to stop her from plunging into what he knew would break her. If he could just get to her, be there, even if it was only to take the blame.

"Nick?"

He'd almost forgotten his brother was on the phone. Nick knew what he had to do. His gut untwisted and let him move.

"I gotta go."

He checked his mirrors. He wasn't that far from Elko. He'd used a charter to shuttle back and forth from Vegas during his winter stays volunteering at a boy's snowboarding camp there. If he turned around now, he could charter the plane, be in Santa Barbara in an hour, and Lompoc an hour after that.

"Meet me at the Santa Barbara airport."

"Santa Barbara? I thought you were on your way to Vegas."

"Just be there."

☙

Nick hyperventilated as the Twin Engine Beechcraft banked southwest and leveled off. Images from the night his mother died and the nauseating waves of guilt that inevitably rose with them were hard to get out of his system once they settled in. He hadn't let them through for a very long time.

He focused his gaze on the ground below, forced himself to breathe slow and even.

From thirty-thousand feet, the solitary highway below was a tiny scratch across the cardboard plain. An anvil of dark cloud stretched its flat top toward the horizon. With his forehead pressed to a cabin window, Nick saw no movement at all. Anyone driving across that desert was completely alone.

"You can move around the cabin, Mr. Berlin." The captain spoke directly to Nick, the only passenger on board the chartered flight. "There's some coffee and soft drinks in the galley. Or something stronger if you'd like."

The captain had ferried Nick many times back and forth from Elko to Vegas, Nick's second home and playground where it was never the wrong time for a shot of good tequila. A drink would settle his nerves. But his next thought was of the last time he'd used tequila to escape. To ease the ache of loneliness. He'd ruined his chances with the only woman who had ever felt real to him.

No. His ragged nerves and the ache in his heart had nothing to do with flying and no amount of tequila would ease the pain.

Chapter 10

"Pretty lonely out there." The voice startled Maddie from her thoughts. The view from the doorway of the convenience store—a dry, flat plain divided by a straight line of highway that seemed to disappear into nothing—had her second guessing the next leg of her journey. The road itself wasn't so daunting. It was the stark emptiness that chilled her. She could be looking into herself.

She shook off a quick flush of goose bumps and stepped into the store. "Beautiful, though," she said, trying to buoy herself up.

The convenience store clerk, her face skinny and gray as a weathered fence post, observed Maddie through doubtful, hazel eyes.

Maddie gave her half a smile and angled past an aisle of junk food, avoiding the woman's stare. It had seemed to Maddie like a good idea to take the road least traveled instead of the Google map suggestion. If she had taken US 80, Nick—or anyone else for that matter—could have easily caught up with her. Instead, she'd chosen a two-lane road that sliced through Tonopah, Nevada on its way to California.

From her view at the top of the incline leading to the highway dividing the shimmering valley below, Maddie had to agree with the clerk. She had never seen such a long stretch of flat brown nothing in her life. At least in Kentucky, you could take a road one hill at a time.

"Done that highway by myself a few times though," the woman said, leaning to look at the yellow Cadillac in the parking lot. "…long's your car's in good shape."

"She'll make it." Maddie angled back up a different aisle, snagging a package of dog treats off the shelf. *Don't know if I will.*

Her few items made her painfully aware of the fact that she was all by herself.

Again.

She pulled a stronger smile from a very shallow reserve, loaded two bottles of water on the counter, along with a plastic-covered, cow-paddy-looking thing that might pass for a bear claw and the doggie treats.

"Looks pretty lonely right here." Maddie gestured to the dusty old buildings and dried up attempt at a flowerbed outside the pay booth. She had never even heard of Tonopah until now.

The woman flipped a short laugh. "Yeah, I know. Nuthin' but tumbleweeds, dirt and a busted silver mine. My husband and I spent our honeymoon night in that old hotel."

Maddie's followed the woman's gaze across the street to a shabby brick building undergoing a facelift.

"Now he's in that graveyard over there." She shrugged. "I've got family here."

The image of her grandfather's casket being lowered into the ground slid through Maddie's mind on thready tendrils. Family shouldn't be just a memory or a piece of land. For as long as she could remember, Maddie had imagined night surf crashing outside her Kentucky farm windows and the scent of ocean spray on the summer wind. Sometimes in the hazy waking moments of morning, half dreaming, she pictured her father downstairs, hunched over a steaming mug of coffee. She could almost smell smoke spiraling from a lit cigarette burning itself out in the ashtray. For once, she was taking the situation in hand. Doing something about it. It would be a lonely drive, but at the end, she would find…

She gazed out at the highway again, the purple mountains stacked in the distance, a chill running down her back. Maybe it was best to take it one mountain at a time.

Maddie pulled a handful of cash from her jeans pocket and stared dumfounded a moment at the wad of bills that unfolded in her palm.

The clerk's eyes widened. "D'you always carry hundreds around like that?"

"I forgot I had them," Maddie said, chiding herself.

"That'll be the day when I forget I have a stack of Benjamin's in my pocket."

"They're not mine. Not really, anyway. I won them playing craps back in Wendover." The image of playful Nick's grin brought a warm glow to her center. Not likely she would ever see that grin again. She pushed the memory away. Best to forget him. He lied to her, used her. Played her just like the dice on his precious craps table. Put your money on as many numbers as you can and throw the dice. *Only this time, you lost, Nick Berlin. Big time.* She slipped a twenty off the top of the stack and folded the hundreds neatly back into her pocket, blinking away an unexpected sting of tears.

The clerk laid the bill on the cash tray and glanced back at Maddie.

"You okay, honey?"

Maddie scooped the bag off the counter and huffed out a sigh. She put on a smile to mask the desolate loneliness that suddenly folded around her like the bare brown mountains on the horizon.

It'll pass, she told herself. Eventually. That empty feeling was familiar territory. *Don't wallow,* Grandpa's voice came through. She was grateful for those memories of him, strong and supportive, when all she wanted to do was cry.

"No." She lifted her chin. "I'm not okay. But I will be."

❧

They cruised at high speed, the Goddess with her convertible top down, Maddie singing along with a Katie Perry song about fireworks, and Bébé crowding her in the driver's seat, her tongue blowing in the wind. Maddie didn't feel much like fireworks, but the singing lifted her spirits.

Didn't even know the guy existed a week ago, so what's the big deal?

But it was a big deal. From the moment she looked across her grandfather's grave to see the handsome stranger step out of that limo, Maddie had felt the impact. This man would be important in her life.

The sun beat down on the straight line of road that stretched out across the valley. The horizon mocked her, a rippling, mesmerizing image that never seemed to get any closer. She didn't notice the vehicle behind her until it was only a car's length off her bumper.

Really? The jerk tailgates on a road without a single other vehicle in sight? She stuck her arm out over the driver's door and motioned the car to go around. The follower pulled within a foot or two of her rear bumper.

Maddie slowed, pulled as far to the right as she could without running off the road. The car persisted. The sun reflecting off his windshield made it impossible to see the driver's face.

"Damn you, asshole," she said aloud, popping the familiar single digit up over her head. "Go 'round, already."

She glanced in the rearview mirror to see that he backed off for a moment, then roared around, kicking up a cloud of dust. When she turned her eyes back to the road, she got the shock of her life.

Preoccupied with the jerk riding her ass, she failed to see the car on the side of the road ahead. Like an apparition materializing out of the dust, a man standing near the back bumper shot up his hands, so close, she could almost read the logo on his work shirt.

Maddie yelped, then cranked the wheel sharp to the left. The Goddess skidded across the broken yellow line in slow-motion, spewing gravel and dust behind her in a wide arc before coming to a stop after what seemed like an eternity, facing the wrong way on the other side of the road.

The man tipped off his sweat-stained hat and wiped his forehead on a khaki sleeve.

Maddie held her breath for several heartbeats before she dropped her head back against the seat, exhaled, and closed her eyes until her chest stopped thumping like a drum. Two cars on this godforsaken road and she has close encounters with both of them? Was this the Twilight Zone or what?

She hoped she hadn't done any damage to the Goddess. Any nicks or dings in the paint would have to be repaired before she could go to auction. Nick would have wagged his finger at her with an "I told you so" frown.

Maddie's anger flared. It didn't matter what Nick would think anymore. It wasn't his car. It would never be his car. She squeezed her eyes tight against the unwanted intrusion.

When she at last opened them, two little pairs of deep brown eyes peered at her from the pickup truck bed. The man pulled off his hat and held it in front of him. "*Buenas diás, señora.*"

"Papa?" The tallest girl pulled her sister under her arm.

"*Sientese usted,*" he told them gently. The girls scrambled back under a canvas tarp tied to stakes at each side of the cab and sat as they were told.

The man was about forty. Circles of sweat darkened the front of his shirt and under his arms, but other than that, he was clean and well-groomed.

Maddie got out of the Cadillac, followed by Bébé who ran her nose up the man's leg, wagged her tail, and got a pat on the head for her trouble.

Maddie smiled and offered her hand. "I'm so sorry. That was close."

"*Es verdad.*"

True indeed. And, she was coming to the extent of her knowledge of Spanish. "You speak English?"

"*Sí*, eh, yes, some," he said. "My name is Xavier Salazar."

"Pleased to meet you Mr. Salazar. I'm Maddie."

His shoulders dropped into a defeated sag as he waved his hat vaguely behind him. "The *trucka*, she's broke good."

Maddie frowned at the New Mexico license plate.

"She got you this far," she said, trying to cheer him.

Salazar shrugged. "Not far enough."

"*Es verdad.*"

She trailed her hand over the old truck's smooth, dusty fender. The dark blue paint was oxidized, but the body wasn't detectably rusted or filled in with Bondo. Good metal on a '51 Chevy five window pickup was a restorer's wet dream, depending.

She knelt to see under the chassis.

The dream faded.

The drive shaft lay in two pieces. Its severed knuckles plowed into the roadside dirt. Minor surgery she might have performed with the tools she kept handy in the Caddie's trunk. But she wasn't equipped to raise the dead.

She straightened. "I don't suppose you have a spare U joint on you?"

Mr. Salazar scratched his head, glanced up to his girls in the back of the trunk.

"U joint?" he asked, lowering his voice.

"How about Triple A?" She cursed herself for not bringing her grandfather's card. What if it had been her dumped by the side of the road?

The man shrugged his shoulders and sat down dejectedly on the bumper, shaking his head. "We go to my sister's in Bishop. It's my oldest daughter's *Quinceanera.* Her fifteenth birthday is next week."

A father who cared. Imagine that. The billowing pile of pink fluff that filled the truck's cab—a dress for her coming out party—probably cost him a month's salary.

The young woman fisted a hand at the waistband of her pleated skirt. "I'll be thirty before we get there."

Her English was perfect.

"*Dios mio.* And I will be a hundred." His proud smile and the light in his eyes said it all. He was prepared to do anything for his dark-eyed beauty. Until his truck broke down.

Maddie brushed road dirt off her hands and suppressed a smile. "Well, come on then. I can at least give you a ride into Bishop and you can send someone for the truck."

She helped the father transfer their things into the Cadillac's spacious trunk, a rather large pile of belongings just to go to a birthday party.

Once the girls were belted in the open backseat, the eldest held Maddie's gaze in the rear-view mirror without mercy, her mouth set in a rigid pout. The father looked down, squeezed his red hands together. "She is just like her mother."

Maddie pulled slowly out onto the empty highway and made her U-turn, careful to keep traction on the rear wheels through the soft shoulder. "She's beautiful."

"Sí. And impatient and stubborn," he added.

The girl's sour mood was perfectly understandable. She was fifteen after all and stuck out here in the desert for who knew how long before Maddie came along. But there was something else in those petulant brown eyes. Something that stretched old scars in Maddie's heart.

You can't fix the world, Maddie girl. Grandpa's words echoed through her mind and he was right. She remembered the occasion vividly. She had been in modeling school in New York when she gave all her expense money to a student who said she had to go home because her father was dying. Turned out she was pregnant and used the money for an abortion. Maddie was fifteen then too. "Fifteen is a rough age."

"Es verdad. And I have another just like her." He sighed, shaking his head ruefully. "They are my life and my heart."

Shrieks of laughter and flowing Spanish erupted from the backseat as Bébé wiggled between the girls, begging tastes of pork rinds they ate from a bag.

Maddie couldn't help herself. "And their mother?"

"Se muerté, miss." His voice came rusty now, choked with emotion. "She died this last summer…of the cancer."

Maddie glanced in the rearview mirror. The ache in her heart turned sharp and cold. At two, she couldn't understand why her mother left her, only the fact that she was gone and Maddie couldn't go with her. She could never picture her mother alive, only the empty place where she might have been. She shook off the memory, but the ache remained.

"I'm so sorry. It must be very hard for all of you right now."

He looked away. After a moment, he stretched his arm across the seat back, his eyes, shining with moisture, gazed over the Goddess's chrome dash and Bakelite knobs. "This is a very nice car, miss."

"Yes. Sí," Maddie said, her heart tightening at the thought of the magnitude of their loss.

"She is worth a lot of dinero, no?"

"Sí. Mucho dinero." She glanced over at him, grateful for the little Spanish she had gleaned from movies and TV, and the slang she'd picked up in the car world. "That truck of yours? She's worth mucho dinero, too."

He shook his head. "Right now I don't think too much o' her."

Maddie laughed. "That's understandable, but believe me, there are people who would pay a lot of money for that truck."

She was thinking particularly of her friends in Cheyenne who had a row of shiny five-windows in their climate-controlled garage. If she was going to make it on her own, she had to think beyond the Flying Goddess to Mad Monkey's future.

"It was my father's." He turned his head away sharply, his pride showing in the set of his shoulders.

Maddie let him have his privacy. After a moment, she flicked on the radio and soon had the backseat bouncing to Miley Cyrus.

Though Mr. Salazar sat mostly silent, Maddie was thankful for his company, which kept thoughts of Nick from intruding on her mind. By the time they crested the pass from the western border of Nevada into the White Mountains of California, Bébé snored between the sleeping girls.

Maddie scolded herself as they wound their way down into Bishop. This family's troubles made hers seem silly by comparison. She was a grown up, after all. Responsible for herself. She was well beyond expecting someone else to take care of her. And perfectly capable. In fact, to hell with this whole damn road trip. It had been nothing but an impulsive, stupid waste of time. She didn't need her father's approval to auction off the Caddie. Or for anything else she did, for that matter. He had given up that right the day he'd dropped her at her grandfather's farm. He hadn't cared enough to show up at his father's funeral, why should he have anything to say about it? As long as she held the pink slip, there was no argument about ownership. She could drop off this poor family, turn around and head straight back home.

But she wouldn't.

She knew there was more to finding her father than confronting him about the car. The rash flared up, itchy and demanding. She needed something, anything, to sooth the pain.

Maddie stood by the door as the girls piled out of the car, a little dusty and hot, but safely delivered to their aunt's doorstep. Mr. Salazar hesitated, watching them fold into their aunt's embrace.

"Muchos gracias, miss."

Maddie eyed the pile of belongings. There wasn't a male item among them.

"You're leaving them here. With your sister." It wasn't a question. She swallowed the urge to light into him. She didn't know this man after all. It was none of her business.

"I cannot give them what they need." He shifted his gaze away from Maddie's, clearly suffering his own pang of guilt. "They need a woman."

The oldest was crying now, her aunt guiding her quaking body indoors.

Not your problem.

Maddie shoved her hands in her back pockets and kicked the dirt at her feet. Her left hand found the folded hundred dollar bills, instantly reminding her of the night she wanted to forget.

The idea formed slowly, argued with Grandpa in her mind. She still had six hundred dollars in her overnight bag, and though she tried not to use her credit card, it was there if she needed it. The money meant nothing to her but heartache and the memory of a man she wanted to forget. Once she sold the Goddess, the Kentucky property would be paid for and Walt and Flo wouldn't have to worry about a place to live. Mad Monkey Motorcars would pay for everything else. But a boost right now would mean everything to this family.

Grandpa smiled his approval in her mind's eye. He'd raised a selfish, irresponsible son, but his granddaughter was made of better stuff.

"Listen to me, Mr. Salazar. I want you to take this." She pushed the money into his hand and folded his fingers over it. "Get your truck towed and fixed."

It was the right thing to do and would rid her of the nagging sense of debt to Nick. "You find work here. Your girls need a mother. But they need you too. Don't ever forget that."

"But miss, I can't take this. How can I pay you back?" he asked, shaking his head.

Maddie fished a Mad Monkey card from her dashboard. "If you decide to sell your truck, you give me a call."

❧

"Out of the way, fat boy." A reed thin blonde in black leather knee-high boots and a matching mini skirt bumped a carry-on past Leon and stepped onto the escalator.

Leon Grange did not like being called fat. He'd lived his first sixteen years in and out of foster homes listening to that kind of garbage and he sure hadn't signed up for a life of crime to take more of the same. Then again, he didn't want to piss off the big boss, and the big boss had sent them here. He needed to stay focused. He had never seen a woman like that in real life. But not even the sight of her tight backside descending the stair in front of him could shake the vision of steel-finned teeth dragging him down by the pants and slicing his legs like pepperoni at the bottom of the stairs.

"Move, damn it." Georgie shouldered Leon forward until he had no choice but to step on the moving stairway. He held his breath and his pants legs until he recovered his balance then took a gorilla grip on the rubber railings.

"She didn't have to call me *fat boy*."

"Life's a bitch, Leon, and in LA, most of 'em are blondes, I guarantee it."

Leon didn't see how Georgie could guarantee anything. He'd never been to LA either.

A lineup of people at the bottom of the escalator held name cards in front of them, some printed neatly and some makeshift. Leon's gaze stopped on a piece of dented cardboard with their names scrawled across it. He punched his elbow back into Georgie's stomach. "Who's that guy?"

The last time they'd seen Nicholas Berlin, he was a foot taller and twice as big around as the scrawny man in a rumpled shirt and tennis shoes who held up the sign.

"I don't know. Just keep quiet."

"He spelled my name wrong," Leon hissed, leaning into Georgie. He didn't like the man's eyes. They were full of bad karma, he was sure of it.

Georgie lurched ahead of Leon as they came to the bottom of the escalator.

"Where's Berlin?" he asked.

The man pulled his lips into a thin line that Leon thought might be a smile, but he wasn't sure. It gave him the creeps.

"George Whitley and Leon Grange?" The way the guy said it, you'd think he was FBI.

"Yeah," Georgie grunted. Leon's longtime friend and partner was seldom intimidated.

"Mr. Berlin is…indisposed." The scant man turned and headed out the sliding door, stuffing the cardboard sign in a trash bin as he passed.

Georgie followed him through the crosswalk against the red light, cars and vans whizzing by on either side them. Leon hunched his shoulders against the barrage of blaring car horns and hissing brakes and waited until the light turned green.

"I was hoping we could get something to eat," he said when he caught up with them at the entrance to the parking garage. "I can't live on *biscotti* and peanuts."

"Shut up." Georgie crossed in front of him, trying to keep up with the skinny man as he double-timed into the parking garage.

"You're not hungry?"

His partner ignored him and kept going.

Leon shrugged.

Their driver stopped at a dusty SUV and pressed his electronic key. The door locks popped. "Gentlemen."

Georgie stood outside the car and checked his fingernails. "So who are you anyway? Nicholas didn't say anything about someone meeting us besides him."

"Let's just say I'm a friend of the family. Now get in the car. We've got some ground to cover today."

He pulled that sickly smile again. What choice did they have? Leon's stomach rumbled and squeezed. He leaned in to Georgie. "You think he'd take us to a drive-thru?"

George ignored him.

Jimmy Ray Montepilier slipped into the fancy Range Rover's leather seat and ran his hands over the wrapped steering wheel. Robert had good taste in women and cars. Too bad he was such a bad gambler. Jimmy Ray checked his watch. They had plenty of time to prepare before they headed north. He smiled to himself. Old Berlin was going to be busy for quite a while. He would get what he deserved someday. Schmucks always did. Nicholas Berlin might have made a fortune off that heist back in Vegas while Jimmy spent a year in jail, but he'd made out okay. Got the best education a petty thief could hope for and the next three stints got him his criminal's Ph fucking D. A stroke of luck meeting good ol' Ross Kerrigan the last time through. Sad about him. He'd been a nice guy. Honest, for a thief.

Jimmy Ray glanced in the mirror at the two idiots in the backseat. "Buckle up, boys. I promised Mr. Berlin I'd deliver you safe and sound."

The tumblers fell into place with the precision of the finest executive safe. This time, Jimmy Ray had the right combination.

Chapter 11

Maddie's cell phone buzzed as she came to a dead end for the second time. Caller ID said "Unknown" but she had a good idea who it was and she wasn't biting. Nick could take his billion dollar bank account and his fancy shoes and shove them right up his handsome, self-serving, silk-underwear-covered ass. She had driven for more than ten hours and had come to nothing but a barricade at the end of the road. The last person she wanted to talk to was Nick Berlin.

She clicked the cell off.

The more she thought about how he'd charmed her, the madder she got. She had driven through Lompoc to the middle of a plowed field without seeing anything but his lying eyes and clever smile, and now she had to retrace her route again. She had missed something, obviously, her mind preoccupied with images of Nick.

"Stop, stop, stop," she declared forcefully, bringing Bébé up out of her drooling slumber. "And you stop thinking about him too."

She turned the car around and retraced her route. No houses, apartment complexes, not even a trailer park, yet her GPS unit blinked at her, a one-eyed beacon insisting she was wrong.

"Dammit. There's nothing here." Nothing. Except the entrance to some sort of government installation. A few more yards and she could read the sign: Lompoc Federal Correctional Complex.

"Perfect." Maddie pulled over. "If you're not safe outside a prison, where can you be?"

Bébé ran her nose alongside of the two-lane road bracketed by fresh turned earth. Shocks of silvered dry grass fringed the asphalt. A warm wind gusted at intervals, driving sandy snakes across the road. Maddie shaded her eyes then scanned the surrounding landscape. Nothing. Nothing but a quivering, disturbing flutter in her gut.

When Bébé bounded back into the Goddess, Maddie turned into the long drive leading to an empty parking lot. She had found the FCC Visitor Complex. Might as well give it a shot. At least they might have a public restroom.

The visitor's lobby was brightly lit. Salmon-colored plastic chairs lined up against one government-green wall, two gray Naugahyde couches against the other. A low counter, perfectly clear, except for a computer and keyboard angled at one end, separated visitors from the reception area where a female officer sat behind a steel desk.

The air smelled of urinal cakes and stale fast food.

The officer, dark hair slicked back in a tight ponytail, wore a khaki uniform over what was likely a bulletproof vest. A heavy black belt with various utilities snapped around it, looked uncomfortable. Maddie tightened her grip on Bébé's leash.

The nameplate on the desk read Veronica Lopez. Her expression read *Don't mess with me.* She spoke in less than sympathetic tones to a young woman at the counter with a baby on her hip, and tattoos down the back of her neck.

Not wanting to eavesdrop, Maddie stepped back and focused on a sign: Visitors Dress Code. No tank tops, tight jeans, or females going braless. She was in violation of all three. Good thing she wasn't here to visit.

"There's nothing I can do, Pauline. You know the rules." The girl whirled away from the desk, and shot a look at Maddie that forced her back a step by the sheer venom in it.

"They don't give a *shit* about families here." She spat the words and swung out the heavy door.

"May I help you?"

Maddie turned back to see that Veronica smiled serenely.

"You have incredible patience. It must be tough sometimes, in this environment." Maddie's eyes went to the badge fixed on the officer's breast pocket. She resisted the urge to add "nice pin."

Veronica's gaze swept Maddie's Mad Monkey tank top. "Sometimes. What can I do for *you*?"

"I'm not sure, actually, I—" Maddie looped her hand around Bébé's leash one more time and straightened her shoulders. Hours on the road alone weighed heavily on her patience, not to mention her stamina. This is the last place she wanted to be right now, but she had run out of options.

The woman sighed. "You've missed visiting period."

She closed a large binder that had been open on her desk and stood. She was much taller, more imposing that she had looked while sitting behind her desk.

"I got that." Maddie took a deep breath, swallowed on a dry throat. In Veronica's place she would likely be impatient by this time of day herself. "This will only take a minute. See. I'm lost."

Maddie fished the letter with her father's address on it out of her purse and flattened it on the counter with the palm of her hand. "I'm trying to find this address, and—"

Veronica came to the counter, scanned the letter skeptically, and typed into the computer keyboard.

"Kerrigan, Ross, 443459."

Maddie took a step back.

"No. It's 3600." She tapped the address again and looked up expectantly. "My GPS unit must be taking me the long way around."

She threw her hands up. Her shoulders felt uncomfortably bare under the officer's raised-brow scrutiny.

At last, the woman sighed, broke her official demeanor, and leaned forward on her hands. "It's not his address, honey, it's his inmate ID."

Her dark brown eyes went straight to Maddie's, full of credible finality, a shot of reality Maddie wasn't expecting. She stared until her body's own demand for air popped her mouth open for a gulp of it. "Inmate?"

She grabbed a handful of Bébé's fur and held on, her gut working hard to catch up with her brain. Her father was in their computer?

"What's your name, honey?" Veronica slid onto a stool behind the counter, hands poised at the keyboard.

Maddie's lips and hands went cold. Of all the scenarios she'd imagined over the years about the reasons for her father's abandonment, the one involving his being in prison had never occurred to her. A woman, maybe. A beautiful woman who didn't like the idea of raising some other woman's daughter. He was a man, after all. A man who deserved the kind of love and attention a daughter could never give.

Or job in a dangerous place like Azerbaijan or Burkina Fazo, a place you wouldn't want to take your kid.

An illness. Debilitating. Terminal.

A witness protection program.

But not prison.

Her feet were lead weights, stuck to the floor, pulling her down. This wasn't happening. If she didn't answer any more questions, she could just turn around and leave. But she knew the options had evaporated. There was no way she was getting out of this one. No impulse run would take her away from the fact.

Kerrigan, Ross, 443459.

"I'm his…daughter …" she heard herself say. "Madonna Kerrigan." The name sounded foreign, like it belonged to someone else. If only that were true.

The woman scrolled through several computer screens, shaking her head. "I'm sorry. You're not on his visitor's list."

Maddie's tongue felt thick and dry, closing off the back of her throat.

"In fact, there's only one approved visitor listed, a Nicholas Berlin. Do you know him?"

The weight of Veronica's words hit her like a giant wave. A crushing, soul obliterating weight. The walls closed in, the light in the room faded for a moment before she punched her way through and opened her eyes.

"Believe me. You're not the first one to learn the truth standing right where you are." Veronica buzzed herself through a gate in the counter and eased Maddie into a chair, pressing a paper cup of water into her hand. She straightened, hands on her service belt.

"I gotta tell you, you still missed the visiting hours and a there's a mountain of paperwork if you've never been here before. Truth is, it can take a while."

Truth. Maddie respected the truth. But it didn't ease the dizziness in her head. She pinched the bridge of her nose and forced herself to breathe.

"I drove all the way from Kentucky," she said more to herself than to the officer.

"That's a long way, I know, but, I can't—"

Maddie raised her hand, then dropped her forehead into it. "I know."

She pressed her fingers to her lips to stop them from quivering.

The woman stepped back to the counter and pulled a brochure out of a drawer. "Here's a motel, just into town. They take dogs. I'll get you an appointment with the warden first thing in the morning. She has to approve all visitors, and then, of course, the inmate has to approve as well."

"The inmate?" Maddie lifted her eyes. "What about me? What if *I* don't want to see *him*?"

Veronica raised a brow. "That's something you'll have to figure out for yourself."

Maddie stared at the motel brochure, her stomach rolling.

Did she want to see him? That question could only be answered after an entire string of other questions. Maddie stood and pressed dry lips together.

"Yeah." She exhaled, pulling Bébé close. "I'll let you know."

ಹ

Maddie barely saw the road in front of her. *His only visitor Nicholas Berlin?*

How on earth did that make any sense? And if that were true, then Nick must have known. Known her father was in prison. Known her mother was involved with his dad. Known about the car. The words chorused through her head like an unrelenting earworm as one nightmare scenario wound through the next, preventing coherent thought until she realized she had driven straight back through town and had reached Highway 101 again.

Tears welled in her eyes. Damn. How had she let herself get so wound up? Defeated and bone tired, she circled back to find the place on the brochure.

The motel could not have been any lower on her list of acceptable places to stay. The doors opened to the outside and the only vacancies were on the ground floor facing the parking lot. She was on her own nickel now so the price was right, but was it a good idea to stay this close to the prison?

"I assure you, it is perfectly safe." The manager's chirpy voice wasn't convincing. She realized his robe and slippers were his regular clothes, not his pajamas. The bluish light of a TV monitor reflected on the wall behind the counter from an adjoining room.

"Most of the visitors to the men's complex are women. Wives, girlfriends," he said waving vaguely at her. "They stay here because it is close and not too expensive and I'm here, twenty-four seven."

He slapped his chest with an open palm as if he were Tarzan.

"Great." Maddie gave the manager a weak smile and ruffled Bébé's ears. "That makes us feel a whole lot better, doesn't it, girl?"

Bébé rolled her eyes, and went into flea scratching mode.

Maddie paid cash in advance plus a deposit for Bébé and parked the Caddie as close to her room as possible, between a faded minivan and a beat-up Honda with an overlarge tailpipe.

At least she wasn't the only one here. Like it would make a damn bit of difference if some freaking convict broke in on her in the shower looking for his girlfriend. Images of the Psycho bathroom scene invaded her calm.

Ironic that the last time she saw Nick, he had invaded her shower. And continued to invade her psyche just like he had from the moment she lifted her eyes to see him in the cemetery. Everything about him had been sparkling and new and exciting. A hopeful beginning discovered on a sad day. An attraction they'd both welcomed, indulged. One she'd have to forget. The sooner the better.

She opened the door to the room and looked around. Yep. It was the Psycho bathroom, complete with dingy shower curtain pulled closed. She found some comfort in exaggerating the moment as she dumped her things on the gray laminate dresser. It was better than focusing on the truth.

Bébé covered the perimeter, checking the shower without incident.

"Well, okay then." If there was a boogey man at the Psycho motel, at least he wasn't in her shower. Her hackles shrank from high alert to an unsettled twist in her stomach. She had been running on empty for hours but doubted she could get a morsel of food past her lips. "Let's go outside for a quickie run before it gets dark and call it a day."

A pink-tinged sky backlit the mountains to the west. They had just enough time to get in a few ball tosses before they lost the light. A Santa Ana wind ruffled at the dry brush along the sidewalk as it kicked up her anxiety. It had been a windy day in October when her father had loaded her into the car for the last trip they'd take together. An unsettling wind that stung her legs and stuck in her memory. He'd talked excitedly about how she was going to love Kentucky and visiting Grandma and Grandpa. How she was going to be happy, how she could have a dog.

He knew what he was going to do. Where he was headed. He was preparing her for a permanent stay, not a holiday visit.

Like Mr. Salazar, masquerading his abandonment as a celebration of his daughter's *Quinceanera.*

Maddie sighed. What else could her father have said? Daddy is going to prison, see you in twenty years? Would she have moved nearby? Visited? Putting herself in his shoes, she might likely have done the same thing.

She let Bébé off the leash, hurled a ragged tennis ball far out into the field and watched the dog bolt after it, dirt flying off her paws.

But did she want to see him?

Beyond the sky turning deeper pink by the moment she imagined the cool blue eyes and broad smile that had lived in her heart next to the resentment and the pain for all these years. She'd been hurt and angry, but she'd missed him too. When he was there, in the comfort zone, her world was aglow with the possibilities. They could take a boat out to the islands for the day, see dolphins, maybe a whale. Or visit the airport and eat grilled-cheese sandwiches with big slabs of dill pickle. She could sit on his lap while he worked at his drafting board. When he retreated into himself, brooding over some inner turmoil, he was lost to her and there was nothing her five-year-old self could do to pull him back.

But she wasn't five years old anymore. She was a grown woman. It had happened without him. He owed her an explanation. He owed her the truth.

Did she want to see him?

Yes.

She would give him a piece of her mind. Tell him how much fun it was never having his face in the crowd at dance recitals and swim meets that were supposed to round her out, give her options, make her happy. Like walking the runway in modeling school in fancy clothes would train the tomboy out of her. Make her pretty enough, smart enough, good enough.

Bébé dropped the tennis ball at her feet. Maddie picked it up and threw it, immune to the slobbery muddy mess in her hand. A moment later, the dog was back, wagging her tail expectantly.

All this time she had felt somehow lacking in herself, something unworthy of love. And all along he was the one lacking. "We know better, don't we girl?"

Bébé *woofed* her agreement.

Maddie tossed the ball out again, fighting the truth that everyone had deceived her. Flo had known, tried to warn her. And of course Grandpa had known. He had agreed after all to raise her as his own. Had he put the letter in his strongbox on purpose where she'd find it after he was gone? Or had he just misplaced it like so many things he had misplaced when the dementia settled in?

The muddy ball dropped on her feet again.

Maddie sighed. Did she want to see him? The question looped inside her mind and got tangled with all the other crap. What would be the point? She could thank him for reminding her that men were handsome and charming, willing to give you the world on a platter, take your heart and your soul and your body spin them up until you could hardly breathe and they got what they wanted.

❧

Maddie lifted her gaze to the mountains. She would put her money on old chrome and steel, like the Flying Goddess. It might start out rusty, but in the end, it made her heart feel full instead of empty.

The sky was a deep purple now. The first star peeked in through the night.

Bébé whined and pawed the ball impatiently. Maddie scooped it up and hooked the dog back to her leash.

"That's it, girl. A quick visit to the prison in the morning and then we turn this road trip around for home."

Bébé balked as they stepped up to the door to the room, the rough of her neck standing in a tight patch. Maddie looked behind her, the back of her own neck frizzed in goose bumps. But there was no one there, just the irritating Santa Ana wind whipping around the corner of the building, rattling dry leaves of fan palms overhead.

But when she pressed the key to the dead lock, the door pushed open on its own. Bébé growled, and pushed in ahead of her. Had Maddie really forgotten to lock it? Again, a rattle, and a scuffling behind her had her turning around. Bébé barked, and Maddie spun back just as the hotel room door slammed. She caught something in the corner of her eye. A jolt to her head sent her sideways and her world went black.

Chapter 12

"Howdy, cowboy." Luke clamped an arm around Nick's shoulders and herded him through baggage claim. "If you're going to channel Johnny Cash, you need to lose the blonde weave."

Nick's half-brother, a dark-haired version of himself, had added a few pounds since he'd seen him last. It softened the angular lines of his face that pegged them as brothers despite their different coloring.

"You've always been jealous of my hair." The black shirt and pants he'd bought in Cheyenne would have to do until they caught up with Maddie. She was his number one priority.

"You going to wear those boots to the stockholders' meeting?"

"If I have to. What's this sudden obsession with my clothing? Are you switching up your game?"

"If it means I can wear silky cowboy shirts with pearl snaps? Maybe." Luke beeped his electronic key and the tailgate of a pricey SUV swooshed open.

"I thought you were driving a moving van."

"Dropped it at The Compound."

"So, you're taking me up on my offer?"

"Temporarily."

"Did you see him when you were there?"

"No. Didn't go up to the main house. Good planning whoever gave that guesthouse a private driveway."

Nick chuckled. No telling what his father had used it for back in the day. Nick had made use of the guesthouse himself on occasion when he didn't want to face the old man with a woman who didn't meet the polo club's debutante criteria. Truth be told, the guesthouse had a better view of the ocean. It was a private refuge from everything Berlin.

He tossed his bag in the back of the SUV and piled into the passenger seat as his brother revved the engine to a powerful, muted purr. The gray-on-gray cockpit was small and dark compared to the Flying Goddess. The sudden, unexpected image of butter yellow leather edged in red piping hit a nerve, adding to a sense of urgency that knotted his stomach.

They rounded the parking lot and pulled up to the toll booth. For a second, Luke's jacket gaped open, giving Nick a glimpse of a gun neatly tucked under his armpit. Luke's gaze flicked to Nick's, to the mirror, and back to the attendant.

Nick waited until the toll gate lifted and released them to the street before he said it. "Seriously?"

Luke glanced at him out of the corner of his eye. "What?"

"I thought you were off duty. Something you want to tell me?"

"Yeah. Fasten your seat belt."

"That's got to be it." Luke cranked the wheel and pulled into the motel parking lot.

"Jesus." Nick shook his head. He supposed staying inside a shabby hotel was better than sleeping in the Cadillac behind the Hampton Inn, but not much. They'd arrived at the prison reception area after ten p.m., too late to catch Maddie, but the night captain directed them there, the only dog friendly motel nearby. The manager charged out of the office door as they stepped up.

"You will have to wait." He waved them aside as he dashed down the walkway.

"My tenants are not supposed to leave their dogs here alone." His nasal, high pitched voice grated on Nick's ears.

A dog barked crazily just a few doors down. Nick jogged after the manager, driven by a sudden twist in his gut.

The moment the key turned in the lock, Bébé exploded out of the room, bowling past Nick as she charged into an empty parking space, her nose working the asphalt in frantic circles.

"Bébé!"

The dog's head came up. She bounded to him just long enough to put dusty paw prints on his black pants, then went back to scouring the ground.

"Where's the lady?" Luke flashed his badge at the manager. The manager's eyes rounded. He shot up his hands as if Luke had flashed a gun.

"I…I don't know. Her car was there…right there where the dog is." Hands still in the air, he danced from foot-to-foot. The poor man looked like he was about to pee his pants.

Luke tucked his badge away. "How long has she been gone?"

The manager's mouth gaped open, his gaze skipped from Nick to Luke. "I don't know. I didn't hear anything."

"I'm sending a unit over to secure the room. Don't go in there or let anyone else in there either."

The manager bobbed his head.

Nick snagged Bébé's leash, hurried her into the SUV, and slammed the door on what he hoped was a just a mistake. His gut told him otherwise.

Luke backed off as he eased out of the parking lot. "We'll just drive around first," he said. His voice went professional, smooth and calm. "Maybe she went for fast food."

"Maddie doesn't eat fast food," Nick said, irritably.

Luke frowned at his brother.

"And, she wouldn't leave her dog." Nick banged his fist on the console. "She especially wouldn't leave her dog on her leash in the room.

Bébé whined at his shoulder, pushed between the seats. Nick ruffled the fir at the back of her neck. "We'll find her. I promise."

Nick's heart rate accelerated with every gear shift, images of Maddie flipping through his mind. Maddie taking off on her own, sleeping in the back of her car, and walking the dog alone.

Maddie being followed.

Taken.

A chain of events set in motion by their fathers more than twenty years in the past.

"Call it in. You can do that can't you? It's a kidnapping for chrissake."

"We don't know that—"

"Didn't you just spend the last ten miles on the phone with your FBI buddy about a sting?"

"Sure, but that sting's going down in Long Beach."

"Look. Someone followed her out of Kentucky. We thought we lost them but obviously we didn't. It's a classic car. A one-off original."

"One-off?"

"One of a kind. I'm serious. If our dear computer-challenged dad got word of this car coming on the market after twenty years, so could a car thief shopping for top grade product."

Luke eyed his brother a moment before he turned his attention back to the road. "Since when did you give a rat's ass about classic cars? It's her, isn't it? The woman *you've* been following all the way from Kentucky?"

Nick cracked his neck, exhaled heavily.

"The woman, the car. What difference does it make?" He dragged a sweaty hand over his face.

"Get your buddies on the phone. If they follow this car, it will lead them to a big pay-off. I'd put money on it."

Luke pressed his teeth hard against his bottom lip. "You're willing to use your girlfriend as bait?"

Nick studied his brother's profile. He'd matured a great deal since the last time they'd been together. "Don't give me that smug *I'm-the-cop-and-you're-the-fuckin'-idiot* bullshit."

"Just sayin'. It could put her in trouble."

"Maybe she did go for food. Or coffee. But if she didn't, she's already gotten herself into trouble."

Nick folded his arms and stared out the passenger window. "She's good at that."

"At least you're excited about something besides commercial real estate, Friday night craps and professional sexologists."

Nick turned away from the window and glared at him. "I'm on vacation, okay? Sometimes it's good not to be me."

Countering with a grin, Luke returned his focus to the road. "You're right. This could be a goose chase or the key piece to a car theft ring with international dimension. Your theory actually fits. Inside skinny says the whole operation is poised to receive something big. A special request before closing the outbound container. Couldn't hurt to alert the Harbor Patrol. Let them decide what to do with it."

Nick sat forward in the seat and drummed his fingers on the dashboard as if it would make the car move faster.

Luke stiffened in the driver's seat. "Catching car thieves isn't on my job description these days."

Nick glared at him, his jaw working.

Luke pulled out on to the main drag, headed for US 101, and flicked his cell phone to his ear. "Patch me through to your team at the Port of Long Beach."

Maddie cursed herself. How could she have been so stupid? Her head hurt where someone had slammed it against the door jam, and her stomach *woozed.* The confined space she occupied was cold, dark, and definitely moving. The trunk of a car. But not just any car. It was the Flying Goddess. Had to be. She knew the smell of every inch of her, from the carpet cleaners she used, to the leather upholstery, to the woolen car blanket someone had placed under her head. Her back rested against the toolbox, right where she kept it. If she could just get her hands free, she could get herself out of this mess, or at least be ready when the time came.

She could hear the constant hum of tires as they plied their way down a smooth road, high speed. She recognized the wheel whine of long-haul trucks and quieter regular cars. But the motion felt oddly disconnected. Where was the thrum of the Cadillac's V8? The sway of her classic suspension? Her smooth hydromatic transmission?

The realization spun her up like a bolt on a wheel. She was inside her trunk, inside a *trailer*, being pulled down the road against her will.

"Damn you, Nick," she tried to say, but a cloth tied around her mouth reduced her intended curse to an agonizing moan. She kicked the floor hard, sending bone-sharp pain through her ankles where duct tape wrapped them tight.

Damn him and the limo he rode in on.

This was his fault. If she hadn't been preoccupied thinking about him, she might have realized something was wrong when she got back to her room. She might have paid more attention to the signs and acted on Bébé's first alert. Blaming Nick took some of the sting out of her anger at herself. The reality was, it was all her fault. If she'd stuck with Nick instead of overreacting and taking off on her own, this wouldn't have happened.

She had actually joked about the Psycho bathroom. The memory of Bébé's anxious bark just before the blow to Maddie's head echoed in her ears. She banged her feet on the trunk floor again. If someone could knock a woman out and stuff her in the trunk of a car, what were they capable of doing to an innocent dog? Her chest tightened. If anyone hurt Bébé, she'd see that they suffered.

The image of Bébé licking Nick's ear from the backseat of the car pushed into Maddie's mind. Another humiliating, preposterous truth jumped up and bit her in the heart. She missed the incorrigible bastard. From his fancy shoes to his Tequila woody to the glint in his eye when he wouldn't take no for an answer.

She growled and kicked and rolled until she had slobbered the cloth in her mouth soaking wet and worked up a sweat that stung her eyes. On her back now, she cocked her legs in preparation to kick the top of the trunk, but stopped before she carried through. What if she put a dent in it? There was nothing she could do unless she could get her hands free. She could get to her tools and…what? Destroy a perfect, original-equipment trunk lid by jacking it open from the inside? Smash out a thousand dollar taillight? Destroy an irreplaceable lock? Exhausted, she went limp. Even if she did get out, she'd still be locked inside a moving trailer.

Her head throbbed, her ears rang, and thoughts went round and round in her brain until they landed in a place that made her really nervous. Maybe this wasn't a random event. And if it wasn't random, it was planned by someone who knew where she was headed. So who knew?

Flo and…*Nick*.

The idea struck a blow to her gut. She'd been sideways since the moment she laid eyes on Nick. She'd gone against her better judgment all the way. Let him weasel his way into her heart. He was charming, but he had dark moods too. Dark enough to do something like this? The idea that Nick would plan to steal her car and kidnap her to do it hurt worse than being trussed up like a turkey in her own trunk. Up until the day she took off with her car, Nick had responded to her whether he would admit it or not. The private moments they'd shared. Those were real. Honest. Whatever intentions he had at the start, he had changed, softened, let his defenses down.

Mr. Fancy Shoes had relaxed into the role of truck driver, unbuttoned his stuffed shirt, and temporarily given over the formality of the boardroom to the freedom of the road. She hadn't made that up. She'd seen it in his eyes, felt it in his touch. He had wanted *her*, not some image fixed in his memory by his father.

Would he really mash her spirit and erase everything that had been good between them? She cocked her feet up again and aimed at the trunk, gritting her teeth until the answer came. No. The Nick she had come to know wouldn't do that.

Which meant she was in more trouble than she could handle.

She had left the only person who could possibly help her back in Wendover. He had known she'd been headed for Lompoc. But he had no way of knowing where she was now. Hot tears welled in her eyes. *Don't wallow*, the mantra started in. But it didn't help. Not this time. She dropped her feet to the floor, defeated, and gave in to the tears.

The constant drone of an engine, combined with the nauseating sensation of riding without feeling her wheels on the ground, lulled her into an exhausted sleep.

She had no idea how long she'd dozed when she woke up to a series of slow lurches. Speed bumps? She braced herself to avoid banging her spine against the tool box until the movement smoothed, then came to a stop.

A new set of sounds. Footsteps. Doors unlatched, turned back against the side of the trailer with a heavy *thunk*. A voice said its owner had to take a piss. Another voice growled approval and the footsteps faded away. She didn't recognize the voices. Certainly Nick's wasn't among them.

The footsteps returned and stopped nearby.

Get ready.

A part of her half wished her captor was Nick. At least she would have a chance with him. But when, at last, the car was cold-rolled down the trailer ramps and the trunk opened, the self-satisfied smile on the face that peered in at her didn't belong to Nick.

Backlit by outdoor lighting streaming bright through a tall, corrugated rollup door, the rangy profile put her senses on alert. Her heartbeat pounded in her ears. He *definitely* wasn't Nick.

The moment her eyes adjusted to the light, Maddie recognized the skin and bones creep. Robert's sidekick at Wendover. What was his name? Ray.

His tongue darted out and slicked over his bottom lip when he looked at her. Suddenly there wasn't enough anger to keep her fear away. *Don't panic.* But the fear was there, right at the back of her throat, waiting to take over her senses.

Not now.

Not while you can still breathe.

He pressed his cold fingers under her chin and lifted her head. "Hello, Maddie. Have a nice trip?"

His eyes, sharp yellow-brown like splintered wood, gazed down over her breasts and lingered. Laying on her side in the trunk and wrists taped behind her back naturally pushed her chest forward. The cold did the rest. She had no defense against his lewd stare.

"Your mother. She was a looker. Just like you."

Maddie stiffened. Her mother? What on earth had she to do with anything? How could this stranger know anything about her mother? A sheen of perspiration spread over Maddie's chest, despite the cold.

Her back ached and her neck was no better after being cramped in the trunk for hours, but she managed to lift up enough to see where she was. The Goddess was parked inside a soaring, steel-walled warehouse, a row of clerestory windows opened to a black night.

He slipped his finger into the cloth at her mouth and pulled it down over her chin. She gasped in a draught of cold air spiked with the ocean's briny bite. In the near distance a fog horn bayed, answered by another much farther away. She shivered, goose bumps rose on her exposed arms.

"What do you know about my mother" She rasped the words. The sides of her mouth stung where she'd worked against the gag.

"Really? You don't know? Your mom and your dad, and Nicholas Berlin and ol' Jimmy Ray were all partners in crime back in the day." He shifted his gaze to the doorway as if looking into the past and straightened his shoulders. The ragged edge of a crude tattoo was visible just above his shirt collar.

"She was the secret sauce." He raised a hip, sat on the extended bumper, and leaned against the continental kit. "She'd strut her stuff across the lobby in those satin shorts, titties pushed up high, and all eyes in the sky would be on her, just like you in that picture of Robert's."

He dragged a strand of his own lank hair behind his ear and grinned at her.

"A sharp guy could scrape a shitload of chips off a player's pile while your mamma had their attention and they'd never know it happened."

"And a stupid one could go to jail." She spat the words, denying the terror building inside her.

His tongue flicked out again as he drew his fingers down her arm.

"Live and learn," he said, glancing toward the warehouse personnel door. "And always have an exit plan."

Maddie pulled her shoulder back, away from his touch. "But how did my father figure in? He was the one who ended up in prison."

"Your daddy? Oh, he was slick as snot back then. Convinced that Swedish woman to stash her stolen loot in the hotel safe. When it all went missing, who was she going to tell? The FBI? All Berlin had to do was set up the car show and let Jimmy Ray and Ross take care of the rest. The old man had the best collection of classics on the West Coast back then. Chevys, Plymouths, Camaros— Too bad about your father. If he had gotten us the car two years ago when I asked nicely, things would have gone…easier."

Maddie remembered the words of her father's letter and tried to mask her quick intake of breath.

… I need the car back to settle accounts, or I'm gone too…

Ray picked at something between his teeth and licked his lips as if he could read her mind, see her making the connection. "But that ad on the internet changed everything, didn't it? Just like ol' Indiana Jones moving that skull in the Temple of Doom. Put that Caddie right back in the spotlight. I'd almost forgotten about it. Old Berlin was holding out on me."

He caressed the iconic taillight. "This Caddie here? She's the best of the lot."

He forced her to look him in the eyes with a finger under her chin. "But it would sure be a shame if I had to ship it to the sheikh without getting that diamond first."

The greasy odor of tobacco on his finger made her want to wretch.

"Diamond?" What was he talking about?

"Yeah, that's what I thought. Your daddy held out on you too, didn't he? Too bad. We might have been able to work something out between us."

"You don't know anything about my father." She shot up her chin in defiance.

"Oh, I know him all right. Better than most," Jimmy drawled, sneering. "But don't you worry your little head. The sheikh is paying me enough to make up for it. That and the rest of Berlin's cars. Nobody holds out on Jimmy Ray and gets away with it. Not even Nicholas Berlin."

Her mind spun in circles, landing on the fact that Ray—Jimmy Ray—was right. She didn't know anything about her father. Not since she was five years old. The truth twisted through her, folding over on itself. It threatened to shatter her composure or what was left of it.

Don't give in. Don't give up, or he wins.

Maddie could just see over the trunk opening into the cavernous warehouse beyond his shoulder. A row of car rooflines told her what was there: A '57 Chevy, a '68 or '69 Camaro, and beyond that, the unmistakable high mounted wing of a Plymouth Roadrunner. There were more, but it was too dark to see any detail. Decent paint, bodies, and popular models. All good candidates for export to the Middle East. She'd read about this on the internet. Stolen classics supplied a steady stream of American steel, each sheikh trying to outdo the next with the best collection. With the money flowing as slick as the oil, sheikhs, only Bedouins five years before, competed to build the biggest and best stable of classic cars as a matter of entertainment.

Maddie's cheeks burned. This was not the fate she had in mind for the Flying Goddess. She pulled her head away, willing herself not to weaken in the face of this pinheaded asshole.

"I doubt the sheikh knows he's buying stolen merchandise," she said.

Don't let him see your fear.

"Stolen?" Jimmy produced an envelope from his jacket pocket, slipped out what looked like a genuine owner's certificate, and held it close to her. His name was listed as the registered owner on a fake pink slip. "You learn a lot spending your life in and out of prison. Make a lot of friends. Got the pink on that Land Rover out there too."

Maddie followed his gaze to see the camouflage green SUV just beyond the rollup door. *Robert's Landy?* It was hard to mistake the custom paint. She had done it herself. The truth struck her now like a freight train. The SUV that had pushed her nearly off the road and into the Salazar's truck had been a Land Rover. She had been too busy trying to recover to recognize the paint job, but it all made sense. Jimmy Ray had followed her all the way from Wendover to the prison. So where was Robert if Jimmy Ray had his car?

Jimmy Ray turned back to her and frowned, but the glint in his eyes told Maddie he enjoyed the game. "Oh, I've got everyone, *Madonna*."

He studied his fingernails and chewed at a cuticle. "Everyone who thought they could hold out on ol' Jimmy Ray. Everyone who made me pay for their mistakes while they took off with the prize," he said, spitting out a hangnail.

"And now…I've got…*you*." He punctuated the words by jabbing his finger at her breastbone. "Although, if you don't know anything about the diamond, I don't really need you, do I?"

She fought to control another wave of panic. Even if she did know about some stupid diamond, he wouldn't let her go. This was more than a carjacking. This was personal. And this guy was more than a creep. He was a sociopath who delighted in teasing his prey. She remembered step three of a segment from a self-defense class. Grandpa, bless his heart, had insisted on her taking it before she went to a New York modeling school over her summer vacation.

Never leave the scene with a carjacker.

It was too late for that.

But as long as she was conscious, as long as she had kick in her, she was ready to go for Step Four: Fight. She worked her wrists against the duct tape, uselessly.

"Robert's got nothing to do with this," she said. *Keep him talking. As long as the trunk is open, you've got a chance.*

"Defending Robert? You didn't seem so keen on him in Wendover. Dumped him for Berlin's son." He leaned in close enough for her to smell his sweat. Maddie fought the urge to recoil. She wouldn't give him the pleasure of her reaction.

"I didn't have much use for him either. Ironic, isn't it? You start out with two big handsome hunks and in the end, you wind up with 'ol Jimmy Ray."

Wind up? Ha.

"You're pretty tough taunting a woman taped up in the trunk of a car." She stopped working her wrists while he paced less than a foot away from her. "What's it going to be when Nick shows up here?"

"Here?" He laughed, feigning a worried look over his shoulder. "Where? Last time I saw Nick, he was towing an empty car hauler down the road to Vegas. Probably keeping his appointment at the Beaver Ranch, you know."

"Fuck you." Maddie had never heard of the Beaver Ranch, but she had a good idea what it was and she wasn't listening. She bored her eyes into the scrawny man's, staring him down until he turned away.

A small victory.

He strode to a low window in the warehouse side door. "Well, *whadayah* know. Here's some old friends of yours come to visit."

A pair of men pushed through the warehouse door, arguing over something. The older of the two eyed her suspiciously as he passed by the open trunk.

"Crane operator's not cooperating," he said to Jimmy Ray. "Says you promised him cash up front."

The moment the larger man came into view, Maddie recognized them both. She swallowed hard on a dry throat. The two guys who had followed her back in Des Moines. She had disabled their car, yet here they were. How? Didn't matter.

As long as they had Jimmy's attention, she worked the tape. If she could just find an edge with her fingernails…

"Leon, stay here with the girl." Jimmy Ray pushed the older man ahead of him out the door. "I'll give that asshole cash, shoved right up his ass."

"But…" Leon held up his hands. "You said we'd get something to eat."

The door banged shut behind the two men. In a huge white t-shirt, Leon slumped his marshmallow frame onto a pile of wrapped tires looking way too much like the Michelin Man to take seriously. "I haven't eaten since breakfast."

Maddie fixed him with a narrow-eyed stare. "Hungry, huh?"

"Yeah. Georgie, he never eats. I don't know how he lives, the way he never eats."

"There's a bag of pork rinds in the back seat of the car." Maddie nodded, pulling a smile. "You can have 'em if you want. Might even be a candy bar in the glove box, or maybe it's in the backseat, I don't remember."

She didn't know what was in the glove box, but she was pretty sure there were no candy bars. All she wanted was him out of her face so she could work harder on the tape while Jimmy Ray was out of the warehouse. The latch on her toolbox might be sharp enough, but she couldn't reach it in her present position. She lifted her hips, but it was no use.

She felt the car dip under the weight of the huge man, then pop up again. Maddie stopped working the tape. A few steps and he peered in at her again.

"Pork rinds," he said. Smiling, he held up the bag. "Want some?"

She shook her head.

"Don't know why those guys always have to be so mean. *It'll all come back to you*, I tell Georgie all the time. One day, it'll all come back."

Maddie frowned at Leon as he devoured the salty rinds like hadn't he eaten in a week.

"You believe in Karma?" he asked.

"Sure. Like, pay it forward."

"Yeah. And don't run over the squirrels on purpose, and never pass up a chance to help someone broken down by the side of the road." He angled a huge chunk of pork rind into his mouth, in one piece, and chewed like a machine.

"Even guys like me got to think about Karma." He lumbered back to the tire pile and sunk down into them.

Especially guys like you. Maybe she could use it.

"How'd you two hook up with Jimmy anyway? He seems a little out of your league, if you don't mind me saying."

Leon shrugged. "I thought it was going to be Mr. Berlin pick us up at the airport. Turns out it was Jimmy. I never seen him before."

"What about Mr. Berlin?" The mention of Berlin had her instincts on their tiptoes.

Leon pulled the last rind out of the bag and looked inside as if he expected a perpetual flow. "We was working for the old guy. Georgie traded him a piece of property near his parents' house for an old forty Ford. Long time ago. Those two go way back. Met in the service, I think. Anyway, when our car broke down, I thought we was done with him, but he sent us tickets to LA. Wanted us to help him get the car back."

He glanced sheepishly back at Maddie.

"I've never been to LA," he added, jamming the rind in his mouth.

Maddie eyed Leon as he looked for a place to toss the empty pork rinds bag. She suspected he wouldn't be a litterbug out on the open road either. Wouldn't be a litter bug, a tattletale or purposely mean.

"All I know is I have to use the ladies room. Jimmy Ray wouldn't let me." She rolled her eyes at Leon.

He glanced over his shoulder.

"C'mon, Leon. Undo my hands and feet so I can go to that bathroom over there." She didn't know if it was a bathroom or not, but a door stood ajar just inside a hallway on the opposite side of the warehouse. A weak light spilled out of it along with the hum of a fan, like the last one who used it forgot to turn it off.

"I promise. I'll let you tape my feet back up so you won't get in trouble. Cross my heart. They'll never know I went."

Leon licked salt off his fingers and sniffed dramatically. "I don't know. Georgie's already pissed off at me for askin' Jimmy to take us to Universal City. I've never been to Universal City either. Have you?"

Maddie exhaled. She understood Georgie's frustration with Leon. "Tell you what. You let me use the ladies' room and, when all this is over, I'll take you to Universal City *myself*."

Leon struggled up out of the tires and took one last peek toward the door. "Okay."

He stripped the duct tape from her hands. "I know you're just kiddin' about Universal City. But it's pay it forward anyway, right?"

"Right." Maddie's fingers tingled as the blood rushed back into them. But just at that moment, the warehouse door burst open.

Jimmy Ray rushed toward her. *Damn.* She put her arms back behind her. He reached up and leaned on the trunk lid with both hands.

"Sorry, Madonna. I was hoping we'd be able to work together, but trouble is, we just ran out of time."

"But wait, I—" A rush of air cut off her plea as the trunk lid whooshed closed.

Chapter 13

The inside of the trunk was blacker than a Harlan County coal mine and just as cold. Maddie's pupils dilated, straining to find any source of light, shadow or shape. She cursed herself for not kicking Leon in the face when she had the chance—something, anything—to keep from being transported to the next place Jimmy Ray had in mind.

At least her hands were free.

She scooted her legs around in front of her, and sat, hunched over, saying a silent prayer of thanks to Harley Earl for designing a car with a trunk that could hold two sets of golf clubs and luggage enough for a week in Palm Springs. The duct tape still tight around her ankles, she stretched forward, feeling for the empty spare tire well where Grandpa had insisted she keep an emergency kit.

Her fingers touched the towel-wrapped bundle and her heart took a little leap. She clawed the contents in a tight package and rolled it up her shins. A moment later, the red-carpeted trunk lit up by the welcome glow from a free standing light. With a box cutter, she zipped through the duct tape around her ankles and exhaled. Her long shafted screwdriver would do nicely to pop the trunk latch if she could just hold it steady. Her teeth chattered so hard she thought Jimmy or Leon might hear them.

She took a moment to rub her bare arms with her freezing hands, then went after the latch again, but it was no use. Her fingertips were numb and her hands shook so hard she couldn't hold the screwdriver steady enough to hit the lever, let alone apply any pressure.

"D-d-d-d-a-a-a-a-m-m-m-m." Her jaws tightened against the chatter. She still wore nothing but the Mad Monkey tank top she'd been sweating in for…What was it now? More than twenty four hours?

Sweatshirts.

She had some sweatshirts left in the trunk, didn't she? Scooting around as much as the tight space would allow, she found a heavy plastic bag in of the corner. Two spare white mechanics suits, a red bandeau top, and her Jimmy Choo stilettos—Flo's version of an emergency kit. Great.

Never know when you'll need a pair of fuck-me red shoes. But finding the clothes gave her courage like finding a piece of herself. She shimmied her Levi's and tank top off and struggled into the tight fitting outfit as she lay on her back. Just the activity warmed her a little.

The feeling was coming back to her fingers when the Cadillac's engine started up.

From the Gerald Desmond Bridge, the container cranes in the distance appeared to Nick like giant electrified giraffes straddling the quays. He rarely traveled to Long Beach, and when he did, it was to the financial district, to some gala event on the Queen Mary, or to treat a group of disadvantaged youth to the Aquarium of the Pacific. While his company owned large chunks of the commercial real estate that stretched before him, he rarely paid attention to details beyond lease values, occupancy rates, or the next high-end acquisition.

Tonight, the view from the bridge gave him a new perspective. He levered the binocular focus until he brought one of the brightly lit cranes into close view. A container moved in slow, silent motion beneath the gantry. It could be on its way to the Gulf Coast or could just as easily wind up in Shanghai, London, or Dubai.

"What am I supposed to be looking for?" His fingers white-knuckled around the binoculars. The thought of Maddie out there somewhere, alone, had his skin feeling too tight for his bones.

Luke bobbed and cranked his head around, scanning the near landscape. "Pier T. Where the railway splits. We stop, call in, and *wait*."

Nick rolled his window down, taking a shot of briny, diesel-tinged air in the face. It was after one a.m. His empty stomach pitched. It was his fault this had happened. He'd volunteered to get her and the car across country safe and sound, regardless of his end purpose, and botched it. Big time. He'd gotten her to trust him. And then he'd shot off his mouth, played the *cool aloof*, and lost.

Nick wasn't good at losing.

For nearly three hours his senses had been on full alert, eyes straining to identify taillights as his brother broke speed limits down the Southern California freeway system. Traffic was thin for LA this time of night. If the big yellow Cadillac was out there, how could he miss it? But he knew better. He knew exactly how. It could be in a trailer headed down the road, or a garage somewhere, already in pieces. It could be at the bottom of a cliff. A chrome-plated, neon friggin' green garbage truck could disappear in this town.

Bébé circled in the backseat until Luke swerved and came to a stop on the side of the road. Nick opened the door, grabbing her leash at the last moment as she bounded out.

The call came ten minutes later. Luke eased the car down an access road, teasing the wheels over the uneven surface, lights off. When they could see the end of the dock, he shut down the engine and pushed a radio bud into his ear.

It was surprisingly quiet out on the quay, far enough away from the freeway and the bridge to hear a foghorn off in the distance. Nick hunched forward in the seat. "Now what?"

"We wait."

Nick wasn't good at waiting either. In fact, nothing he'd done in the past week seemed to be in his area of expertise.

Luke touched the earbud. "They're reporting activity in the warehouse. Crane operator's FBI," he said, his voice low and even.

Nick's pulse ramped up a notch. He pointed his night vision hand-held down the quay because there was nothing else he could do. "So we're on?"

"*They're* on. I've been ordered to stay well back. This isn't my gig, so don't get any ideas."

"But there's no ship at this dock."

"No. Just containers. MO's they load the containers, the forwarder signs off on the paperwork, then they seal the container up here, transfer it to a semi then over to the loading docks and the ships. They get the thieves, the forwarder, everybody, but not until the crane lifts that container off the ground."

Nick could care less about catching thieves. His only concern was Maddie. No way could he sit by and—

A wedge of light opened a crack in one of the buildings, then spilled wide across the quay. Nick's hand shot to Luke's elbow.

Luke's binoculars came up. "I got it. Two guys leaving the base of the crane."

Nick levered the two men into focus. One older, gray hair showing at the edges of a dark watch cap. The other was much younger, heavy, maybe three hundred pounds, bareheaded, his back to them.

From the side of the building, a floodlight blossomed, spotlighting two containers side-by-side, doors pitched wide open. A semi with a flat-bed trailer waited, motor running like a sleeping dragon ready to spring at a moment's notice.

A third man strolled out of the doorway, thin arms cocked at his hips. He could pass for a dock worker or a wharf bum, but either way, something about the profile sent a jolt of recognition from Nick's scalp to the soles of his feet. He'd seen him somewhere. No question.

Luke followed the third man with his binoculars. "He doesn't look too happy."

Bébé nuzzled her head out Nick's window from the backseat, ears perked forward, nose straining.

Nick sat up higher to see around her. "Your guy is coming down the crane elevator."

"Looks like they're ready to move. So three guys, that's it."

"Unless there's more inside that warehouse. Can we get closer?" Nick was more concerned that Maddie might be in there, tied up, injured, or worse. His hand gripped the door handle.

Luke tossed the binocs onto the console. "You know. I really like my job, brother. And I'm doing you a favor here, so don't *Nick out* on me, okay?"

Nick out? But Nick knew what he meant. Nick was never good at taking orders, least of all from his little brother. Sitting on the sidelines was not his forte. Bébé trembled, shouldered forward enough to get her paws on the window frame. Nick figured she wasn't much of a sideliner either. They had that in common.

"She's in there. I know it. Bébé knows it."

Luke shot him a warning look. "And the FBI, the harbor patrol, and the LBPD are on it. Sit tight."

Nick crossed his arms and hunkered down as the heavy man disappeared into the warehouse. The other two shadowed the crane operator to the elevator where they continued an animated discussion until the thin man pushed a large package into the crane operator's chest.

"I know that guy. I'm sure of it."

Luke looked at him and waited.

An image took shape in his memory. The casino. Wendover. The guy with Maddie's friend. What was his name...?

"Hold that thought. Here he comes."

The lanky man sauntered toward the warehouse door, wound up like he was going to deliver a pitch, followed through and pointed to an open container. A bright blue

Camaro rolled out of the warehouse, made a wide turn, and nosed deep into the container closest to the door. A moment later, Fat Boy lumbered out of the way as a Plymouth performed the same maneuver, pulling in behind the Camaro.

The Plymouth was dusty, the orange paint had lost its shine, but the black stripes across the hood and the unmistakable body style triggered a memory inside Nick's skull. His dad had a Roadrunner at The Compound just like it. Plain hubs, no special marks. Still the image of the car parked among the other classics in his father's near-forgotten garage persisted.

"Luke?"

"Yeah. I remember it."

Nick sniffed. "Lots of those around though. They're not rare by a long shot."

"Yeah." Luke relaxed a little. "The Camaro too. Lots of 'em."

Nick closed his eyes a moment, trying to picture the interior of his father's Montecito garage. Had there been a blue sixty-nine? "I don't know. Maybe, I—"

The next car out cut the words out of his mouth and covered his scalp in goose bumps. He sat forward in the seat as a gray and salmon Chevy sedan pulled out of the warehouse.

"Holy shit."

Luke's jaw dropped.

It was the fifty-five. The ugly duckling of the lot. He'd once entertained the notion of restoring it himself. That was before his father had reported the car stolen when Nick took it out for a spin with his little brother in tow. They'd spent the night in juvenile hall without so much as a call or any acknowledgement that their parents knew they were there. The night the cops pulled him out of the car in his own driveway was the last time he'd set foot in that *frigging* garage. "Odds on all three of those cars being here together are pretty slim."

"Yeah. We better call the old man." But Luke made no move to pick up his cell phone.

"I'm not calling that bastard." The thought of his father brought a bad taste to the back of Nick's throat. "Makes more sense he's in on this deal. He's probably in the warehouse."

Fat Boy slammed the doors closed on the first container. Nick and Luke both jumped. Bébé strained in the window, intense, trembling.

"Keep her quiet, man. She's gonna give us away." Luke hissed at Nick through clenched teeth.

"Where's the Cadillac? It's got to be here, if it's not, we're..." Nick rolled the window up to half, hoping to restrain the dog. "Wait. Wait! Here she comes."

A polished chrome bumper broke the plane of the warehouse door. Like Hollywood royalty making an entrance, the huge bullet tits caught the light as she emerged. Dagmar bumpers, Nick remembered, his heart rate ratcheting up. Fat Boy at the wheel, the Flying Goddess eased out through the warehouse door, making the turn. Nick swallowed on a dry throat. Where was Maddie?

Skinny Man walked along behind the Cadillac, a shabby escort. The moment the continental kit cleared the back of the container, Fat boy cut the engine, hurried out and shut the doors, then leaned on the levers to secure them. Skinny backed away, giving the thumbs up to the crane operator high above them.

The crane's huge engine roared to life, a set of nylon straps tightened on either side of a pair of stretcher bars, and the container with the Cadillac and the Chevy inside lifted off the ground as the operator slowly cranked the crane toward the waiting trailer.

It was more than Bébé could take. She pushed all the way through from the back seat. Before Nick could grab hold of her leash, sixty pounds of raucous, barking dog squeezed out the half open window and sprinted for all she was worth off across the distance between them and the loading dock.

Skinny jerked his head up and instantly made them.

Nick caught his breath. He knew he'd seen that face before. "It's that asshole, Ray."

"Who?"

Nick threw his seat belt off and bailed out the door at a run.

"Aw shit." Luke slammed out of the driver's seat and took off after him. "No!"

But it was too late.

Headlights blared on, men spread out into the floodlit yard, weapons at the ready. Bébé hurtled herself at Skinny, tore through his pant leg and had him screaming. She wrenched at his knee before he kicked her off and got away. Nick tried and failed to grab her leash before a pair of gorilla hands clamped down on his shirt and hauled him up short.

"That's as far as you get, buddy." The crane engine slipped into idle mode.

One officer tried and failed to corner Bébé. She skittered away and charged beneath the container, barking and wailing like a hound dog in heat.

"That guy," Nick yelled, stabbing his finger in the direction Ray had run. "He's getting away."

"Shut up." A boot came down hard on the middle of his back. "The harbor patrol's down there. You just worry about yourself."

"Son of a bitch." Nick tried to turn over, only to get another shove.

The officer pulled out his baton, leaned down and poked it into Nick's face. "Don't make me use this."

"Hey, hey. Wait." Luke sprinted to Nick's aid, his badge held out in front of him. "That's my brother."

The officer glared at the two of them. He dragged Nick up to his feet, cuffed, but otherwise unharmed. "I don't give a shit who he is. This is my scene and I'm callin' the shots here."

He shoved Luke and Nick against the wall of the first container. "Stay put or I'll have both of you in cuffs."

"You're grabbing the wrong guy," Nick said, his anger fading to defeat.

An LBPD van pulled in front of the container.

Nick wiped grime and blood off his bottom lip with the back of his hand and heard a pitiful yelp. He cranked his head around to see one of the harbor patrol officers had snagged the old man bumbling down a dockside stairway and shoved him against the side of the van. Fat Boy whimpered as an LBPD officer nearly as big as he pinned his arms high up between his shoulder blades and chopped on a pair of cuffs.

"Tell your dog to shut up," the officer ordered.

"Ain't my dog. It's hers." He nodded up at the container swinging slowly over their heads.

"Whose?" A tall officer in a business suit strode out of the shadows and moved in close behind Fat Boy.

"There's a lady. In the trunk of that Caddie," he whined.

He pushed the Fat boy's face hard into the side of the van. "I don't see any fuckin' Caddie."

"It's in the container," Nick said, snarling. "What? Were you sleeping when they loaded it up?"

"I told you to shut up." The officer's baton poked Nick in the kidneys and he doubled over.

"Hey, Jake." Luke pushed away from the container and stuck out his hand. The suited officer ignored him.

"Somebody shut that dog up," Jake yelled over his shoulder. Then he looked at the officer who held the heavy guy against the van, "Keep 'em here together till we get this sorted out."

"Just check it out man. The brains of the whole thing is getting away." Nick ground out the words between clenched teeth, catching Jake's attention. The big officer clamped his hands on Nick's shoulders and pushed him toward the van.

Jake looked him up and down. "Who is this guy, anyway? He's not on my watch list."

Nick shook his shoulders free of the officer's grip, stared back at the suited man, despite the pain searing his back.

Luke stepped forward. His smile looked forced. "Hey Jake. Been a while."

Nick was already in college when Luke and Jake had played on first string on the football team in high school. They'd spent the first two years in the police academy together before Jake transferred to Quantico for basic training. Nick had never met the man, only heard about their adventures through Luke's stories. One thing he knew for sure, no matter what the relationship, Luke's old friend wasn't happy that Luke and Nick had busted their cover before they were ready to move. Getting charged with obstruction of justice was not entirely out of the realm of possible outcomes.

"I told you to stay back until you heard from me."

"Yeah. Sorry," Luke said. "This is my brother, Nick. The one I told you about?"

Jake's gaze shifted from Luke to Nick then back to Luke. "Tch."

"There's a third guy," Luke said. "The dog had him just before he broke away, and—"

"First you fuck up my sting, now you try to tell me how to clean up?"

Luke held up his hands. "No. I just think—"

Jake's eyes narrowed. He made no move to release Nick. "That your dog too?"

Nick said, "No, she's—"

Luke spoke over him, "Yeah. She's mine." He shot Nick a warning look. "Sorry, I—I'll just get her."

The big officer pushed Nick over to the van with his baton still at his side. "Put your hands on the vehicle."

Nick obeyed, watching over his shoulder as his brother retrieved the barking dog from under the suspended container. Jake gave the signal to lower it and the crane whirred back to life. A few moments later, the container was lowered on the ground and the doors opened.

The crane operator climbed down, crossed the tarmac to the group of men and shook hands with Jake, then clamped his arm across his shoulder. "Shut that dog up, will you?"

Luke hauled Bébé away from the Caddie's continental kit one more time. "I think she's scenting her owner. Fat Boy over there says there's a woman in the car."

An LBPD officer sidled down the side of the Cadillac, checked to see if the car was open or if there were a set of keys on the dash. He came out empty handed. Bébé wasn't letting up.

“Okay, get a crow bar or some jaws or something,” Jake ordered. “We gotta open her up before this dog rips off somebody’s leg.”

With a heavy hand at his back, and another sliding down the legs of his pants checking for whatever, Nick lifted his head to see what was going on.

An officer jogged over to the Cadillac with a large reflector-strapped duffle over his shoulder, no doubt holding cop-approved break-in tools. The FBI agent pawed and jerked at the continental kit as the officer unzipped the bag and pulled out a huge, evil looking crowbar. The sight of it sent a jolting rush through Nick’s eardrums.

“If you so much as put a scratch on that car, I’ll sue you, the FBI, the Harbor Patrol, the Long Beach Police Department and your mother if I have to.”

All heads turned to see a tall, chop-haired brunette in a white mechanic’s suit emerge from the container. Nick’s heart jammed into his throat. She spun a set of car keys on her finger.

“Move this goddamn van out of here so I can take my car and go home.”

She looked triumphantly over at the line-up of men at the van. Until her gaze locked onto Nick’s.

Chapter 14

"I'm afraid I can't let you do that, ma'am." An FBI agent stepped forward.

Nick wasn't close enough to see the color in her eyes, but the look she gave the agent would have withered a bowling ball. *Better him than me.* How would he explain why he was standing there in handcuffs?

"Maybe you didn't notice, officer, but I'm the *victim* here, not one of the *criminals* lined up against that van." She made a deliberate point of staring straight at Nick when she said it. Her voice had that don't-mess-with-me edge to it, but he was relieved to hear it. He didn't blame her. Under the circumstances, how could she think otherwise?

Luke let go of Bébé, who went nuts the moment her mistress appeared. She bounded across the open pavement. Maddie knelt to embrace her, then buried her face in the dog's fur.

Jake moved in closer. His unveiled admiration of Maddie's backside sent a rip of fire up Nick's spine. Catching the action at the van, Jake stepped in front of her and flashed his ID.

"All the more reason for you to come with us, ma'am. We need your statement, and all the cars will be impounded as evidence, of course."

Nick dropped his chin to his chest. He hadn't seen that one coming. Finished with the frisking, the officer pushed him into the van. He moved through to the backseat, careful not to make eye contact with the other two chumps which might lead to further complications.

By rights, they should have un-cuffed him once they knew he wasn't involved, but the fewer waves he made right now, the better it would go later. At least that was his hope as he looked out the back window to see Maddie cave in on herself, shoulders shaking under the weight. A female LBPD officer threw a dark blanket around her and guided her toward a waiting black and white, followed by Bébé and one of the LBPD team.

He doubted now, as the cruiser drove away with Maddie, if there were any words to explain how this happened. Words she would listen to and accept. Any explanation that could erase all the mistakes he'd made. Take them back to that moment in the front seat of the Goddess when they'd melted into the rich leather upholstery and into each other.

Maddie huddled deeper into a plush terry cloth robe and watched the sunrise play out on the Pacific for the first time in twenty years. Gauzy clouds absorbed the dawn and reflected slippery pools of pink across the water like silver stepping stones. Santa Cruz Island pushed up on the horizon, catching the light on its highest peaks. Its tattered sister, Anacapa, remained a blue shadow but clearly visible from the heights of Montecito. Maddie didn't know the names of the islands when she was a little girl riding her father's shoulders over the sand, but she remembered the floating mountains, knew their shapes, and marveled at the way they came and went like magic in the mist.

At first, she had refused to come to the Berlin estate. The ride home with Nick had been hard enough without ending up at The Compound, as he called it. But Nick's brother had insisted and, after all that had happened, she was simply too exhausted to argue. Truthfully, where else would she go? Back to that oily hotel in Lompoc?

No.

It might be emotionally uncomfortable, but it was physically safe here, and in the interest of safety, if not sanity, she decided to stay put. Funny how being cramped in the trunk of a car for hours not knowing if you'd live or die puts things into perspective. A smarter Maddie was in control. More deliberate, sensible. A woman who thought things through, weighed them against her goals, and made informed decisions.

Stop *pushing the river*, Grandpa would have said. She sensed he was with her now. At her shoulder, in her heart. A hillbilly scholar and self-appointed philosopher.

And he would have been right. She was pushing the river. Her father certainly wasn't going anywhere and she could live without her cell phone for another day. *Stay put and take what's offered if it will get you closer to what you want.*

What she wanted was to get her car back and start the application process for auction in Carmel. She couldn't let Nick, her father or anything else distract her from that goal. She felt a little like one of the cows on her property at home, pushed up against the fence by the rain. Running away was no longer an option.

She took a deep breath and let it settle as the sun ticked up a notch. Her senses were raw with the fatigue of an adrenaline hangover. It didn't help that she knew Nick was nearby, up in the big house. The knowledge created an annoyingly delicious tension at her shoulders and a frizz at the back of her neck.

Bébé heard it first. Her ears perked at footsteps padding on a packed-dirt trail. Maddie turned her ear toward the sound as it progressed to the stone patio behind her. And then, as if she had conjured him from her subconscious, he was there. She opened her mouth slightly, drew in a slow, shallow breath, anticipating.

He was at her shoulder, she could feel him. She cut her gaze over just enough to see steam drift through his fingers as he set a mug of coffee on the table next to her.

"You're up early," he said.

Three simple words. Heavy, cool and hesitant, like the marine layer over the shoreline.

She didn't blame him. Seeing him handcuffed in the lineup of thieves sent her into a rage even the cops had trouble subduing. It was irrational, but how was she supposed to react after being tied up in the trunk of her car for hours? Since then, she'd seen him released outside the office, where she'd given her statement, met his lookalike brother, and received assurance from the FBI that Nick's detainment was an unfortunate mistake. He was innocent. She'd known that all along. She owed him an apology.

But her uneasiness wasn't a question of guilt or innocence. The tension between them ran deeper than that. She let her gaze lift to the open French doors to the guesthouse's master bedroom.

"I never went to bed."

Nick exhaled deeply as he slid into a weathered, Adirondack chair and settled, gripping his coffee mug between his hands. His shoulders hunched, he still had on the black clothes and cowboy boots he wore the last time she'd seen him. A rumpled traveler not quite home.

He stared out over chaparral that spilled down the hillsides to the ocean. She couldn't stop herself from following the contours of his jaw to his pulse, visible at the triangle of skin above his open shirt collar, to the silver belt buckle at his waist. The sunlight, just up over the horizon now, touched the hairs on the backs of his hands.

Heat rose from her neck to her ears.

And there was *that.*

Since the moment she left him in Wendover, a place inside her felt vacated, abandoned. Not simply empty, but painfully so. It was easy to deny her need when she had a mission to accomplish. But now that there was nothing to do but wait for her life to come off hold, the ache grabbed a hold of her. More than anger, more than fatigue, more than anything else she may have thought or felt about Nick up until this moment, she wanted to slip in behind him and run her hands down the inside of that shirt. Feel the warmth of him next to her again.

Never let go.

"Nick?"

His jaw muscles bunched.

Maddie scooted up in her chair and lifted the coffee mug to her lips, refusing to accept rejection.

"I don't blame you for being angry with me. I used every vile name I could think of in front of the police, the FBI, the harbor patrol, and your own brother. When I heard Bébé barking outside the container I thought things had turned in my favor. I didn't know how, but somehow, I was saved. Then I saw you handcuffed with those guys…"

No reaction.

"I'm so sorry I dragged you into all this. It can't be good press for you. Your company."

No response

"Nick?"

"I'm not angry with you," he said at last, his voice still distant, not fully engaged.

She had only known this man for a few days—a few intoxicating, tumultuous, maddening days—but she knew him well enough to recognize the set of that jaw. He was a million miles away in another skin in another place. A place she had no right to intrude.

She sniffed the coffee, the first she'd had in what seemed like an eternity, the aroma rich, warm, and enigmatic, like the man she knew him to be.

Sometimes.

She accepted the coffee as a conciliatory gesture, one that would have to do for now.

Let the river flow by itself.

"How's your father?" she asked, taking a different tack.

He sipped his coffee and stared at the liquid light expanding over the ocean, sucked in a deep breath and exhaled on the words, "Sedated. Sleeping."

Nick's shoulders relaxed.

"He's been slipping for a while, I guess. Gina says the bouts of anger and acting out could have been the start of it. Being tied up with his hands behind his back on the kitchen floor for twenty-four hours didn't help. Dehydration and lack of food probably pushed him over the edge. Sometimes the elderly lose it when they've been put in a stressful situation. The doctor said he could improve."

He set his mug down, rested his forearms on his thighs, and laced his fingers into a tight grip.

Maddie leaned back in her chair. "But you don't think so."

"No."

He closed his eyes and did a slow neck crack, first to one side and then the other, then exhaled as if these acts could rid him of whatever it was that clouded his mind.

His gaze lifted to hers for the first time since he'd joined her, a brief acknowledgement, before he turned away again. She'd come to recognize the signs. He pulled inward when he talked about his family. About his father. Something they had in common.

"It would explain a lot of things," he said.

Bébé sauntered over from the door mat, where she'd taken up residence and pushed her nose into his hands until they opened and massaged her ears.

"Dementia's complicated," Maddie said. "A person can be perfectly rational one minute and slip into something different the next. In the beginning, it's hard to tell and easy to deny."

Maddie knew. She'd lived through the nightmare with her grandfather.

When at last Nick lifted his eyes to hers, their rich ocean green color was tinged with the sheen of bottled up emotion. A private battle, she imagined, raging inside his mind.

"He was a despicable bastard. Deserved everything bad that's ever happened to him. But this last year? I avoided him. Avoided coming here. This thing with the car? It was all my fault."

Maddie felt heat rise in her cheeks. She had been thinking only of herself. Of her needs. Her future. But Nick was hurting too. She saw that now. He could have run back to Vegas. To his croupier or the Beaver Ranch. Instead, he was here.

With her.

Needed her.

Trusted her.

He may not be able to put that in words, but what man could? The revelation swelled in her breast and suddenly the question that had haunted her through the wee hours of the morning expanded and dissolved like the islands on the horizon.

She no longer had to ask. She knew. Nick was there for them. What they were together. None of the rest of it mattered. It was her turn to lift him up.

She scooted forward in her chair and matched his pose, holding her coffee in her hands. "So your father gets Alzheimer's and all is forgiven?"

"What?" His head came out of his private rabbit hole.

"You're blaming yourself for what he did all that time ago. For what he was. None of that has changed."

He turned to her, his face contorted with pent-up emotion. His hair pasted to his head up on one side, his five o'clock shadow from yesterday extended to six o'clock this morning.

"I might have seen his behavior for what it was. Stopped him before he ruined another person's life. Instead, I hid out in Vegas. Ignored the signs."

He pushed out of the chair and went to the wood railing at the edge of the veranda. "I mean, look at this place."

His eyes went wild, flashing as he gestured toward the acreage behind them. A sprawling mission style home nearly covered the crest of the hill. She had seen it there when they arrived last night but hadn't realized it belonged to this property.

"He's fired all the help—the gardener, the housekeeper, the pool guy. He's been holed up in there eating food out of cans with his fingers like a homeless person. Nicholas Berlin, the real estate baron of Montecito."

His back stiffened, the muscles worked in his jaw. "I *listened* to his bullshit about how your mother ruined our family. Blamed *her* for my own mother's death."

"You were just a boy then. You didn't—"

He held up his hand to stop her.

"I knew. In my heart, I *knew* he pushed her. I never told a soul, not even Luke." He forced the words out through a tightened throat.

The words struck Maddie in a place she rarely let herself go, where she held the memory of her own mother. She had blamed the same man for the same thing. Fury rose in her like hot lava, ready to explode. And then the anger dissolved into anguish. It had happened so long ago, but there was no statute of limitation on pain for a child who loses a mother. They had that in common too.

She got up slowly, moved closer, talking as she went, as much to herself as to Nick. "And now he gets off because he's sick? It's cruel, and certainly not fair, but it's still not your fault. You don't owe him a thing. Least of all your grief and guilt."

When he turned to her, it was difficult to endure the torment on his face.

"I'm sorry, Maddie. I'm so sorry for what he did to you. To your family. Your mother. "

"My mother was no angel. She knew Nicholas was a married man. She was young, but she wasn't stupid." *And she had something on him, knew where his money came from. That knowledge may very well have been enough of a threat to distort his father's judgment.*

Maddie studied the furrows in Nick's brow. How much of what Jimmy Ray had told her was true? How much of it did Nick know? She moved close to him and rested her hand on his forearm. There was no use going over what couldn't be changed.

"We are not our parents. We're not responsible for what they did. And we certainly don't have to relive their mistakes over and over."

"Maddie—"

"Shhh…" She lifted her hand to his face, tracing the taught skin over his jaw, remembering the conversation they'd had in a roadside restaurant only a few days earlier. How her heart had ached for the boy who'd suffered under his father's twisted view of life. She stroked her hands over his shoulders.

Lifting her face to his, she kissed him, a tender, healing kiss meant for the boy who haunted the man. "We can't change our past. It's what we do now that matters."

She kissed him again, a deeper kiss for the man he was now.

❧

Nick drew in his breath as if breathing for the first time that day. The eyes that had captivated him the moment they first looked into his stopped his heart. Like clear water over dark slate, they picked up the morning sun and reflected back all the emotion he felt. Saw into him. Through him

Cradling the back of her head in his hands, he lifted her mouth to his and kissed her gently, asking only what she was willing to give. Eyes open, she answered him with a deepening heat. His lips slanted, opened, his tongue sought hers, hesitant, fearful if he pushed too fast, she would evaporate like spindrift over the sand. He wasn't about to push her away again.

He circled his arm around her and pulled her close, savoring the surrender of her embrace. He'd been afraid he'd ruined everything. Afraid he'd lost her. Uncertainty lingered like the morning cold, clouding his way. He wanted to take her to a new place. One without fear and uncertainty. Without conditions or pain from the past. A place they could explore together. Nudging her away, he caressed her face in his hands. "Can you forgive me Maddie?"

She rolled her head down and leaned her forehead against his chest.

"That depends," she said, her voice deep, lusty. She pushed away slightly.

Nick inhaled the fragrance of her skin, his hands poised at her neck, then he traced her collar bone with two fingers, slipping inside the shoulders of her robe. "On what?"

A tear slipped down her cheek as she lifted her eyes to his, "On who you see right now. Is it me, Nick? Or is it a ghost from your father's past?"

Her eyes caught him, convicted him, forcing him to look inside himself, demanding the truth. He swallowed the pride, the uncertainty, the loss, and grief. Layer on layer fell away under her gaze.

"It's you, Maddie." The fist of anxiety in his stomach relaxed its grip. "It's been you since the moment I saw you in the cemetery alone. There was something vulnerable about you that day. Open, honest, like a clear bell ringing in my head. I didn't know any of the rest of it then. All I know is the ground shifted under my feet that day and a new place opened in my heart. The rest of it crowded in later."

He dropped his forehead to hers.

"That morning I woke up alone in Wendover and you were gone…" He brushed her hair off her forehead with the backs of his fingers, drawing her gaze to his. "I never felt so alone. I should have come straight after you then. Instead, I ran in the opposite direction like a stubborn jackass. I wasted precious time and I almost lost you."

"S-h-h-h-h," she said softly, pressing a finger to his lips.

She popped the pearl snaps on the front of his shirt and slid her arms around him. "Hold me Nick. Just hold me and don't let go."

He pressed his cheek to the top of her head, enveloped her in his arms the way he'd wanted to do since the moment he'd seen her safe on the docks. He breathed in the scent of her and let it soothe his doubt.

She pressed close against him, her breath catching jagged against his chest when she felt his hardness.

She looked up, the blue in her eyes turned to darkest slate. "You made me crazy that night too. I had let myself believe you wanted me. Made me want more than I knew you could give. So when you said my mother's name, something snapped inside me. I felt betrayed, humiliated. I couldn't bear the thought that you had used me. That what you really wanted was revenge."

"I'm so sorry. I never meant to hurt you. There was just too much crap swirling around in my brain, not to mention too much tequila, but I won't use that as an excuse. I was wrong. I put you in danger that night. I should have been with you when you found your father. I tried to catch up. If I'd been there—"

She pulled away, her tears flowing. "I know, Nick. I know. And if you hadn't gone after me when you did, I'd be locked up in a container on a freighter somewhere on the ocean."

He cupped her face in his hands, rubbed tears away with his thumbs. Without water or food or heat, she might have died. The pressure in his chest expanded until he thought he would burst.

"But you haven't answered my question," he said, his lips moving against her forehead.

She curled her lips in the beginnings of a smile.

"I could forgive you…possibly…if…"

"Anything," he whispered, his voice cracking.

"If you take me inside before I freeze to death."

His brows drew together until she widened her smile. Then, in one, sweeping move, he bent, circled his arm beneath her knees and lifted, covering her mouth with his. He carried her through the open doorway and into the bedroom, kicking the doors closed behind them.

Laying her reverently on the king-sized bed, he stroked a hand over her hair and lingered, content for the moment to have her near, though he wanted more. He wanted everything. From now on. He exhaled. *Take it slow, Nick.* He lowered his forehead to hers, nipped her bottom lip.

"How about we try a do over?"

"A do over?"

"Yeah. Starting with a shower. It's been nearly two days since I had one and I haven't been able to get the last one off my mind."

She stretched luxuriously, then propped herself up on one elbow, letting the front of her robe slipped away from her breasts. She patted the bed next to her. "How about we start right here?"

Nick gave her a slow smile.

"Can't argue with that," he said, his gaze taking in the length of her.

A moment later there was nothing but the heat of passion between them. Slow, freshly washed, reverent love would come later. Right now, all he wanted was to be deep inside her, filling her up, feeding his need. She gripped his legs and pulled herself tighter against him as he picked up the rhythm, erasing the distance between them, until they moved as one creature hell bent on breaking all the rules.

Maddie gasped, her lips swollen and open, her eyes wide. She reached up to touch his face, lose herself in the gaze she had thought only a few hours ago she would never see again. Running off alone was likely the single most foolish thing she had ever done, and very nearly could have cost her life. Her eyes stung and she blinked to clear them.

"Nick." Her throat closed off at the thought of almost losing him.

He leaned in to kiss her eyes, her cheeks, her lips, then pulled away again, smoothing her hair back from her face. "Don't think about it," he whispered, as though he read her mind.

Then he stretched his body full length against hers and started to rock, slowly at first, then building until she gasped, her arms falling free, her insides closing around him in rolling waves of pleasure.

When she could use her arms again, she wrapped them around him, urging him on. She felt the low moan build within his chest as he surged into her without restraint until the moan became her name. *Her* name.

The sun had angled higher in the morning sky by the time she stirred, casting its light across the bedroom floor. She raised her hand and watched its shadow play on the wall next to the bed. Nick moved his head on her tummy where he'd collapsed, exhausted and slept.

"Maddie?" he asked, his voice groggy.

"Hmmm."

He moved up her body and planted a salty kiss on her lips. "I really think we should move this *do over* to the shower."

She ran a hand over his wild hair, content for the moment just to feel him next to her. The *do over* had a much happier ending. She rolled slowly on top of him and returned the kiss, not surprised to find his body responding. She arched her hips lazily against him and her contentment turned to urgency.

"Good idea," she said, circling him in a tender caress. "We don't want to let this go to waste."

Nick's closet made Maddie's at home look like the racks at the thrift store. She had poked her head in to see if she could snag one of his shirts to wear when the sharp aroma of cedar pulled her inside. She flipped on the light and caught her breath. The space was nearly as large as her bedroom.

On the left, a dozen pair of slacks hung on neat wood-clamped hangars. Along the back wall were long and short sleeved shirts and sport coats in several colors and styles. On the right, tuxedo suits, vests, cumberbunds and a lineup of shoes that looked new. An assembly of drawers and bins occupied the center of the room, along with a soft olive green upholstered chair.

This was the well-stocked closet of a man with impeccable taste and the places to take it. Flo would have been impressed. Maddie ran her hands over the shoulders of pressed shirts, her mind wandering. She half expected to find some forgotten piece of women's clothing but there was none. Not entirely disappointed, she slipped a rusty orange golf shirt off a hanger and held it up to her body. It was a little short. Nick would like it. She smiled, letting another layer of stress slough out of her shoulders.

A loud knock startled her. Was that the front door? She turned and stepped out of the closet. She wasn't sure how much time had passed, but the sun that lit the bedroom floor when they started now filled the room with yellow light. They were well into the morning. She suddenly felt vulnerable in nothing but a bathrobe.

"Nick?" She could still hear the shower running. A chill ran through her. Events of the past few days had left her nerves rattled, scared of her own shadow. *Don't be silly.* It was probably Luke or one of the detectives assigned to the crime scene at the big house.

The knock came again more persistently. Definitely from the front of the house. She hauled in a deep breath to bolster her courage, cinched the robe belt tighter around her waist, and went to the front door.

A pair of narrow, leaded glass windows flanked the heavy oak door at the guesthouse entry. Maddie couldn't resist the urge to peek through one of the clear panes. A woman as tall as herself stood on the front porch, one hip cocked out. She balanced a tray of Bloody Mary's on the palm of a hand. Flaming red hair the color of the drinks was caught up in a ponytail that reached halfway down her back. A set of aqua nurse's scrubs did little to conceal her ample curves.

Maddie stepped back, biting her bottom lip. Apparently the man radar was alive and well in Montecito. Nick arrived home in the middle of the night and an off-the-chart gorgeous woman arrived at the door for breakfast.

Maddie's ears heated as she opened the door, her hand holding the collar of the robe together at her neck. "May I help you?"

With the skill of a Vegas casino server, a smile full of perfectly straight teeth, and a startling pair of amber eyes, the woman pushed past Maddie into the entryway, dragging an overnight bag behind her.

Chapter 15

"Wow. Luke said you were a knockout, but he says that about anything in a pair of tight jeans." The redhead sailed into the entry hall like she owned the place and slid the drink tray onto a Craftsman-style console table against the wall.

"Gina," she said, offering her hand. "Luke's *ex*-fiancée."

The *ex* came out with a flair that took the edge off Maddie's pique. She exhaled and found her smile.

"Maddie. I'm *really* glad to meet you."

"But he was right. You *are* about my size and you *are* a knockout." The room blazed with energy as she ran the bag over to a white leather couch in the center of the room and unzipped it.

"These should hold you over until we can get you to Nordie's."

Maddie lowered herself to sit on the edge of the couch and ran a hand self-consciously through her bedroom hair, switching gears. "Nordie's?"

"Oh, honey…" Gina pawed through a stack of folded sweaters and leggings and came out with a lacy bra and a pair of matching underwear. "… when Luke told me what happened, I couldn't believe it. Here. Take these."

She piled a soft Pink hoodie and pair of ivory leggings into Maddie's lap.

"Everybody says I make a mean Bloody Mary. Just give me a call if you two want more. I'll be taking care of Nicholas Sr. for a few days until we can get him evaluated."

Maddie eyed the drinks. It was a nice gesture but not her usual breakfast fare.

"Those will be fine, I'm sure," she said, a little overwhelmed. "Things have been so crazy, I was only just realizing I had nothing to wear." She smoothed her hand over the appliquéd lettering on the zippered jacket, shaking her head. "I never dreamed I'd be in this position. Thank you. This was really thoughtful."

Gina waved away the words as if she loaned her clothes to strangers every day. "I just did my laundry. It was easy just to grab a stack."

"You're a nurse?" Maddie folded the bra and panties on top of the pile.

"LVN. Guess the old man finally went over the edge. I told Luke something was up the last time we came by, but he stays away from here, pretty much. He only checks up on the place because of Nick. Ancient history. Anyway…"

Maddie smiled and settled back onto the couch. It had been days since she'd felt human. After a couple hours in Nick's arms and a few minutes with Gina, she began to think she might even feel a little like her old self. "So…not so *ex* then?"

"Three years is long enough to be engaged. I gave Luke the old ultimatum, and he moved his stuff out of my condo." She nodded to the U-Haul parked in the circle driveway in front of the house. "Notice, it's not unloaded yet."

She tipped Maddie a sly grin.

Maddie laughed. "He seems like a levelheaded guy."

"I'd like to level his head sometimes." Gina pursed her lips. Then she shrugged and her eyes lit up. "Truth is, I can't get enough of him. Nick's a great guy too, despite his moody exterior. Luke says Nick's crazy about you."

She laid out another sweater and a pair of stretchy jeans. "I think these may fit as well. But you and I can go shopping later. That is, if…well. I don't mean to be pushy."

Maddie stood. "I'll be getting my things back soon, but thank you. These will save my life until then."

Gina jumped up and spun to the door. "I've got to go. Luke said he'll be down here as soon as the detectives leave. They're still fingerprinting in the kitchen where they found Nicholas Sr. and that other guy tied up. What a mess."

She was through the door and halfway across the driveway before Maddie fully caught her breath.

Luke says Nick's crazy about you.

Nick emerged from the master bath to see that the bed was empty. His stomach lurched. He spun around, ready to charge out of the room naked, until he saw her standing in the doorway. There was a relaxed glow about her, something he knew was there, but was usually hidden under a cool, defensive patina. Her half-zipped hoodie sloughed maddeningly off one shoulder. He couldn't resist touching her there.

She offered him a Bloody Mary. "Luke's *ex*-fiancée brought these by."

He pulled his hand reluctantly away from her shoulder.

"To Gina." He held up his glass and waited for Maddie.

She moved in, circled her free arm around his waist and pressed her hips close to his.

"To Gina," she said, tipping her glass. "And to the difference a day makes."

Maddie sipped, grimaced, and put the glass down. "If I drink that, I'll be horizontal for the rest of the day."

Nick took another sip. "That was my plan."

Maddie sucked the liquid off the end of a celery stalk and put the glass on the dresser.

"Boy, give him an inch, and—"

"Anybody home?" Luke's voice echoed in the entryway.

Nick rolled his eyes. "Be there in a minute," he yelled, then delivered a kiss that left Maddie gasping for air.

Her eyes went unapologetically to the towel tucked low on his hips.

"Hold that thought," he said, pulling away. He turned her around and gave her a gentle push out the bedroom.

&

Luke had made himself at home in the kitchen and emptied a bag of groceries on the stainless steel chef's table. He'd changed clothes, sporting a pair of baggy shorts, a plaid shirt, and a vest loaded with pockets like a man ready to take a hike in the chaparral.

"There's dog food, water, coffee, avocados, limes, jalapenos, tequila…all the necessities."

"Bloody Marys for breakfast and Tequila for lunch?" Maddie's brows drew together. "This feels like a conspiracy."

Luke grinned at her and tossed a bag of bagels on the granite counter in front of a toaster oven. "Do those meet with your approval?"

Maddie nodded with a smile. "Absolutely. Thanks. This certainly beats that flea bag motel in Lompoc."

"We aim to please."

Bébé trotted in from the patio, her nose drawn to the dog food bag.

Maddie poured kibble into a plastic bowl she found in a cupboard under the counter. Bébé vacuumed it up in less than three seconds. A moment later, Nick appeared in the doorway in pressed tan pants, the rust-colored golf shirt Maddie had planned to wear before Gina saved her dignity, and a pair of very fancy loafers. Casual compared to the first time she'd seen him, but his expression was all business.

"Where are we?" He directed his question at Luke.

"Looks like you're home, big brother." Luke helped himself to one of the coffees. "At least for a while until we get this mess straightened out."

Luke gripped his brother's shoulder as he crossed the kitchen to the table and sat. "It's going to be interesting, that's for sure. The detectives say whoever took those cars had some major equipment at their disposal. Some heavy truck tire imprints in the decomposed granite down in the grove. Auto transport most likely. The way Robert and the old man were taken without much fight says they must have known the person. Let him in."

Maddie rubbed her wrists, still bruised where she had fought against the duct tape. The thought of Jimmy Ray's hands on her brought on a pressure in her chest she wanted to forget.

"Fingerprints will confirm it, no doubt, if he's got a record," Luke added.

Nick glanced at Maddie, and then attacked the pile of groceries, putting items away like a man who knew his way around his kitchen. "I appreciate your help, Luke. Really. This couldn't have come at a worse time for Central Coast. I can't just put things on hold because a bunch of thugs decide to get revenge on our father. The year-end stockholder's meeting is on Wednesday, and I'm locked in on this Jonathan West event next week…" Nick squeezed a package of cream cheese nearly in half.

Luke put up his hand. "I know, I know. My money's in Central Coast too. I've got this covered."

Maddie laid out bagels on the toaster oven tray, shoved them inside, and flipped it on.

"I hate to be selfish amid all this brotherly love, but what about my car?" She snatched the cream cheese away from Nick. "When do I get it?"

Luke leaned precariously in the kitchen chair, pursed his lips a moment, and then stretched out his legs. "It's the weekend. The FBI will probably turn the cars over to the LBPD, they've got two guys in custody they'll be questioning, and Christmas is next weekend, so…the wheels of justice will be caught up in holiday magic."

Maddie's senses went on alert. "Wait. *Two* guys?"

"Yeah. Unfortunately, one of the guys got away during the circus we started." He shot Nick an accusing glare.

Nick stood behind Maddie and compressed the muscles supporting her neck in a soothing grip. "Jimmy Ray."

"They found a small boat—one of those open aluminum jobs—at the bottom of the stairs at the end of the dock. It had a plastic bag with a change of clothes and some cash on board, but nobody made it there. Harbor patrol's still searching the dock and the area around the scene."

"His exit plan," Maddie said softly.

Nick came around and sat next to her. "His what?"

"Exit plan." She clasped her hands on the table in front of her and stared at them. "That's what Jimmy Ray told me before he shut me in the trunk. He was the only one caught back then when they pulled their heist in Vegas, because he didn't have an exit plan."

Luke rocked forward, propped his elbows on the table. "They who? What are you talking about?"

"More than twenty years ago. Jimmy Ray, your dad, and my parents. You didn't know about this?" Maddie shifted her gaze back and forth between the two brothers. Their remarkably similar features took on the same astonished expression. "I better make us some more coffee."

The coffee and bagels were gone by the time Maddie finished telling them the story.

"So that's what he learned from it all. Always have an exit plan?" Nick shook his head.

Maddie's skin felt like insects crawled under it. The idea of Jimmy Ray still lurking out there launched a fresh set of chills over her scalp. "He won't stop. Not until he gets what he thinks he's owed. He thinks there's jewelry hidden in the car. He kept talking about a diamond."

Nick scooted in, wrapped his arm around her, and rubbed the goose bumps away with his hands. "A diamond?"

"A big one. Part of the old heist," Maddie said.

Luke fingered the sides of his mouth. "Tough to unload a large diamond."

"He would have made a fortune off selling the Cadillac to the sheik, but now he's got nothing." Maddie swallowed a mouthful of coffee to soothe her dry throat. "He'll be back."

"You're safe here. We'll get him." He glanced up at Luke as if to confirm the possibility.

"If there's a diamond in that car, the boys'll find it," Luke said.

"Boys?" Maddie shot out of her chair and stalked to the sink, then turned on Nick, her palms against the counter. "You can't let them touch that car."

"They have to Maddie. It's part of the investigation. This thing is bigger than you now. You don't get to call the shots."

"But there's no jewelry in it. There can't be." She pushed away from the counter and back to the table. "Grampa and I did a frame-off restoration. Stripped everything off her bones, even the paint. If there was anything in that car that didn't come from the factory in 1953, we'd have found it."

Luke rubbed stiff fingers over his face, pulling them together under his bottom lip. He focused on Nick first then shifted his gaze to Maddie. "Maybe I can get you in to supervise the process."

"Supervise!" She threw up her arms and looked to the ceiling, moisture brimming in her eyes.

Nick captured her in his arms and guided her into her chair. "It's going to happen, Maddie. Whether you're there or not, so you might as well be there."

Maddie huffed out her frustration. Maybe it was better she didn't watch. She was that exhausted.

Luke got up from the table and put his empty plate in the sink. When he turned to face them, his expression was grave.

"Let's go sit in the living room. I'm afraid that was the good news."

Maddie settled in on the white leather couch and tucked her legs under her. Morning sun streamed in through the wide bank of windows. Colored panes at the top and sides of the entry door sent an amber glow on the walls, highlighting the rich wood cabinetry and thick, wool area rugs on oak floors. The room had been designed to give a feeling of warmth, but it wasn't enough to stop her hands from shaking. Nick slipped in between her and the armrest, adding what comfort he could.

Luke cleared his throat.

"I did some checking at the prison. That's the first connection I knew of between Jimmy Ray and Ross…" He glanced at Nick, "…Maddie's father."

An image of her father hunched at the kitchen counter filled Maddie's mind and sent another chill through her body. He'd been a troubled soul back then, like he already knew what was coming.

Luke paced across the room, his hands shoved in his back pockets. "Ross got twenty years for his involvement—whatever it was proved to be—in the embezzlement from Dad's original real estate company. A rough sentence for a white collar crime."

He turned back to them and leaned against the console table in front of the window.

"Jimmy Ray was small time. In and out of county jail on various charges over the years. He graduated to check fraud about five years ago, landed in Lompoc, working on a three-year sentence. He was nearing his release date when he screwed things up for himself and got two more years for assault.

Nick uncrossed his legs and scooted forward. "But I thought Lompoc was a minimum security prison. Guys running around in white shorts playing tennis. No violent criminals."

"Back in the sixties it was. Prisoners like H.R. Haldeman of Watergate fame and ex-football player-turned-drug-dealer Chuck Muncie were treated well, as were doctors and lawyers who'd gone to the dark side or small time drug dealers who turned over bigger fish. But with overcrowding in the California prison system, they added units taking more violent offenders, starting in the nineties."

Maddie's head came up. "So, Jimmy Ray and my father were there at the same time?"

Luke fisted his hand at his mouth and looked at his hiking shoes. "Yeah. For three years, until—"

Maddie couldn't breathe deeply enough. A cool sweat budded on her face. "The assault."

Nick put his hand on her knee and pulled her closer as Luke continued with the story.

"Jimmy Ray was working in the farm area. Inmates grew vegetables used in the prison's food supply. There was an accident in the field. An inmate ended up with a fractured skull.

One witness said Jimmy Ray went after him with a shovel. But others stuck with the accident story. In the end, Jimmy Ray was transferred to the medium security unit with two years added to his sentence."

"And the other guy?" Maddie stiffened, sensing what he was about to say.

"Brain injury. He's suffered a series of strokes since then."

Maddie covered her mouth, tears brimming in her eyes. "My dad. It was my dad, wasn't it?"

Luke picked at a stray string on the pocket of his shorts and avoided her eyes.

"Oh my god, the letter." The words of the letter she'd found among her grandfather's things echoed in her mind.

I need the car to settle accounts or I'm gone too.

"It was Jimmy Ray. *He* wanted the car. Not Daddy." She gave Luke the short version of how she'd found the letter from her father among her grandfather's things.

Nick laced his fingers behind his neck and pressed his shoulders back. "So, all these years, Jimmy Ray stews that he got aced out of the loot in the heist. Maybe he learns something from Ross about the jewelry while they're still bosom buddies in Lompoc, and Jimmy Ray puts the pressure on him to get the car."

Maddie sighed. The story was getting complicated but it began to make sense. "Grandpa keeps the letter to himself, wanting to preserve my ignorance of Daddy's…situation. He just stuffs it away."

Luke pushed off the table and crossed the room. "And two years later, after getting no response, Jimmy Ray gets out of Lompoc, madder than hell."

"Just about the time I put the ad on eBay."

"Yeah. Maybe he's an internet buff. They have limited access at the prison. So, he decides to pay a visit to the only other person in the original group left," Luke said. "Our father."

Nick huffed out a laugh. "I should have known Dad had help with that. He can't even pick up his voice mail."

They sat blinking at one another, not saying a word, until Luke broke the silence. "Can you get me a copy of the letter?"

Her mind raced. Too many thoughts from too many directions crowding in to the finish line.

"Sure. It's in my…" She glanced over at Nick. "…my bag. In Lompoc."

Nick gathered her into his arms. "Looks like we're going for a drive. Is the prison open for visitors today?"

Maddie leaned into his side, one safe place in what seemed like a tsunami of fear and dread. What were those visiting hours, anyway? She squeezed her eyes closed, trying to visualize the sign in the prison lobby, but it was no use. "Honestly, I don't even know what day it is."

"It's Friday." Luke popped open his cell phone and punched in some numbers. "I'll have my assistant check the hours for you. Besides, I actually have to check into work if I want to keep my real job."

❧

Two hours later, Maddie's stomach churned as they walked into the prison visitor's lobby. The memory of the first time she'd been here and what happened after had left visceral wounds in her psyche. Nick kept his arm firmly around her waist as they approached the counter. She didn't recognize the person at the reception desk. The woman she remembered, Veronica, must have had Fridays off. This woman was petite, gray-haired and looked more like she belonged in a Christian Science Reading Room than a federal prison.

Maddie had recovered some of her energy after spending the rest of the day before snoozing and eating while Nick caught up on his emails and phone messages. But now that they were here, her legs felt like noodles ready to splay out on the floor beneath her.

"I spoke to a Miss Lopez yesterday…" She glanced up to Nick. Had it really only been one day since she was here? "She was going to start visitor's paperwork so I could see the Warden?"

The tiny woman's eyebrows went up. "Miss Kerrigan?"

She popped out of her seat and came to the counter. "Veronica told me you'd be here."

She slipped an envelope from under the counter and passed it across to Maddie. The woman's smile faded to a look of concern. "I hope you're not too late."

"Too late?"

Nick grabbed the envelope and pulled Maddie away from the counter to the bank of plastic chairs and sat her down. "Just open it. Whatever it is, we'll deal with it."

Maddie slipped her finger under the sealed edge, popped it open and flattened the folds of the document out on her lap, reading the important words as she scanned the page. "He's not here."

She squeezed Nick's hand, her throat closing on disbelief. "He's been taken to a convalescent hospital, for…for…hospice care."

An attendant at the nurse's station on the third floor of the hospital came around and greeted her. "You're lucky, Miss Kerrigan. The warden relaxes visiting rules for inmates in hospice. I'll take you to his room. He's not communicating now you understand."

Her eyes, a cool dark brown complementing smooth olive skin, conveyed compassion and competence.

Maddie didn't understand. Why hadn't they told her when she was at the prison? How is a person transferred to hospice care without notifying the family? Her heart worked to justify what her brain already knew. Her father hadn't listed her as his next of kin. Hadn't even listed his own father. She slipped her hand into Nick's and followed the attendant down a hallway as she wound her way among carts loaded with sheets, plastic water containers, bedpans and diapers. A cold fist of fear closed tighter around Maddie's heart with each door they passed, until the woman turned into a darkened room.

Maddie stood in the doorway as the attendant pushed vertical blinds away from a wall of windows, spilling morning light across a bed in the corner where a lone figure rested. Bon

Jovi played softly on a beat up boom box next to the bed, partially masking the sound of a unit pumping oxygen through a cannula resting on his upper lip. Nick stepped behind Maddie, his hands firm, reassuring on her shoulders as she moved slowly into the room.

The withered figure on the bed looked nothing like the man she remembered, except for the deep blue of his eyes, which matched her own. His breath came shallow, intermittent, like he didn't need it anymore.

The attendant backed toward the door. "We don't know how much he understands. He doesn't respond to any of us. He's sipped apple juice today, but he's refused food for the last few days, which is…natural…so…I'm so glad you're here."

"Let me know if you need anything," she said and then slipped away.

Nick slid a chair near the bedside. Maddie moved closer and sat. "Daddy?"

The eyes, flat and dull as battered beach glass, stared into the space over the bed. Nick moved behind Maddie again, resting his fingertips on her shoulders. She covered the mouse-thin hands folded across her father's chest as it rose and fell almost imperceptibly.

The thought of him wasting away in that room after years of prison hit her hard. Days when she'd hated him for not being there—dance recitals, graduations, holidays missed—he'd been in prison. Days when she'd cursed him for not caring enough to even send a card on her birthday. When she'd imagined him off in the world enjoying a carefree life without the responsibility of a daughter. When she cried for him, missed him, remembered the times he held her close—he'd been in prison, taking the blame and the burden for what they'd all done.

She was overcome by a wave of guilt, tears brimmed hot in her eyes and blurred her vision.

"Daddy, it's me. Maddie," she said, barely able to push the words through her lips. She brushed her hand over the thin, salt and pepper hair that was curly and full on the day he'd left her with her grandparents. When she got no response, she gripped her hands in her lap and closed her eyes.

"Maddie…" Nick squeezed her shoulder. "Look."

She opened her eyes to see her father's eyes clear, searching, and shifting in her direction. When at last they focused, the light of recognition was unmistakable, accompanied by a sharp intake of breath. His gaze lingered there, taking in the sight of her, a slight pull at a corner of his mouth. A tear spilled down over a pale cheek and onto the white sheet covering his chest. He took three more breaths, slow and shallow, then lifted his head an inch off the pillow, eyes wide.

"M-a-d-o-n-n-a-h" He exhaled her name like a prayer, long and sweet on breath that smelled of apples. When he lay his head down and closed his eyes, his lips stretched into a thin smile, and he was gone.

Chapter 16

The pre-dawn fog was wet and cold, making Jimmy Ray's fingers ache and his knee hurt like a son of a bitch where that stupid dog had sunk its teeth into his skin. He peeled back the piece of T-shirt he'd wrapped around the wound during the night. The skin over the outside of the swollen joint had already turned a sickening yellowish green.

He stretched out stiff legs and climbed over rough planks, painfully making it to the stairs. *Fucking halfwit Leon.* If he hadn't run down the quay stairs Jimmy Ray would've been across the bay right now sleeping at the Holiday Inn. Instead, he'd been stuck for hours on a narrow, tar-stinkin' board high up in the rafters under the pier while the cops frenzied over his dingy like seagulls on an all-day fishing boat.

Best case scenario had him driving off in Robert's Land Rover before the doors closed on the containers, free and clear, with the promise of a fat paycheck from the sheikh once the cars made Dubai. A paycheck fat enough to make up for what those shysters Kerrigan and Berlin had stolen from him back in Vegas all that time ago. Then that rabid dog came outta nowhere and damn near ripped his leg off.

He'd watched from a crack between planks as the cops loaded the Land Rover onto the last of the tow trucks removing the cars he'd stolen from Berlin's garage. And then all was quiet.

Now he was stuck with the old Datsun pickup he'd stashed in the parking lot behind the railhead on the outside chance things went totally south.

Which they fuckin' did.

Jimmy Ray rubbed his leg above the dog bite but it did nothing to relieve the throbbing pain. The only consolation was that he'd tossed a change of clothes in the Datsun, just in case. Teeth chattering, he exchanged his wet, shredded pants for dry ones. He riffled the stack of IDs from his wallet until he found the one he wanted.

Warmer in a set of sharp-creased workmen's Dickies, dry socks and work boots, he shoved the IDs in his back pocket and tossed Jimmy Ray Monteplier's shredded pants and wallet into the drink.

Always have an exit plan.

Exit plan.

Exit Plan.

The words circled in his mind as the Datsun's heater struggled to find a bit of warmth. A fresh stab of pain shot through his leg. He would need some antibiotic for that soon. A deeper pain drove him now—a worm of fire, squirming in his brain.

He was back to square one, gawd *damn* it. Square *fucking* one.

Nick guided the nimble Jaguar over banks and turns in the road as it wound through a forest of live oaks and leafless sycamore trees. Maddie huddled near the passenger door, her forehead against the glass. His heart ached for her, but he knew there was nothing he could do but hope the quiet countryside would work its soothing magic. She hadn't said a word since she'd cleared through prison security as Ross Kerrigan's legitimate next-of-kin, with the help of an official fax from the Santa Barbara DA's office. The shoebox containing her father's personal effects sat unopened on her lap like the voicemails waiting on her cell phone.

She stared out the window into a world closed off from Nick. He'd hoped a detour to Jalama Beach would give her a chance to decompress. So far it wasn't working.

"I'm going to have to hire an auto transport to pick up the vehicles I've left strewn across the country in the past few days." As much to soothe his own churning psyche as hers, he opened a one-sided conversation.

He sighed, his gaze sliding over to the back of her head. "There's the Beemer at LAX, my *new* truck and trailer over in Elko, and the Prius at the Vegas airport…"

Maddie hunched against the window and clung to the shoebox like a woman overboard.

He cleared his throat. "We'll get the Flying Goddess back soon, Maddie. Luke assured me it's complicated by the Christmas break, but they'll waive the impound costs, and—"

She let go a shuddering sigh, the first sound he'd heard out of her since they got in the car. "I'm sorry. I've really messed things up for you."

Nick pressed the gas pedal down and let the Jag do her thing as he steered through patches of sunlight and shade at way over the posted speed limit..

"How do you figure?"

"*Nick Berlin, CEO of a Montecito real estate investment firm, detained in international car theft sting operation...* That's going to go over really well at your board meeting."

"They know me and how I operate. They trust me."

At last she faced him. Her eyes were dry, but still red and swollen, her response from the churning, heart wrenching events of the morning.

"Do they? Will they trust you when they learn the connection between us? Between our parents?"

She turned back to the window and rested her head against the glass. "Your best bet will be to drop me at the airport and be glad you're rid of me."

The Jaguar topped the bluff. The tossed, sea-green of a powerful south swell dominated the view. Nick pulled across the road, parked, and shut down the engine. Bébé stirred in the tiny back seat and got to her feet. When the door opened, she lunged out, her nose in high gear.

Nick focused on the woman in the seat next to him. He had seen her in so many moods as they'd traveled across country and crashed into one another. Tough, sexy, angry, sweet, and all of them tinged with fire. But right now, there wasn't even a hint of a spark. The fight had gone out of her, leaving a fragile shell in its place.

He reached across the seat to stroke the back of her neck. "A wise woman told me not long ago that I wasn't to blame for what my father had done. I believed her. Are you telling me she was wrong?"

He shifted his gaze to the scene out the window. "I like to gamble, to play the odds. But one thing you need to know about me is I don't hedge my bets, and I don't plan on starting any time soon."

Maddie sniffed and sighed, turning her attention to the wide expanse of ocean that lay before them as if realizing where they were for the first time.

He stroked up the side of her neck, grazing her cheek with his thumb until she leaned into the caress. "See there? My odds just improved."

Maddie straightened, her eyes wide open, deepening the blue. "What odds?"

"That you'll stay." His voice thickened with emotion. "With me."

His words shimmered in the electrified space between them, until at last, she reached for his face, her hand warm against his cheek. He breathed in the promise of it.

But just as quickly as she'd responded, the light in her eyes cooled and retreated.

"You'll lose, Nick. I have to go home. I don't belong in your world. How will it look at your next big gala event having a grease monkey on your arm? The daughter of a criminal. A felon. A man who died in prison. As much as I want it," she hesitated, her eyes slowly returning to his. "I don't fit into your world any more than you fit into mine."

He brought her hand to his lips and kissed her palm gently.

"Ah, but that's where your wrong, Maddie," he said, brushing a curl behind her ear. "You shouldn't believe what you see on the internet. The balls, the galas, the guest lists of the rich and famous. We never really fit into that crowd. My father was new money. An outsider. But he had a handsome son. He used me to insert himself into a society where he had never belonged. Ancient history."

He took her in his arms, pulled her close.

"This is where we belong." He lowered his mouth to hers and kissed her gently. "This is what fits."

Maddie shuddered softly, remembering the waves of pleasure his touch could bring. That they belonged together was all too magical. Surreal. A dream they both knew they'd awake from and realize their mistake. But she couldn't bear to pull herself away, her need was too urgent, too great. Her heart swelled with it, her mind reeled with it. As his lips gently covered hers, traced down her cheek, to her throat, to the rise of her breasts, her battered, grief-ridden soul expanded to let him in.

She lifted his face to hers. He was open, wanting, ready to give of himself. Irresistible. Pushing his knit shirt up to his arm pits, she nuzzled the soft hair on his chest. Not the public road, or the gear shift console between them, or even the shoe box sliding off her lap to the floor could deter her from the thrilling passion that rose in her center.

His hands strong and warm against her skin slipped under her sweater and caressed her back as he pulled her closer into his arms. His eyes searched deep into hers, sharing strength of a man who'd turned a corner in his own life. Then he shifted in the seat and let go a soft laugh, his slacks tented with his desire. "I miss the Goddess more than you know right now."

Maddie caught her breath and a shudder shook her to her soul. She had hardly noticed her hip cocked over the console, the gear shift pressing into her side.

"I suppose I could give you a rain check," she murmured, her lips tracing the sharp line of his chin. "But it doesn't look like rain."

His mouth grazed her lips, her cheeks, her throat. "We can pretend if we have to."

"We have to," she whispered, and eased herself over into the passenger seat.

Excited, he pointed out the window to a set of breaking waves backlit by the sun. A trio of dolphins arched through the jade water, surfing the wave.

"Can we go down there?"

"That's why we're here. Dolphin therapy."

Nick slipped out of the driver's seat and held the door open. "Bébé, let's go."

And like she'd been his dog all along, Bébé bounded up from a stand of dry sage and ploughed into the car.

Nick snoozed, shirtless in the slanting December sun. Maddie had awakened, her head in the crook of his arm, her hand spread over the flat of his stomach and her fingers resting just under his belt buckle. Bébé frolicked far down the beach, chasing after a flock of seagulls that seemed as much into the game as she was.

Back home, Flo would be preparing for a white Christmas, a flurry of baking and cleaning for the inevitable guests invited from the surrounding community. Their extended family. All that seemed so distant now. Artificial. But above Maddie's head was blue sky with jet contrails tracing the routes of travelers headed for San Francisco, Seattle, and beyond. The wind, still tinged with Santa Ana warmth, had picked up a notch, frosting the surface of the water off shore.

Lying on a blanket Nick had pulled out of the Jaguar's trunk, between sessions of passionate lovemaking on the deserted beach, they'd watched the dolphins surf overhead waves for most of the afternoon. It was easy to imagine for a moment that they were here, on the edge of a great continent, alone. No troubles, no history, no baggage. Just two lovers on a beach, caught in a timeless moment like tangled seaweed abandoned in the ebb tide. But a large kite rising near the more public section of beach ended the fantasy. With the wind came the kiters, as Nick called them. Soon they'd sail within easy view of Maddie and Nick's lovers' cove.

Gazing over at Nick, her heart expanded with the possibilities. But she knew once they left this place reality would check back in. She took a deep breath and sat up, savoring the moment as she pulled the shoe box into her lap, slipped her fingers under two yellowed strips of Scotch Tape, and lifted the lid.

Chapter 17

Nick awoke to a grating noise which turned out, he discovered after reluctantly opening one eye, to be the sound of Bébé gnawing a piece of driftwood in the sand inches from his ear. Hovering near the horizon, the sun had lost most of its warmth behind a veil of cloud. An offshore breeze popped a frizz of goose bumps over his bare stomach. He sat up, suddenly missing the weight of Maddie's head on his shoulder. Would he ever wake again without missing her presence? Controlling the unreasonable panic, he turned to see her at the edge of the blanket, hunched over the shoebox.

"*Whatcha* got in there, Mad?"

She lifted her tear-streaked face and her gaze met his. The light in her eyes had faded again, along with high color of recent sex on her cheeks. The scrap of newspaper she held between her fingers caught in the wind and fluttered across the blanket. Nick trapped it long enough to read the story title: *Honor Student Lands Modeling Scholarship for the Summer.* A seventeen-year-old Maddie smiled at him from the faded newsprint. She handed him another: *Madonna Kerrigan graduates Magna Cum Laude, University of Kentucky*. Maddie in a cap and gown.

Next came a handful of old photos.

Twelve-year-old Maddie, the young ballerina in a Nutcracker cast, taking a recital bow.

Six-year-old Maddie riding a pony with a huge red bow around its neck across a field dusted in Christmas snow.

Mad Monkey Maddie in her signature white mechanic's suit and red scarf, leaning an elbow against the door of the Flying Goddess.

She lowered her forehead into her hands, shoulders caving in.

"Maddie," he whispered, his heart aching for her. "Let's put them away for now. We'll take them home and—"

"No." She got to her feet and flung the rest of contents of the box into the wind. Scraps of paper and photos skittered across the sand. Nick rose to go after them before they reached the water. She stopped him with a hand on his knee.

"Let them go."

❧

Grief broke over her, ragged and powerful like swells breaking over rocks down the beach. Nick gathered her into his arms, kissed the top of her head, and held on tight as year after year of loss and pain pounded her breathless. How she'd longed to have her father there on those occasions. Wished she'd had an address to send pictures to. And all along, someone else had been doing just that, without her knowledge, without her participation, without the joy that would have come from knowing he cared even if he couldn't be there with her.

She circled her arms around Nick's waist and turned her burning face against his shoulder. The fresh memory of her father's frail body lifeless on the hospital bed assaulted her and tore at her spirit. To finally find him and have him slip away so fast was like losing a part of herself. But having the image she'd carried in her heart replaced by the one in the hospice room was like losing what little she'd had of him before he went away. Yet in the scrap pile of her life there wasn't one picture of her father. Would she ever be able to see him as he was again? As she remembered him?

Worst of all, the thing that took every ounce of punch out of her and kicked her in the gut was the knowledge that the people who claimed to be her family had deceived her. It was a betrayal beyond comprehension.

They had erased the memory of his handsome face—his intelligent blue eyes, his smile—as completely as death had done. Surely the knowledge that he was in prison but alive and cared for her was better than not having him at all? No matter how hard she tried, she could not call up the living memory of her father's face, and that was the worst blow of all.

She tried to breathe out of it, to let it go, but finally there was nothing to do but give in to waves of grief. On and on they came, swelling, rising, and breaking as Nick held her close, absorbing her misery and her pain. The sun had laid a crimson path across the ocean by the time she settled, exhausted against his chest.

"I'm sorry," she whispered. "I'm not usually so weak."

"Weak? You found your father today only to lose him a moment later. That's a monster storm of hurt, and there's no way around it. The strength comes from getting through it."

She wiped her eyes with the back of her hand and straightened a little.

"Oh, I hurt all right. I hurt so much I can hardly breathe. I thought I knew grief. When my father never came back. When Grandpa died. But I was wrong. This grief is full of anger as well as loss." Her throat tightened. She pounded her fist on her knee and fought to pull herself together. "My grandfather, even Flo and Walt, they all had a hand in this."

She slipped the Mad Monkey picture from his grasp. "And this picture? I would never have sent this picture. Not if I knew—"

"But you didn't know. And neither did they." He pulled her closer in his arms. "They thought they were keeping you safe, protecting you."

"I was never safe. Not as long as this picture was out there where Jimmy Ray could see it." Maddie shuddered under another wave of conflicting emotion.

Nick tipped her face to his and kissed her softly. "You're safe now, my love."

She held him tighter, stroked his chest and breathed in his musky fragrance. *His love?* She swallowed hard against the sting at the back of her throat. The echo of his statement warmed her soul. "If love was all I needed to be safe, I'd never be afraid again."

The blue-green in his eyes intensified and settled the little nagging in her heart.

He stood and pulled her up to his side. "My only fear is that you'll do something rash, like run off again where I can't be there to protect you."

"You don't trust me and I don't blame you." She had thought about running. Jimmy Ray wouldn't think twice about hurting Nick to get to her. Now that his plan was ruined, he would be plotting his next move. Of that she was sure. "You didn't see the evil in that creep's eyes. Hear the menace in his words."

"He wouldn't dare come back at us again." Nick slipped his shirt over his head and pulled it down. "Not after what happened in Long Beach. The police and the FBI are looking for him. He's got to know that."

"Us. I like the sound of that." The promise of it eased some of the tension in her shoulders, some of the grief. "I only hope it will be enough."

Maddie hesitated at the bottom of the terra cotta steps leading to the main house. From the Craftsman bungalow below, she had seen that it was an imposing structure. Up close, it overwhelmed, not only in size but in character. An echo of California's mission period. Fingers at her elbow, Nick urged her forward. He led her through the entry, apologizing for the cold. "Apparently, my father had the heat turned off. Told the gas company to go fuck themselves because their prices were too high."

"I'm all right. I'm used to Kentucky cold, remember?"

Gina met them in the formal foyer. "He's in the parlor, grumpy as ever. I cut back on his medication to appease Luke. He couldn't stand to see him drool. But I don't know. Whatever's going on in your father's head has got him stretched as tight as a blister ready to pop. The sooner we get him into a protected environment, the better off he'll be."

She slipped in behind Luke who stared out the window with his hands clenched behind his back. "And the better for you and Nick as well," she said, glancing meaningfully over at Nick.

Maddie stood in the doorway with Nick at her side. She didn't want to insert herself into family business or disturb the tender moment shared between Gina and Luke.

"I can't put this board meeting off," Nick said softly in her ear. "And I've got a lunch with Jonathan West afterward."

"I'll be fine," she said, still admiring the room. "I'm a big girl. I can take care of myself."

"You guys are going to have to make a decision soon," Gina told them. "We can't keep him on Atavan forever."

"It can wait until dinner," Luke said. "I've got to at least make an appearance in the office before the DA decides to find another boy."

"Tonight then. At dinner. Here," Gina said.

Maddie liked Gina's style. She took control when it was warranted, but had a softer, tender side that warmed Maddie's heart. Luke was an idiot to play games with her, but she had to admire his swagger.

But most of all, her eyes fell on Nick as he prepared to leave. He was dressed like he'd been the first time she'd seen him. Impeccably-cut, dove-gray suit and ivory shirt. A fuchsia-colored silk tie, not every man had the nerve to wear, was perfectly knotted at his neck. A gold cufflink winked at her when he raised his wrist to straighten his tie in the antique mirrored wall behind the piano. Flo would have approved of the high polished shoes. What Nick lacked in swagger, he made up in refinement. The brothers had turned out well despite their father. Testament, Maddie supposed, to Luke's mother, whom Nick had also adored. When their eyes met, Maddie felt the heat return to her cheeks, and everything else around them faded away.

Nicholas Senior was halfway across the room before anyone realized what was happening.

"You," he yelled, his forefinger stabbing the air in Maddie's direction. "You bitch!"

His yell expanded to a frightening bellow filling the room with his contempt. He stumbled forward to the piano, pulled a beaded shawl down as he tried to steady himself, bringing a set of silver candlesticks with it. "How dare you come here? *My* house!"

Gina jumped toward him and ducked to avoid the first picture frame he flung across the room. A shower of books spilled from the bookshelves as he grabbed another heavy-framed photo and threw it at Maddie's reflection in the mirrored wall, shattering the glass.

"Get out of my house. You can't come back here. My wife. My family. *My* car, you fucking whore. How dare you come here."

Luke grabbed him from behind, pulled his arms back. Gina ran for her supplies as Nick leapt to his brother's aid and together they wrestled their father to the floor.

"I'm still here, you fucking bastards," he bellowed. "You won't get away with it."

Maddie froze in the doorway. She had no idea what to do.

Gina ran past her into the room. "Pull up his sleeve," she ordered as she prepped a syringe.

Nick stretched the old man's arm out, sliding his silk pajama sleeve up, ignoring the vile accusations. "Hurry. I don't want to break his arm."

Gina pricked her patient's skin with the needle and emptied the syringe.

"You...you," he chanted, the bellow fading to a whimper until at last he was still.

Satisfied his father could do no more damage, Nick released his grip, rolled back on his heels and exhaled. "Jesus Christ."

He pressed his thumbs against his temples and squeezed his eyes shut. Maddie knelt beside him. "Nick?"

"God, that was like a flashback moment. He thought you were *her*."

Maddie covered her mouth with both hands. "Oh my god. I'm so sorry. I shouldn't have come in here. I didn't mean to upset him."

"Upset him, my ass," Nick growled. "I'd like to break his friggin' neck."

Luke got to his feet and shot his brother a warning look.

"Okay," he said, in his official peace officer voice. He glanced up at Gina for a moment, getting a nod. "I think we can hold off on the neck breaking for a little while."

Gina slumped down on the piano bench and blew out a breath. "One thing is for sure. I can't take care of him here. Not if he's delusional. I could help you arrange respite care, until we see how this all shakes out. It may just be that he's stressed after all that's happened. Or malnourished. Who knows?"

Nick went to Maddie's side and pulled her next to him. "I think we could all use a respite."

Nick adjusted his tie, chafing at the restriction after having taken the longest vacation he'd allowed himself since launching his business more than ten years before. The four men and one woman sitting around the black lacquer table were all well known to him. People who'd served on his Central Coast board for many years. They were savvy, solid, and he trusted their judgment implicitly.

His nerves were understandably on edge after what happened before he left home for his offices in downtown Santa Barbara. Maddie was shaken but bearing up well. Still his stomach churned at the thought of leaving her alone for the first time since the night on the docks. Not that he was worried. She and Gina had become fast friends in the week leading up to the holidays. As official LVN at the house for the next two weeks, Gina had latched on to Maddie like a long lost sister. She would be okay for the day, he assured himself, but that wasn't what had his jaws gritting.

And there was no anxiety about the business. They'd done well this year, despite the ongoing housing crisis. The Central Coast REIT had invested in high-end commercial properties that averaged ninety-six percent occupancy even during the economic downturn. They couldn't complain. Sure they'd had the usual rash of takeover letters from Palmer and White, but that was to be expected. Fishing for short sales and playing on stockholder fears was P&W's business and they were thorough at it. Central Coast had never lost an investor to them because of wise and swift action by the people in this room.

No. The business wasn't the source of the prickling at the back of his neck when he walked into the room. Something else was in the air. Something new and disturbing.

He had barely gotten himself seated at the head of the table when Elizabeth Moore confronted him. Liz and he had been close when they were teenagers back at Cate School, where the rich and famous parents sent their kids. Both A students, she led the girls Lacrosse team, he was the varsity football running back. Their long standing, friendly competition continued to spark his board meetings with the energy they deserved. Wife of a bank president and owner of the successful real estate brokerage house that often gave Berlin Real Estate its fiercest competition, she never left the house without her power suit and high heels, never declined when a local charity called on her, and never held back when he asked for her opinion.

But today, despite the heathered-lavender tailored suit and perfect bob of white-blond hair swinging at her ears, she looked tired. By the set of her brow, Nick knew he was about to hear exactly what was on her mind.

"Nick, I know you have a good explanation for this," she said, throwing down a tabloid paper. "But I need to hear it and quick because I don't want to lose any more sleep over this if I don't have to."

The newspaper spun around on its way across the table, the headline almost verbatim what Maddie had predicted. But worse than that, the words were printed in glaring red across a picture of him, shirtless, in the front seat of the Goddess, his shocked expression framed in a flash of light.

Nick felt the blood drain from his face but managed to get out a nervous laugh. "Why, Liz, I didn't take you for a tabloid reader."

"Don't play with us, Berlin." Jonathan West was a professional surfer and founder of a locally-grown international surf equipment company and one of Nick's Pepperdine alumni. West and Nick had hosted Winter Break, a popular surf school for disadvantaged youth, for the past ten years running. Fine lines around his eyes sharpened as he pulled off his sunglasses, opened a high tech briefcase, and threw another copy of the tabloid trash on the table. "This isn't the kind of publicity I'm goin' for, pal."

Ben Rausch, Christopher Hennings, and Robert Pirelli, longtime associates with the kind of financial credibility Goldman Sachs only wished they had, produced their own copies of the rag and fixed equally perturbed stares on Nick.

"You mean to tell me you all got caught in the tabloid gauntlet at the checkout stand?"

Elizabeth poured herself a glass of ice water from the pitcher on the table. "It was mailed to my home in a plain envelope, hand addressed, as was John's and the others."

She slipped off her jacket and draped it haphazardly across the chair back next to her. The diamond and ruby necklace at her throat bounced with her elevated heart rate.

Nick took a deep breath and cracked his neck, trying to put the pieces together. The camera must have been in the car. He had forgotten about it. The names of his board members were public record. Their home addresses weren't listed on the website, but a savvy person could get them in a number of different ways.

"May I see one of the envelopes, please?" he asked, losing the flippant tone.

Elizabeth slid her envelope across the table. The address was hand printed with a thick black marking pen. He turned it over in his hands, dropped it back on the table, then stepped away to think a moment, running his fingers through his hair. Heat rose up his neck.

"Okay." He attempted to explain, laying out the events of the last few days as simply as he could, but the longer he talked, the more ridiculous the story sounded and the more color rose on Elizabeth's cheeks.

Before he could finish, John West cut him off. "All right, all right, listen. Your private life is your own. None of us has ever questioned who you romp in the sack with, least of all me."

He picked up the newspaper and slapped it on his hand. "But I don't know how our stockholders will feel if…when…they get ahold of this. And this woman you're…*aligned* with. She stole a car from your father? And she's staying at your house?"

"Romp in the sack?" Nick's pulse rushed in his ears. He glanced behind him. "Wait. Am I in the wrong room here? Because I thought this was my board meeting, where we exercise mutual respect."

John dropped his gaze to the table and pursed his lips.

"It doesn't have to be true, Nick." Elizabeth stabbed a polished fingernail at the paper, ignoring John's remark. "It only has to be in print to be talked about and shake people's confidence. Your personal life is your own, but you can't play reckless with it when you're CEO of a billion dollar organization."

"Play reckless?" Nick fumed. "If anything, I've played it too safe for the last ten years. First to satisfy my father, and now, apparently, to satisfy *you*."

He resented the comment, especially from Liz, who had tried to set him up more than once with one of her college sorority girlfriends, one of whom had actually dragged him into a bogus paternity suit.

"Since when do people believe what they read in the tabloids?"

Liz straightened in her seat. "Since gossip became news, that's when."

Nick seethed. "No one's going to dump their Central Coast shares because some hack picked up a story on the police blotter and ran with it. It happened, Liz. I was there. But I wasn't implicated in any way, and I can prove it. End of story."

I wish. He gulped down a mouthful of water.

Jonathan gathered his papers into his briefcase.

"I'm sure you can, Nicky boy. But in the meantime, maybe you should take yourself on another leave of absence. A vacation. We can cancel the benefit. At least until after the first quarter stockholder's meeting. We don't need any disruptions. Things are bad enough as they are."

"What things?" Nick jumped to his feet and banged his fist on the table.

"If we could get on with this meeting, you'd all confirm that we're doing better than most in this environment. And, my dear friends, last time I checked, a person is innocent until proven guilty in this country. If I take a leave of absence it will look like I have something to hide."

Elizabeth sighed heavily. "Do you, Nick?"

She leveled her gaze at him and clicked her pen cartridge in and out.

Nick shifted his weight back away from the table, setting some distance between them. "What? You think I've decided to give up a respected investment firm worth six billion dollars to become a car thief?"

He couldn't believe what he was hearing. Had Maddie been right about them? He stepped over to the window and ran his fingers along the sill.

It was a warm winter day on the central coast. The kind of day most people in the country only dreamed of this time of year. There were expensive yachts in the harbor. Pricy restaurants on the pier. In recent years, even cruise ships anchored, bringing visitors from all over the world. He had a good life in Santa Barbara, one that he could be proud of. He'd worked hard to keep his father out of his business and mostly out of his life. Then along came Maddie Kerrigan and everything went in the crapper? His mind snapped hard at the thought. No. Maddie had nothing to do with it. If anything, she had helped him see that he was better than his father.

Stronger.

Worthy of respect.

He'd be damned if he'd let his father's past interfere with their future. He took another breath and turned back to face his team.

"I don't know what's in that paper. I haven't read it and I don't plan to. I've spent the last month heading down a different path than usual, I know. Trying to right a wrong. One I had nothing to do with. And neither did Madonna Kerrigan. That path led me from a farm in Kentucky to Long Beach, to that scene on the dock. It was inconvenient. It was dangerous. I didn't create it, I stumbled into it. If I hadn't, a young, innocent woman would probably be dead right now, or close to it. If that's reckless, then yeah. I played reckless."

He pulled back a notch, armed with the knowledge that he knew what was best for his future. He paced the carpet at the end of the table, fists clenched.

"And I'd do it again if she was in trouble."

"No one knows the whole truth about the relationship between Maddie's father and mine. Apparently some contraband was stolen from a casino, a long time ago. Thieves stealing from other thieves. According to my brother, Luke, who works for the DA in Santa Barbara, in case you have forgotten, nothing's ever been recovered and no one's ever been charged. But some maniac thinks my father held out on him. Who knows? Maybe he did. But it was more than twenty years ago. I wasn't even ten years old at the time.

"The true crime here, and you won't read it in that frigging paper, is what my father stole from us. From Maddie and me. Our childhoods, our innocence, our mothers. Pieces of our selves. There's not a punishment strong enough to make up for what he's done." *Unless you count losing your mind.* Nick counted that as getting off scot free.

"I can live with what he stole from me," he said, taking a moment to control the emotion straining in his voice. He filled his glass again and drank.

"In the long run, I believe it made me stronger. I've made a success of myself despite my father's constant ranting to the contrary."

He raised his eyes. Five faces told him they saw something unexpected, unfamiliar, and shocking in the man that stood before them.

He took a deep breath, exhaled, and gripped the back of his tall, leather chair, deliberately taking time to make eye contact with each one of them. "*We've* made a success of this organization."

He lowered his head and waited for his heart rate to slow before he spoke again.

"The statute of limitations will protect my father from what he did all that time ago." *Not for what he may have done to my mother.*

"And Maddie's father passed away last week in a federal penitentiary doing time for a crime he very likely didn't commit. I can't tell you how sorry I am that Maddie suffered her whole life for something my father did. But I can tell you this. My goal from the time I was a very young boy was to grow up to be nothing like my father. I have never invested a dime of his money in our business. Never misrepresented one fact to this board. Never hidden anything from any of you. I have conducted my business with the highest integrity in every transaction, every report, every acquisition, every single act of my life from the day I opened the doors of Central Coast.

"If you can't live with that…" He swallowed a hard stone of remorse in his throat. "If *any* of you feel that you can't support me through this…this…ridiculous piece of crap passed on by a criminal and some low-life hack…" He caught the corner of the tabloid and spun it back to them. "…then I'll resign right now. I don't want any of you to suffer on my behalf, even if it isn't warranted."

Elizabeth's mouth slowly closed. She placed her pen quietly on the table, pressed shaking fingers to her lips. Rausch and Pirelli exchanged nervous glances.

John scanned the faces of his colleagues, and slowly, deliberately, began to clap his hands. After a shattering moment of silence, the rest joined in.

Nick straightened, then loosened his tie a notch. "If there's nothing more on this new business, I have one more thing to announce before we start the official proceedings."

No one breathed. Elizabeth stared at her hands, shook her head quickly as if to take back everything she had said.

"You should know that I plan to ask Maddie Kerrigan to marry me. My shares in the company will go to her in the...end."

Elizabeth's head popped up.

"But you hold the majority of the shares…she would be—" she said before she checked herself.

"As I said, if you can't support me, I'd be happy to purchase your shares at the current value." Nick fixed each of them with a mirthless smile. They all knew they would have to ride out the slump. No one would be selling. Not for a while.

"I know. It's too sudden. Too *tabloidy*" He wiggled his fingers in the air, regaining some of his humor.

"But I assure you, I know exactly what I'm doing. I'll be drawing up papers soon to ensure that no matter what her answer to me personally, she will benefit from my profits on CCREIT. It's not about love or passion or 'romping in the sack'. I can never repay the loss she's endured because of my father. But this will be a start. Making a real family one day will be the frosting on the cake."

Again, silence filled the room like a giant elephant with red eyes, until John cleared his throat.

"Well," he said, undoing his tie. When that didn't relieve the tension, he pulled it all the way off. "I move we shelve making any kind of a response to this article then, unless it would be to kick the ass of whoever dropped this story to the press to begin with."

"Believe, me, that's being worked—n-not by me." Nick waved his hands in the air to emphasize his innocence.

After the meeting, John clapped him heavily on the back on the way down the hall.

"Does this mean you'll be shutting down your Vegas operation?" he asked. His tone clued Nick he was referring to the Beaver Ranch.

Nick laughed softly, relieved. "Not all of it. Maddie's pretty good at shooting craps."

The iron gate at the street stood open long after the ambulance cleared the cobbled driveway. Jimmy Ray would bet his left nut it carried Nicholas Berlin. He'd left him in pretty bad shape the other night. Old bastard. Served him right.

Jimmy Ray snorted back the beginnings of a head cold and considered his options. He could follow the ambulance to see where it landed, or slip through the gates, take a look around, and see what had changed now that the boys were back in town.

He took another bite of the stiff bacon and egg hockey puck he'd bought the night before. It lodged in his throat like a rock until he washed it down with cold coffee. Fucking stomach would act up. Just when he was getting back on track. He had to hand it to guys who went on stake out. They must have iron stomachs.

He craned his neck to see up the winding driveway. Apparently no one was going to follow the ambulance. In the rearview mirror, he watched it take the turn toward the Pacific Coast Highway at slow speed. Either the person inside was dead already or out of danger. Jimmy Ray had to know. He finished off the stale sandwich and started to throw the wrapper out the window, but thought better of it and dropped it instead on the truck's floorboard.

"What they don't know won't hurt 'em," he mumbled to himself. "Yet."

He cranked up the old Datsun, hung a U-turn, and followed the ambulance.

Chapter 18

"Don't let the Berlin drama scare you off." Gina's tone turned from playful to serious as she dropped Maddie in front of the big house. "With the old man gone, this house may very well become the home it was meant to be."

Maddie pulled her bags from the backseat of Gina's Volkswagen and thanked her for the impromptu shopping trip. "I'll keep that in mind."

She stood on the steps of the main house and collected her thoughts as Gina drove away. It would have been far more productive to spend the day checking her emails and voicemails now that she had her gear from Lompoc. She did, after all, have a business to run. But with the Goddess still in impound and no transportation of her own, it wasn't a hard decision to choose Gina's offer of retail therapy over work. That and the fact that she was wearing borrowed underwear, thanks to the Lompoc Motor Hotel *losing* her overnight bag. At least her purse and her laptop had been spared.

She should have asked Gina to drop her off at the guest house, but when they'd pulled up to the sprawling mission style mansion instead, Maddie hadn't protested. She was drawn irresistibly to the home where Nick grew up. Once under the arching portico, there was no going back. She traced a finger over the intricately woven design in the wide terra cotta panels that framed the double entry doors. With her hand on the levered handle, she half hoped it wouldn't move and she could spare herself the embarrassment of someone catching her mid snoop.

But the door opened.

The house seemed to breathe in and hold it, silent and pensive, as if it too waited to see what would happen next. Maddie let her packages fall to the floor in the foyer and stepped inside.

The salon to the right of the entry was just as they'd left it earlier, turned upside down. Books were strewn across the floor and broken glass littered expensive area rugs where a heavy silver picture frame had shattered a mirrored wall at the south end of the room.

Maddie's heart rate ticked up to beat in her ears.

Don't let the Berlin drama scare you off.

Trouble was, she was part of the drama. An elemental part. She couldn't separate herself from that fact. Her gaze drifted to the stairway that must have led to Nick's childhood room. For a fraction of a second she entertained the thought of going up there.

Maddie had wanted to clean up the mess before Nick returned home, but Gina insisted they leave the minute the paramedics took Nicholas Senior away.

Now, she traced quaking fingers over the grand piano and straightened the shawl that had been pulled off the top. She picked up one of the frames, turned it over and brushed broken glass from the photo.

The image took her breath away. She had seen it from the doorway just before Nick's father exploded. Her mother, standing against the Cadillac, those frayed Daisy Dukes, that provocative smile. The same photo she had cherished all these years. The one Nick had seen in her bedroom back home. Maddie pressed her fingers to her lips and squeezed her eyes shut against the new wave of pain.

It was one thing to learn about their families' connection from Nick. It was quite another to see the evidence first hand. In the image, her mother had been younger than Maddie was now, but somehow, whether it was the style of the day, or the photo faded over time, Corinne looked older than her years.

No one had expected what had happened that morning when Nick brought Maddie up to the big house before leaving for his office. No one could have predicted Nicholas Senior's reaction when he saw her from his chair in the parlor. No one had known how far his mind had gone off its tracks, or if it would slip again. Inside this room, she could still hear his curses ringing in her ears. Hopefully, she would never have to face him again.

She bent to restore one of the candle holders to its round footprint on the dusty piano.

"You don't have to do that."

Maddie spun around at the sound of Nick's voice. He dropped an armful of papers on the piano and scooped her into his arms.

"I won't have you cleaning up the mess he made."

Maddie fit herself against his side, breathing in his scent. She stroked the length of his silk tie. "I have to do something. It was my fault. He was sitting calmly until he saw me."

"He is a psychotic bastard. He's never done anything calmly."

Nick turned her face to his and traced across her brow with his fingertip. "I called the housekeeper back this morning. I can't believe he fired her after all the years she put up with his crap. You'll love Isabel, she's—"

"But look at these books." Maddie picked one off the floor, *Interview with a Vampire*. "This is a signed by the author. What if it was damaged?"

Nick let go half a laugh and gazed up at the wall of books. "My father had these bookshelves added and insisted they be filled with first editions. I doubt that he ever cracked one open."

He took the book gently from Maddie's hands. "My mother used a decorator to help her fill these shelves, though I suspect this one belonged to Luke's mother."

He smoothed a section of dog-eared pages and slipped it reverently back on the shelf.

"She was fond of Anne Rice long before vampires started turning up in the local singles bars." Nick turned Maddie back to the piano. "This Steinway? Luke's mother played it beautifully. Toward the end, as her cancer sapped her strength, playing the piano was the only thing that gave her comfort. The old man refused to allow it when he was home. He said she had no feel for the music, no talent. It was just another thing to give and then take away. Broke her spirit in every way he could."

Maddie slipped her hand into Nick's and felt him tremble with a fury long suppressed.

"That portrait there?" He tipped his head toward an oversized painting of Nicholas Senior in a riding outfit complete with crop, smiling down from the entry way. The resemblance to Nick and his brother was remarkable. A strong jaw line, that elegantly straight nose and a high forehead. But there was something else. Something behind the eyes that lent a lie to the smile. Perhaps the sins of his own father somewhere in his makeup. The thought sent a chill to her core.

"He had that done as a present for Luke's mother. I think he did it to terrorize her even when he wasn't home. Even when he was off with…"

He lowered his head and puffed out his breath. "Sorry. I—"

"No. It's all right." She slipped her arm around his waist and fit her hips against his. "So much went on in this house…"

She smoothed her hands up to rest on his chest and smiled into his eyes, letting the warmth of his body melt into hers.

"We have a lot in common. We're hardwired to our past. What your father did destroyed three women and made your young life hell. But it made you stronger. Made you fight to make everything he said and did a lie. And you won."

Nick inhaled his anger and exhaled some relief. His gaze roamed the room, memories playing through his mind from the time he was a small boy to the events of the morning. Old hurts tightened his jaw, the tendons in his neck and his fists.

Maddie squeezed his hand and brought his eyes back to hers. "It's over. He's gone. It may take a while to clear the memory of him out of this house, but he will never rule your life again."

Nick gave his neck a slow crack to relieve the tension. When the beautiful woman looking up at him raised a disapproving brow, he returned a half smile. "I think it will take a bulldozer."

"There's hope for you, Berlin. As soon as all this crap is cleaned up and I'm out of your hair, everything will go back to normal and you can get on with your life."

Her words shocked him awake. He thought they had worked that out. He circled his arms possessively around her and pulled her close. Dark slate eyes drew him in and suddenly the room that held so many memories faded away and all he could see was her face. The face of the woman he loved.

"I don't want normal Maddie." He lowered his forehead to hers, brushed a kiss across her lips, and her eyes darkened further still. "Normal for me has meant living a lie. I don't want that. Not the way it was before all this happened. The way it is now, with you."

Maddie shook her head, her eyes squeezed shut.

"Don't you trust me, Maddie?"

She leaned away and toyed with the beaded shawl on the piano. "How can I not trust the man who came after me, putting his future in jeopardy?"

"Then what the hell are you afraid of?"

Maddie angled her shoulder away, putting more distance between them. "The ones I've trusted the most—the ones I loved—they all betrayed me. All I've ever wanted is a normal family and every way I've tried to put that together, the people I loved and trusted were the ones that pulled it apart."

He lowered himself down on the piano bench, captured her hand, and brought her attention back to him. Her gaze lifted, touching the ache inside him. How could he convince her that he needed her more than this house or his business?

"Not this person, Maddie. Not this time."

"I've got more at stake." He brushed her lips with his, his voice deepening with emotion. "They were all concerned for your welfare. I'm looking out for my own."

He kissed her again boldly, unapologetic, his arms closing around her.

"You can trust me to protect you, to love you, because, when I'm away from you I can hardly breathe. If you weren't here right now, I'd be tearing this room apart, and that would be just like *him*. Because I have you with me, I can let go of the past and plan a future. Imagine what that might hold? Trust me Maddie. Think about building something new."

"You make love sound so easy. Something people just fall into without giving it a second thought."

"And you think too much."

❧

She nodded in agreement, lifted the old familiar photograph from the piano, and studied her mother's face, so like her own.

"I used to think I would grow up to be just like her—seductive, reckless, irresponsible—it scared me to death. I've lived my entire life doing everything I could to make sure I didn't repeat her mistakes."

"Like you said, we have a lot in common." His smile drew her away from the memory.

"I do look like her. Your father bore witness to that." She let her hand drop and dangled the photo at her side.

"I'm not like her, though. I want more than anything to start new," she said, searching deep into his eyes. How could she explain to him what she hardly understood herself? "But I can't just jump off the deep end hoping there's water in the pool. I'm hardwired to resist."

He lowered his mouth to hers, kissed her deeply this time, pulling her inside his spell.

"Oh, there's water in this pool. Deep enough for all of us."

"All of us?"

"You, me, Bébé, some puppies…a couple of kids…"

Nick played a simple minor chord on the piano.

"You were right about that headline, by the way." He toyed with the piano keys, walking his fingers up the scale, and then tilted his head to call her attention to the newspapers he'd brought in.

She slid one off the stack and gasped at the photo on the front page.

"Oh my god." Her hand went to her mouth and she clenched her eyes shut, trying to erase the image from her mind. But when she opened her eyes, Nick grinned back at her.

"How can you laugh? They must have thought the worst."

"Oh they did." He told her about the incident at the board meeting and how they wanted him to take a leave of absence. Then he jabbed a discord on the piano keys. "That's when I knew."

Maddie cocked her head, confused.

He took a hand in his again.

"If they can't accept me the way I am—with you—I can walk away without a second thought. But if you walk away…" He swallowed hard and looked back at the keys a moment. "Without you, nothing of who I am makes sense anymore."

Her heart expanded beyond herself, the loneliness of her childhood and the confines of her fear. She had never wanted to run away. Not really. Not since the cold wintry night he had tapped on her car window in the parking lot of the Hampton Inn. There was something solid about Nick Berlin, even then. Something irresistible and safe about him, even before she knew who he was. It was too good to be true, but somehow it was true. She had seen all the sides of him and none of them—none of them—showed her a man who would cut and run.

She felt her mouth relax into a smile despite her fears and self-doubt. "You've thought this through."

Nick nodded.

"Puppies? Really?

Nick's smile broadened and his blue-green eyes brightened.

"And a couple of cars, maybe? Old ones?"

"There's a garage full of them waiting right out back."

Maddie hesitated just enough to tease a hint of worry in his eyes, and then her laugh came bubbling up through the doubt. She threw her arms around his neck and kissed him quick. "Now that sounds like a pool I could jump into. Head first."

With the full force of his passion, Nick covered her mouth with his, and slid her into his lap, his hands running down over her shoulders, the small of her back and her thighs. He breathed her name into her ear—

A loud bang at the entry startled them both stock straight, Nick's arm slamming the piano keyboard.

"*¡Madre de Dios!*"

Nick nudged Maddie to the bench beside him and cleared his throat. "Isabel."

The woman who stood in the doorway couldn't have been more than five feet tall, including the thick fist of shiny black hair knotted on the top of her head. Her bearing and the keen focus of her dark eyes lent her a much larger presence in the room.

"Oh. Mr. Nick. I didn't realize anyone was here. Am I too soon?" She turned to pick up the vacuum hose extension she'd dropped in the doorway.

"No, of course not. Here, let me help you with that." Nick glanced quickly at Maddie with a cautions grin, then scrambled to haul the vacuum equipment into the room, along with a cartload of cleaning supplies, brooms and plastic bags.

"Isabel, this is Maddie." With the display of passion the housekeeper had interrupted, he didn't have to explain any more.

She gave Maddie a knowing smile full of energy and female camaraderie.

"Ah. I am *surprise* to see you. Nicky, he doesn't bring his friends around here much. In fact, I don't *see* him in this house in a long, long time."

She waved a disapproving finger at him as she easily pulled the vacuum out of his hands.

Maddie worked on regaining her composure, the last few moments, the revelations, and the consuming, conflicting flood of emotion had her trembling.

"*Is* a shame about your father," Isabel said to Nick, diffidently. Turning to survey the damage in the room, she clicked her tongue. "Mmmmm. Maybe *no* such a shame."

"I agree, Isabel. You don't have to be polite. You can blame it on his condition, but I think you've been around here long enough to know better."

"Maybe, he *get* what he deserve, eh?"

Maddie gasped.

Isabel only fisted her hands at her hips and sniffed. "Just look at that mirror, *tch, tch, tch.*"

"I'm sorry he fired you. If I'd known I would have stopped it."

"No worries, Mr. Nick. I would have quit anyway. He was such a devil lately. More than usual."

She picked a candlestick from the floor and placed it next to the one Maddie had put on the piano earlier.

"Jose and Miguel? They went back to Mexico for the holiday? He say, 'You go, you never come back'. So they went. And they didn't. But me? I have family here, eh?" She sent Maddie a complicit wink.

"I don't blame them," Nick told her. "I'll get you some more help soon. In the meantime, the grove house is at your disposal, as before."

She grinned at Nick, then beamed it over to Maddie. "He's a good young man, your *friend*, Mr. Nick."

Maddie fit her hand back into Nick's and laced his fingers with her own. "Yes he is."

❧

The Silver Palms nursing home was a cluster of red-tile-roofed cottages surrounded by a high stucco wall that dominated most of a rural block and dead-ended into a horse stable. At the farthest end of the parking area, Jimmy Ray rolled his window down and flinched at the aroma of fresh manure. Ironic that

Nicholas had finally ended up where he belonged. Hopefully, the old man had enough thoughts left in that brain of his to tell Jimmy what he wanted to know.

Lifting a pair of drug-store field glasses to his eyes, he could see that the decorative wrought-iron gate beyond the entrance could be accessed only through a not-so-decorative steel reinforced one in the stucco wall. Just inside the gate, he caught a glimmer of water dripping from a three-tiered fountain in the center of a large courtyard. A crow, magnified in the glasses to look as big as a vulture, rose from the top tier of the fountain and flew straight at him.

Jimmy Ray jumped, dropped the field glasses, and banged his knee on the steering wheel, delivering an excruciating shock of pain to his whole leg. He had noticed a red streak running up the inside of his thigh when he woke in the front seat of the Datsun this morning, but first aid would have to wait.

His number one priority, the one that had kept him out here in the middle of fucking nowhere overnight, was finding a way inside the rest home. From what he could see, someone on the inside buzzed visitors through either the front gate or a service entrance at the side of the main facility.

Jimmy Ray had just blown his nose on a candy bar wrapper and pitched it out the window when the P-Trap Plumbing Company van turned into the side entrance. A gray-haired man who looked to be about eighteen months pregnant struggled out of the driver's seat and opened the tailgate of the van. He fisted his hands at his back and stretched like a man in pain.

Jimmy sympathized.

"This is it," he told himself out loud. He would have to move quickly, even if his knee complained.

He started the Datsun, pulled in behind the plumber's truck, and hobbled out.

"Here, let me help you with that." The extra weight would send a hell of a pain through his knee, but he would just have to suck it up. Gritting his teeth, he pushed past the old man and dragged a heavy toolbox toward the van's back bumper.

Caught off guard, the man gaped at him. "You work here?"

"Yeah, I volunteer," Jimmy lied with a wide smile. He spotted a dirty ball cap next to the toolbox and stuffed the bill of it in the back of his belt. "I figure I gotta do my bit to help society, you know. Pay it forward." *Thank you Leon.*

The man shook his head "Gotta hand it to you."

He sauntered slowly to the back entrance with Jimmy following close behind and rang the buzzer. "It's a good thing this place is next to a horse stable. The manure blocks the smell of the inside."

"You get used to it," Jimmy said, shifting his weight to his good leg. "It comes with the territory."

The gate buzzed open and Jimmy Ray followed the plumber in to a large service area where bundles of sheets and other laundry lined stainless steel tables on both sides of the room. Jimmy's luck held. A young Hispanic woman explained to the two of them that P-Trap Plumbing was called in to fix a problem in the laundry, then to do a service check through the whole facility. Jimmy Ray hung back, setting the toolbox on the steel counter. The plumber followed the woman into a utility room. Jimmy Ray waited to make his move until the rumbling equipment muffled the sounds of their voices, then he jammed the ball cap on his head, picked out a wrench from the toolbox, and headed for the residential area.

Once inside, it was a simple matter of asking a large man in stained, blue scrubs for the new guy's room. The plumber's hat and heavy wrench said the rest.

Nicholas's head came up the moment Jimmy opened the door. A good sign. At least he was conscious. The old man looked out of place in the gray-walled room in his silk pajamas, smoking jacket robe, and sheepskin slippers. He sat in an expensive leather recliner Jimmy figured had been brought in by his family.

"What happened to you?" Nicholas asked, his eyes registering alarm. "You look like shit."

Jimmy's brows wrinkled. "Proud talk for a man shipped off by his own sons to a rest home."

Nicholas's gaze roamed the room as if reminding himself where he was. "Yeah, well, I guess they thought I needed some."

Jimmy sidled in, closed the door behind him, and folded his arms across his chest. Except for the old man's labored speech, the threat in his eye still set Jimmy Ray on edge. He leaned against a heavy, wood dresser that had taken a beating over the years.

Nicholas eyed the wrench, the ball cap, then Jimmy's face. "What are you doing here? I thought you were in prison."

Jimmy pursed his lips and scratched under his chin. How does a guy not remember being punched in the stomach and tied up in his own kitchen by an old friend? Jeez, it had only been a few days ago. The old man was playing coy and Jimmy didn't have time for it.

Jimmy Ray stalked across the room, kicked the recliner lever with his foot to bring it upright, and nearly shot the old man out of the chair. "You son of a bitch, you know why I'm here, so don't fuck with me."

Nicholas's eyes rounded. He pressed his head back into the cushion as far from Jimmy as he could get. He reached for a buzzer control attached to the chair, but Jimmy knocked it away before he could get a grip on it. "The diamond, you fucking fuck. Where is it?"

Jimmy Ray took pleasure watching his old partner's face drain of color until it nearly matched the gray walls in the room. His mouth worked, but nothing came out.

"It wasn't in her garage in Kentucky and it wasn't in the car. Ross is dead without a penny or a stitch of his own, and now you're stuck in here. I'm the only one who can benefit from it."

Nicholas's face contorted in confusion. "Ross is dead? I just saw him yesterday."

He sat forward suddenly, his eyes focused past Jimmy's shoulder as if someone stood behind him. The old man's hands white knuckled on the arms of the chair. "Son of a bitch took her away from me. Stole her. *They've* got it now."

Jimmy straightened. He fingered the wiry tendrils of his chin beard. Maybe the old man *was* stark raving. Slipping in and out.

His madness could work in Jimmy's favor, if he played it right. If he calmed it down.

"Relax, man. We're old friends. We can work this out." He spotted a tray with coffee cups and a thermal pitcher on a bedside table. "Want some?"

He glanced at Nicholas. "Cream, sugar?"

"Cream." The old man relaxed his grip on the chair. Some of the color returned to his cheeks.

Jimmy poured himself a cup, loaded it with real sugar, sat on the bed, and stirred the liquid. *Keep it calm.* "I'm here to help you. I can get the diamond before they take it, cut it up, and sell the car."

Nicholas scowled at Jimmy a moment, his eyes wary. Then he shook his head and sipped his coffee.

"They'll never find it," the old man said, his voice a low growl in his throat. Self-satisfaction oozed from his grin.

Jimmy laughed softly, not wanting to break the mood. Patience, he'd been told a hundred times, wasn't one of his strong points. He rubbed his knee and scooted forward on the bed.

"Yeah, yeah. You're clever. I'll give you that. You were smarter than all of us. Managed to keep yourself out of jail."

"Outlived all of them…" Nicholas said. He gestured with the cup in his hand, spilled some down his front, and looked at it as if he'd forgotten how it got there. He stared at the blank TV screen until Jimmy wondered if he was falling asleep.

"Hey, hey. Over here," Jimmy said, clapping his hands.

The old man jumped and cranked his head around.

"JR? How'd you know I was here? I thought you were in prison."

Jimmy Ray exhaled.

"I bet you'd like to see that diamond again, wouldn't you," he said, steering him, working it.

"The diamond?" Fire returned to Nicholas's eyes.

"I could get it for you," he said, a friend consoling a friend. "Just tell me where it is."

Nicholas refocused on Jimmy with the old intensity that used to scare the shit out of him.

"Hiding in plain sight," he said at last, his eyes narrowing to straight slits. "Right under their noses."

"Ho ho, that's great." Jimmy leaned closer. He clamped his hands on the arm of the chair. "Where?"

Nicholas pressed back a little, confusion taking over his expression again. Jimmy Ray scooted in, his knees nudging the arm of the chair. "Just relax. You'll get it." *Don't go out on me now you old fuck.*

Nickolas rolled his head and looked Jimmy in the eye again. That sly smile returned to his lips.

"I had a medallion cast with her initials in it. Hers and mine. Made the mold myself. A steering wheel knob. Sealed the diamond up inside and capped it with the medallion. That stupid bitch touches it every day she drives," he said, then mumbled something unintelligible before his smile faded.

It didn't matter. Jimmy had heard all he needed to know. His fingertips tingled. He'd touched that knob himself only a day or so ago. And he'd touch it again soon.

Nicholas sat up so quick Jimmy never saw it coming. The old man grabbed Jimmy's knee with the strength of a wrestler. "You get that car back for me, Jimmy, or I'll have you back in prison so fast you'll wish you…wish—"

Jimmy Ray cried out in pain, clenched the old man's wrist and bent his arm back in his face.

The door opened suddenly. Jimmy Ray dropped Nicholas's wrist and spun around.

"Everything okay in here?" The same attendant he'd spoken to earlier filled the doorway with his bulk.

"Uh, yeah. Whew!" Jimmy Ray stepped away from Nicholas. The pain in his knee shot through his entire body and exploded out the top of his head. He had to catch his breath before he could speak.

"He was choking on some coffee, I think."

The attendant glared at Jimmy Ray, thick brows converging over his eyes.

"He's okay now, but you might want to check him over." Jimmy took a step back, pointing at Nicholas.

The moment the man shifted his attention to Nicholas, Jimmy Ray slipped out the door.

❧

Nick held the back door of the guest house kitchen open for Maddie. She breezed through and stacked her bags on the kitchen table. Bébé trotted in and nosed Nick's hand, wagging her tail.

"Well, how quickly loyalties change." Maddie raised an eyebrow at her dog. The fragrance of pine overwhelmed her senses. "It smells like Christmas in here."

Nick slipped his hand in Maddie's. "I did a little shopping after lunch today myself. I hope you don't mind I did it without you."

He led her through to the dining area where a fresh cedar filled the corner of the room and nearly reached to the top of the cathedral ceiling. There were no decorations, but a large oblong package wrapped in metallic gold paper and tied with a gigantic red bow had been tucked under the lowest branches. Visions of *Pretty Woman* danced flip flops through Maddie's stomach.

"You'll need to open it now. I know Christmas is a few days off, but you should try this on so we have time to get the right size if we need to before the benefit."

"Benefit?" Maddie checked her pique before she ruined the moment. Nick was so animated, so excited, she hated to revert to old resistance after they'd had such an emotional day. But her stomach got the better of her. Opening her heart a crack didn't mean she would give up herself.

"Just because you've got me captive in your castle doesn't mean you can take me to the ball."

His grin was sly, boyish. Tantalizing Nick was in the house. He lifted his shoulder. "Suit yourself. But I think once you see the outfit, you'll change your mind."

"Vera Wang couldn't design me a dress that would get me to parade on your arm in a room full of socialites. It would be embarrassing. For me *and* for you."

"Oh, it'll probably be embarrassing. I won't claim otherwise, Miss Maddie. But I can guarantee you, *this* benefit is not hoity toity."

"Nick, I just—"

He tipped her off balance just enough to plop her on the leather sofa, then shoved the package into her lap. "Just open it. Trust me."

Maddie raised her brow at him, a half smile curling at the corners of her mouth. *Live a little, kid.*

Exhaling her exasperation at a man she knew would not be denied, she pulled at the big, red bow and opened the lid, then sent him a confused look.

"A wet suit?" She lifted it out of the box and held it at arm's length.

"A Jonathan West. All the debutants are wearing them these days. It's the latest thing."

Nick stepped to her side, grabbed the suit, and held it up to her body. "Wooo, I think I nailed it."

"Wait. You're not thinking you'll get me out on a surfboard?"

"It's the Sixth Annual Jonathan West *Winter Breaks* Benefit, sponsored by West Swell and the Central Coast REIT."

"I don't know whether to be relieved or scared to death."

"Both. You won't be alone. The rest of the attendees are twelve-year-olds." He pulled her to him and planted a kiss on her lips.

Maddie ran her hand across the front of the suit. Her Mad Monkey logo had been stenciled just below the neckline. "You've been busy behind my back."

"My favorite place. But…don't think about that now. We've only got a few minutes to get ready. It's an hour up to Bacara."

"Bacara?"

"We promised to make a decision about my father tonight, remember? Doesn't mean we can't do it somewhere special. I know you've got something in those bags in the kitchen you'd like to wear."

He flipped out his cell phone.

"Luke and Gina will meet us there."

The sun set fire to a dappled sky for barely sixty seconds before it flamed out and over the edge of the planet. The sunsets. They were one of the things Maddie missed most about the West. The sunsets, the ocean, and the food. *Miro's* Mediterranean cuisine and the impeccable attention they got as friends of the chef at the Bacara Resort were enough to keep the four of them distracted well into a dessert plate of gold-foiled chocolate truffles.

Maddie and Gina emerged from the posh ladies' room to see the brothers' heads together.

Gina flipped her silky red hair behind one ear and slid into the booth next to Luke.

"This looks like a conspiracy in the making."

Luke dropped his napkin and raised his hands in a mock display of innocence.

"Luke's been filling me in on the case." Nick took possession of Maddie's hand as she scooted in next to him. "At least what he knows of it."

He nodded to their server.

"Bring us some espressos, Rubio." Nick bumped his shoulder into Maddie's. "And a little pot of that Kahula whipped cream. Oh, and some more of those truffles."

Maddie stretched her smile out. "I guess you're planning on being up for a while."

Nick dropped his gaze to the table, that familiar tension tightened his jaw. He had tried to keep the conversation light, but Maddie sensed he was losing the battle. She touched his knee. He turned and blinked at her in slow motion, the light coming back up in his eyes.

"I brought us here, away from the house, to make some decisions, took the liberty of reserving us some rooms. A little pick me up now, and later…"

Gina's brows raised. "Us? You mean, *all* of us?"

"It's a long drive home. Two rooms, four people. I assumed the usual human pairing," he said, grinning at Luke.

Luke rolled his eyes then looked back at Gina who made a show of scooting away from him.

Maddie kept her eyes on Nick. He was only half engaged. The other half of him still brooded.

"You made yourself quite an assumption, didn't you?" Gina couldn't hide her smile.

Nick lifted a shoulder. "Same assumption as always."

Maddie felt her insides settle and let herself enjoy the mood. It was good to be here. At that table. With this family. On what had been a jarring day. Despite the fact that Luke and Gina were *ex*-fiancés at the moment, and Nick had been absent from their day-to-day lives, there was a rhythm to the way they interacted. The way they cared for each other. Trusted one another.

Family.

The brothers managed it well, despite their father's abuse. A tribute, Maddie observed, to their mothers. She squeezed Nick's hand under the table. Nick nodded at Luke to continue.

Luke sat back and waited for the server to distribute the coffees, then started in.

"So, none of this is really my jurisdiction. The DA's office doesn't usually get involved until after the perps are arrested. But because of my former position as detective—"

Nick twirled his hand in front of him. "Can we dispense with the preening and skip to the facts?"

"These are the facts. I spent a long time on the streets. A detective gets no respect—Ow!" Luke jumped in his seat. Gina gave him a smug smile.

"All right. All right. Enough about me. We can talk about me later."

He spooned a dollop of whipped cream into the tiny cup in front of him and stirred. "Really? You pay extra for this miniscule cup?"

Maddie hid her smile behind her hand. She wasn't ready to get serious either. She'd had enough serious for one day. But she straightened as Nick leveled his gaze at his brother.

"Get on with it, pal."

Luke held up his pinky and sipped, leaving a trace of whipped cream on his upper lip. Gina whisked it off with her finger.

"So. It was out of my jurisdiction, even if I was a detective. It was first of all, in LA County. And falsifying documents for international freight, kidnapping…" he sent Maddie a look that said how sorry he was, "…and transporting stolen goods across state lines. That all belongs to the FBI. The fact that it was in the harbor added another layer I'm not privy to. And, international freight forwarding, that's US Customs. You've got yourself a regular Christmas Policeman's Ball cluster fuck...excuse my French."

Gina knuckle punched him in the shoulder.

"What?"

Gina rolled her eyes over to Maddie. "Never mind."

Maddie appreciated the interruption. She had managed to push the memory of the events that led to the Goddess being impounded out of her head. Now the thought of how close she had come to losing everything including her life had her nearly hyperventilating.

Nick tucked her under his arm. "Go on."

Luke eyed Maddie a moment, then continued. "But when Jimmy Ray showed up at Montecito, hogtied your boyfriend Robert and our father together on the kitchen floor and drove off with three of his cars on a double-decker tow truck, he was in the venerable County of Santa Barbara. Right in our own back fucking yard. Literally and juris-*dictally*, if that's a word.

"Not." Gina scooted closer to Luke, stole a tiny spoonful of doctored espresso, and sipped loud and slow.

"Anyway, you can thank Nick and your dog for getting the show rolling ahead of schedule or Jimmy Ray might have gotten away. Oh, wait. He *did* get away." He shot a scornful look over at his brother.

"That wasn't Bébé's fault," Nick said. "She knew Maddie was out there. She just went for it."

Luke held up his hands. "I'm just sayin'."

Maddie toyed with a truffle then put it down. Outside, the beach was wide open. Anyone could be out there, watching them. Even now. Watching and waiting. The thought put an edge on what had been until now a relatively pleasant evening.

"For the record, Robert is not, and never was my boyfriend. Still, I don't understand what he had to do with all this," Maddie said. Better to change the subject than feed her fears. "It just doesn't make any sense to me. Robert shows up out of nowhere in Wendover and next thing, he's buddies with the FBI?"

Nick rested his hand on her thigh, a possessive gesture that told her he knew what she'd been thinking.

"Not so out of nowhere," Luke went on. "Apparently, he hooked up with them some time last year. The FBI had been onto Jimmy for a while. He'd staged the same show on the East coast. Put together a container of classic cars and shipped it out of New Jersey. He'd contacted Robert to purchase one of those cars. Fished him a little and found a sucker to help him shop for American steel on a regular basis."

Maddie shook her head. "Robert worked for Jimmy Ray? I don't believe it."

"Maybe not *for* him as in actually stealing cars and loading them on trucks. Jimmy was working him, more likely. Lining up cars on Robert's advice. For a small cut. Robert knew classics, knew where to find them, and what they were worth."

Maddie sat up to the table, despite Nick's hand on her thigh. "Robert was a nerd. The kind of guy smart girls ditch by excusing themselves to the ladies room. Harmless and clueless but not dangerous. I've seen him wrangle a cheap price on a classic car from an old lady, playing on her sympathy, then flip it around for a huge profit. He used to brag about getting an old Chrysler for seven hundred dollars because he was a dead ringer for this woman's son."

"Is that good?" Luke helped himself to another truffle. "Seven hundred?"

Maddie huffed. "*Obscene.* A pristine Chrysler 300 is worth at least a quarter of a million dollars today. Maybe more."

The server came, refilled their waters, and glanced at Nick for instructions. When he didn't get any, he backed away silently. Luke took a long drink.

"Maybe he was hungry. The classic car market's been down lately, right?" He shot a look at Nick.

Nick swallowed his espresso in one gulp. "Everything's down. That doesn't make it okay to steal cars and ship them out of the country."

"We don't know that he actually stole anything. Only that the FBI made the connection and contacted him. Made him an offer he couldn't refuse."

Gina shifted in her seat and tucked a leg under her. "You mean like, stick with Jimmy, keep us informed, or we tag you with conspiracy."

"Now that makes sense." Maddie popped the chocolate into her mouth. She was starting to breathe normally again. "Robert was just enough of a nerd to get off on that. Feel important. He'd eat that up."

"And just enough of an amateur to let Jimmy give him the slip." Nick let go a laugh, then nodded to Maddie. "Sorry."

"No. I agree. He bit off what he thought was going to be an adventure. Jimmy Ray is kind of a small, *weasely* guy you might think is harmless." Her gaze slipped away to the next table where a young couple oblivious to anything in the room besides each other were seated and given water and menus. "But he's… not."

"Which is why," Nick added, "we have to be careful. I've got an idea he's not one to let go of a bone once he tastes the meat."

He tapped his spoon on the saucer nervously. Maddie covered his hand.

"They found his clothes or what was left of them after Bébé shredded his leg. They washed up near a pier adjacent to the takedown. His wallet, his ID—"

"His exit plan," Maddie said on an exhale. "Layer upon layer of exit plans."

Nick sighed and sat back against the plush banquette. He glanced at his watch, then cleared his throat. "Which leads me to the next item on our agenda."

"We have an agenda?" Luke ran a hand over his mouth and cut his eyes sharply at his brother.

"What to do with our father." He rearranged his silverware, his cloth napkin, and his water glass.

Gina uncurled her legs and sat forward, her eyes full of concern. "I'm not the expert, but I'd say he's incapable of living on his own."

Nick glanced up at her. "What makes you say that?"

"The change in habits. Mistrust of family, hired help. Blaming. "

He popped out a laugh. "That's no change. He's always been that way."

"True, but I'd say he's slipped to another plateau. Before Maddie set off the spark, he was complacent, vacant. Like he's in and out of reality."

Maddie recognized the LVN kicking in. Gina had deliberately softened her tone. Their father had been an asshole, a monster, and was likely responsible for more mayhem than any of them had imagined, but he was their father and Gina treaded lightly. Maddie had to give her credit for her skill.

"The lack of personal hygiene, holing up in the house, failure to cook and clean. I'd say this outburst of uncontrolled delusional anger will shift him to another plateau. You can wear yourselves out, put yourselves at risk trying to take care of him, or you can leave him where he is. Safe for him, safe for you. I'm not his doctor. But if I were, I'd recommend he stay right where he is. I've seen it. I recognize it. If he's headed where I think he is, he's got two years, maybe less, and he'll be gone. But if you try to keep him home, he'll take you down with him."

The brothers looked at each other, speaking volumes in the way that brothers can.

Maddie sat forward and rested her elbows on the table. "I'm not really part of the family here, but I know something about caring for someone who is declining mentally."

She glanced at Nick and his brother in turn. She could see they were considering what Gina had said.

"I loved my grandpa with all my heart. Would have done anything to make him happy. Make his life easier. Even so, taking care of him for the two years it took for him to die nearly killed every human feeling I had inside me. Put my life on hold. Tore me apart. Your father—"

"—was an asshole," Luke said. "I'm with Gina. Let someone else wipe his ass. I was done with him a long time ago."

Nick drummed his fingers on the table. He lifted his gaze to Gina. "What does it take? To put him away?"

Maddie caught her breath. With her grandpa, there was no question that he would stay home, be cared for by loved ones in a familiar environment. But she understood how Nick felt and didn't blame him.

"His mental assessment score was below twelve. He didn't even know what year it was. Add that to the behavioral issues? He definitely can't continue to live alone. "

Nick rubbed his hands over his face and looked at his brother for several heartbeats. The background noise in the dining room—murmured conversations, silverware tinkling on plates, soft music—faded away until Maddie could hear her own heart pumping in her ears. The seconds stretched to a minute and maybe longer as the brothers stared. Maddie and Gina exchanged glances.

At last, Nick raised a finger and caught the server's attention. "Bring us four brandies, please."

When the squat glasses of golden liquid arrived, Nick picked his up and motioned for the rest of them to do the same.

"To the gift of peace in the family. I have a feeling this will be the best Christmas we've had since…" he closed his eyes for a moment, sucked in a breath and exhaled, "…for a very long time."

Nick sipped his brandy and turned an uncertain smile to Maddie.

"To the gift of peace," she said. Nick's jaw relaxed and the light came up a shade in his eyes.

"Amen, brother." Luke lifted his glass, sipped.

"Oh," He patted his coat pocket. "Speaking of gifts…"

He pulled out a manila envelope and handed it over to Maddie.

Chapter 19

Maddie slipped a thick stack of official looking documents out of the envelope and scanned the pages. Her shoulders slumped against the banquette and she tossed the package on the table in front of her.

"Well," she said. A week ago she would have been thrilled to find out the Goddess had been released from impound. Now the news hit her with a sour note. It was time to move on.

Nick scowled at Luke.

"What? She'll have her car by January fifth," Luke said, raising his hands in defense. Then back to Maddie, he continued. "I forwarded your restoration log and photo documentation on the Cadillac to the team. Pled a case for special circumstances to expedite the investigation and release of the vehicles."

He lifted his shoulders and exchanged worried looks with Nick.

"I thought she'd be happy." He turned to Maddie, "You can get the car ready for the auction."

Maddie waved away his concern. "Thanks. Really. Both of you. For everything."

The words had no force behind them. "It's just…will you excuse me please?"

With an apologetic glance at Gina, she slipped out of her seat.

In the ladies room, she leaned into the sink, feeling suddenly off kilter. A glass of wine, several dark chocolates, and likely the finest dinner she'd ever had, put high color on her cheeks. In contrast, the discussion around the table brought her solidly back to reality. No matter how much she wanted to jump into Nick's fantasy pool, she still had to sell the Goddess. With the car being released, she was a step closer to that goal.

Less than a month ago she was hell bent on getting the car sold and getting on with her business. It had been wonderful to build the car with her grandfather, and she'd come to the realization that it didn't need to define the rest of her life. With the money the car would bring, after she repaid Nick, of course, and paid off the ranch, she would be the mistress of her own destiny. Mad Monkey would have an infusion of cash she could build into a brand everyone in the car restoration business would recognize, admire and respect.

Every day that passed put distance between herself and the doubts and fears of her childhood. Having Nick at her side added a layer of healing salve to old hurts and fresh grief, like new paint on an old Chevy.

Brought healing to both of them.

The fact that Nick loved her, needed her, couldn't breathe without her, and that she needed him, gave her new strength. But it didn't make selling the Goddess any easier. She realized she'd pushed the thought of it to the farthest netherworlds of her mind.

The papers in front of her brought the reality, full force, to the *now*. It felt like someone had pulled the plug on her resolve and let it drain out messy and sad, over every good thing that had happened.

She had a commitment in Kentucky, a debt to pay, a legacy to preserve. Once the application was submitted to the auction in Pebble Beach, once the financials were signed, there was no turning back. The car would be sold and the fantasy would be over.

She pressed a linen napkin under her eyes as the tears brimmed and spilled.

"Maddie?" She turned at the sound of his voice.

"Nick! You can't come in here."

Nick glanced behind him as the door to the ladies room closed. "Looks like I just did."

She turned to the mirror and repaired a smudge of mascara under her eye. "I'm okay. I'm just—"

"Thinking too much." He smoothed his hands over her shoulders and caught her eyes in the mirror. "Tell me, Maddie. Dump it on me. After all we've been through, it can't be that bad."

She steadied herself against the sink, and then looked into his sea green eyes. He was right. It couldn't get much worse than what had already happened.

"When they impounded the car, I was so angry. I'd made the decision to sell her and I was damn well not going to let anything stand in the way. Walt and Flo needed a place to live. I couldn't let the bank take away what they and my grandfather had worked so hard to build."

Tears brimmed again. She swept them away with shaking fingers.

"I know. They're lucky to have someone care for them the way you do. And the farm will be watched over—"

Maddie threw up her hands. "But it won't. That's the problem."

Nick leaned in, rested his forearms on his thighs, and clasped his hands together. "Am I missing something here, because I don't get why--"

"Because they're leaving!" Maddie told him about a message she'd retrieved just before they left for Bacara. "Like Grandpa and my dad. Just up and take off without even consulting me."

Hurt flashed in her eyes, the child in her lashing out.

She dropped down onto a velvet-covered bench and slumped against the wall.

"Walt has cashed in on his pension and bought a house in Pensacola near his brother. They're moving as soon as the escrow closes."

Nick sat beside her and circled her shoulders with an arm. "But that's good news, isn't it? I'll get someone to take care of the place until—"

"That's my Nick. The great fixer. Just throw a wad of money at a problem and it all goes away."

"Really, Maddie. How hard can it be? There must be dozens of people who—"

"You can't just buy another family." Her voice echoed off the walls in the marble-floored room.

"They were all the family I had left," Maddie whispered, afraid her voice would carry outside the door.

Nick took her hands in his. "People move. Things change."

She exhaled at last. "I thought I had it all figured out. Under control. Thought it was my call."

"It is your call, where you're concerned. But you can't huddle everyone around you forever any more than I can buy a family. They haven't abandoned you. They've set you free."

That crazy pinball game started in her middle. Confusion, anger, guilt, and fear.

"But I can't just let the farm go into foreclosure."

"No, *you* can't. That's what I love about you. You're responsible, trustworthy and loyal. You don't have to give that up. But you have choices. You can pay it off, keep it, sell it…do whatever you want with it. Walt and Flo gave you that choice *because* they love you, *and*…and this is a very big *and*…because it was best for them too."

The room, silent as a cocoon, insulated them from the murmuring voices in the dining room, their responsibilities, their fears, and the rest of the universe. Nick stroked the column of her neck with his fingers, giving her the time she needed to work things out in her head.

After a long moment, she slipped her hand in his on a shuddering sigh.

"She's been like an old friend, the Goddess. Always there, the only family I have. Until now, that car has defined my life." His hands warmed hers, the warmth spreading to her heart.

"You're right. I do have a new freedom." She dragged in a deep breath and released it along with a degree of the tension in her face. "If she's the price I have to pay for that freedom, then…I *can*…let her go."

❧

The last of her words came on a whisper, touching a soft spot in his heart. He was fond of the old Caddie himself. The Goddess had brought them together, caught him up in her spell and forced him to turn a corner in his own life. The idea of selling her—of watching Maddie go through that—left him feeling helpless. He could pay off Maddie's mortgage in a heartbeat and the whole problem would go away. But he knew that wouldn't do.

You can't buy family.

Maddie would have to do this her way.

Nick slipped his arm around her shoulders and leaned them back against the wall. When she turned her face to his, he marveled at how his entire world could come down to the blue slate of her eyes. The way her chin came up under a challenge, the way she could spin herself up, hit an emotional peak, then reverse, fall, and somehow land on her feet. It was a trick he hoped to learn and master. He needed that kind of balance. It humbled him. And it aroused him in a way that was dangerous to think about in a public place.

Yes. Maddie would have to do this her way.

Or at least think she was.

He smiled at the scenario playing in his head and stood up.

"What do you say we get out of here, before I have to take you right now on this velvet bench?" He levered her up, spun her out into a quick pirouette, and then back up against him.

Maddie eyed him sideways and he hesitated long enough for the stress lines on her face soften into the grounded woman he'd come to admire. At last, she lifted her chin.

"Don't even think about it."

Suppressing a laugh, he guided her out the door, fingertips at her elbow.

"Too late," he said close to her ear as they wove their way to the table, his rising passion grazing the back of her skirt.

She angled her head toward his shoulder. "Maybe, we should just make our excuses and say good night."

"Hmmm."

Luke stood as they approached the table. "Ha! The old run-to-the-bathroom-when-it's time-to-pay-the-bill routine."

"It didn't work, I see."

Gina scooted out, slipped her arm through Luke's as Nick drew his arm around Maddie's shoulders from behind.

An eyebrow arched, Gina split a look between them. "And what took you so long?"

"We were discussing…family matters," Nick said. He signaled the waiter over Maddie's head.

"Liar." Maddie shoulder shoved him, feeling suddenly like a teenager at the prom. "We were talking about giving you two the slip, but it looks like you're beating us to it."

"Can't let a terrace room go to waste. Especially when Nick's paying," Luke said.

They looped arms and started away until Luke turned back and gave his brother a two finger salute before he rounded the corner and out of sight.

Maddie smoothed her hands over the thick, satiny sheets. Luke had been right about the room. The view from the terrace was spectacular. "A girl could get used to this."

Nick let go a deep laugh, slipped out of his jacket, his shoes and socks, and his pants. "Sure it's not too hoity-toity for you? Because we're pretty close to Lompoc. We could head back there and save me a bundle of cash."

"Too late," Maddie said, mimicking the tone of his earlier comment. She shrugged out of her black-sequined, cropped jacket, thanking Gina silently for pushing her to buy it. She kicked off her shoes. "We're already half naked."

A gold bandeau top came off next.

"I knew you were hiding something under that thing." He snapped off the light at the bedside. "Now you're wearing nothing but moonlight."

A three-quarter moon cast silvery light into the room, lending an aura of fantasy to the moment. Maddie's mind danced into new territory, no longer restricted by dialogs of the past. January fifth was two weeks away. She no longer had to worry about Walt and Flo. Clay was manning the shop, happy as a raccoon in the melon patch, she imagined, without her peering over his shoulder. Her grandfather's passing left a tender spot in her heart, but the constant pounding of grief had subsided. She had made peace with her father and said her goodbyes. Nick's father, whatever his involvement in the progression of events, was no longer a threat. She was in sunny California, away from the wet and the snow, and right now, this room was filled with the intoxicating musky scent of male.

It was their time.

Nothing from the past could come between them.

It was her call and she was going to enjoy every second of it.

She knee-walked across the bed, grabbed him by the tie, and pulled his face close enough to see the gold flecks in his sea green eyes.

"These are only the first course," she said, her nipples peaking under his gaze. "Wait till you see what I've got for dessert."

The heat that ignited the moment they entered the room flamed higher as he joined her on the bed. Covering her lips with his, he gently probed, tasting, teasing, taking her to the next level. She gasped as his hand slipped between her legs, coaxing them apart. His fingers found her wet and ready, his to explore. And explore he did, circling the swelling nub of her desire as the first waves of pleasure expanded. She savored and gave, loving the feel of his fingers inside her, the way he possessed without taking, owned without force, led her to the brink and brought her back until her body begged for release. Every cell ached to give without hesitation all that he asked, all that she had to give.

"Nick," she moaned, barely able to breathe. *Nick. Nick. Nick.* The sound of his name echoed through her soul, familiar, like an anthem she'd known all her life. Building, calling, bringing her home.

Under his expert skill, she rose higher and higher until she nearly collapsed against him. She broke away. "Wait…just let me…"

With trembling fingers, she urgently worked the buttons down the front of his shirt, fully aware of his hand still cupping her heat, his eyes devouring her, his lips ready to begin again.

She pulled the shirt off his shoulders and sailed it across the room. The silvered light fell across his body, already slick with the heat of their passion. She ran her hands over his strong shoulders. The tendons bunched and stretched as he reached for her again.

She slowed herself down, relishing the moment, the soft hair swirling under her fingers as she trailed them down over his chest, over the hardened muscles of his stomach. She nipped his lips playfully, then deepened her kiss as her fingers continued, beneath the band of his silk shorts.

"I think you're ready now," she whispered into his mouth as her hands pushed silk fabric aside.

"I've been ready since I first saw you."

She grasped him hard, matching the intensity of his desire before gently, breathlessly, guiding him toward the overwhelming ache that longed to be satisfied.

Maddie pushed him down on the bed and took the lead. She straddled him, never taking her eyes from his. No hesitation, no doubts, no *over thinking*. Just bodies moving together in a perfect dance.

He needed her. The heat in his eyes told her he longed to take control, to take possession of her. Instead, he allowed her to set the pace, to set herself free. She luxuriated in the scintillating pleasure of his fingers feathering up her sides, his hands cupping her breasts, his thumbs teasing her nipples to tighten and burn, every inch of her stretched to the limit until she lowered herself, ready to take him in. She bent low, and gently kissed him.

"Don't you want to put on your life jacket?" she asked.

Nick slid his hands down over her back side and pressed her closer. "My life is in your hands now. I'm not afraid of the water."

She melted against him, his hands guiding, adding force and rhythm. Her hands splayed over his chest, she arched back, giving in to her own need until she collapsed against him. Gently, he pulled her down, covered a nipple in the heat of his mouth and teased it with his tongue as he rolled them over.

She wrapped her legs around his body as he drove, deeper, faster, to a place she had never dared go before. A place where there were no doubts, no fears, no barriers. A place she could call her own. Her hands gripped his thighs, holding on until the world and everything in it disappeared and it was just the two of them falling through space, in a weightless spiral of pulsing heat.

Maddie lost track of time. The moon had completely disappeared over the edge of the Earth when she raised her head from his shoulder to find him staring down at her. He bent and kissed her brow. "I love you, Madonna Kerrigan," he whispered.

His words filled a place in her heart that had ached for healing. There was no pleasure like the feel of his skin under her hands, no peace outside of his arms, and no limit to what she would give to hear those words over and over again.

"And I love you, Nicholas Berlin."

He smiled and spooned her against his body. She pressed herself to his chest, listening to the slow, powerful beat of his heart as a calm descended over her, erasing everything that had gone before.

Christmas at the Berlin's was indeed the best Maddie could remember since before she learned the truth about Santa. Luke, Gina, and Nick surrounded her in their natural warmth, connecting with her the way lost children often do. They were all orphans in one way or another. But together, they made a family.

Ignoring *Christmas Story* playing on the TV in the background, they played craps on a felt tablecloth on the floor. Nick ended up with all the chips, of course. Luke ordered pizza and Bébé made off with a piece before they caught her. Flo had managed an overnight delivery of her famous gingerbread cookies. Once the four of them consumed all of Santa's peppermint schnapps cocoa, Maddie was content to see Gina and Luke pack themselves off to the big house.

Curled up in bed, Maddie basked in the warm glow of the evening as Nick lit the fire in the bedroom.

"Merry Christmas." She pressed a lingering kiss on his lips. "I can't remember when I've had a better Christmas Eve."

"It's not over yet." He slipped a small package from behind his back.

Maddie stiffened. Her mind jumping to conclusions.

Nick hesitated. "No. Wait. This isn't what you think."

"How do you know what I'm thinking?" But somehow he could.

"You're thinking ahead, and I've got special plans for that." He sat next to her. "But I also know Christmas is a sad time for you. Especially this one. Reminds you of what you've lost."

He scooted closer and leaned in to her side. "It's sad for me too. Makes me think of people who should be around but aren't."

She lifted a shoulder. "I'm okay. You and your family are enough for me. For now."

He handed her a package about the size of a deck of cards. "I wanted you to have this tonight. It might help."

Maddie took it from him, her face losing some of the tension she'd felt earlier in the evening. "But I didn't get you a present."

"You're my present," he said, impatiently. "Just open it."

Maddie slid off the gold satin ribbon, unfolded the silver paper and dropped it in her lap. A picture frame. Gilt, with rich purple velvet on the back. She ran her fingers over the soft fabric, lifting her gaze to his.

Nick looked at her sternly under his brows. "The picture is usually on the other side."

Maddie nodded, turned the little frame over in trembling hands, and caught her breath. The eyes of her father smiled back at her from a tiny black and white photo. Laughing eyes, full of life, love, and promise. The way she had always remembered him. A two-year-old version of herself perched on his shoulders, her arms wrapped around his forehead. She was young enough in the picture that her mother might have been the photographer. An image to hold on to. An image to replace the one of a frail man dying in a prison hospital.

Her heart swelled at the care Nick had put into the gift. His gesture brought tears to her eyes. "Where did you get this?"

Jumping to the dresser, he opened a drawer and pulled out a box no bigger than one that held recipe cards. It was pink, decorated with tiny filigreed flowers that looked like ladies dancing. "It was in here."

Maddie laid the picture in her lap and took the box from him.

"I found it under the front seat of the Jag. It must have gotten bumped under there the day we went to Jalama Beach."

"This was mine." She turned the box over in her hands, her thoughts racing along corridors of childhood memories.

She glanced at Nick.

"He took me to Santa Barbara to see The Nutcracker the Christmas before our trip to Kentucky. He bought it for me at the theater. I guess I forgot about it."

She lifted the lid with her thumbs. The tiny ballerina she remembered was there, reflected in a mosaic of mirrors, a pink fluff of tulle circled her waist.

"He must have kept it all this time." Her throat closed on the words.

Nick slipped an arm around her shoulders. "With the picture in it."

Her eyes glistened a moment before she smiled at him. "It plays *The Waltz of the Flowers*."

She turned a lever to wind up the music box, but it simply spun around. "Darn. It must be broken."

She shook the box gently, the mechanism rattled heavily in its sealed compartment.

Nick took it from her, tried the lever, and rattled the box again. "Maybe we can have it fixed."

Maddie threw her arms around his neck.

"Oh, don't worry about it. It's just a toy." She kissed him warmly. "The picture is what's important. You were right. I needed it tonight. Thank you."

Nick held her long into the night. The cozy fire in the bedroom fireplace dwindled to glowing coals before they exhausted themselves making love and fell asleep in each other's arms.

"Nick? I need help with this zipper."

Music to his ears.

Watching Maddie don the wardrobe she and Gina had put together was a bonus he hadn't planned on. Day after day the payoff was better than throwing dice at the crap table. But this morning the outfit was a gift from his business partner, Jonathan West. They were in a hurry, but that didn't stop him from taking time to appreciate the moment.

Maddie stood at the French doors to the veranda outside the bedroom, the strap on the wet suit zipper dangling over her runner's ass like a cat tail, exposing a delicious slice of white.

He ran his hands appreciatively up her bare skin, kissed the back of her neck, and pulled her hand behind her.

"Just grab a hold of this," he murmured close to her ear. At her sharp intake of breath, he dropped the zipper strap in her hand and guided her arm up.

She turned and poked him in the chest. "You have a one track mind."

"Me?"

"Yes you. But what do you think? Will this work?" She stretched her arms over her head.

"You look good in Neoprene."

"I wasn't thinking of how I look. I saw on the Net the water's fifty-three degrees today. Will this keep me warm?"

"The warmest. How's my stock doing, by the way?"

"What?"

"You spent so much time on that laptop this morning, I figured you were checking up on me again."

Maddie laughed as she used the strap to undo the zipper. "Last I saw, it had plummeted to fifty cents a share."

Her words sent a prickle through his chest before he realized she was joking.

Nick helped her peel the suit over her shoulders. "Good thing you're about to become a Kentucky land baroness. If my stock ever goes to fifty cents, I'll be begging for a place to live."

For the first time since Flo told her the farm was in trouble, Maddie felt a sense of relief.

She'd filed the papers with the Pebble Beach auction in anticipation of getting the Goddess back in time to enter. She'd be committed to a sale if bidders made her one hundred eighty thousand reserve. Enough to pay off the farm and Nick. Enough to finance a new start.

She dismissed a little twinge of sadness at the thought of saying goodbye to the Cadillac. *Things change, people move, life flows on.*

She pulled a Mad Monkey sweatshirt over her head, rolled up the wetsuit and another set of clothes, and stuffed them in a large tote bag she'd found in the kitchen, along with towels, kibble, and fresh water.

Through the kitchen window, she could see her love-struck dog following Nick. Tail slapping back and forth, she shadowed his every move as he loaded surfboards and other gear into a custom van. The sight made Maddie smile, took away the melancholy. Nothing in her experience had led her to believe in fairy tales, until now.

❧

The sun came out from behind the clouds in the little cove, instantly warming Maddie's face and hands. She sat in a beach chair Nick had brought her, admiring the way the kids in his surfing school responded to him. Even the rowdiest, more boisterous of the lot snapped to and listened the moment Nick led them out into the water.

Jonathan West was their idol, a surf icon known for his quick moves, cutting edge gear, and a *take no prisoners* attitude. He'd supplied all the surfboards, wet suits, booties, towels, and food.

But Nick brought something else to the day. A discipline built on respect for the water and respect for each other. Not an idol but a mentor. The father most of these kids didn't have, the one Nick had always wanted.

When the last boy had ridden his first wave, Nick sauntered up the beach and sat beside her, his wetsuit peeled down to his waist.

"That kid there." He pointed to the smallest one of the group. "He's a natural."

"You give them self-respect and dignity." She dug a water bottle out of her tote and passed it to him. "I take it these kids don't get much of that at home."

"These kids? They don't get much of anything. Some of them will end up in juvenile hall. No doubt about it." He tipped his head back and drank.

"And the rest?"

He reached to caress her neck. "The rest might learn to take a chance. Push themselves. Today, they've done something they didn't think they could do. Conquered their fear. They risked falling down and getting smacked in the face by a ton of water. But they kept trying. Trusted their instincts."

Maddie lowered her eyes and scrubbed a piece of driftwood into the sand at her feet. "You'll make a good father one day."

Nick grinned at her broadly. "I'm workin' on it."

Maddie shoulder bumped him. "Speaking of fathers, I got an email from one this morning."

She should have told him earlier. She'd been getting messages from Salazar's daughter for several days. This morning's confirmed their arrival—today. She told Nick about Mr. Salazar and his daughters, the five-window pickup, and how she'd helped them get to Bishop. "It was the least I could do. But here's the thing. He never found work."

Nick ran fingers through his hair, squeezing out droplets of water. A familiar glint of the fun loving Nick brightened his eyes. "And you thought you might get a chance at fixing up that truck if he came and worked for me?"

Maddie threw back her head and laughed. "You know me too well."

She drew his face to hers and kissed him discretely. "But you do need a groundskeeper, and they need a place to live…"

"I suppose we could give him a try. Isabel would certainly love having the girls around."

"Thank you." She moved in closer and kissed him again.

He nicked her chin with his knuckles. "And you're stalling. Zip up your suit."

In her wildest dreams, Maddie never imagined herself surfing during the week between Christmas and New Year's, back home on a California beach. Like the boys he mentored, with Nick by her side, she felt she could conquer the world.

Bébé slept all the way home, exhausted from chasing seagulls and Maddie was close behind. But when Isabel met them at the door of the guest house, Maddie snapped to attention, sensing something not right. "What is it? What's wrong?"

Isabel wrung her hands.

"I don't know. Nothing maybe." She cast worried glances back and forth between Maddie and Nick. "There was a man here, in an old, gray truck. Said he was looking for work."

Maddie laughed light-heartedly. "That would be Mr. Salazar and his daughters."

She pulled Isabel to her, gave her a squeeze, and glanced up to Nick. He pursed his lips, then broke into a warm laugh. He may have looked like his father, but he was definitely made of better stuff.

"You'll love them, Isabel. And Mr. Salazar, he needs someone to look after them while he works," Maddie said. "He made good time getting here."

She scooped up her tote and headed into the house.

"Well, that may very well be," Isabel said, following her into the kitchen. "But this man? He was no Mexican. And he was all by himself.

Chapter 20

Maddie clutched her tote bag tight as the familiar pressure pushed into her chest.

"This man, what did he look like?" Nick frowned, his tone serious. He dropped his sports bag to the ground and pulled out his cell phone.

Maddie and Nick exchanged worried glances.

Isabel's bottom lip quivered. The color drained out of her cheeks.

"He was a *gringo*. Skinny. Not as tall as Maddie. I *tole* him Mr. Nick would be right back. *Tole* him he'd have to leave. He just drove down to the big garage anyway."

Nick craned his neck to see down the gravel drive.

"When was this?" he asked, turning his attention back to Isabel.

"About an hour ago. He drove down there and I started to run after him and here he came back, nearly plowed me over, kicking up dust, then out the driveway. *Vrooom*!"

She clamped her hands to her temples and dug her fingertips into her hair. "*¡Dios Mio!* I knew he was wrong. I knew it."

"It's not your fault, Isabel. I'm glad you were here and that you're safe," Nick said, lifting his phone to his ear. "We should've had that gate fixed by now."

Luke's voicemail message came over the speaker phone. "He's back," Nick said.

Maddie covered her mouth with trembling fingers.

Remnants of yellow crime scene tape fluttered on the hinges of the double garage doors, reminders of the police investigation following the stolen cars from the Berlin collection. The building was larger than Maddie expected, situated down a gravel road near the center of the property. *Secluded. He had to know it was here.* She stood in the doorway, arms folded across her chest, watching Nick survey the area.

"Looks like he lost control in front of the garage when he beat it out of here." Nick pointed out deep grooves in the dirt and a spray of pea gravel over the edge of the circular drive. When his cell phone jangled, Nick answered quickly.

"I thought we decided he wasn't coming home." Maddie heard Luke's voice over the speaker phone. He sounded annoyed.

"Not *Dad.* Jimmy Ray. He was here." Nick's certainty showed in the set of his jaw.

Maddie turned away and peered into the garage as Nick filled Luke in. The idea that Jimmy Ray could reach her in The Compound, as the family fondly called the Berlin estate, put her stomach in distress. She had been naive to think she was safe there. Jimmy Ray got in before, what was to stop him from coming back? He must have been out there, watching. Waiting for them to leave. She shivered at the thought.

Stepping across the threshold, she flipped an industrial lever on a junction box near the door. The overhead shop lights, once state-of-the-art, were dimmed by layers of dust and cob webs, creating an eerie glow horror film set decorators would kill for. It was a car lover's nightmare…or fantasy…depending on your point of view.

Maddie was drawn like a magnet to steel. A dozen old cars were parked haphazard under thick, gray blankets of dust.

Most from the fifties, a couple older. Near the door, three cars had obviously been removed, leaving clean patches on the garage floor where their tires had sat. Jimmy Ray hadn't been picky. He'd grabbed the three vehicles closest to the door.

At the far end of the space, two cars hunkered under tarps. Maddie couldn't resist. Taking a quick peek outside to see that Nick was still on the phone, she headed straight for them.

The first tarp, its folds encrusted with cobwebs, undisturbed for who knew how long, covered a 1953 Oldsmobile Starfire, an early General Motors Motorama gem. Maddie's excitement grew as she peeled back the tarp. She covered her mouth and nose with her sweatshirt sleeve as billowing dust assaulted her lungs.

The metallic green paint and body were in excellent condition. Piles of mouse droppings around and under the car told her the wiring and other soft elements might need some attention.

Like the Flying Goddess, '53s were highly collectible as original Motorama tour show cars.

Maddie dragged back another tarp, protecting her mouth and nose in the crook of her arm. "Holy shit on a shingle."

There was no mistaking the iconic fencing-mask headlight covers of the earliest Corvette.

Some idiot had covered the rare car with the top off and windows removed. The only consolation was that this mistake allowed her to reach under the dash and pop the hood. The sound sent a zing of excitement to places she wouldn't admit to a soul.

Toes carefully inserted into the spaces in the chrome grill, she stepped up, braced her hands on the radiator, and peered into the engine compartment.

Nick stopped halfway through the garage, his heart in his throat. It was the first time he'd been in this place since the night his father had him arrested and taken to juvenile hall, but that wasn't what took his breath away. Maddie's backside propped high over the front end of a white sports car stopped him in his tracks.

A classic, if he'd ever seen one. He pulled out his cell phone and tapped the camera icon.

"Wait. Don't move."

"Nick!" The flash caught Maddie's shocked expression in mid yelp. She shifted to an even more provocative position. "You scared the bejesus out of me."

He snapped another shot. "And you're killin' me."

He moved in, lifted her off the bumper, and set her down. "Looks like you found a little prize."

"Not your typical barn find." She brushed dust off her hands and pants. "This is a first class collector's dream. Not the power plant Corvettes are famous for. V8s came later, but…"

She leaned over the engine compartment. "…this is a Blue Flame Six. Extremely rare."

Forehead compressing over her brows, she brushed at loose debris scattered over the car's manifold, her lips pressed hard together.

"…and rat infested like the rest of the cars in this place."

When she turned to him, he couldn't help sweeping her from head to toe with an approving gaze. Eyes shining bright, high color on her cheeks. Maddie on a tear was a thing to behold.

"Are you listening?"

"Absolutely." He smoothed damp hair off her forehead, trying to reel her in as he realized this was more than a tear. She was agitated in a way he hadn't seen before.

"It's cute," he said, trying to diffuse the tension he saw building in her expression.

"Cute? There's probably less than two hundred and fifty of these left, if that."

She pushed away from his embrace and scooted to the other side of the car. "Help me lift this cover the rest of the way off. Careful. Try not to dump the dust into the cockpit."

Nick complied.

"It's a crime the way these cars have been left to disintegrate." He could tell that she was winding herself up into a major tailspin, and it had nothing to do with the cars. The appearance of Jimmy Ray had set him off too, and he had taken steps to remedy the problem. But for Maddie, it went deeper. He would need to tread lightly.

"Maddie…"

She swiped a cobweb off the classic steering wheel, eyes already threatening to tear. "I doubt there's a wiring harness intact in the whole place."

"Look at this." She pulled at a hole in the upholstery obviously eaten by varmints. Her tone escalated from disbelief to anger.

"Maddie." Nick rounded the front of the car and caught her away from the wrestling match she'd started with the end of the tarp.

"Who leaves cars to rot like this?" She shot her arms over her head.

"Maddie." He gathered her in against him, felt her trembling, and held her close until she sobbed out her frustration. At last, she raised her head and looked into his eyes.

"He came after me, Nick. He said he would and he did."

"Luke's posting a black and white at the front gate until Jimmy Ray's behind bars. You are safe," Nick said, though he wasn't entirely convinced. He tucked her against him and rubbed the side of her arm. "I won't leave you alone until we've got him."

"I suppose this was a good thing. A heads up." He could hear the doubt in her voice.

"A slip up if you ask me." He guided her out of the garage. "He's getting reckless, making mistakes."

Together they pushed the doors closed. "Let's go get changed. Luke's on his way over with the sheriff. We'll figure it out."

❧

Maddie's shoulders hunched up around her ears. The detectives had swarmed over the area for hours, shot photos of tire tracks from every friggin' angle, and grilled poor Isabel until she was ready to drop. They warned the family to lock their doors and put a temporary lock on the front gate. The sun had nearly dropped below the horizon by the time they left.

Great. Jimmy Ray was an "A" student of Criminal 101. She doubted locks would stop him from getting what he wanted. She pulled her knees up to her chin and wrapped her arms around them, but that didn't stop the shaking.

The day had started out balmy. One of those magical California days impossible to imagine in the Midwest. But, with the dusk came a change in the wind's direction. The highs of the desert fought with the lows of the Pacific, and the ocean had won. Despite the chilly breeze, Maddie's shaking had nothing to do with the cold. He was out there. Watching. She knew it.

She could almost smell the oily tobacco on his fingers and feel him touching her skin.

She had been living a fantasy. And the fantasy had come to the end.

"Luke's right, Maddie." Gina's voice startled her. She looked up from the lounge on the guesthouse veranda to see the three of them staring at her. Had she been that far away? Inside her fear? She forced her knees down and rolled her shoulders out of a cramp.

"He's not after you, honey, he's after the car." Gina's voice was soft, assuring. Maddie appreciated her concern.

"Which is a good thing," Luke suggested. "The Cadillac wasn't here."

"But he *thought* it was," Nick said. He threw a blanket around Maddie's shoulders. "And he'll keep coming back until he gets what he wants."

Maddie squeezed her eyes shut and pressed her fingers hard between knitted brows.

"Let's have a fire." Nick lit the gas burner in the firepit and they all huddled toward its warmth.

"The bad news is," Luke said, hesitantly as if he were unsure how his message would be received. "The cars *will* be here tomorrow…"

Maddie's teeth still chattered. She raised her hands to the warmth of the flames.

"It's good news, Luke. You can relax. Life goes on, things change, people move on."

She sent Nick a meaningful look.

Luke stood and shoved his hands in his pockets. The eucalyptus logs snapped, sending their fragrance up in smoke. "I've got some other information that might shed a light. The detectives in Long Beach had a little chat with the boys we arrested down at the docks."

"Georgie and Leon?" Maddie asked.

"Yeah. Seems Leon was upset at the way Maddie was treated. And hungry. Spilled his guts. 'Paying it forward', he kept saying. His price was a couple of Big Macs."

Maddie suppressed a smile, then shook her head. "He's a victim…A crook, for sure. But I'd say he got exploited by the crooks *and* the detectives."

"The detectives have a job to do," Luke said, defensively. "Anyway, for whatever reason, he rolled on Jimmy Ray, big time. Says he was crazy looking for something in the Cadillac. Wouldn't tell Leon or Georgie what it was. Tried to buy more time from the crane operator, but got slapped for it."

Nick poured Maddie a glass of cabernet. She took it with a steady hand. "I'd say maybe Jimmy Ray was glad the authorities interrupted the deal because the car's still in the country."

She sipped her wine. "Jimmy Ray said they'd cheated him out of his share. They, meaning our fathers and Corinne, stole from him. I assumed it was money. But he did talk about a diamond."

Nick sat down next to Maddie again and circled his arm around her shoulders. "Whatever it is, he's bold. I mean, showing up here in broad daylight? That's nuts."

"Desperate," Maddie said. "Maybe the sheikh put the pressure on. After all, he didn't deliver the goods."

Luke paced around the fire.

Gina followed him with her eyes. "A sheikh on the other side of the planet is not enough of a threat. There's something visceral about the guy. He almost gets caught and comes back to the scene of the crime? Makes a show of it?"

Maddie shrank down into herself again. She wanted it over. Wanted him gone. Nothing wonderful that had happened to her since connecting up with Nick would continue as long as Jimmy Ray was out there. Not selling the car or saving her grandfather's property, or launching her career, or even, falling in love. The fact that Nick was willing to give up his past and his present to make a future for them was totally and completely negated by the knowledge that Jimmy Ray was still…out…there.

Maybe even watching them at that very moment. The pressure in her chest crowded her heart into a corner. She stared at the fire, forcing herself to breathe. The circle of light around the veranda rendered the surrounding chaparral that much darker, more threatening.

The police had done what police do but offered no real solution. All this blah, blah, blah was getting them nowhere. A spark of anger launched a growing heat in her center. If she had to wait for someone else to do something, she'd explode. She would not be made a victim again.

The idea hit her in the gut first, pulling her to the edge of her seat. She threw the blanket off.

"He wants the car," she said, touching each of them with her gaze, "…let's give it to him."

Her voice sounded more confident than she felt.

"Don't you worry." Luke waved her idea away like annoying smoke. "We don't have to take a risk like that."

Maddie shot out of her seat. "Don't patronize me. I mean it."

Gina's eyes widened. "You want to set a trap for him?"

"Yeah. No black and white at the gate. No visible changes at all. Make a big show when the cars come back from Long Beach. Draw him out. Leave her right out in the open, where he can see her. Then catch him in the act, whatever it turns out to be."

Nick exchanged worried looks with his brother. "Can you get guys to cover it?"

"It could work," Luke said. "Or it could go wrong ten ways from Sunday."

❧

"Oh, I see where *this* is going." Nick moved in and nuzzled her neck. He circled his arm around the slim beaded waistline of her fifties classic gown. The lights in the hotel mirror framed them in a warm glow. Maddie admired the contrast of her white skin against the aquamarine gown and had to admit she was excited about spending a formal evening with Nick. She had taken extra care to give her short bob a fifties flair and added a layer of gloss to deep red lipstick. Nick kissed her where a pearl clasp at the nape of her neck was the only thing standing between sanity and oblivion. She felt him harden against her.

Maddie turned in his arms and straightened his bow tie. "Too late. The lipstick is on. We're already a bit tardy."

"This is unfair you know." Nick rolled his eyes to the ceiling and let go a deep sigh. He held a full-length beaded wrap, a purchase, along with the gown, she'd made at a vintage clothing boutique in Carmel.

Maddie turned to the mirror, letting him slip the wrap around her shoulders. "How so? It's just dinner."

"To benefit the United Way and the Boys and Girls clubs," he said, his tone playfully mocking. "You vowed never to be cheesecake on my arm at a hoity toity benefit, now here I am a penguin on your arm."

Maddie's eyes glittered at him in the mirror. "And a very handsome penguin you are. I just hope we haven't overdone it."

Her outside was wrapped in sparkle and shine, but her insides shivered with nagging fear, and it wasn't pre-auction jitters. Jimmy Ray hadn't taken the bait. From the moment it arrived at The Compound, the Cadillac sat in full view in the guesthouse carport.

The real Mr. Salazar had arrived with his daughters, to Isabel's delight, and a professional cleaning company had been hired to clear twenty years of dust from the car garage. Two of the workers were undercover police officers assigned to the case. Detailers worked in the carport polishing the Goddess to perfection. If Jimmy Ray had been out there watching, he'd kept himself out of sight. The night before the auction, Jonathan West had insisted they use his Surf Expo transport to deliver the Goddess to Pebble Beach and Nick had agreed. It was easy to load a vehicle inside and the type of vehicle that naturally drew a crowd. Even if Jimmy Ray saw them load the Goddess, he would think twice about making a move on her in transit.

Maddie's stomach churned. If only the situation had been resolved before the auction. She could have done without the added stress.

This evening's event, billed as a pre-auction gala, was like none Maddie had ever attended. Nick called it right when he suggested they do a little shopping in Carmel before dinner. The soaring white tent was a thing of grandeur. Inside were linen covered tables adorned with china and fresh flowers, women in full length gowns, and champagne glasses floating in bejeweled fingers. A parade of Michael Bublé tunes covered soft murmurs of conversation. Maddie pulled in a deep breath and stalled at the entrance.

"I guess the joke was on me. It doesn't get any *hoity toitier* than this."

"Wait until somebody asks me a car question. The only answer I have memorized is 'Dagmar tits'."

Maddie tightened her grip on his arm, put on her smile, and looked straight ahead. "That was Dagmar *bumpers*, smart ass."

Nick guided her into the crowd. "Let's get some champagne."

"Maddie? Maddie Kerrigan."

She turned her head toward the man's voice. Who on earth would know her in this place? But she immediately recognized the thick white hair combed to perfection, bulky torso cinched by a silver-buckled belt, and fancy stitched cowboy boots.

"Marsh," she said, extending her hand. "I never expected to see someone I knew in this crowd."

"We usually come here in the summer, but my company was tagged as one of the sponsors for this special event, so..." He pulled a glowing silver-haired woman to his side. "The auction was a special treat added in. You remember my wife, Ilene."

"Of course. So nice to see you again." Maddie smiled at her, glad for a break in the tension that had, until now, made it difficult to put on a pleasant face.

Ilene shook Maddie's hand and glanced immediately to Nick, as had nearly every other woman in the tent. "This is my…friend…Nick Berlin. Nick, Marshall Whiting, from Cheyenne. I restored a forty Ford for him last year."

Marsh clapped Nick hard on the back. "Mad Monkey is the best in the country, if you ask me."

He turned to Maddie. "I was real sorry to hear about your grandpa. Forgive me for saying, but I heard he had a heart attack sitting right in that Cadillac of yours. Is that true?"

"Thanks, Marsh. Yes." The image of her grandfather slumped behind the wheel came up in her mind's eye and passed through, leaving her with only thoughts of fondness. She was making progress.

"I think he knew he was going and wanted to be with her. The Goddess is in the auction tomorrow, in fact."

"No." Marsh stopped a waiter passing with a tray of champagne flutes, scooped one up, and waited for the others to follow suit. "Well, to the Flying Goddess then. Good luck, Maddie."

"To the Goddess," Nick said, his eyes smiling brightly into Maddie's. She'd handled the moment better than she expected. *Things change, people move on.*

"Shall we find ourselves a table?" Nick said. "You know, Maddie and I were in Cheyenne not long ago."

She bumped him with her elbow as they slipped into the crowd.

❧

Too good to be true. After only an hour of hanging around the edges of the parking lot trying to figure a way in, Jimmy Ray spotted it on the ground. Someone had dropped their event ticket and lanyard next to a portable hand washing unit. Jimmy froze and surveyed the surrounding area. No one rushing to look for it. He strolled over as best he could on a leg that screamed with every step, snagged it up, and looped it over his neck as if it were his own.

A *lookiloo* ticket, not a bidder's registration. That was okay by him. He was just going to *lookiloo* until he found what he was looking for.

No hurry.

No mistakes.

Lucky for him this wasn't the official *Concours d'Elegance*, or there would be much greater security. Still, it was good to have a ticket and a lanyard. He would blend in with the crowd in his boxy silk shirt and brown pants.

He circled around behind the tent where the rich folks were having their kick off soirée, to the larger viewing tent where the early arrival cars were stored. The public event would not open officially until the next morning. That worked in his favor. There would be fewer people around. Still, he would have to work fast. At least now he knew what he was looking for. If his luck held, he could remove the steering wheel knob without drawing attention and be on the road before midnight.

The Cadillac had been one of the first to arrive. Jimmy figured she would be near the back of the tent, and his hunch paid off. When he slipped through a junction in the heavy fabric, she was only two cars away.

Smart asses. Thought they could fool ol' Jimmy Ray.

Didn't know who they were dealing with. You don't spend half your life in prison without learning a thing or two about set ups. And that fancy surf show semi? Just made it easier to follow them down the road. Jimmy Ray was in his prime. Ready for the party. It was part of his exit plan.

Know the rules of the game.

Know the players.

Follow your instincts.

❧

Nick spotted Louise from across the room and caught his breath. She wasn't supposed to arrive until the auction. Maddie and Ilene sat next to him at the table, their heads together deconstructing the sauce on the rack of lamb. Wiping his mouth with his napkin, he stood. "Will you excuse me a minute please, ladies?"

Maddie's head came up. He motioned to the bar area. "I'll just be a second."

He wove his way across the tent through tables and clusters of guests and came up to stand behind his old friend.

"What are you doing here?" Nick asked, his impatience undisguised.

Louise's eyes lit up.

"Well, hello. It's great to see you too," she purred, and lifted her mixed drink in a mock toast. She leaned in close and her gaze shot in Maddie's direction. "Is that *her*?"

Nick glanced over his shoulder. Maddie was still in serious conversation with Marsh and his wife. "Yeah. I'm sorry. I just didn't expect to see you until tomorrow."

"Come on. How could I pass this up?" She gestured with her glass at the elaborate display of desserts on a banquet table next to the bar.

"Turn around. I don't want her to see me talking to you."

Nick pushed out a sigh. His friend was likely tired after driving straight through from Vegas. Seeing her there ahead of schedule was a shock, but he was glad to see that she'd made it. She looked lovely, and somehow in character in her white silk blouse, and long, black skirt. Replace the pearl choker with a black bow tie and she could be running his favorite craps table. He lifted the plastic folder at the end of her lanyard. "I see you've got your bidder's ticket."

"Yup."

"You understand how this is going to go, right?"

"Perfectly. Nicky Boy is finally ready to gamble everything on love."

Caught. He pressed his lips together, then grinned. Louise had been a good friend, filled a void in his life while he worked on his image as the up and coming executive.

"You were right all along, Louise. You know me too well."

"No bid too high?"

"Go through the ceiling if you have to," he said, glancing quickly over his shoulder. "See you tomorrow. We'll all get together at the end of the event."

He had just turned to see Maddie scoop a spoonful of crème brulée into her mouth when the commotion started. Their eyes met over the heads of seated guests. She shot up, tipping her folding chair over and ran a zigzag pattern toward the exit. Nick caught up with her there.

"Stay here," he said, pushing past her, even though he knew she wouldn't.

❧

Jimmy Ray had his Slim Jim halfway inserted in the Cadillac's driver's side window when he spotted the attendant. "Shit," Jimmy said under his breath.

"I'm sorry sir, you can't…what are you doing?" The man's face contorted, sliding from confusion to fear. Jimmy Ray swung the Slim Jim. Dark red bloomed instantly from a gash along the man's cheek. He went down and shielded himself from further blows.

Worthless has-been rent-a-cop.

Jimmy needed to work fast. He crammed the tool back inside the door panel until it caught, then he pulled up, popping the door lock.

Shouts came from outside the tent.

"In here," the old man yelled.

Jimmy Ray knelt down and gave him the stink eye. The shouts grew louder and the first of the security guards broke through the entrance.

"Fuck, fuck, fuck." Jimmy didn't have time to use the screwdriver. The backup plan was more destructive, but faster. He pulled a ball peen hammer out of his belt and whacked, succeeding only in spinning the knob.

"Over there," one of the guards yelled. Footsteps coming. Jimmy panicked, hyperventilating. He hated that about himself. He pressed his hand against the man's mouth, glared into his eyes, holding the hammer like he'd waylay him if he had to. The old man's eyes widened and he shook his head.

No time. Jimmy Ray had to make his move or it was all over. He sprang back to the steering wheel, took another whack, and the knob went flying, bouncing once on the seat before Jimmy juggled it into his hand.

"You! Stop where you are!"

He could see them now. Uniformed guards. A taser. Shit!

Whirling, the hammer still in his grip, he inadvertently struck out a window on some prohibition era coupe before throwing himself down.

He crawled back to the wall, the pain so intense in his knee he could hardly breathe. He used the hammer head to clear the tent's weighted edge and scooted under. He could hear men shouting orders to circle around as he hobbled for the parking lot, the steering wheel knob in one hand, the hammer in the other. More voices joined the shouting. Jimmy's heartbeat went into overdrive but his knee was not cooperating.

He wouldn't make it all the way to his car, but if he cut through the line of Porta Potties…

Nick caught up with Maddie as she stopped to kick off her heels. "I saw him. At the back of the tent," she said, gasping.

Nick leveled his gaze on her eyes.

"I've got this." He gripped her by the shoulders. "Stay here. Just…please."

He angled across the lawn anticipating Jimmy Ray's goal. When Jimmy burst out between the Porta-Potties, arms flailing, Nick was waiting for him. He caught Jimmy Ray under the chin with a forearm block.

"It's over, asshole," he said, rubbing his arm. "Don't make me do that again."

Jimmy Ray gasped and clutched his throat, then defiantly scrambled to his feet.

"That's pretty big talk for an office boy," he said, panting. He wiped blood off his lip. "Now look what you went and did. That's assault."

"Yeah, and this is payback." Nick shot a right to Jimmy's chin, taking him all the way down. He wrestled the knob and the hammer from Jimmy's grip.

"That's mine. Your father and your bitch's mother stole it from me."

"You're willing to go to federal prison over a fucking steering wheel knob?"

Jimmy stuck out his chin defiantly. "Not the knob, *Junior*, the diamond. My idea, my share."

People were coming. Maddie's voice was among the shouts, giving directions. Nick clutched the knob in his fist and studied the swirling pattern on the top.

"A diamond, huh?" He remembered now. His father had told him about the knob. How it had Maddie's mothers initials on it. Cast it himself. Proof that the car was the one his father had bought for Corinne. The car Corrine had kept and left to her daughter.

He turned it over in his hand, ran his thumbnail over a crude seam down each side. Whatever his father had done, someone had done him one better.

"Let's just see about that."

Balancing the knob on the cement sidewalk, Nick reared back and whacked it as hard as he could with the hammer, splitting it in half along the seams. It was true. A large stone was lodged in its hollowed out center.

Jimmy's eyes grew wide. "It's mine. Just give it to me and I'll let you go."

"*You'll* let *me* go?" Nick laughed as he grabbed the stone and held it up to the parking lot lights. A poorly executed perfect cut, the stone reflected back nothing but rainbow hues. A dead giveaway to a fake. He and Louise had entertained themselves after hours many times debating the value of casino patrons' oversized chunks of glass. He turned back to Jimmy, yanked the lanyard off his neck, and laid the stone on the plastic-covered ticket envelope. A real diamond was nearly impossible to read through the way it refracted light. Nick shook his head.

"Mr. Wasserman will be glad someone found his ticket," Nick said, eyeing the little man on the ground. Jimmy Ray's eyes gleamed with contempt.

Nick held the stone up to the light again.

"This is a huge rock, Jimmy Ray. Seventy, maybe eighty carats. Big enough to set you up for life." He huffed a breath over the stone, which immediately fogged up. "If it were real."

At that moment, Maddie ran up, along with the two uniformed guards and a following of curious guests from the dinner tent.

Nick nodded to Maddie and held his hand up. "Keep them back."

Jimmy moaned, holding his knee. "You're full of shit. Your father put it in there himself. It's a real as it gets!"

"Shall we find out?" A diamond would shatter under the hammer's blow just like a fake, but Nick already knew the truth. He raised the hammer high for effect.

"Noooooo!" Jimmy wailed.

Maddie gasped and covered her mouth with her hand. Nick slammed the hammer down. The stone smashed under the blow, half of it was a jagged chunk, the other half disintegrated into a pile like sea salt.

Jimmy Ray rolled onto his side and moaned. He grabbed his knee with one hand and held the other out to fend off the guards. "I'm injured. Be careful," he said as they dragged him to his feet.

Maddie rushed into Nick's arms.

"It's over," he said softly, kissing the top of her head. To the guards he said, "This is the guy I told you about. Get him out of here."

Chapter 21

"Is it working?" Maddie rose partially out of the steaming water and refilled their champagne flutes. Nick dipped his fingers into the delicate cleft between her legs to find the source of her heat, increasing the pressure until she arched against him.

"Seems to be," he said, his voice lazy, absorbed in the activity.

Maddie exhaled, trying desperately to postpone her pleasure. "I was talking about your hand."

"Oh this?" Nick raised his right hand out of the ice bucket, stretched his fingers a little, then plunged them back into the cold. "I'll never play piano again, but I never really played before, so…"

His eyes shifted to the layer of bubbles caressing the upper curves of her breasts.

"I still can't believe you smashed that diamond without knowing for sure it was fake."

"I was sure enough," he said, sliding deeper into the water. "Fakes throw off color in the light." He shifted his eyes down and to the left. Maddie raised a brow at him.

"Interesting concept," Maddie murmured against his lips. He was holding something back, she was sure of it.

She moved her hand, agonizingly slow, from the hollow just below his rib cage down over his stomach and beyond. She gripped him there, tightened, and slid her hand out. By the look on his face, she imagined she had emptied his brain of all but one thought.

"So what do you think happened to the real one? If there *was* one?" She lifted up, allowing her breasts to break the surface of the water. His gaze triggered an instant response.

He drained his glass and set it down. "Can we talk about this later?"

Maddie smiled into his eyes, pulled his face close and kissed him deeply. "Any time you're ready."

She let herself melt into the moment, play the siren, knowing where it would lead.

Nick answered with his own searing kiss, his tongue teasing, drawing hers in to play. Her body was slick in the soapy water. He smoothed his hands over her stomach to cup her breasts, graze her nipples with his thumbs, and trail his lips down the column of her neck.

By the time they'd finished covering every inch of each other's anatomy, spent their last ounce of energy, and melted into a searing release, Maddie's skin had pruned and the water had cooled.

"Let's move our operation to the bed," Nick suggested. "Before I dissolve and swirl down the drain with the bath water."

Sated beyond her wildest dreams, Maddie snuggled under his arm. "I never figured you for a tough guy."

Nick snorted a soft laugh. "I haven't run a forearm block on a guy since college football."

"But you have an effective right."

Nick raised his hand. "I have a bruised right and I'm not thinking of using it that way again anytime soon."

Nick slid his arms around her, pulling her into a perfect spoon. She settled her hips against his. How had she ever slept without him? How had she breathed? How had she lived?

He lifted her hand to his lips and kissed her palm.

"I love you, Maddie Kerrigan," he said, his voice husky with desire. She turned in his embrace, slid a leg between his, and folded into his heat.

ං

The announcer's voice echoed through the sound system in the soaring main tent as the Goddess rolled forward. Bright stars flashed on the pointed tips of her Dagmar bumper and took a slow, synchronized spin as she pulled under the lights on the main auction stage.

"Next up, top billing on our 2012 Carmel *Classix* Charity event, number tee-*wenty*-nine on your brochure, the Mad Monkey Restorations' 1953 Cadillac Eldorado. Folks, this is a frame off restoration by one of the country's up and coming artists."

Maddie glanced at Nick and took a deep, trembling breath. He could see the anxiety in her eyes. Everything she had worked for, everything she had sacrificed and traded off, her past and her future, was caught up in this moment. With a confident smile, he squeezed her hand, and the moment expanded in his eyes. This was not the end of a dream, it was the beginning.

"Some of you may recognize Maddie Kerrigan below the podium here," the announcer went on, "The owner and genius behind Mad Monkey Restorations. Maddie come up and give everybody a wave."

Nick let go of her hand and stepped back to admire the woman who had restored his faith in love. The sight of her took his breath away. She worked that practiced, runway walk across the front of the stage. The tantalizing curve of her runner's ass and her own set of Dagmar tits wrapped up in a sharp pressed white mechanics suit. The searing red bandeau top peeking through the unbuttoned front matched her *fuck me* stilettos, glossy lips, and the filmy silk scarf tied around the long column of her neck. He could almost feel the testosterone building in the room as she took the few remaining steps to the platform. A cheer and a few whistles went up when she turned and waved to the crowd, her smile beaming self-assurance and, damn it, raw sex appeal.

"All right, let's get the bidding started…" The announcer's voice left off and the auctioneer began his chant. *"I have a starting bid of fifty thousand, fifty thousand, do I hear sixty? Fifty thousand, someone give me sixty…"*

❧

Maddie's gaze shifted from the car to the crowd. This was it. The real thing. Nearly all of the cushioned folding seats in the oversized tent were filled with bidders. She had to force herself to breathe.

"Only fifty thousand?" Nick leaned down and whispered in her ear. "What is he doing? You said the car was worth at least one eighty."

Maddie's hands twitched but she held them at her sides, and kept a smile pasted on her face. The auctioneer's cadence sped up. "Don't worry. They start low to get the action going and more bidders involved. I set the reserve at one eighty, so we're guaranteed not to sell below that."

The auctioneer's assistants spread out among the crowd, visually tagging the active bidders. Maddie also noticed that one of the phone attendants had gotten a call.

"…I have one hundred in the back of the room. One hundred, who'll give me one ten…"

Marshall's hand shot up. "One fifty."

"…I'm bid one fifty, one fifty folks for this one off 1953 Motorama Classic Cadillac…" The auctioneer worked the room driving the bidding at a faster pace.

A woman in the front row sat at attention with a white-knuckle grip on her bidder's paddle. She had missed a few bids at the beginning, but was getting into the swing, her main competition a caller at the phone desk, a gentleman standing on the sidelines in the back of the room, and Marshall.

"…I'm bid one fifty, who'll give me one eighty…"

Maddie's racing pulse shot adrenaline through her veins. An assistant came down from the podium and stood next to her. *Predictable.* The auctioneer would try to push the bidding over the reserve if he could, but his assistant was at the ready in case Maddie got desperate.

She was nervous. And she was scared. But she held her chin high, her smile firmly in place. Nick slipped his arm around her waist. She would never feel desperate again.

At last, the lady in the front row broke the lull, raised her paddle and called out, "One eighty."

"…I have one hundred and eighty thousand dollars down in front. One hundred and eighty. Ladies and gentlemen, the reserve is off and this fifties classic dream car will have a new home today…" He changed up his cadence to push the crowd at tongue-twisting speed.

"One hundred and eighty thousand, who'll give me two? I've got one eighty, who'll give me two. One eighty is the bid, have I got two?…"

The nod came from the phone desk.

"Two *hundred* thousand," the auctioneer sang.

The woman's paddle went up. "Two fifty."

Maddie grazed Nick's hand, pulled it tighter into hers, and dragged in a breath. The man on the sidelines sat and waved the auctioneer's assistant away.

"Two seventy-five." Marsh gave it another try. Maddie let out her breath. She'd love Marsh to have the car, but she didn't want to feel that he'd underwritten any part of Mad Monkey Restorations when all was said and done. He was a friend, but also a shrewd businessman.

"I have two seventy-five one time. Two seventy-five, do I hear three? I have two seventy five, two seventy five…" Marsh's eyes gleamed.

"I have two seventy-five one time, two seventy-five the second time…"

"Three hundred." The call came from the phone desk.

The woman in the front row sat on the edge of her chair. "Three twenty-five," she countered with a satisfied grin.

Marsh gave Maddie a little salute and shook his head at the attendant who had been standing by to take his bid.

"…I have three hundred and twenty five thousand dollars," called the auctioneer without breaking his song, *"…Am I bid three fifty?"*

"Four hundred." The bidder on the phone upped the ante again. The room fell silent, and for a fraction of a second, the auctioneer faltered. Nick squeezed Maddie's hand so hard she thought her fingers would go numb.

"Four…hundred…thousand is bid. I have four hundred, going one time… four hundred…"

The woman in the front row bowed her head for an agonizing moment and Maddie's heart stopped. It shouldn't matter to her at all. But somehow it was better to see the person's face. The person who would ultimately drive away with the Flying Goddess. Maddie swallowed hard against a sting at the back of her throat.

"…four hundred for the second…"

Maddie's heart stopped. The Goddess was almost gone.

The woman hesitated, then shot out of her chair. "Four fifty."

The murmurs that started when the bid hit four jumped to a rumble that spread through the room like a wave. Maddie covered her mouth with her hand. She knew the Goddess would go for more than one eighty, thought it might go to two, but she never dreamed the bidding would go to more than twice that much.

"Four hundred and fifty thousand for this 1953 Cadillac Eldorado fifty year anniversary edition, an icon in the automotive world. The Flying Goddess, ladies and gentlemen, and worthy of her name. I have four hundred and fifty going one time, do I hear another bid? Four hundred and fifty thousand dollars, going for the second time…"

The gavel slammed down.

"Sold! At four hundred and fifty thousand dollars to the lovely lady in the front row, congratulations…"

Maddie blinked. That was it? Congratulations? Shouldn't the world be coming to an end, or at least stop turning? But there was nothing but the sound of her heart beating in her ears.

Nick squeezed her hand. She let go a long sigh that purged twenty years of sorrow from her soul.

"How can you eat?" Maddie slipped back into her red high heels. They pulled into the restaurant parking lot. She had changed into a curve hugging, long sleeved black dress and at

Nick's suggestion left the bandeau top on underneath to span the plunging neckline. "My stomach is so woozy from all the excitement. I don't think I can eat for a week."

Nick guided her along a low, stone wall to the restaurant entrance. "You don't have to eat if you don't want to. I just want you to meet a friend of mine for a drink."

Maddie fell into a syncopated rhythm with his walk, melding to his side as if they were born that way. "Oh! There's the woman who bought the Goddess. Look, out on the terrace."

Nick craned his neck in the direction she nodded. "You're right. That's her. Shall we say hello?"

"Oh, no, I don't want to intrude."

"But it seems like she's alone. Let's go over." His fingers went to the small of her back and urged her forward.

As they arrived at the table, a waiter brought three menus. The woman, older than Maddie first thought, rose and extended her hand.

"Miss Kerrigan. What a surprise." Her eyes twinkled like a mom meeting her son's prom date.

Maddie shook her hand and returned her warm smile. "I hope we're not intruding, I just wanted to say congratulations personally. You got yourself a beautiful automobile, Ms…"

"Louise." She glanced at Nick. "It was a privilege to bid on her."

Maddie dug into her clutch bag for a Mad Monkey business card. "I know they gave you the complete package and a voucher to repair the damage to the steering wheel, but if you ever have any questions, feel free to call me personally."

The woman hesitated and glanced at Nick again.

Maddie sensed something in the exchange. "What? Is there a problem?"

Nick pursed his lips a moment, then grinned at the two of them.

"No. No problem." He slid out a chair for Maddie. "I think you should sit down though."

The waiter brought over a champagne bucket stand. A bottle of Dom Perignon rested in the ice.

Maddie let go a nervous laugh. She cocked her head first at Louise, then to Nick who waited patiently while the server popped the cork and filled three flutes.

"Thank you." Nick dismissed the man with a gracious smile. When he had gone Nick turned to the women and lifted his glass. Maddie followed his example, baffled but ready to play the game. Whatever it was. The day had been full of mixed emotions but overall, things had turned out according to her plan. She would learn how to deal with the consequences.

"It's a beautiful day." Nick looked away at the Pacific spreading beyond the green rolling hills on the bluff.

"Oh, for heaven sakes, Nick, just tell her." Louise lifted her glass and sipped.

Maddie's heart felt like it had opened up, her life blood blowing through without stopping to beat. *What on earth?*

Nick shifted his gaze to the table in front of him for a moment and finally to Maddie's eyes. "Louise was working for me."

Louise let out a little laugh and an apologetic grin. "I'm sorry for the deception, Maddie. It was nearly as exhausting as the bidding itself."

Nick sighed as if a burden had been lifted. "Don't give me 'exhausting'. You were enjoying yourself playing loose with someone else's money."

Louise's eyes gleamed and she winked at Maddie. "I've made a career of it."

Maddie set the champagne flute down on the table, her arms suddenly weak. "What?"

She watched in disbelief as Louise fished in her handbag and then dropped a familiar set of keys on the table. The keys to the Flying Goddess.

"Consider her your engagement present, Maddie. The Goddess and every other car in The Compound garage, the house, the property, and everything I own, including my heart. I want you to marry me."

Maddie lifted the keys and closed her hand around them. "But you paid nearly half a million—"

Nick held up his hand. "You'll need to make a donation. To the Boys and Girls Club."

Then his eyes softened, the tease gone out of them. "Marry me, Maddie."

History was repeating itself. The car was once used as a bribe to keep Maddie's mother as Nicholas' Senior's mistress, now Nick was doing the same, with one all important twist. He had put his heart and soul into the bargain. It was there, crystal clear in those maddening blue-green eyes.

"Does this deal include the Corvette?"

Nick let go a throaty laugh and gave the red scarf at her neck a playful tug. "You drive a hard bargain, Maddie Kerrigan. I was hoping I could keep that one for myself, but…oh hell yeah. Why not?"

She picked up her glass and waited for them to do the same. "Then, yes, Nick Berlin. I will marry you." She threw her arms around his neck and kissed him.

"And I'll let you drive the Corvette. *Sometimes.*"

Chapter 22

Highway one stretched out before them, a flowing ribbon of road hugging the cliffs along the central Pacific Coast. A classic car on a classic lovers' drive. With the heater on and the top down, they cruised toward home.

"Pull over here, Nick. Let's watch the sunset." In an inset cove, a veil of water fell into the aqua blue of the ocean below. "Isn't that the most beautiful thing you've ever seen?"

Maddie knew her excitement was over the top, but she couldn't hold back. Her joy was so thrilling, his love so complete, the only thing left to do was to bask in it and hope she could fulfill his dreams as well.

Nick steered the car to the side of the road, shut down the engine and studied her face. "It's nice. But not the most beautiful thing I've seen by a long shot."

Maddie felt the heat rise in her cheeks. He brushed wisps of hair away from her forehead and kissed her there.

"Oh, I nearly forgot. There's something else for you in the glove compartment."

Maddie lifted her brows. "What?"

He handed her a small package.

She slid across the seat and opened it. Inside was the pink music box her father had kept. She gave Nick one more questioning look and rattled the box.

"Just open it," Nick said on a laugh.

Maddie lifted the lid with her thumbs. The little ballerina danced to the tinkling music. But it was the ring tucked between folds of pink velvet that took Maddie's breath away. A large sapphire, the color of her eyes sparkled in a nest of diamonds. He lifted it out and placed it on her finger. "You can't exactly wear the Flying Goddess."

"It's beautiful. And you fixed the music box." She wound it up and let it play again. "It still rattles…"

Nick glanced away for a moment as if collecting his thoughts. "Yeah. It still rattles. But it plays perfect, just the way it is."

Maddie cocked her head, caught the faraway look in his eye. Mysterious Nick. She loved that part of him too. "Thank you, Nick. For everything."

"It's just like the first time, Maddie. The first time we sat together in this car, it was like slipping into a dream. A magical car and a beautiful woman with the longest legs I'd ever seen."

He laid his arm across the seat back, stretched out his legs, and lifted his eyes to the sea. Feeling his heart beat next to hers, Maddie leaned her head on his shoulder and toyed with the buttons on his shirt.

"When I was a little girl, I was fascinated by the hood ornament on the front of the car, a flying goddess made of chrome. I asked Grandpa why the lady was there. He told me that's why he named her the Flying Goddess. 'Follow the Goddess' he would say, 'and you'll never lose your way'."

"I used to sit behind the wheel, pretend to drive, and dream about all the places she would take me, the things I'd see…." She swallowed a twinge of sadness and let it pass.

"Today when she was sold and all the papers were signed, before I knew about Louise, I had resolved to let her go with a light heart because she had done her job."

She slipped her hand inside his shirt, remembering how on that first day, the heat of his skin had radiated through her and lit a fire in her heart that had never gone out. She lost herself in golden specks of color in his eyes, a calming sea of blue-green deep enough to dive into and never find the bottom. "He was so right."

Nick lifted her chin, caressed it with his thumb, then he kissed her softly. "Who was right, my love?"

"Grandpa." She returned his kiss, deep with the promise and passion only lovers know. "The Flying Goddess led me straight to you."

Nick let go a rich laugh. "That she did and I'll be eternally grateful. And you know something else?"

He teased the bottom of her chin. "Your father was looking out for you too. Although I'm not exactly sure what we're going to do about it."

Maddie sat up, her breath came shallow and her heart nearly stopped. "What do you mean?"

Nick slipped the music box out of her hands. "A gift, of sorts."

He peeled a piece of thick tape off the bottom of the box, slid the base open, and dropped the contents into her hand. The huge diamond caught the last rays of the sun and reflected a sharp glint of white.

"Oh my god." Maddie touched it with the tip of her finger as if it might disappear under pressure. "It's real?"

Nick folded her fingers around the stone and clasped her hand in his. "Not as real as this," he said, and he covered her lips with a searing kiss. "Never as real as this."

Did you enjoy **Mint Condition?** If so, please go to Amazon or Goodreads to post a short review, then check out **One of a Kind, A Classic Car Romance, Book 2**

More Books by Kat Drennan

The Love on the Faultline Romantic Mystery series
Borrego Moon

Love on the Faultline Historical Novella
Lies In White Satin

Love on the Faultline Standalone Romance
High Tide

Serpent's Coil Historical Time-Travel
The Cloisonné Brooch
Lesidi's Coin
The Serpent's Coil

A Classic Car Romance - Romantic Suspense
Book One - Mint Condition
Book Two - One of a Kind
Book Three – Hotrod Lincoln
Book Four – Five Window Pickup Coming Soon

Award-Winning Women's Fiction
The Goddess of Undo

About the Author

Kat Drennan writes sensual stories from the heart of the Golden State.

From the curling surf at the edge of the continent, to the granite sculptures of the Sierra Nevada; from San Francisco to Death Valley and all the way to the Mexican border, California's unique landscape and history step forward as characters in each of her novels.

She is an alumna of the Squaw Valley Community of Writers, as well as a member of Romance Writers of America.

Based in Ojai, California, with her husband, Fred and Remi the mini-aussie, Kat loves the beach, a challenging bike ride, cooking for a crowd, and traveling to wherever her two granddaughters are.

Kat loves to hear from her readers. You can follow her at www.katdrennanbooks.com, sign up for her newsletter to find out about new releases, or follow her Facebook page at www.facebook.com/KatDrennan.

www.ingramcontent.com/pod-product-compliance
Lightning Source LLC
LaVergne TN
LVHW020659110826
845149LV00012B/2049